ABOUT THE AUTHOR

Susi Fox lives in Australia with her family,
where she works as a GP.

PENGUIN BOOKS

Mine

SUSI FOX

PENGUIN BOOKS

PENGUIN BOOKS

UK | USA | Canada | Ireland | Australia
India | New Zealand | South Africa

Penguin Books is part of the Penguin Random House group of companies
whose addresses can be found at global.penguinrandomhouse.com.

First published by Penguin Random House Australia Pty Ltd 2018
First published in Great Britain by Penguin Books 2018
001

Printed in Great Britain by Clays Ltd, St Ives plc

A CIP catalogue record for this book is available from the British Library

ISBN: 978–1–405–93464–0

To those who understand

Out beyond ideas of wrongdoing and rightdoing,
there is a field.
I will meet you there.

– Rumi

BEFORE

I thought I'd love being a mother.

I was wrong.

I don't enjoy it at all; not even for one moment. I know I'm bad at it. My life as I know it ended the day I gave birth. Being a mother is the hardest thing I've ever had to do.

All of this has been a big mistake.

I don't want to do this anymore.

I can't do this anymore.

I will fix what I have done. I will make everything okay again – for you and for me.

And, please, I beg you: forgive me for what I'm about to do.

DAY 1, SATURDAY DAYBREAK

A thin band of light falls in a strip of yellow on the floor beside the bed. My brain is full of static, my tongue a pad of steel wool in my mouth. Beneath the tucked sheet my legs are a tangle of pins and needles. I press my feet against the cotton and try to tug them free.

It's difficult to inhale the thick, hot air. The window on my right is out of reach. The curtains are striped and drawn together, with only a pale line of sky littered with treetops visible between their folds. A beeping monitor stands beside the bed, flashing red. Silver rails are locked in place on either side of the mattress, running from my feet to my torso. A white hospital gown cloaks my chest.

Surely Mark should be here, by my side? I haul myself onto one elbow and scour the room. Empty. There's no chair. No cot, either.

Cot. The realisation hits me. *The baby.*

I pull the sheet back and hoist the gown to my neck. A thick pad is taped above my pubic bone. My belly is smaller than before, and wobbly. I'm empty.

I ease myself back down against the mattress, sucking in air. There's a flash of memory from the moments before I was put to sleep: a mask held over my face, the pressure of it against my cheeks, the smell of musty plastic. The anaesthetist's pinpoint eyes. Mark, staring down at me, blinking in slow motion. Then coldness in the back of my hand, stinging like a nettle.

I lift my fingers to my eyes. My vision pulls into focus. Clear liquid dribbles through tubing into a vein. I yank at the plastic taped fast against my skin.

There's a call bell on the bedside table. I thrust my arm over the rail, knocking a cup of water to the floor in my haste. The liquid pools on the matted carpet, then begins to soak in, forming a jagged mark. I catch the cord of the buzzer and manoeuvre it onto my lap. I dig both my thumbs into it and listen as a loud ring resonates in the corridor outside my room. There's the squeak of a meal trolley. A baby whimpering from a nearby room.

But no one comes.

I press the buzzer again and again, hearing the echoing chime outside my door. Still no one answers.

A red light flickers on the buzzer, the colour all at once too familiar. Blood. Was I bleeding last night? Why can't I remember? There's something far more wrong now. Where is my baby?

'Excuse me,' I shout in the direction of the corridor. 'Is anyone there?'

I try to steady my breathing and take in my surroundings. Everything about this place feels unsettling. There's a thread of cobweb stretching high against the ceiling, a sliver of a crack in the plaster above the skirting board by the door, a dull brown stain on the bed sheet. I shouldn't be here. This isn't the Royal, with its homely birthing suites and clean, airy rooms. There the midwives are attentive and caring. Soothing music is piped along every corridor. The Royal was where I was supposed to have our baby girl.

This – this is the hospital down the road, the one with the *reputation*. The one I'd insisted on avoiding in this town big enough to have a choice, small enough for me to know individual obstetricians. As the local pathologist, I'm the one who writes up the autopsies of babies that don't make it. I've seen the work of each specialist. I know more than anyone how much can go wrong.

A wave of nausea sweeps over me. *That* hasn't happened to my baby. Not after everything. It's not possible. It can't be.

The door pushes inwards, the silhouette of a broad-shouldered woman backlit by the lights from the corridor.

'Help. Please,' I say.

'Oh, but that's my job.'

The figure steps under the downlights: a midwife in a navy pinafore. *Ursula*, the badge at her waist reads.

'I do apologise. We've been so busy,' she says. She dumps a cluster of folders on the end of my bed, picks up the closest one and peers at it through spectacles hung on a thin chain around her neck. 'Saskia Martin.'

'That's not me.' My heart quivers inside me. 'Where's my baby?'

Ursula inspects me over the rim of her glasses, then thrusts the folder back onto my bed and picks up the next one in line. 'Oh. You're Sasha Moloney?'

I nod, relieved.

'So you're the abruption.'

Maroon clumps on asphalt rise, steaming, before my vision. The stench of metallic clots, bled out from behind the placenta, peeling my baby away from the inside of my womb before it was time for her to emerge. So, the bleeding was real, not solely from my imagination.

'My oh my. You lost of lot of blood.'

I don't ask the volume. 'My baby. Please tell me?'

She skims the file.

'You're thirty-seven years old.'

'Yes, I am.'

'And this is your first baby.'

'That's correct.'

From the corridor now comes the sound of babies wailing in unison. Finally, Ursula lifts her head from the file.

'You had an emergency caesarean at thirty-five weeks. Your baby boy was sent to the nursery. Congratulations.'

Boy? I draw a sharp breath. 'I thought I was having a girl.'

Ursula flips through the file, sticks her finger on the page.

'Definitely a boy,' she says.

It takes me a moment to understand her. Not a daughter, but a son. This is most unexpected. But there's a small chance the ultrasound – and my maternal intuition – could have been wrong.

'You're sure?'

'Quite sure. It says *boy* right here.' Her jaw tightens. 'Oh,' she mumbles. 'Hmmm . . .'

Oh, no. Any baby, any gender is fine, as long as they're okay. Please, please, let them be okay . . .

Ursula scrambles through the notes, then inspects me again through the lower half of her bifocals.

'It looks like he's alright. The files are so difficult to read these days. So many babies. And so many mothers to care for. We'll get you to him as soon as we can.'

Relief floods my body. My baby is alive. I am a mother. And somewhere in this hospital is my newborn son. My heart is still a drum beating behind my ribs.

'Can I see him now, please?'

'Hopefully soon. We're extremely busy.' She gives a theatrical sigh. 'I'm sure you understand.' She checks the file again. 'You're a doctor, am I right?'

I'm not sure if she's playing some sort of perverse game. Perhaps she's merely run off her feet. I've heard the stories about this place: a constant victim of budget cuts, perpetually short-staffed, doctors and nurses overworked.

I nod. 'Well, I'm a pathologist . . . But can you at least tell me how he is?'

Again Ursula drags a finger down the page. 'It's not immediately clear from these notes.' She eases the folder shut.

I scrunch the bed sheet into a ball beneath my palms.

'I need to see him. I need to see him now.'

'I understand,' Ursula says, placing the folder on my bedside table. 'Of course you do. I'll be back with a wheelchair as soon as I can.'

'Mark will take me. My husband. Where is he?'

'He must be with your baby. I'm sure you can see him when we get you upstairs.' She removes my mobile from the top drawer of the bedside table and hands it to me. 'You can call him. Tell him to come to the desk for a wheelchair.'

A buzzer screeches from a room nearby. Ursula frowns as she steps into the corridor.

I find Mark's number and press the phone hard against my ear. It rings out. I call again. This time I leave a message in a voice I barely recognise, begging him to come and get me straight away, to take me upstairs. I tell him I need him. That I need to check on the baby.

I've worked in hospitals for years. I know the systems, the faults and flaws. On the face of it, I should be more comfortable here. But being a patient is different to being a doctor. Now I'm the observed rather than the observer; I'm the one being dissected, examined, judged. I can spot incompetence like a watermark. And, worst of all, I know how easy it is to make mistakes.

Nurses titter in the corridor outside my room. Muffled wails of newborn babies filter through the air. My uterus seems to tighten inside me. I'm starting to get some feeling back in my legs as the tingling fades away. My muscles soften with the last of the opioids and I gasp at the sticky, hot air, willing myself to stay here, stay conscious, there's no time for sleep, but the room tilts beneath me, and I swirl into a vortex as the walls collapse in on themselves and the room disintegrates to black.

DAY 1, SATURDAY BREAKFAST

The clatter of a tray wakes me. There's a stale sulphur smell about the room, a hint of bleach beneath. I peel open my eyes. Pale yellow scrambled eggs on a slice of soggy white bread. Acrid bacon alongside, flecked with charcoal. A woman stands over me. Her name flickers into my mind: *Ursula*.

Then: *the baby. The baby boy.*

My limbs stiffen as I remember that I'm a mother now; that I'm alone. So is my son. And where is Mark?

'Please . . . Is my baby okay?'

I should never have fallen asleep. It's my first failing as a mother. Correction: my second. My first failing was my inability to keep him inside until forty weeks.

'I checked with the nursery while you were asleep. He's stable. But he's little. I'm sure you guessed that.' She indicates my chest; my milk hasn't yet come in. 'What he needs right now is some colostrum from you.'

Colostrum. The first milk. It's full of antibodies, fats, all the vital nutrients. I want him to have it, right away.

'After we get that, can I see him?' When I see him, I'll know how he is. How I am, too.

'Things have settled down on the ward. I'm sure a visit can be arranged. You'll be able to see your husband in the nursery.'

Mark. He should be able to calm me, help me forget the images of deceased premature babies flickering through my mind, the ones I've dissected at post-mortems over the years.

'My baby will be alright, won't he?' I remember his gestational age. 'I mean, thirty-five weeks is okay, isn't it?'

Ursula lifts my gown. 'He should be fine.' She places her thumb and index finger either side of my nipple, first squashing it against my chest wall, then squeezing it like she's juicing a lemon. I wince, but say nothing.

'You understand we need to stimulate your breasts, to get your milk flowing? You know breast pumps won't work yet?'

I nod.

'Good, then.' Ursula squeezes harder. 'You've picked a name for him?'

The child on the ultrasounds had an upturned nose, pouting lips and a sloping chin. I'd been delighted to discover we were having a girl. After all, I'd saved my childhood dolls, my *Anne of Green Gables* and Malory Towers book collections in a box under our bed, for our future daughter. Mark had been happy enough, too, even though I knew that, deep down, he'd wanted a son. He'll be ecstatic now we've had a boy.

'We had decided on Gabrielle for a girl,' I say. 'So, I suppose Gabriel, then.'

Ursula raises her eyebrows. 'Your turn to try.' She untangles my arm from the IV line that trails to a hanging bag of saline. Then I pump my breast, fingers thrusting back towards my ribs, clenching together like she has demonstrated, crushing the nipple as hard as I can until it's the colour of a bruised strawberry. Nothing comes, not even as my hand stiffens into a cramp.

'Let me,' Ursula says.

I've always admired breast tissue under the microscope; something about its branching channels, like a tree growing within. In lactating women, the ducts are filled with smooth pools of milk, stained a salmon pink by the dye. I'd assumed my lactiferous ducts would fill of their own accord. I had never anticipated the need to express the milk into being with brute force.

Ursula twists and squishes my breasts, trying to extract even a single drop. I focus on the babies' cries through the walls, through the open door, through every inch of this room until, finally, there's a pearly bead of yellow on the tip of my nipple, shining like a jewel.

'He'll need this,' Ursula says, sucking it up into a syringe. 'Well done.'

I'm not sure if she's talking to me, or to herself. My breast throbs. I wiggle my toes against the cool sheet, then with tingling fingertips trace the edges of my thighs up to my sagging abdomen. There's a new lightness in my limbs, an ease of movement that I've missed these past months. My belly, though, feels hollow after all the constant kicks.

'Can I go to the nursery now?'

'One thing at a time. I'll be back as soon as I've delivered this to the baby.'

'You don't know where Mark is?'

Still pumping at my breast, Ursula uses her chin to point out a vase on the shelf opposite the bed. 'He sent those down. He said not to wake you. He's upstairs with your baby.'

Twelve blood-red roses. The florist must have mixed the colours up. Mark knows white roses are my favourite. The cotton pillowslip chills the back of my neck as I press my head into it.

Ursula holds the syringe up to the peeling cream ceiling, examining the straw-yellow contents. 'That should be enough for now. Their stomachs are only the size of marbles, you know. And we'll need more in another two or three hours.' She snaps the bedside rail back into place and walks out of the room.

Oh God, no. This isn't what breastfeeding is supposed to be like. I stare up at the paint flecks on the ceiling. None of this was on my birth plan. I was supposed to have a peaceful vaginal birth, Mark beside me massaging my shoulders, whispering encouraging words in my ear. Pain relief if I needed. A healthy baby girl. It was supposed to all go right for me, after everything that had gone wrong before. I'd written my birth plan in minute detail during the hormone-induced bliss of pregnancy. Maybe that was the problem: I never should have written one at all.

The bedside rails are jail bars, pinning me to the narrow mattress. I must wait for Ursula to come and fetch me, and take me to my son.

DAY 1, SATURDAY MORNING TEA

I'm gripping the wheelchair armrests as we pass the nurses' station directly opposite my room. Why did it take them so long to answer my calls? Ursula pushes me down long, tunnelling corridors with metal handrails fixed to the pale pink walls. Overhead, flickering fluorescent lights hang in unbroken tracks. The scent of disinfectant, mingled with quiet murmuring, wafts out from adjacent rooms. The footsteps of staff strike hard against the laminex. Is it because I'm in a wheelchair that people seem to glance away as we pass? Twists, turns, corridor upon corridor; it seems as if I'm being transported into the centre of the earth.

The chair clamours to a stop in front of an elevator and the doors scrape open. Inside, Ursula thrusts her thumb against the button numbered five. The lift is filled with a potent antiseptic smell, suggesting it has been recently cleaned. Mirrors reflect my face from every angle: straggly fair hair and bloodshot eyes emerging from a white hospital blanket slung over my shoulders, images of my blotchy face repeating infinitely. My fingers tingle on the armrests. The air is still thick. My chest starts to heave and shift. Is this what panic feels like?

The lift jolts to a stop. As I'm wheeled out, the hollow inside of the lift reminds me of a receding womb. We move down the corridor and I see a plastic fern beside a row of chairs, a pinboard of smiling baby photos opposite. We reach a small annexe. Faint baby mewls are audible. A long, shiny metal sink is attached to one wall, numerous taps without handles perched above it. An opaque glass door beside the annexe sink is labelled in thick black font: *Special Care Nursery. Wash your hands before entering.*

'Mind you don't forget,' Ursula says. 'Infections can spread quickly. We've had issues before when people didn't wash their hands.'

The water comes on with an automated spurt as I place my fingers beneath the tap. I lather purple liquid soap in my palms and use a nailbrush to scrub at the tinges of blood coating the side of my fingers until I've rid my skin of all the stains. I'm very careful. I know, more than anyone, how dangerous infections can be.

The door slides open with a rasping sound to reveal the cacophony within. Bleeping monitors, crying babies, apnoea alarms reverberating off the bleach-white walls. Hitting the back of my nostrils, the scent of starched linen. The sweetness of newborn faeces. The reek of latex gloves. It's all too familiar, back from my rotation as a junior doctor in a nursery in the big smoke, when I had no clue how to slide needles into the miniature babies' veins or how to thread tubes into their tiny lungs. Back when I had no experience of how sick a baby could get.

Ursula pushes me over the threshold into a low-ceilinged room. Mark must be here. My baby, too. My stomach knots.

To the right of the L-shaped nursery, humidicribs – plastic boxes illuminated with white lights, each containing a miniature baby – are trimmed with leads and monitors attached to flashing screens on the benches beside them like a perverse Christmas display. Two lines of the cribs stretch down a long corridor, about five on either side. The small window on the far wall is the only source of natural light. Open cots, for the larger, less sick babies, cluster close to the nurses' station in the smaller arm of the ward to the left. With two separate wings, I imagine it's hard for the staff to keep an eye on all the babies at once. I can only hope they're taking good care of my son.

A gaggle of nurses survey me from the desk beside the door as I'm wheeled towards the corridor of humidicribs on my right. The nurses here are overworked, indifferent, hostile even; I can see it in their narrow eyes and tight lips. Another mother who has made more work for us. Another mother who has failed her baby.

As for the building, it is shabby, old-fashioned, a tad unclean. It feels backward compared with the progressive city hospital where I worked as a junior doctor; where I first met Damien, the baby from years ago who I'm still trying to forget. That hospital had a completely different atmosphere, an aura of calm, modernity and efficiency pervading the entire organisation.

Ursula points down to the end of the row.

'Your baby is this way. We'll get a doctor to come and let you know how he's doing very soon.'

Is it because she knows I'm a doctor that she doesn't feel comfortable telling me herself?

'And Mark?'

'I believe he's just headed off. I'm sure he'll be back any moment.'

Where could he have been going? Downstairs to see me?

'You've worked in a nursery before, I take it?' Ursula says.

I nod, even though it was only for a short time and long ago, during my paediatrics term as a medical resident. Like all young doctors, I rotated through multiple specialties, trying to find the one that suited me best. Obstetrics, paediatrics, emergency, psychiatry, among others. Ursula doesn't need to know how little I remember of those early days; how much I've blocked from my mind.

There must be twenty or so infants in here. I have no idea where my baby is.

'Here we are,' Ursula says, tugging me to a stop beside a humidicrib on the left, beside the window. 'Your baby.'

My heart skips a beat. Part of me doesn't want to look. I fixate on the outside of the humidicrib. It's an unfamiliar model: matt-grey base with a rail strung along the side, see-through plastic over the top like a snow globe, enclosing another world. A rectangle of blue card is sticky-taped to the cot wall in front of me, coming unstuck at one corner.

Name: _____

Baby of: Sasha Moloney

Sex: Male

Then a list of numbers: his weight, date and time of birth.

I have to bend around the card to see him. There are wires taped to his chest, a tube emerging from his nose. He's tiny – smaller, even, than the teddy I bought him, waiting in the cot back home. His chest sucks in between his ribs, his abdomen flailing with each breath. He doesn't look comfortable. His arms and legs are kindling-thin, with wads of padding at the knees and elbows for him to grow into, his skin almost translucent with purple streams of veins beneath.

He looks like he's struggling. Like he knows he should still be inside my womb. Him being born prematurely – I blame myself. As his mother, the one who was supposed to keep him safe, I know it's my fault. Yet despite my guilt, there's no stirring in my chest, no tightening of my heart. He doesn't look like the baby who appeared in my pregnancy dreams. I stare at him as I would any other premature newborn. I don't feel like his mother at all. Fleetingly, I'm struck by a terrible idea: what if this isn't my baby? But I reorder my thoughts, pushing that inconceivable notion to the back of my mind.

Ursula is back at the desk, chatting to another nurse. They both stop speaking to glance up at me. I give them a cursory smile and turn back to my baby.

I understood it would be love at first sight. That's what I'd heard other mothers describe, what I'd read, what I'd always believed it would be like. It's strange, I suppose, but I find this baby unappealing. He has a flat-bridged nose, wide-set eyes that are blue-grey in colour – different from Mark's, and my own – and ears that protrude like a monkey's. A few tufts of dark hair jut out through pocks of dried blood on his conical scalp.

I'm waiting for a maternal connection to kick in, a sense of certainty to settle over me, but as the seconds tick past nothing changes. This could be anyone's baby. Shut away behind plastic, with no way to reach him, no way to touch him, no way to feel the texture of his skin – he's barely more than an outline of a child. This isn't what I've been spending months planning for.

This isn't what I believed motherhood would feel like at all. I wish Mark were here. I need him to tell me that everything is going to be alright.

Around me, several mothers stroke their babies' backs, cooing and ahhing and smiling in delight. A father a few cots over tickles his newborn under its chin as it snuffles and gurgles. I observe them, trying to figure out how they are able to touch their children. Of course – the portholes. I can't believe I've forgotten.

I fiddle with the latch on one of the two round portholes lining a side of the humidicrib, pressing the catch firmly until it releases with a pop and the door springs open. This is the moment I had dreamed of. Skin on skin with my baby, for the very first time. I lean forwards in my wheelchair and ease my hand over to my son.

The sole of his foot is squishy, like mincemeat. I recoil. The other mothers are still massaging their own babies. I reach for him again, edge my thumb into the arch of his foot, but he thrusts his leg at my hand, kicking me away. I extricate my arm from the porthole and snap the door shut.

I'd imagined my baby's body on my chest, nuzzling into my breasts; hardly the vision now before me, of a skinny, skeletal mound struggling to breathe, unaware I'm even here.

I remember one of my patients, a new mother, years ago, when I was a junior doctor. In her shared postnatal room she had been trying to put her newborn to her breast, but the baby kept pulling away.

'This is the worst,' the woman had complained to me, staring down at her son as he lay on the blanket, perched long and restless between her outstretched legs. 'How can I love him when he doesn't even seem to want to know me?'

I'd clicked my tongue. 'It's not that he doesn't want to know you,' I'd said. 'He's learning. Breastfeeding is a learned skill for both of you.'

'Then why is it so goddamn hard?' the woman said.

With no personal experience of babies or motherhood, I didn't have an answer for her back then. I thought she was the one with the problem. I had no idea how right she was; how hard this could be.

Beside me, the small window provides the nursery's only viewpoint to the outside world. The pane has been tinted black to soften the glare. I can still see out, but no one can see in. The town's main road runs directly below, cars gliding over asphalt. Across from the hospital, a playground glistens, ringed by a black fence. There's a clump of gums at the far corner of the park. Beyond the trees, red rooftops stretch like blood-flecked breakers into the distance towards the hills where the bush begins.

The park is where I want to be right now. Away from this sterile, noisy place. Away from this tiny baby who might live, or who might die. But no one would understand my desire to flee. This is my child. And he needs me.

A siren blares from the road as a fire truck weaves in and out of lanes, lights blazing. The memory comes to me in a scatter of broken images: our car lurching across the road. A dark shape rising through the windscreen. The pulsing blue lights of an approaching vehicle. I was brought here by ambulance. Mark called the emergency services from the roadside.

On the humidicrib panel, two numbers flicker red amid the dials and knobs. Oxygen, twenty-nine per cent. Temperature, thirty-four degrees Celsius. A grey monitor is fixed to the wall above my head, displaying more numbers on its screen.

Heart rate, respiratory rate, oxygen saturation – all flashing in lurid blue, red, green.

Beneath the clear plastic, the baby's bellybutton stalk is cherry-red, oozing yellow. Should I call a nurse, warn them about the possibility of infection? But the staff are capable professionals – I should focus on being a mother, rather than a doctor, for now.

I inspect my son closer. His fingers tapping against the cot sides are pudgy, his palms thick; both out of proportion to his scrawny body. It has been a while since I dealt with living, breathing babies. Aren't they all unattractive, a little hard to bond with? Maybe I just need more time to feel something for mine?

The residual sedatives loosen my muscles, turning my limbs to liquid rubber, thickening my eyelids even as I try to prop them open. Ursula is behind me, her hands pressing on my shoulders, offering to take me back downstairs. I try to resist – I should be here, waiting for Mark – but Ursula is firm.

'You need some rest,' she says.

She wheels me back out through the sliding nursery door, into the shiny elevator, then along the long pink corridor to my private maternity room. She shuts the door behind her, guides me into bed and tucks me in tight. The babies in the other rooms are quiet now. Fluorescent lights hum above my head. When Ursula flicks them off, I try to fight against the endless blackness, the mind-numbing promise of not having to think or feel, even as my body limbers into stillness. As sleep engulfs me, I feel like Mark could almost be at my bedside, scratching the itchy spot between my shoulders that I can't quite reach, smoothing down my hair, whispering that he loves me, that everything is going to be alright.

DAY ZERO, FRIDAY, APPROACHING SUNSET

I'm thirty-five weeks pregnant. We're cruising home along country back roads. In the cocoon of the car, with the sun piercing the clouds on the horizon and spilling pinpoint shafts of light onto distant hills, I make the promise again to myself and to my unborn daughter: *I'm going to be a perfect mother.*

Mark is in the passenger seat, the whiskey from his Friday-afternoon work drinks hot on his breath. A lock of hair is curled over his forehead and the top button of his favourite shirt is undone as he sings along to Billie Holiday in an off-key falsetto. When the song ends, he leans over to me and presses his lips close to my ear. He has something good to share with me when we get home, he whispers, then strokes my swollen belly with the flat of his palm. I smile to myself and nudge him away with my elbow.

On the side of the road, near the approaching curve, a grey figure comes into view. A kangaroo, bouncing towards us.

There's no time. I hit the brakes. There's a sickening thud on the left bumper as the car shudders to a stop.

Clutching the steering wheel, I try to slow my racing mind. My heart is hammering. I don't want to see the damage I have done – I wish I could just leave, keep driving, forget this ever happened. This isn't me. I'm not a person who has accidents, not a person who makes mistakes or causes intentional harm. I'm the person who always tries to do the right thing.

'Pull over, pull over,' Mark says, his words slurred.

My fingers tremble as I ease the car onto the shoulder of the curve. I can feel myself starting to hyperventilate.

Mark flips open the glove box and pulls out the small animal-rescue kit we keep handy. Although he's been a chef since his early twenties, he likes to play the amateur vet when he gets the chance. I got him into it during the early days of our relationship, taught him the ropes. Until now, lumps by the dirty roadside have always been caused by someone else.

'Baby's alright?'

I place my hand on my tight abdomen and nod. He passes the kit across to me. 'Then I suppose we'd better check on this roo.'

We've been stopping for animals for years now. Our 'rescues'. Seeing Mark at times like this still reminds me of how he was all those years ago, when we fell in love. Early in our courtship, I had established that I never wanted to have children. Growing up without a mother for most of my life, I was convinced I would be inadequate at the job. Mark had quietly acquiesced. Then, one day, I saw him pull a newborn kitten from a box behind our garden shed, its eyes still fused shut. As he cradled it in his palm, I had a sudden flush of icy-cold certainty that spread from my chest along my arms, to the tips of my fingers. This man was built to be a father. I would never be enough. He would always be wishing for more than me.

Fortunately for Mark – for both of us – a few years later I started paediatrics training. The first birth I attended was for a baby expected to require resuscitation. As I sidled into the room, I found the mother pushing, a sweat barely breaking on her brow. Before I could arrange the resuscitation cot, the baby slid out of her straight into the waiting obstetrician's arms. As the newborn was placed on the mother's chest, I saw how they both lit up: the mother's face was ecstatic, the baby's serene. He was already breathing, his inhalations perfectly aligned with his mother's. It turned out there was no need for me to be there at all.

At first, I didn't notice that my ovaries had kicked into overdrive. But with each new birth I attended, each newborn baby I examined and handed to its glowing mother, the idea of having my own baby began to seem more and more possible, less and less unappealing. I could be like these women. With Mark's support, maybe I could be a good enough mother, too.

Mark was delighted, his enthusiasm contagious. He said he'd known the best way for me to come around was to allow me to arrive at the same conclusion myself. I didn't even let his patronising tone bother me. We would have a baby. Why cause unnecessary argument? Soon, getting pregnant became all I could think about. Mark certainly didn't complain as my conception attempts began to take on the fervour of a religious zealot.

But what followed was eight years of blindsiding infertility. Two miscarriages. Every test known to Western medicine revealed it was me – my eggs and my endometriosis – that was the problem. Mark's sperm were top-notch. Then we tried every possible medical intervention, short of the IVF Mark refused to attempt. We had exhausted our supply of hope. Not only was I devastated, but I had also let down the man I loved in not being able to give him what he wanted most. Until, finally, this: our miracle pregnancy. And a marriage that hadn't quite recovered from the years of infertility, despite our attempts at marriage counselling. Maybe if the waiting hadn't gone on for so many years, I wouldn't have been contemplating asking Mark for a trial separation just before I discovered I was pregnant. But none of that mattered anymore. Everything would be better between us once this baby was born.

I ease myself out of the car. The kangaroo is lying on its side, legs askew on the gravel. She has a pouch: a female. She lies still, watching me with panicked eyes as I approach. Her left leg is twisted at a terrible angle. Blood oozes from a deep cut near her knee, pooling on the asphalt, her front paws scrabbling at the dirt beside her.

Mark crouches down and shuffles closer, whispering reassurance. Her paws stop clawing the ground, her head lolls back onto the road and her eyes glaze over. We're too late. Mark's face creases. It's been a while since I've seen him at a rescue. Lately, we've rarely been in the car together. He rolls his shirtsleeves up to his elbows, pulls on plastic gloves, then passes me a pair. Time to check the pouch. Kneeling on the gravel, he reaches down into the fuzzy pocket. His hand seems to snag on something. I hope for his sake it's not a pinky – a joey too small to survive. Mark hates having to kill them, even though it's the humane thing to do.

He grasps the leg and tugs the joey up towards the surface. It's still suckling on its mother. But it's more than twenty centimetres long; large enough to be given a chance at life. I reach for the surgical scissors in the kit as Mark clutches the joey. After I had taken some weekend classes from the local animal shelter, I taught him about the way joeys grasp tight to the teat, continuing to suckle, long after their mothers are dead. Pulling them off damages their jaws, making it impossible for them to survive. The only way to save them is to cut them out. I've sliced through dozens of animal teats over the years, as well as far worse things in my patients: cancers and pus-filled boils and maggoty wounds. Yet tonight the thought of cutting through the tag of spongy flesh turns my stomach. Clenching my teeth, I bend over and stretch the teat long with one hand, then snip through it with a single snap.

My finger prickles.

Blood dribbles out through the plastic glove, running over the curve of my wrist. I rip off the glove and drop it on the ground. Shit. I'm not paying enough attention. I've cut myself.

It's a deep cut, through the skin, down to fat. Damn. I press my hand into an old pillowcase from the kit, meant for the joey, trying to stem the blood.

The joey is cupped in Mark's palms, curled into a ball, its jaws gripping tight to the displaced teat like a child sucking on a lollipop.

Mark glances at me. 'Sash, what have you done?'

'It's just a little cut.'

He wraps the joey in a towel and draws it to his chest. 'Please take care,' he says, with concern in his voice.

I smile sweetly, pressing harder on my finger. 'Why do I need to, when you do such a good job of looking after me?'

Mark bites at his bottom lip. Once it was confirmed this pregnancy was likely to continue, he began attempting to treat me like royalty, carrying in the groceries from the car, drawing me deep baths, cooking me nourishing food for every meal. I'm lucky, I suppose. I'm always trying to remind myself how lucky I am.

A thin trickle of fluid slides down my inner thigh. 'Crap,' I say, 'and now I've wet myself.'

Gathering the pillowcase into a clump to wipe at my leg, I look over at Mark, expecting him to be grinning at me, but his eyes are globes, the whites shining. When I lift the pillowcase to my face, I see it's stained with bright red blood, the colour of a fire extinguisher, or a matchbox.

'It must be from my finger,' I say. There's another gush. This time it feels like a lump of jelly sliding out of me, into my underwear. It's not coming from my finger.

I survey the road. There's now so much blood pouring out of me that large clots are glistening scarlet on the gravel, trembling like my fingers as I lean towards Mark, grasping for something I can hold on to.

'Mark,' I call out.

He is standing, the joey still clutched to his chest in one hand, reaching out for me with the other. As I crouch on the asphalt, one palm grazing the rough stones, I scrabble the other hand to the skin of my abdomen but no matter how hard I try to feel a kick of life from inside, my belly remains firm, silent and frighteningly still.

DAY 1, SATURDAY LATE MORNING

An oxygen saturation monitor bleeps staccato time with my heart, the pitch of a car alarm. I try not to analyse the rate. It hits me quicker this time: where I am, what has happened to me. The incision across my belly – the proof that I'm a mother now. But I've been asleep again, when I should be by my son's side. I'm failing him even though his life has just begun.

A fragment of my medication-induced sleep intrudes on my consciousness: my dream-baby. I have been visualising her – what I thought was a her – for months now. Her head, covered with tufts of brown hair. Peach-coloured cheeks, shiny blue eyes. She never makes a sound. Yet her face is so different to the baby in the humidicrib upstairs. That child still feels like a stranger.

A low thrumming starts up in my head, the persistent buzz of a memory. A news segment, reporting a story of babies mistakenly switched in a US hospital. I had heard the piece on a radio show years before. At the time I had been enthralled, listening in horror and fascination. Baby swaps weren't uncommon, the reporter had said, quoting examples from every corner of the globe.

A shiver runs down my back, coursing like rivulets of rain across my skin. I'm suddenly terrified. Could they have given me a boy instead of a girl by mistake? Ludicrous. I need to get a grip. I take a deep breath, try to calm down.

As if sensing my discomfort, Ursula's broad frame appears, casting a shadow over my bed. There is brown lipstick smudged on her front teeth, dark circles below her eyes. She scrawls notes in a red folder and doesn't look up as I shuffle about on the mattress. Above me, the fluorescent lights buzz a warning.

'Sasha. Sasha's my name,' I say.

She squints down at me through her bifocals.

'I know,' she says, but she glances down at the name label in the top corner of the folder to check. Is it possible that she, or someone like her, could have been responsible for a serious mistake? In the case on the radio, it was the fault of a midwife; a simple error. One baby looks much like another. Staff are busy. Procedures aren't followed. Mistakes are so easily made.

'Your breastmilk is with your baby. You'll be wanting to head up there again now, I suppose.'

I nod. It seems she recognises my anxiety, at least.

'I could have sworn I was having a girl.'

'It's not uncommon for the ultrasounds to be wrong,' Ursula says.

'I know.' What I don't say: my baby *felt* like a girl to me.

'Are you disappointed?' Ursula stares down at me.

Perhaps that's all this is – my paranoia is disappointment.

'Because gender disappointment is quite common. You can work your way through it.'

No, I realise, it's not gender disappointment. I didn't mind having a boy *or* a girl. My concerns are for something far, far worse.

'Was someone with my baby the whole time after he was born?'

She inspects me with narrowed eyes, then presses a button on a beeping monitor beside my bed. The alarm instantly silences.

'Of course. We never leave babies alone.' From my wooden bedside table, she produces a plastic kidney dish the colour of bile and removes a large syringe from it. 'We'll get you down to him as soon as you've had your meds.'

'What meds?'

'Morphine. Your pain relief will be wearing off any time now.'

I'm not in that much pain, though nausea loops through my stomach like a roller-coaster. My head is still fuzzy, but I have to keep my brain switched on. The last thing I need is more medication.

'No, thank you.'

Is her glare one of fury or shock? She removes a second syringe from a see-through dish.

'Antibiotics, then.' She offers a stern smile. 'Standard procedure at this hospital. I was on the hospital committee that introduced these protocols after we had an infection outbreak a few years ago. We don't want you getting sick now, do we?'

I don't have an infection so there's no need for antibiotics, no matter what their protocol says. I extract my arm from her reach, secrete it under the white cotton sheet.

'I'd prefer not. I need to get to the nursery right away.'

She replaces the syringe in the plastic dish with a clatter.

'Excuse me while I have a word with Dr Solomon,' she says, not looking behind her as she leaves the room.

My bedclothes feel like a straitjacket. I push the sheet to my ankles, hoist the hospital gown to my neck. My belly is still protruding, almost as prominent as when I was pregnant. I can't believe I didn't pay more attention to the women's bodies after their births. I suppose I was so focused on the wellbeing of the babies that the mothers almost seemed to merge into their children, until there was nothing separate, nothing left of their bodies that was their own.

I trace the stretch marks, shiny slivers, down to the firm, rubbery lump of my uterus concealed beneath puckered skin. The layers of my body the obstetrician, Dr Solomon, has sliced through: yellow globules of fat, tense white fascia, then the bulky mauve muscle of the uterus that failed me. Obstetricians don't always stitch up all the layers afterwards; some are left open to find their own natural ways of closing. Fluid oozes between tissues, sometimes into places it shouldn't. I know this from the autopsies I've performed on postpartum women over the years. The images of their bloated bodies, swollen breasts, don't bother me as much as the dead babies I've dissected – whose tiny bodies, seeping maroon fluids, still haunt my dreams.

A flash of red in the corner of my eye. The roses from Mark, on the shelf. I need him here. I need his opinion about all of this. Right now.

I lean for my phone on the bedside table. It tumbles from reach, onto the floor. With a stretch, I catch the overhead handlebar and try to haul myself to sitting. A spark of heat sears from beneath the dressing. I press into the wadded bandage with the heel of my hand as I try again. This time, it feels like a hot skewer. I collapse back against the mattress with a groan. I'm going to need help to get out of bed.

I ring the call bell, the buzz reverberating down the corridor. A choir of babies wail from distant rooms, screaming in distress. Where are their mothers? Why isn't anyone answering them?

Ursula sweeps back into my room, holding a new kidney dish – this one transparent plastic – aloft like a butler.

'Can you please pass my phone?'

She bends to the floor and lifts it into my lap, then leans over the bed, inspecting the crooks of my arms. Her face is flat, her voice even. She's hard to read.

'Dr Solomon requested I take some blood.'

'I really don't want a blood test.'

'He insists. Remember, you lost a lot of it.' She holds my gaze with a thin smile. I'm first to look away.

My fingers turn pale, then blue, then indigo, dammed like a river below the tourniquet. Finally, she finishes labelling the tubes. She holds the syringe up, ready to plunge it into me.

I stare up at the light above my bed, a solid glow like a light-sabre. I don't expect to feel anything – God, I've had enough blood tests during the years of infertility to start my own pathology company – but she strikes a nerve and an electric shock runs the length of my arm, causing my hand to jerk and dislodge the needle from the crook of my elbow.

Ursula jumps back, still holding the syringe. 'Sorry,' she murmurs.

Heat pulses through my arm, my hand tingling with pain as a blue-ringed bruise rises on my skin.

'Jesus!'

It's Mark. He's wearing the olive long-sleeved shirt I bought for him in New York several winters ago, his cheeks flushed as he approaches the side of my bed.

'Sash. Are you okay?'

Ursula pushes the syringe into the almost-full sharps container then snaps the lid shut.

'I need help,' I say. 'I'm so glad you're here.'

Mark takes hold of my hand and turns it over so the inner flesh of my elbow is on display, the swollen bruise of bluey-black almost ready to explode.

'Is that okay?'

Ursula nods, her mouth cut in a firm line.

After all the long hours spent in waiting rooms, medical appointments and hospital cubicles trying to conceive, Mark and I know what each other's hand signals mean. *I can't take this anymore, Mark. Get me out of here.*

He squeezes back, scrutinising Ursula. *It'll be okay, no matter what.*

'We'll need to repeat the blood tests later,' Ursula says. She gives Mark a pointed look before heading out the door and leaving the two of us alone. I wait until I can no longer hear her footfall in the corridor.

'I don't know what she has against me.'

'Don't worry, Sash,' he says. 'Our beautiful son is here. A bit early, but he's okay. And you're okay. I was so worried I might lose you, too.' His face has collapsed in on itself like a crumpled paper bag. He leans in close and hugs me tight, perhaps tighter than he should, given my condition. I run my hands through his hair and take in his almond-scented shampoo.

'We had a boy,' I say quietly in his ear.

'Isn't it great?'

Just as I thought – he's happier with a son. 'Tell me what happened after they put me to sleep.' I pat the mattress beside me.

He takes a seat, a little further away than I indicated. The bedspread crinkles under him. I take hold of his hand and bring it to my face, inhaling the familiar smell of garlic beneath the hospital soap.

'Have you been making lunch?'

He shakes his head and presses into my warm thumb with his cool one. His nails are cut into neat moons, the dirt from last weekend's work on the veggie patch dug out from beneath them.

I run my hand over his sandy-brown hair again, damp under my palm. I try to phrase my next words delicately, without recrimination; I don't want to spoil our reunion.

'Where have you been? We agreed in the birth plan that if I needed a caesarean, you'd stay with her . . . I mean *him* after he was born, until he was stable. You did, didn't you?'

He presses deep into my palm. His thumb feels like the nub of a walking stick, solid, dependable. It's the pressure he always gives to let me know he's telling me the truth.

'I stayed with him, Sash, the whole time.' With his free hand, he fiddles with a loose thread on my bedspread as he details the resuscitation, the cannulation, the oxygen mask pressed fast against our baby's face in the nursery.

'The whole time? But you weren't there when the midwife took me up to him.'

'I had to go to the bathroom, Sash.'

I smile for the first time since the birth. I'm being ridiculous. I trust the man I married. Why would Mark lie about this?

'And the joey. Did it make it?'

Mark nods and kisses my cheek. I lean into him, his stubble rasping against my forehead. The warmth of his body seeping through my hospital gown onto my flushed skin is just like the feel of his hand on mine the night we met. Despite everything we've been through these last ten years, his presence still soothes me.

'Thanks for the roses,' I say.

His brown eyes crinkle. 'The florist said she ran out of white ones. I figured you wouldn't mind. They're nice though, aren't they? Like our handsome boy.'

My breath tugs inside me like a bell-pull.

'Who do you think he looks like?'

'Like both of us. He has your nose.' He points at my face, then his own. 'And my eyes. The shape of them, at least. Don't you think?'

The lines between Mark and the wall behind him are blurring. Surely he's noticed there's a problem too? I try to focus on the edges of his cheeks, his chin, his earlobes, parts of a whole that define my husband's face.

'I'm not sure,' I say uncertainly. He pulls away before I can add anything more.

'I knew you wouldn't like hospital food,' he says, reaching for a bag on the floor beside the bed. Extracting a plastic container, he gives it a shake and places it on the tray table beside me with a clatter. 'I bought you lunch from the cafeteria. Your favourite. I'd have preferred to make you something myself, but that hasn't been possible yet.'

It's a prosciutto, haloumi and asparagus salad. I try not to look disappointed, even though Mark really should know that it's not my favourite. Ever since I got pregnant, the texture of haloumi has made me gag – squeaky and sour on my tongue. I push the container to one side.

Mark doesn't notice. He is too busy setting several magazines, *Delicious* and *Taste* and *Saveur*, still wrapped in plastic, on the small table by the bed. 'I left these in the car yesterday by mistake. At least now you'll have something to read.' Annual magazine subscriptions, a Christmas present from his parents, more for Mark than for me. They've been buying them for years, since Mark told them about his plan to open his own café. Glossy photographs of braised lamb shank with a wobbly mint jelly, confit duck leg with cannellini beans and a chocolate cake oozing ganache icing. It's nothing like the food Mark has planned for his café: simple yet delectable organic fare. I don't think his parents have ever really understood what he's wanted to do.

'Thanks,' I say. Right now, I'm hungry for his simple gnocchi, the curtness of the butter entangled with the gentle tang of sage, cooked until it almost melts in my mouth. We've made it so many times together, side-by-side at our kitchen bench, rolling the small balls, pressing our thumbs into the dough to make a dent, licking our floury fingers to taste the salt. It's the dish that reminds me most of us, of him, and of his hopes and dreams.

Mark takes my hand again. 'He'll be able to come off the drip tomorrow if he's okay with the formula.' His mouth is drawn, as if he knows what's coming next.

'Formula?' My voice cracks.

Mark has crossed the room to the window and tugged open the curtains to dark clouds slipping across the sun.

'I didn't want to wake you,' he says. 'They started him on

some baby formula a few hours ago through the tube in his nose. He needed something in his tummy, they said.'

'But we didn't want baby formula, remember?'

In the container on the tray table the prosciutto is already starting to curl at the edges.

Mark continues to jabber on.

'I didn't know what to do, Sash. I was torn. I haven't been through everything you have. I don't know how it feels. The nurses said he needed formula and you weren't there. I'm trying to do the best I can, really I am.' He pauses, returns to the bed to take my hand, and uses his fail-safe method to distract me from my anxieties: the same cheeky grin he gave me at the jazz club all those years ago. I can't help but smile back.

'Sash, please. I'm worried about you,' he says.

For a brief moment I hope there *has* been a mistake. That the nurses have got it wrong – that this baby isn't ours. And when I'm reunited with my real baby, I'll hold her – or him – in my arms and feel that flood of maternal love wash over me. The slate will be wiped clean. I'll have another chance to be the perfect mother I desperately want to be.

I fill the silence with questions I didn't even know I needed the answers to: 'Does he look like you imagined? Whose ears do you think he has? What about the shape of his mouth? Did you check if he has your webbed toes?'

There's an awkward pause before Mark begins to speak, slowly, in the voice he uses when he likes to make sure I'm paying attention.

'I didn't check his toes. He does have my attached earlobes. You know, like my father's, joined directly to my head. The ones you hate.'

I inhale, hoping Mark won't notice. There would be only one thing worse than a mistake about the baby's identity: that the real mistake is in my imagination; that I will continue to feel nothing for my son at all.

'He has your skin, your pale skin. I would recognise his face anywhere, Sash. Let's visit him now, together. It'll help you feel better.'

'There's nothing the matter with me. I'm just tired.'

'Well, let's go now, then,' Mark insists. It seems I no longer have a choice.

THIRTEEN YEARS EARLIER

MARK

Life with Sash began unexpectedly. All the guys except Adam and I had pulled out of the boys' night we'd been planning for months. In the dim jazz club, a veil of musty cigarette smoke hovered in the air above my head. I sucked down the dregs of my lager, warm and flat in my mouth, as the quartet stepped away for a quick break. Adam had started chatting up a brunette near the toilets. I was alone, stuck on a table up the back, starting to wish I'd stayed at home like the other guys.

I approached the bar. Beside me, a woman pulled up a stool. Her blonde hair was clipped short against her head, her face slender with a pointed chin, like a pixie. She wasn't my usual type, but she was what other men would call beautiful.

'Having a good night?' I said.

'Sure.' She pointed over at Adam and the brunette, now entwined on a couch by the far wall. 'I think our friends are hooking up.'

She was right. Adam and the unnamed brunette were sucking at each other's necks. It looked like they were going to have a damn fine night.

'Would you like a beer?' She was forward right from the start. When I nodded, she called the barman over, ordered me a lager. She chose my favourite brand. 'I trust your friend treats women well.'

'Of course.'

'Bec's had a bad run, that's all.' The band piped up, drowning out whatever she said next. I slurped my beer, rested my elbows on the bar, trying to appear like I was following the subtleties of the solo. She raised her voice above the saxophone.

'What do you do?'

'I'm an apprentice chef. But my real dream is to start my own café.' I'd never said it aloud until that moment, but something about this woman demanded ambition. Courage. Vision.

'Hey, that's really cool,' she said. 'Tell me more.'

I thought fast. 'I'm scoping out sites for an organic food café. It's been my dream forever to set one up.'

'I love organic food.'

I grinned. 'And you? What do you do?'

'Nothing special.'

'Nothing special sounds great.'

Her cheeks, her eyes, lit up. Before the end of the song, her hand was cupped around my ear, her warm breath on my neck. 'It's too loud for me. You want to get out of here? I don't even like jazz.'

I'm still not one hundred per cent sure what it was about her that made me say yes without hesitation. Perhaps it was the warmth radiating from her skin, maybe the flash of her silver earrings in the wan light, or the smile that danced freely on her face.

We ended up down by the bay, on the thin strip between footpath and water. She walked by my side, close to the lapping waves, as our soles padded against the shore.

'You seem quiet somehow. I don't know, like you're sad,' she said softly.

I tried to keep my face blank, kicked sand into the air.

'My brother died recently.'

'Your brother? I'm so sorry.'

'My twin.'

She stopped, looking out at the twinkle of lights on the other side of the bay, and seated herself on the sand.

'That's awful. I'm sorry. What was he like?'

I sank down beside her, found myself telling her the whole story of Simon. The cancer in his blood. His stoicism as needles pierced every part of him. The hair in clumps on the pillowslip, caught in the drain. The doctors who insisted on just one more test, one more treatment, until they had no promises left. She listened, nodded at all the right places. She seemed to get it. I was pretty sure Simon would have approved of her.

Then she told me about her mother. It wasn't the whole story, I know that now, but it was enough to understand that Sash had suffered and come out the other side lighter, alive and beaming, her skin warm as she reached for my hand.

That's where it all started, I suppose, as the stars fell over us like a blanket, her head resting in my lap, water licking the sand.

DAY 1, SATURDAY LUNCHTIME

A line, the colour of a cleanly sliced wound, is sewn into the white wool blanket perched on my lap. I pinch at it as Mark pushes me through the automatic door to the nursery. Buzzing conversation fades to a flatline. Parents and relatives have turned to look at me, the newest mother here. The nurses are observing me too, their mouths set in smiles.

Close to the nurses' station we pass a door labelled *Resuscitation Room*, which I didn't notice last time. I hope I'll never need to enter that space. Babies are squawking across the nursery, their cries rising in non-harmonic discord. The air is filled with a sickly sweet smell, from the formula room I realise as we sweep past the labelled door. I hope I'll still be able to breastfeed. Then again, it may be one more thing that's out of my control.

As we near the end of the corridor of humidicribs, Mark pushes me to the right instead of the left.

'This is the wrong side,' I say.

'They've moved him since you visited. Another baby needed

his humidicrib, for the lights.' He pulls the wheelchair to an abrupt stop.

The card tacked to the crib is unchanged, with my name and a blank space for the baby's. I peer through the plastic. I'm not sure what I was expecting until I feel my chest deflate. It's the same baby from this morning.

On the other side of the narrow corridor, our baby's old humidicrib is lit up in electric blue. There's another baby inside. The phosphorescent light beams up through the plastic, casting wavy blue shadows against the nursery walls, as if we're under the ocean, too deep to see the sky.

A petite, slender woman with porcelain skin sits straight-backed beside the blue cot. A bundle of red wool is arranged in her lap, grey knitting needles in her hands. Her delicate feet are slipped into sandals beneath her hospital gown. She's singing a lullaby, almost to herself, as she picks up stitch after stitch. *My Bonnie lies over the ocean.* There's a deep crease of worry between her eyebrows, but the woman's eyes, small and deep-set like a bird's, brighten as she catches sight of me.

I smile at her, my plastered-on smile cracking as I realise I'm not the only one finding this all too much. She smiles back, revealing a wide, innocent gap between her two front teeth. Then she lowers her eyes to the square of wool perched in her lap and brings the needles together with a quiet click. An introvert. Perhaps a potential ally. Or a friend.

Our baby's new humidicrib is illuminated in insipid light that casts dark shadows in the corners. I reach to turn up the dial in order to examine him more closely, but Mark places his hand on mine.

'They told me to keep the lights on low, Sash. We don't want to stress him out.'

The baby is already crying, not the throaty squeal of a newborn, more like the high-pitched squall of a seagull. His eyes are scrunched closed, his face sunburnt-red. Turning the lights up briefly won't affect the baby, but in this moment I'm too overwhelmed to explain that to Mark. He believes he's doing the right thing by following the nurses' instructions to the letter. I sniff back the hint of tears threatening to spill down my cheeks.

Mark opens the humidicrib doors – how many times has he done this already? – and nestles his hands around the baby, one cupping his skull, the other resting on his back, the same way he cradled the joey. 'He likes it,' Mark says, and indeed, the baby stops wailing, his cries easing into sniffs, then softening into silence. I hadn't realised Mark had a skill with babies, hadn't known he would have any idea what to do to settle them. It should be appealing, this trait in him. And yet it feels cruel, somehow, that he already has more of a bond with this baby than me.

The baby is lying on his stomach, his neck tilted to the side with his head lolled towards me. A flush of heat shimmers in my chest, a tidal wave of disappointment. I was right the first time: he's nothing like the baby in my dreams, or in the deepest recesses of my mind. The elongation of his head appears to have eased since this morning, although his dark hair is still coated with vernix. The bruising on one hemisphere of his scalp has deepened from maroon into violet. His wide-set eyes, rimmed by stubby eyelashes and dark eyebrows, are unfocused, motionless. Downy black hair coats the olive skin of his shoulders. He's more ape than human.

'He's cute, isn't he?' Mark says.

'He's kind of ugly.' The moment it's out, I know I've said the wrong thing.

Mark's mouth gapes as if he's about to berate me, but instead he takes a controlled breath and turns back to the crib.

'Are you still okay with calling him Tobias? Toby?'

'But we decided Gabrielle. So, Gabriel for a boy, right?'

'I don't know, Sash. Gabriel doesn't seem right for him. He looks solid to me. Kind of strong. Tobias is a powerful name. Masculine. It was top of our boys' names, remember? I think he looks more like a Tobias. What do you reckon?'

I shrug. We can always change it, I suppose.

'Once it's set, I don't think we'll be changing it, darling,' Mark says lightly.

I can feel my face flush – did I say that aloud?

'You make the decision,' I mutter.

'Toby it is, then,' Mark says. 'Maybe it's time you held him.'

He goes to get a nurse to help us, glancing over his shoulder at me and giving me one of his smiles as he walks away.

Mark has left the humidicrib doors open. I inch my fingers through the holes until both hands rest on the baby. His skin is cold and moist, like a frog's. His back arches and he emits a low-pitched whimper. I run my hand over his slimy skull, rubbing at the vernix with my fingertips, then bring my palm to rest on his ribcage, at the back. With the other hand, I reach down to his feet to check the webbing. An absence of webbing would be a hint that he's not Mark's son. All at once, before I can prise his toes apart, his breath begins to rasp in and out of him like a rattlesnake. I pull my hands from the portholes and shut them with a loud snap.

'They hardly look human, do they?'

It's the woman beside the blue-lit cot across the walkway, her face alight with an affable smile. Above her, the light dances on the nursery wall.

'And they're so fragile. It feels like even touching them could break their skin.'

At last, someone who seems to understand. Someone I might be able to connect with. Someone who can answer the question welling up inside me like a flood.

'That's exactly it,' I say. I don't add that the prematurity, at least, must be my fault.

She rests her knitting on her lap. 'I'm Brigitte. My son is Jeremy. He was born this morning, thirty-seven weeks, four pounds, nine ounces.'

'How much is that in kilos?'

'Hmm, I don't know. I do know it'll take him a long time to get into this.' She indicates the square of knitted wool on her lap. 'I was planning to have it finished before he was born. I was expecting him to be bigger. At least now I have more time to get it done.'

I can't knit, can't even sew. I really should have learned how before now; it's a motherly thing to do. Brigitte is like the parents I was envious of when I worked in paediatrics, the women born to be mothers. The women who always seemed so comfortable caring for their offspring. Who always knew exactly what to do.

'This is Tobias.' The name catches at the front of my mouth, almost stutters out as I pronounce it for the first time. I choose to recite his statistics from the namecard. It seems to be the way new mothers introduce themselves. 'Emergency caesarean at thirty-five weeks, one point nine kilograms.'

Her eyes glaze. No doubt she considers me a failure for having had a caesarean. I tuck my fingers into my palms.

'There was a lot of bleeding. Clots. Hence the caesar.' My only other memory as I lay soaked in blood was the voice of Bec's mother soothing me from within. *My darling, oh my darling. Just breathe.* I wish she were still alive, so she could comfort me in person.

Brigitte recoils from my description of the blood, shuddering.

'Ugh. It sounds horrific. That's why I studied naturopathy. What do you do?'

Naturopathy. Better if I don't discuss my beliefs about natural medicine with her. And she probably won't approve of my work.

'I'm actually a pathologist.'

At first, I presume the breath she draws is in disgust – I know how naturopaths are about doctors. Then she begins to gush.

'Wow, that's just brilliant. You get to see everything. I must say, I do love those TV shows. Is it really like *CSI*? Fingerprints, DNA tests?'

'I'm an anatomical pathologist. Not forensic. Most of my work is staring down microscopes at pink splodges and purple dots and writing reports that people skip over. I have to write the conclusions in capitals so they're not overlooked.'

'So, you love your work, then?' she says with a grin.

'I suppose. Some days. I don't like the dissecting dead babies part.'

The first baby I dissected had been found by her mother in her cot, a suspected SIDS case. Her body was stiff as I shifted her into position on the steel tray. She looked and felt like a hard plastic doll; not like a real baby at all. As I sliced through her skin, her guts spilled out of the slit, slippery on the steel. I gagged. I resolved to quit right there and then. Not just pathology, but all of medicine. I was never coming back.

It was my supervisor who led me from the locker room back to that dissection room, to the baby waiting for me on the steel.

It was my duty, she said, to find out why this baby had died. To give her parents the answer they so desperately needed. It was the best thing I could do, for them and for her.

So that is what I did; what I still do from time to time. Cutting through the babies' wafer-thin flesh, digging deep into them, searching their shelled-out cavities for something or someone to blame. I don't pretend it's pleasant. I try not to talk about it to my friends when they become new mothers. I don't think they'd understand.

Brigitte is staring at me now with a look of horror on her face, as if I might be contemplating dissecting her baby. With the heat of the nursery and the fatigue muddying my brain, I realise abruptly that I've said the wrong thing.

'Sorry. I shouldn't have mentioned that. I've just got babies on my mind.' I flash her a weak smile, which feels more like a grimace. The muscles in my face ache with the effort.

Brigitte frowns back at me, before looking down at her thin hands, clasped together in her lap.

'I lost faith in Western medicine years ago. I only trusted natural remedies. That's why I became a naturopath. Then, last year, I developed a new appreciation for doctors when my cousin's baby was born at twenty-four weeks. They didn't think he was going to make it. Somehow, thanks to the hospital, he pulled through. And it looks like he's going to be fine long-term.'

'Poor parents,' I murmur. Thirty-five weeks feels bad enough.

'It was tough for them.' She nods. 'They're through the worst of it now, though. As for me, I can't wait to get Jeremy out of here. I'm looking forward to taking him home. A new start.'

Brigitte's lips are blue, almost cyanotic. I want to reach for her wrist, check her pulse, make sure she isn't becoming one of my corpses, before I realise it's the humidicrib lights tainting the colour of her skin. Still leaning forward, I almost whisper the question that burns in my chest.

'Is it normal to feel nothing?'

Brigitte's eyes soften.

'For the baby? Probably. The social worker told me bonding is harder when they're in the nursery. I mean, I'm sitting here, but I could be anywhere, right? How would my baby know? I can't even hold him yet. It's harder to love them when they're behind plastic.' She smiles kindly.

Maybe that's why I'm finding him ugly. Maybe all premature babies are. Maybe all mothers think the same thing.

'You're normal,' she says reassuringly. 'It's your husband who seems unusually keen. He's been here most of the morning. I mean, I guess you're lucky, right? Is he that attentive with you, too?'

I shrug. He hasn't always been, but I'm not about to disclose that to a stranger, no matter how trustworthy she seems. 'What about you?'

She sighs. 'John is more like a part-time husband. He's a fly-in, fly-out engineer. I've been trying to call him all day to tell him the news. Remote sites. They're the worst.'

A hand on my shoulder, the weight of a dumbbell. Mark, with Ursula by his side.

'I can help you with your first hold with Toby before my lunch break.' Ursula opens the whole sidewall of the humidicrib and adjusts the leads and tubes. 'You're ready?' Before I can answer, she lifts Toby high into the air, the leads draped over her arm as she delivers him into the crooks of my elbows.

He's lighter than I expected, nearly weightless.

He lies motionless in my arms. There's a metallic scent wafting off him, perhaps from the antibiotics, perhaps his natural smell. His eyes are pinched shut, as if the industrial scent is being emitted from me.

I look up at Mark. He is gazing at Toby in adoration.

I begin to peel the wraps from Toby when Ursula taps my shoulder.

'You need to keep him warm.' She places the blanket over him, then checks the watch hanging from her breast pocket on a silver chain. 'Lunchtime.' She raps me on the back. 'Good luck.'

Why do I need good luck? Does she say that to all the new mothers, or is that a warning just to me?

I glance over the walkway, but Brigitte's chair is empty. She didn't say goodbye.

From the wheelchair beside Toby's cot, I can see a woman out the window, standing at the bus stop opposite the hospital. She has a baby cocooned in a carrier on her chest, her chin resting on the baby's head, her hands wrapped around it like ribbons tying a present.

I lift Tobias upright, place him on my shoulder, then encircle him in my arms, to make it look as though I'm snuggling him. The fuzziness inside my brain is diminishing. I can almost feel the drugs being metabolised inside me, chemical compounds concentrating in my sweat and urine, soon to be expelled. Slowly and surely, I'm turning back into myself.

'Do you know how many other babies were born today?' I whisper to Mark.

'No idea. Why do you ask?'

I'll have to tell Mark of my concerns soon, I suppose. It's the right thing, the best thing, to do. Holding the baby now has confirmed my fears. My lack of attachment towards Toby is far beyond the normal maternal response. I'm doing everything right, but it still feels all wrong. It isn't 'normal' like Brigitte suggested, nor do I feel at all depressed. I can't explain away this feeling about the baby. The only possible explanation is that there's been a swap. A mistake. My real baby must be in the nursery, somewhere. I'm going to need Mark's help to examine the other babies, to track down our real child. I know he'll support me in this.

An alarm screeches from a monitor nearby, echoing down the long corridor to the nurses' desk. Red lights flash on the screen. It all happens too quickly and before I can deduce that it's Toby's monitor emitting the alarm, a cluster of nurses has surrounded me. They snatch him from my arms and replace him in the humidicrib. Then they take turns listening to his chest with stethoscopes, plugging and unplugging monitor leads. Mark stands beside me, staring with wide eyes.

The alarm has stopped long seconds ago. Toby is breathing fine now, apparently. Did he even stop at all?

'An apnoea.' Ursula clips the side of the humidicrib back into place. 'It's not unusual for babies this small to stop breathing for short periods. It can be positional, if their head bends too far forward and blocks their airway. They've got very small airways. But I'm sure you know that.'

If only I'd realised what was going on, I could have fixed it myself.

'Did I do something wrong?'

No one answers. Not one of the nurses will meet my eyes.

As the nurses dissipate, Mark is still staring at me.

I glance to the desk. The nurses are standing in a huddle, observing me from afar. Is this some sort of test of my mothering abilities? A cruel prank for the new doctor-mother: see if she can identify that she has been bestowed a false baby? Surely not – it seems too far-fetched, even given the situation. The mix-up can't be intentional. With a flash of clarity, I recall Ursula making an error with my name. It's their fault. The hospital's.

Against the cotton sheet, Toby lies motionless. Looking at him now, I feel nothing. Holding him, I felt nothing either. I catch Mark's fearful eyes. There are things I need to say.

'I know you've bonded with this baby. But just because I haven't doesn't mean there's something wrong with *me*.'

It's beyond Toby's prematurity, all of this, beyond my guilt and fear, far beyond rationality and love. I know I'm right. That my baby, who appeared to me in my dreams, needs to be trusted, needs to be honoured and believed.

'Mark. I know what's wrong.' The words that will change everything crystallise in my mind, as Toby's face blurs into the baby from the ultrasound, the baby I knew we were destined to have before I realised I even wanted one, the baby I committed to by becoming Mark's wife.

'This is not our baby. Mark, listen to me. This baby is not our son.'

TEN YEARS EARLIER

MARK

What was our wedding day like? It was perfect.

I mean, almost.

Sash wasn't on her side of the bed when I woke up. She insisted on staying at Bec's. Tradition, apparently. I can't say I understood. Adam – Bec's partner since they met at the jazz club, and my best man – showed up around twelve. We got into our tuxedos, combed our hair and sat down with a beer in front of the footy. He gave me a few jibes about being under the thumb for the rest of my life as we watched the pre-game show. I warned him he was likely to be next. He shut up after that. Besides, Sash wasn't anywhere near high maintenance. She's always let me do whatever I liked. In fact, back then she was constantly encouraging me to go out, live a little, try to have more fun.

The limos were taking a long time to arrive. Sorting out the cars had been my job for the wedding, Sash said. It was all I had to do. It got to one o'clock. The players were starting to warm up on-screen when a text came through from Sash.

Are the cars far away?

I'd booked them for twelve-thirty. They were definitely running late.

I rang the limousine company. No answer. I called the mobile number from their website. Nothing.

'Fuck, man, did you speak to them recently?' Adam said.

Nearly there, I texted back. The rosebud in my lapel was already turning brown at the tip.

'You're both going to have to get a taxi to your wedding,' Adam said, shaking his head.

I checked my emails. The limo company had sent through confirmation of the booking. Two limousines, twelve-thirty, Saturday 14 February 2002. *2002?* That was next year. I hoped like hell they wouldn't have taken reservations a year in advance.

I pulled open the front door, peered into the empty street. Adam was on the porch, ordering a taxi. Not a sniff of a limo. Simon wouldn't have made a mistake like this. What would he do now? I stepped back inside to think.

Dad had an old blue Chevrolet in the garage. It was rusting out in places, but he still ran it from time to time. He'd offered to take Sash for a ride when we first visited their house. She politely declined; antique cars weren't really her thing, she said. The car might have been old and small. But I had to call Dad, even if he'd already left for the church. That car was my best hope.

*

Sash looked stunning as she walked down the aisle. Her smile was dazzling, her braided hair glistening. I don't think I'd ever seen her look quite so beautiful. At the altar she turned to face me and took my hands in hers, squeezing them tight. Then she smiled her radiant smile at me again. I knew she had already forgiven me for stuffing up the limos, for having to drive her to the wedding, for seeing her before the ceremony began, for getting her to the church more than half an hour late.

With the sunlight that filtered through the stained glass playing on her face, I could hardly focus during the ceremony. I even stumbled over the vows. We'd written them the week before – Sash did most of the work, but I'd been happy to go along with the sentiments. Something about honesty. Something about love. It didn't really matter what we said, anyway. All that mattered was that we loved each other. That we didn't want to spend our lives with anyone else. That we'd be together *'til death do us part*.

In retrospect, I probably should have said more: all the reasons I loved Sash. Her compassion, her thoughtfulness. Her passion for anything she set her mind to. Her integrity, to a fault. She was someone I could depend upon, someone I could trust; who believed in me and my wild dreams, who I wanted to create a family with. I couldn't wait to start our lives together, to be everything Sash would want, give her everything she could ever need.

After the formalities were over and we stepped out of the church into blinding sun, Sash leaned against me, a hand cupped against my ear. 'Great work with the car,' she said. 'That's one of the things I love most about you, Mark. You never quit. You always find a way around problems. And you never give up on me.'

DAY 1, SATURDAY LUNCHTIME

I shrug the woollen blanket off my lap, down to my ankles. It's a relief to have finally said it.

Mark's mouth snaps shut. He leans in closer, checking whether any of the staff or visitors have heard.

'Not our baby?' he hisses. 'That's not funny, Sash. Is this supposed to be a joke? Like that April Fools' Day when you convinced me there was a brown snake in the bathroom. This is a joke. Right? *Right?*'

The baby is asleep before us, resting on his side like a marooned boat. I gawk at his translucent skin.

'He's not ours,' I say again in my serenest tone, the one I would employ with patients when they were agitated or upset. It's the same voice I used when I spoke with Damien's parents on that fateful night eleven years ago, when I was still training to be a paediatrician. Seated on his mother's lap in the emergency department, Damien had red, tear-stained cheeks.

His chubby limbs thrashed against me like a wild animal as I examined him. I was reassured by his energy and his normal observations. His temperature had settled with medication. He even gave me a miniature smile as I made a funny face.

'He's okay for now,' I recall saying to his parents in my most placid voice. 'I know you're worried. Why don't you take him home, see how he goes overnight. You can always bring him back in the morning if you're still concerned. Yes?'

His father nodded, taking in every word. His mother cradled Damien in her arms. I thought they were overreacting to his fever, like so many other parents I had seen before. I thought that reassuring them was the right thing to do. How could I have known he wasn't going to be fine at all?

I catch Mark's eye and force him to hold my gaze.

'Mark, I'm being completely serious.' I point at the sleeping child before us. 'This is not our baby.'

'Jesus.' Mark's eyes widen. 'How ... I mean ... Shit, Sash. Are you sure? Because this could be very tricky. It's not something to joke about.'

'I'm not joking. You have to believe me. I'm certain.' My calmest voice again.

'But how the hell could that have happened?'

'I'm not sure. Easily enough, I suppose. Particularly if some-one isn't paying attention.' Anatomical specimens get mixed up, mislabelled, lost in the system, all the time at work. Pathology reports, too. 'And I know it has happened before, in the States. Lots of other places, too. And now it's happened to us.' There's a lightness in my chest now I've said what I needed to.

He scrutinises my face.

'And you're sure about this?'

I nod and grasp at his hands.

'He isn't ours. And now we need to find our real baby.'

He squeezes back. *Don't worry. I believe you.*

His hand in mine is warm and smooth, like that first night we met, seated on the beach in the moonlight, cool sand on our calves. After he told me about his brother, Simon, I told him the story of the last time I remember seeing my mother. He didn't laugh or look incredulous. Instead, he listened as I described my mother's hair, gleaming golden under the porchlight. She had turned and placed her finger across her lips as if binding me to silence before she slipped away into the night.

Mark has gone, striding across the nursery before I can say any more. Trying to stay calm, I hunch down in the wheelchair and retrieve my phone buried in the pocket of my dressing gown. No messages. I guess Mark hasn't yet had time to send out the birth-announcement text we crafted together a week ago to our friends and family.

The nurses aren't watching me. I can't see where Mark has gone; presumably he's tracking down a midwife. Slowly I punch the words *'Baby mix-up'* into the search engine with unsteady fingers. I nearly drop the phone as the page loads. Fourteen million results?

My mouth gapes as I scroll through the search finds. It's like I told Mark, except it's more prevalent than I realised. France. Brazil. Poland. South Africa. Canada. Every state of Australia. High-profile cases before the courts across the world. Nearly always accidental. The mothers often knew instantly, and when the authorities believed them, their babies were returned immediately. Yet sometimes the mistakes took hours to recognise and rectify. In the meantime, women were left to feed the wrong babies. And, sometimes, the women weren't believed by authorities for years. Or at all.

It's already been hours since our baby was born. At least she won't have been fed by the wrong woman. She might have been given her milk, but she won't have been able to breastfeed. She's too young to have sucked the milk from another woman's breast.

I scan through more pages for anything that could help. The hospital administrators are quoted in the news articles with sincere apologies, promises to fix the system. Snippets of dialogue from court cases, quotes from the children themselves as adults. Nothing from the mothers. Why aren't they speaking out?

Maybe I should call the media, lawyers? No. Better not to make waves. Mark's more than capable of sorting all this out. He's stuck with me, believed in me through everything, even when I thought I couldn't go on. And doctors are reasonable. They believe other doctors. I have to trust it'll be put right, that we'll have our baby back any time now.

A chill comes over me. I tug the blanket from my ankles up to my lap. I'll expect a sincere apology, of course, once I finally have my beautiful baby in my arms. But the hospital should be glad this has happened to someone who understands how fallible humans are. How easily mistakes can occur. Even if they hardly ever happen to me.

At least half an hour later, Mark still hasn't returned. Presumably he's on the trail of our baby. But I can't just sit here helplessly. I need to do something, find my own proof. After all,

I'll recognise my baby instantly – really, I'm the best person to look.

Hauling myself to my feet, I nearly double over from the fiery ache in my guts. I should have accepted at least a small dose of morphine, I suppose. I begin to move jerkily from one humidicrib to the next. There are ten of them in total lining both walls of this corridor; I've counted them three times to be sure. The girl in the first humidicrib beside Toby's has a downy scalp and stubby nose. The second girl along, tubby fingers and curled-up toes. I can see Mark again, engrossed in a conversation with Ursula at the desk. I quicken my gait, glancing through the perspex of each crib as I pass, focusing more on the babies with pink namecards. So many children, each of them needing love. I'm surprised their parents aren't by their sides. When I find my baby, I know I won't be leaving the humidicrib for even a moment. I continue up the row.

Thin legs, dark skin. Stuck-out ears, jutting chin.

I round the corner of the nursery's L shape, clutching my aching belly as I stumble between the open cots in the smaller wing, all eight of them.

Black eyes, ruddy face. Dark hair, chubby waist.

Next cot, then the next, then the next. Finally, I'm at the end of the nursery. I can't have missed any of the babies. So how is it possible that none of them looks like mine?

I sink against a nearby bench, clinging on to remain upright despite the pain, which is now a sword stabbing deep into my guts. Behind me, there's a squeak. Ursula, directing a wheelchair towards me.

'You shouldn't be wandering around in your state,' she says. 'Most women can't even walk the day after their caesar.'

She levers me into the chair and wheels me back through the nursery. 'I'll take you back to your room shortly. Mark had a chat with me. We'll sort this out. Do you need some painkillers in the meantime?'

'I don't need painkillers. I just need my baby,' I say, my heart hammering. 'Right away.'

'Of course,' she says, parking me in front of Toby's cot. 'In the meantime, I suggest you spend some time by *this* baby's side.'

Before she steps away, an idea comes to me, a way I can begin to assemble irrefutable proof. I lift my head and try to compose myself.

'Can we weigh this baby, please?'

Ursula's mouth forms a neat red bow. 'Oh, but he's already been weighed today.' She points to the sign at the end of his cot as she pulls up the wheelchair. 'One point nine kilograms. He's a healthy weight.'

'It won't take a moment.'

'You wouldn't want to disturb him unnecessarily, would you? He needs all the growing time he can get.'

It was Ursula who got my name wrong at the start. Could she have something to do with this?

'I'm just a little concerned, that's all. I'm not sure they weighed him correctly.'

Ursula tilts her head. 'You missed the first weigh. I understand. I suppose just this once.'

The trolley clacks over the lines in the vinyl as she wheels the scales from the formula room. She places Toby on the metal like a netted fish. He doesn't make a sound. The numbers flash red until they come to rest: 2070 grams.

'I knew something was wrong,' I say, adrenaline thrilling through my limbs as I indicate the discrepancy between the two weights. 'This is not my baby.'

Ursula bundles Toby back into the humidicrib and snaps the side shut.

'I should have said. The nasogastric tube and the connector leads all add a little mass, you understand. We subtract the estimation for them in our calculation of your son's weight.'

She kneels beside me, rubbing her hand on my forearm. I nearly recoil from her touch, from her change in manner, but stop myself just in time. 'It's a shock, isn't it? They look different when they're premature. He'll grow into his wrinkles and his skin, you'll see.' Her tone sharpens, almost imperceptibly. 'You need to believe this baby is your son.'

I want to slink down, pretend none of this ever happened. Instead, I straighten my spine against the back of the wheelchair.

'Is there something you're not telling me?'

Ursula steps back from the chair, her lips thin.

'I have to be honest: I am very concerned for the health of your child. And for yourself.' She points at the humidicrib with a stern finger. 'This is your son, Sasha. Look – his wrists and ankles, both labelled.' She leans for his file on the bench and, with the writing facing me, flicks through the pages. 'All the documentation, in order.'

'That means nothing,' I say. 'You should know that. All I want is to find my baby. Surely that's not too much to ask?'

Two nurses approach from the desk, their jaws set. They stop a few metres away from me. Are they afraid to get too close?

'You need a hand, Ursula?' one says. 'You want to call a code?'

A code. They're asking if Ursula wants to call hospital security.

Ursula eyes me from where she stands beside the bench. 'Call Dr Niles,' she says.

'You're going to shut me down, is that it?' I screech. 'Call me crazy?'

There's a stirring among a few visitors seated around other nursery cots. A low murmuring rises in the hot air. Am I speaking louder than I should? Or are these parents sick of being ignored as well?

'You must know the case in the US,' I say, raising my voice as Mark approaches me. Where has he been? 'It was a midwife error. There have been many other cases, too.' My voice falters. All at once, I can't recall any details.

Mark shakes his head at Ursula, holding his palm up to her. She and the other nurses step away. He kneels before me on the laminated floor, his hands resting on my knees, his eyes frozen as if in fear. His voice is the one he uses during animal rescues, when he's trying to placate injured wildlife.

'Darling, you need to calm down. There's someone come to see you. Someone you can count on.'

A shadowy figure looms behind Mark and comes into focus.

'Congratulations, you two.'

It's Dad standing above me, his gravelly voice thinner than normal as he bends down to the wheelchair and plants a dry kiss on my cheek. He's clutching a green shopping bag and a newspaper, the deep wrinkles on his hands folding in on themselves like rippled waves approaching shore.

Mark walks off, to give us privacy I presume. The nurses return to the desk. The scattered visitors remain beside their newborns. Dad is staring at me like he did when I would occasionally misbehave as a child. No sense telling him about the baby mix-up. He's still traumatised from my birth all those years ago. He wouldn't believe me, anyway. Plus he couldn't possibly understand what I'm going through.

Dad leans towards the humidicrib and peers inside.

'Your baby looks just like you when you were born.'

Dad has never had much of an eye for faces.

'I'm not sure, Dad.'

He doesn't seem to hear me. From deep in the shopping bag he retrieves a quilt that he lays with ceremony in my lap.

'Thought you might like this for him.'

It's my childhood patchwork quilt. The cotton is cool under my fingertips. Some of the patterns are familiar – teddy bears, whales, fire trucks – and others I don't recall at all. As a child, I used to hold it to my nose and rub the material across my skin, inhaling the various smells embedded within the fabrics. It was my main source of comfort.

'I don't think I ever told you, but your mother made it for you. When she was pregnant.'

I trace the outlines of the octagons, stitched together with tiny white threads, and spread the quilt across my lap. For a moment, the drama of the day feels far away. My mother made this just for me.

'Did she always sew?'

'Rose used to make pottery when I first met her. But she made such a mess with the clay, I suggested she move into sewing.'

He produces a photo album from the bag. There's a pink giraffe on the cover.

'Your baby album. I dug it out, too. Thought you might be interested.'

I haven't seen one like this for years: photographs adhering to the sticky, yellowing backing paper, clear plastic folded over to hold them in place. After all this time, the plastic is coming unstuck. Some of the photos have slipped down the pages, slid underneath the plastic covers as if they're trying to escape.

'Dad, what was Mum like after I was born?'

His face breaks out in a creased grin. 'Overjoyed.' Then his eyes drop.

I flick through the images. I'm a newborn, swaddled in blankets and a knitted beanie, my mother clutching me in an awkward embrace as she stares at the camera from under her eyelids, unsmiling.

'She doesn't look . . . overjoyed.'

Dad seats himself beside the humidicrib and puts his bag on the floor between us. He unfolds the newspaper, then refolds it in a complicated pattern so only the crossword is visible.

'These days they might have diagnosed her with something. They love doing that, don't they?'

I clutch at the quilt.

'What do you mean?'

Dad fills in some letters across the top line.

'That postnatal depression thing, I suppose,' he says. 'Everyone has it these days.'

I scrunch up my eyes. 'You never told me that. And you never showed me this album before.'

'I thought I had.'

The photographs swim before me. Me, as a toddler in a wading pool; pushing a wooden toy wagon; naked in a bath. My mother has disappeared. I'd always assumed it was because she took the photos. I press the album closed.

'No. You never told me.'

Glimpses used to come to me from time to time: visions of my mother's pale face in the mirror of her bedroom dresser. She would be running a brush from her roots down to her split ends, or dabbing on foundation, or plucking stray hairs from her chin with tweezers. She never noticed me sitting beside her on the dresser stool. Her face began to glow, and I would reach out my hand to the mirror, but before I could touch her reflection the picture always fractured into shards.

I push the quilt and photo album back into the shopping bag. The fusty smell of mothballs hits me, the scent of my mother's sewing chest. The quilt must have taken hours and hours to make, tiny threads stitched into place with an image of me held in her mind as I kicked away at the inside of her. Some of the stitches are pulling loose and patches of material are fraying like old cobwebs. It will be my job to learn to sew, otherwise the quilt will fall apart.

Dad lifts his pen from where it has leached a small pool of ink onto the newsprint. He won't meet my eyes.

'Rose was in a psychiatric ward several times. You were six months old the first time – too young to remember. I don't know why I'm telling you all this now. It's all coming back.'

Coldness flows through me. He has definitely never told me this before. I shiver and clutch my arms to my chest. Dad is still speaking. He pauses, running his eyes over my face, my hands.

'Of course, you'll be fine. A natural. You're nothing like her.'

He's always bluntly forthright, so I can usually trust his assessment of me. But if I'm not like my mother, who am I like?

He folds the newspaper up until it's small enough to squeeze into his pocket.

'You always seemed so . . . well adjusted after she left. It never seemed to have affected you much.'

Heat rises behind my eyelids. 'I guess not.'

He leans to kiss me goodbye.

'I got the nine-letter word today, by the way. *Exonerate.*'

He's leaving already? Even though he's always been out of touch with his feelings, emotionally repressed, he's still an ally. I need him here. I turn my head so his lips graze my ear.

'Can't you stay a little longer?'

'I'd love to, but I've got a golf match. By the way, this is for Toby.'

The crinkly yellow cellophane sticks to my damp fingers.

'I bought it from the Women's Auxiliary downstairs. Rose was a knitter too, you know.'

His shoes squeak on the vinyl as he shuffles towards the nursery door.

I rip the sticky tape from the cellophane. Inside is a soft blue woollen cardigan with a cable-stitch neckline and pearly buttons down the front. It's simple but lovely. I hold it up against the perspex of Toby's cot. It's still a little big for a premmie. Down the track, it'll look lovely on our baby – when we find her, that is. I'm hoping the staff will listen to Mark, take him seriously. He'll be able to track her down. I only hope it won't take him too long.

DAY 1, SATURDAY AFTERNOON

Mark gives me a smile as he returns. I'm not sure how long has passed since Dad left.

'Everything's going to be fine, Sash,' he says, with more confidence than I feel. He takes hold of the wheelchair handles. 'They want us to head back to your room to have a chat.'

The corridors, the lift back down to level one, crowd in as Mark guides me back to the maternity ward. I'm Alice in a nightmarish Wonderland, growing larger and larger as the hospital walls shrink around me. Babies squeal from each door we pass, their cries echoing through my skull like foghorns. I can't help wishing one of these healthy term babies would suddenly reveal itself as my own missing child.

In my room, Dr Solomon is waiting for me, clad in a shiny suit with a tie hanging straight down the middle of his starched shirt. His hands are thrust into his pockets. He taps a buffed boot on the dusty carpet at the side of my bed.

Ursula stands beside him, her harsh gaze following me. Mark pulls me to a stop and helps me up onto the bed. I bite my lip so as not to scream from the piercing pain in my gut. I don't want to show any sign of weakness right now.

As my head is propped against the pillow, my eyes fall on the van Gogh reproduction above the bedside table. I hadn't noticed it earlier today. *First Steps*: a mother, supportive, holds her child beneath his armpits as he takes tentative steps towards his father in a field. On our New York trip, while Mark frequented hip cafés for inspiration, I wandered through the Metropolitan Museum of Art and stumbled on this painting. My eyes had filled with tears as I'd stared at the figures, envisaging myself as the mother sacrificing everything for her child, Mark as the father beckoning to his son.

Dr Solomon folds his arms and enunciates his words. 'I believe there is a problem?'

'Yes,' I say. 'We need to find our baby. Please help us.'

Mark sits at the foot of the bed, grasping so tight to my hand that my knuckles ache. 'Please,' he echoes.

I tell Dr Solomon everything: the medications, the blood test that went awry, the general anaesthetic, the protracted time Toby spent away from me, his lack of resemblance to Mark or me. Dr Solomon stands very still, uncrossing his arms every now and then to scratch his nose or smooth down his hair. Ursula stares at me from the other side of the room.

When I finish, Dr Solomon gestures for me to lie down. Mark helps me into a recline. Dr Solomon raises my gown. With his brisk, cold hands on my belly, pressing hard to ensure my womb is still contracted and checking my dressing, I feel a little like a corpse. He pulls the covers back across my naked skin, grunting with satisfaction.

'I apologise for any misunderstandings with the nursing staff,' he says in a gruff voice. 'I inspected Toby in the nursery before coming here. He is the baby I delivered in the early hours of this morning. I know you were expecting a girl, but you definitely had a little boy. Your baby was labelled with two name bands at birth, ankle and wrist, as is standard protocol. Because of his gestation, a midwife transported him from the theatre to the nursery.' He signs my medical file and places it on the tray table beside me.

He hasn't heard anything I've said.

'But it was supposed to be a girl,' I murmur.

Dr Solomon shakes his head back and forth.

'I presume you know that no test in medicine, including an ultrasound, is one hundred per cent correct.'

'I was convinced,' I say with more certainty now. 'It felt like a girl to me.'

'Uh-huh.'

This is what they do, doctors. Dismiss the pieces of the puzzle that don't fit. Dismiss female intuition, too.

'Was our baby left alone at any stage?' I ask. Mark squeezes my hand tight. *Easy, Sash.*

'You were with the baby the whole time, weren't you?' Dr Solomon says, indicating Ursula.

'Oh, yes,' she says, running the chain of her glasses between forefinger and thumb. 'He was never left alone.'

'But she got my name wrong,' I cry, pulling myself to sitting with the overhead handlebar. The stitches on my belly, and the cut on my finger from the kangaroo rescue, prick and burn.

Ursula picks up my file and makes a show of inspecting the

pages under the lights. How can she be allowed to get away with this? How can any of them?

'I just need proof. Can't we do DNA testing?'

'He's not an IVF baby, is he?' Dr Solomon says.

During the months that stretched into years as we tried to conceive, I'd pushed and pushed Mark to start IVF. I asked in the car, I asked over the dinner table, I asked in bed. Mark resisted each and every time. Finally, one morning over Mark's poached eggs, I'd exploded.

'Don't you even want a baby?'

He'd carefully tipped the plastic ladle, egg inside, to drain water back into the saucepan. 'More than anything.'

'More than me?'

He shook his head. 'Sash, come on. I don't want you having invasive medical stuff. Not after watching Simon. All those needles. In his arms. His spine. His hip. I told you what he went through, right?' He slid the egg onto his slice of toast. 'You know I can't stand hospitals.'

I thrust my knife into my own egg. Yolk oozed out like bodily fluids, spilling over my spinach, weaving its way around the mushrooms.

'Plus, there's been enough going on in recent years with . . . you know,' he'd said. 'That baby who died. I don't want to be responsible for causing you more stress.'

I dabbed the tines of my fork into the yellow goo and spread it over the edges of my plate.

'I'll do *anything* except IVF,' he said.

We didn't speak for three days. In the end, Mark won. We did what he wanted. Waited. Hoped for a miracle. I never had a choice.

'There was no IVF,' I say to Dr Solomon now.

'Then there can't have been any sort of mix-up in a petri dish or a lab. There certainly hasn't been a mix-up here. So there doesn't seem to be any need for DNA tests, does there?'

Dr Solomon's voice sounds ominously grave. I'm confused. Then concerned. Surely something terrible hasn't happened to my baby. They would have had to say something, wouldn't they? And yes, I feel my baby is missing, but there are a finite number of premature babies here in the hospital. We just need to work through the options systematically. But everyone's looking at me with such pity that I feel nauseated. Have I missed something? What is Dr Solomon saying?

I can feel my breathing quicken. None of the cases I've heard about involved cover-ups of dead babies. It would be unfathomable. Yet doctors prefer to hide their mistakes. Bury them, in fact.

Ursula spoke about something going around the hospital in the past. An infection. It comes to me for the second time, a terrible lurch – is it possible my child could be dead?

'Has something happened to my baby?' I ask shakily.

Dr Solomon and Ursula exchange glances.

'Of course not, Sasha,' he says at once.

The relief floods through my body until I realise with a start that I'll have to be more careful. I shouldn't make any more accusations while my baby is still missing – not until I know the truth.

I give Mark's hand a firm squeeze. *Help, please.*

'Couldn't we check Toby's DNA, to be sure?' Mark says.

Dr Solomon smooths down his tie.

'All the documentation is in order. There's nothing further that needs to be done at this stage.'

'Why won't you respect my wishes?' I say, almost crushing Mark's hand in mine. 'Why aren't you helping us find our baby?'

'Sasha, we're all trying to help you.' Dr Solomon reaches for the drug chart hanging on the end of my bed. 'There's an order for sleeping tablets, two before bed, and Valium as required. And do make sure you take enough painkillers. That should make you altogether more comfortable,' he says.

Mark presses my hand between his palms. *Everything will be okay.* Mark listens to doctors, but what he can't understand is that doctors aren't always right.

Dr Solomon hangs the chart back on my bed with a clatter and heads for the door, Ursula following him.

'Please,' I say, struggling not to yell. How can the conversation be over? 'Can't you call my specialist from the Royal? Dr Yang. She'll tell you what I'm like. She knows I wouldn't make up something like this. Mark will tell you, too. Mark, tell him.'

Before Mark can say something, Dr Solomon speaks. 'I've already spoken with Dr Yang. We felt it would be best for you to speak with a colleague of mine. I've asked her to come and meet with you as soon as possible, to sort everything out today.' He turns to Mark, sitting stony beside me. 'I'd like a word with you outside if I may.'

Mark gives me his best attempt at a reassuring smile as he trails Dr Solomon and Ursula out the door.

I'm alone, again.

Maybe they're right and I'm wrong. A hospital conspiracy is definitely far-fetched. And how could there have even been a baby swap, or a death, when Mark was there with Ursula the whole time? Maybe I should be listening to the doctors. Believing them. Doctors usually know what they're talking about. Don't they?

Breathe, I tell myself. *They've listened to you. They wouldn't lie to a patient. You're tired, you're sick . . .*

I've been wrong before. My intuition about Damien was wrong. After him, I feared I wasn't safe to take care of children, believed I wasn't responsible enough. Even before that, I'd already doubted my ability to be a good enough mother, questioned whether I even had the right to try given my own mother had walked out on her parental responsibilities. I feared I'd inherited some sort of bad-mother gene.

I suppose there's a simple solution: I just need to spend more time with Toby, try harder to be his mother. Even if I'm still far from convinced that he's my child, I need to try to love him, in the same way I was able to love the other babies that stopped growing inside me without even thinking. It's not Toby's fault that he's trapped upstairs in a plastic box. How hard could it be to try to give him love?

I've never felt more alone than I do right now. I wish Bec's mother, Lucia, was here with me, squeezing my hand. Illuminated by fluorescent lights, the mother from *First Steps* holds her child upright in the painting above my head. But I'm not the mother at all, I realise with another surge of nausea. I'm the child just learning to walk. And where, I wonder as acid burns the back of my throat, is my mother, holding my hand as I go?

TWELVE YEARS EARLIER

MARK

After that first night on the beach, Sash barely spoke about her mother again. Rose had walked out when Sash was young; at least, that's what I was told. I tried to bring it up with her a few times, but Sash always changed the subject, her eyes blank, her mouth a slack line.

Sash was happy enough to talk about her childhood, though. Lucia had been like her surrogate mum, taking care of Sash after school, cooking her dinner, teaching her the ways of the world. Her daughter Bec was almost a sister to Sash. They spent their childhoods playing Lego and Barbies after school, racing each other up trees and sprinting their bikes through the local park on weekends. As for Bill, Sasha's father, he sank into his work, almost forgetting he had a daughter at all.

I met her father for the first time after Sash and I had been dating a few months. I'd just moved into her apartment the week before. There was a ring at the doorbell. Bill stared over my shoulder as I pulled open the front door. Sash had showed me photos of him, so I knew what he looked like, but he clearly had no idea who I was. I was surprised Sash hadn't mentioned me. But then, Sash never told him much at all, and I had moved in with her pretty fast.

'Does a Sasha Jamieson still live here?' he said.

I extended my hand.

'I'm Mark. You must be Bill. Sash is stuck at work. Please, come in.'

Bill shuffled on the doorstep. 'I don't want to intrude.' He handed over a bag. 'I was cleaning out her bedroom. Thought she might want these.' He stepped backwards, almost tripping over his feet. 'Please let her know I called by.'

'I will.'

I sifted through the bag. It was full of square, black-and-white photographs of a serious woman in front of instantly recognisable backdrops: Eiffel Tower, Leaning Tower of Pisa, Colosseum. The woman was beautiful, a younger version of Sash, but with a longer, narrower nose. It could only have been her mum.

I had shut the bag and stuffed it on the top shelf of the cupboard in the spare room. Back then, I thought it would cause Sash harm to view the photographs. I justified it at the time by promising myself I would show her one day. To be honest, I'm still waiting to pull them out.

Sash met my parents early on for dinner at a fancy Italian restaurant. As we walked in the door, Mum stood up and held out a stiff hand to Sash. 'Pleased to finally meet you,' Mum said. 'I don't think I've seen my darling son quite as smitten with his previous girlfriends.' She turned to me. 'Except maybe that girl Emma.' She tittered as though it were a joke and returned her focus to Sash. 'Emma broke his heart back in first-year university.' Then, with narrowing eyes, 'I suggest you take things slow with our son.'

My cheeks burned. Dad only nodded a greeting to Sash as she slid into the chair next to him. She bumped her cutlery with her elbow, knocking a knife to the floor. Dad raised his eyebrows at me.

'Sorry,' Sash said, reaching for the knife. I didn't blame her for being flustered. My parents could be a little intimidating at times.

'I promise I'll take good care of Mark.' Sash folded her hands in her lap. 'And we'll take things slowly.'

'Well, good then. It's nice to finally meet the woman who seems to be making our son so content.' Mum's voice softened. 'It hasn't all been happy families, you know.'

Sash gave a sympathetic smile.

'So, welcome to the family,' Dad said in a neutral tone.

As we sipped prosecco and slurped at pasta, I could see Sash was trying hard to use her best table manners. Normally, with her long hours, she was so starving by the time she got home to me that she was almost ready to inhale her food. This night, she wound the spaghetti around her fork, pressed against her spoon. She paused between mouthfuls, nodding at my mother's inane stories and smiling at my father's attempted jokes. When she placed her knife and fork together on her plate at the end of her meal, I saw Mum give a satisfied nod to Dad.

By the time we left the restaurant and wandered back to our car under the glare of streetlamps, I could tell my parents had been impressed. Frankly, so was I. Impressed that this woman, who had endured such an unusual childhood, yet was so accomplished in her own right, could find a place in a family as dysfunctional as my own.

DAY 1, SATURDAY AFTERNOON

A slim woman, nudging her mid-forties, ambles into my hospital room. She places her cracked leather briefcase on the floor and smooths down her white linen suit. Then she leans over the bed's handrails and retrieves my medical file from the tray table. Glancing at the front cover, she tips her head, her cropped ginger hair catching the afternoon sun streaming through the glass.

'I'm Karla Niles,' she says, eventually taking a seat at the end of the bed. 'I'm sorry for the delay. I came as soon as I could.'

I frown. 'You're not from Administration, are you?'

She uncaps her fountain pen.

'I'm a psychiatrist.'

My hands begin to shake. I bunch them into fists and tuck them into my armpits. I suck in air, my lungs tingling.

'I don't need a psychiatrist.'

'I apologise in advance for the intrusive questions. It's imperative I speak with you.'

It's clear that I need to appear relaxed. Sensible. Sane. I rest my head back against the pillow and paste a tranquil smile on my face.

Dr Niles asks questions about the pregnancy, the birth, the appearance of my son, and notes down my answers in the medical file with the shiny fountain pen. The minutes drag on.

'Is all this relevant?' I ask.

She pauses, the nib poised above the paper.

'You know, your husband says your baby looks like him.'

My stomach hardens. 'You've spoken with Mark?'

She clears her throat. 'Just for the record,' she says, her voice docile as she winds one leg around the other, 'I'm here to help.' Then she delves into unexpected territory, asking about my own family history.

I'm confused by the nature of her question but, after a moment's hesitation, I launch into the story of my own birth, the one my father recounted so many times growing up, the only story he'd tell about my mother. It's a story I prefer to keep to myself, recount to myself when I'm missing her – but it seems pertinent to the current situation.

For the first twenty hours after I was born, my mother wasn't allowed to see me. The staff were too busy. She was too weak from blood loss. But she was determined. She demanded I be brought to her; threatened to take herself to me. She loved you so much already, *Dad always said.* She couldn't bear to be apart from you . . .

Dr Niles jots down a few further notes, her slender fingers gripping the fountain pen like a spear, her nails filed to talon-like points. Then she proceeds to the standard mental-state examination questions, the ones I used to ask as a junior doctor on my psychiatric placement years ago. Have you heard any voices that don't seem to be from people in the room? Have you seen anything unusual? Are you receiving any messages from the TV?

No, no and no. I wipe my clammy hands on the bedspread as I deny suicidal and infanticidal ideation.

'I want to find my baby, not kill her – him,' I say, tripping over the words.

'Standard questions,' she says, her voice lilting now as though she's singing a lullaby to pacify a baby. 'There's only one more question I need to ask. I understand that your foetuses used to speak to you. Before the miscarriages?'

I'm stunned into silence. Mark is the only one I've ever told. Dr Niles inspects me with hooded eyes.

'It was a silly thing I used to say to Mark. A bit like a joke. I'm surprised he mentioned it.'

'I see,' Dr Niles says, although she doesn't really appear to see at all. She shuts my file with a snap, then launches into a description of the decor of her mother–baby unit – calming paintings, gentle music, quiet bedrooms – without disclosing what I know it to be: a part of the psychiatric ward.

I interrupt her. 'I know what a mother–baby unit is. But there's nothing wrong with me. You must believe me.'

Her red hair glints again in the light.

'Your baby will be able to join you as soon as he's discharged from the nursery.'

My limbs feel like they're shuddering. I only hope she can't see it.

'I really don't think I need –'

Ursula appears at the door. 'There's an urgent phone call for you, Karla,' she says without looking at me. 'Something about a rescheduled embryo transfer?'

Dr Niles excuses herself and walks out with Ursula, their voices fading as their footsteps pad down the hall. Her briefcase is still beside the bed. My medical file is lying closed on the tray table. I have the right to read it, surely? To know what they're saying about me.

All remains quiet outside my room. The babies must be feeding, or asleep. I manoeuvre myself to the edge of the bed and lower my feet to the floor. Heat sears through my belly. I bite my tongue to stifle a groan and shuffle to the door. The nurses' station opposite my room is deserted. The corridor is empty. I turn to the tray table. As I reach for the file, Dr Niles' fountain pen crashes to the floor. I pause and listen. Nothing.

I seat myself on the edge of the mattress and flip open the folder. My fingers turn numb as I stare down at my name, printed in thick black capitals in the corner of the page, next to a six-digit identification number.

The top piece of paper is a Request – the first of two forms that would need to be signed off by two doctors to certify a patient mentally ill. They're not seriously thinking I'm unwell? I'm usually a speed reader, but today I need to run my finger under the words to make sense of them. At least I can discern the information I need from a medical file quicker than most.

At the bottom of the page, the Request is signed. *Dr Solomon*. The page beneath is a Recommendation. There's a blank space next to Dr Niles' name, ready for her signature.

Fucking hell.

If Dr Niles signs this, I'll be sectioned. Forced against my will into the mother–baby unit. They'll be observing, keeping track of me. I won't be able to leave. And when I do find my baby, being a psychiatric inpatient might mean they're reluctant to return her to my care.

I flip through the rest of the pages, the words pulling into focus as my vision tunnels. My admission, the caesarean, the anaesthetic. It's all there in scribbled medicalese. I read every line, trying to retain it, with the pervasive sense that this is all happening to someone else. Not to me. Surely not to me.

This morning's nursing notes are towards the back of the folder.

0700: *Mother confused about sex of her baby.*

I can't believe they've even documented this. My questions were based on medical tests. I wasn't confused at all.

1200: *Patient agitated, refusing medications and attempts at blood test.*

Did I ever misrepresent patients in this way?

1330: *Special Care Nursery staff reported that patient's baby experienced an apnoea while in her care. Exact circumstances unwitnessed.*

Except by me. Surely they don't think I was trying to hurt him? I shudder, my breath catching in my throat. I turn the page, to the notes Dr Niles has made today.

'Just knows' her baby isn't hers.

Denies suicidal/infanticidal ideation, but note midwives' concerns re: same.

Tears catch behind my eyes. I blink them back. I'm going to need every inch of my strength for what is to come. They listened to my mother in the end, took her to her baby after her repeated insistence. For some reason, right now, they're choosing not to listen to me.

From the dark peripheries of my brain, a thought clarifies. I could track down the birth register, the enormous black book containing the list of every newborn, the details recorded in longhand. At the hospitals I've worked at, it's always been stored at the nurses' station. It will have recorded the date and time of every baby born in the hospital. Thank goodness the health system is so far behind every other industry with digitisation. My own baby's details will be in hard copy in that book.

My abdomen throbs as my feet scud across the carpet. My legs are swaying sticks under me, ready to give way at any moment. I steady myself against the wall as I go.

The nurses' station is still empty, the ward eerily quiet. No one is about. Presumably they're taking their afternoon-tea break, the one I never had time for as a junior doctor. I peer over the faded brown laminex ledge. No sign of a birth register on any desk.

'What are you doing up and about again?'

Ursula steps out from the back office, her hands pressed against her hips.

My tongue thickens. 'I wanted to check the birth register,' I say. 'I was interested in who was at the birth.'

Ursula frowns. 'All that information is in your baby book. You can read it in the nursery. But, right now, you need to get back to bed. You need rest, Sasha.'

'Where's the birth register?' I try to sound casual.

She looks nonplussed. 'It's all stored on the computer these days.'

How much has changed since my obstetrics rotation; and how much hasn't. I stumble back to my room, Ursula's eyes like an owl's, trailing me.

Back in bed, the sheet chills my neck as I flick through my mental contact list. Bec is the only one I can think of who could support me, who might understand.

At school, Bec tended to hang around her own group of friends in the centre of the quadrangle. They played elastics, British Bulldog, and later, towards the end of primary school, the whole gang of them would hang out in the sun, gossiping and laughing. I used to eat my Vegemite sandwiches alone under a gum tree in the far corner of the yard. The other girls never seemed to like me. It didn't bother me much. I knew I didn't belong.

One day at Bec's house after school, she switched the TV off at the end of *Neighbours*. 'It's not that the other girls don't like you,' she explained. 'It's just that you always come top of the class. Maybe if you didn't try so hard, they might let you in the gang.'

I didn't want to be part of their gang. Playing with Bec most days after school was enough for me.

High school was more of the same. I focused on my studies, spent my lunchtimes in the library. At the end of year twelve, I entered med school. Bec, who had glided through school without appearing to study much, decided to pursue a career in law. At the last minute, she changed into medicine too. At uni, Bec partied a lot. I tended to stay at home on weekends. I shared my lecture notes with her, helped her with her studies.

It was only when we hit specialty training that we went our separate ways.

Bec moved to London to complete her emergency physician fellowship. She and Adam got married, settled over there. With oceans between us, our friendship gradually trailed off. In our occasional correspondences, I would always encourage her to come home. 'Maybe next year, Sash,' she used to reply.

It was at Lucia's funeral that we reconnected. Bec disclosed the trouble she was having falling pregnant. Mark and I had also been struggling to conceive. Bec and I picked up our old friendship, contacting each other after every failed cycle, and after my miscarriages, to commiserate. We spoke over the phone several times a week for years, discussing every test result and brainstorming every possible option. That is, until I discovered I was pregnant. I texted her right away with the news, before anyone, even before Mark. She didn't ring, not that night, or the next. It took me a few weeks to realise she might never call again.

When she finally phoned several weeks later, all she said was, 'Congratulations, Sash. I guess you were always first to the finish line.'

Since that night, it's been hard to contact her. She's been busy: work, IVF consultations, family functions. I haven't wanted to push it. After all, I know more than anyone what she's going through. But this time she picks up on the first ring.

'Sash!' She yawns. 'My God. It's 6 am here.'

'I'm so sorry, Bec – I didn't know who else to call.'

'Please don't stress. My roster's all over the shop at the moment. And I'm supposed to be on this morning anyway. So how are you coping?'

I tug my childhood quilt from the bag beside my bed and place it on my lap. *Coping?* Mark must have told her.

Bec was also the first person I rang all those years ago when Mark refused to do IVF. He didn't want any child of his starting life in a test tube. Petri dish, I corrected him. And he didn't want to see me suffer. I'm suffering now, I'd said.

It always seemed as if there was another reason he wouldn't go ahead with IVF. I sensed he was holding back, yet I couldn't get it out of him no matter how much I pushed. I wasn't Simon; I didn't have cancer, I didn't need chemotherapy, I wasn't going to die. So did he even want to have children with me? Of course he did, he insisted. Then why not give IVF a try? Each time I asked, he would shake his head and turn away.

'What's more important, Sash,' Bec said at the time, 'a husband or a baby?' I knew I didn't want to be a single mother. So I stayed. And hoped. And waited. Persistence, patience and Bec helped me through the years of infertility. Despite the distance over the past few months, I feel sure she'll have my back with this baby mix-up too.

'So, you know the whole story?' I say into the phone.

'What story?'

'Mark hasn't rung you?'

'Should he have? What is it, Sash? Is something wrong?'

I lift my quilt to my nose. It smells of my childhood. It reminds me of my mother, and of Bec.

'Oh, Bec. Everything is ruined. There was an accident. I'm okay, but I had to have an emergency caesar. I had a general anaesthetic, so I was asleep during the birth. After I woke up, I realised the baby they're saying is mine isn't mine. I have no idea how it happened. It's a mix-up – a mistake. But all the staff won't believe me. Even Mark won't listen. They think I'm mentally unwell. But I'm not, Bec, I'm not. I know he's not my baby.'

She exhales down the phone.

'Wow, Sash. God, okay. I don't even know what to say. This is huge. I mean, I thought you'd finally have everything you wanted.' I wonder fleetingly if any part of her is happy to hear things have gone so wrong for me. 'Hang on, did you say "he"? Did you have a boy, Sash? I thought you were expecting a girl.'

I almost sob. 'The ultrasound said a girl. It felt like a girl, too. But the hospital is insistent I had a boy.'

'That's so weird. And you're one hundred per cent sure the baby isn't yours?'

I sniff back my tears. Even if no one else does, I need Bec to believe me.

'You remember that boyfriend of yours you thought was gay?'

'Daniel.'

'And the other guy years ago, the one you just knew was cheating on you? This is the same. I know I'm right. It all feels wrong, Bec. The baby feels wrong when I hold him. When I look at him.' Even as I say it, I realise how it sounds.

'It couldn't be first-time-mother nerves? The baby blues? Postnatal depression? Something like that?'

'No.' Though that's what Mark must think. The psychiatrist, too. But I know myself. I'm not depressed, or confused, or delusional. And I know my baby. I carried this life inside me for the last eight months. Toby is not my child.

'Have you checked the other babies yet to see if yours could be elsewhere in the nursery?'

'I checked them already.'

'Are you certain? Only once? You've got to check again, Sash.'

'Okay.' Thank God Bec is onside. I desperately need her optimism. I don't want to revert to my state of mind during those dark years of infertility, when I was starting to lose hope not only in my chances of a baby, but in my marriage, too. There had been a time when I felt I had failed Mark so completely I could barely look him in the eye. I even told him he should think about leaving me. He shushed me, of course, said I was being ridiculous. I wouldn't have blamed him if he'd wanted to, though. My parents' split had taught me from a young age that sometimes love just isn't enough.

Early in this pregnancy, at our scan appointment with Dr Yang, I sat straight-backed at the opposite end of the cramped couch in the waiting room, my legs crossed away from Mark, flipping through *Time* magazines as I sneaked glances at the other, happier couples also waiting. Mark's foot tapped on the carpet while my heart steeled in anticipation of a crumpled foetus. Dr Yang emerged from her room and, with an extended arm like an usher, directed us into the sterile space where I undressed behind a curtain and slipped into a hospital gown. I sat astride the plastic examination chair, which stuck to the back of my thighs, Mark beside me so I could clench his sweating hand in mine, my legs splayed to either side, the physical contact the closest we'd been to having sex since I'd conceived. I gritted my teeth as Dr Yang placed the lubricated probe inside me.

'Ready?' she'd said, and she showed us an image of the foetus on the screen, indicating the beating heart, the nasal bone, the spindly limbs – all good signs, all things we'd never seen on our ultrasound before, and I tried to smile, really I did, and Mark smiled back, and I hoped then that the chasm between us wasn't too wide to bridge now that things were working for the first time.

Afterwards, as we walked out into the sunshine, I had grasped Mark's hand, daring anyone who came across us to notice how hard I was trying to pretend that our marriage was really, absolutely, one hundred per cent fine.

Bec's voice jolts me back to the present.

'Look, Sash, I believe you. I'm completely behind you – I know you'd be behind me if I were in the same situation. It's a mother's instinct. And you don't get things wrong. It makes sense why they're not believing you. It's classic, isn't it? You've seen the studies? Women's pain getting dismissed in emergency departments. It happens all the time here in the UK, too. And didn't you see it happen in paeds? You know, they label the mothers anxious, then their child's illness is dismissed. Or the staff suspect the mothers are trying to make their children sick.'

'I haven't done anything wrong,' I say.

'*I'm* sure you haven't done anything wrong,' she says soothingly. 'You've got to make sure *they* know it, too. Those studies from med school – you remember?' She details the Rosenhan experiments, where research assistants pretended to hear voices. As soon as they were admitted to psychiatric wards, they denied hearing anything. They were locked up, couldn't talk their way out of there for weeks, until they were finally able to convince the psychiatrists of their sanity. Bec pauses to put on her most serious voice. 'Once you get a label, it's hard to shake. So, for them to believe you, you've got to act completely sane. No – correct that. Beyond sane. You got it?'

'I'm trying.'

'I'm sure you are.'

Our years of shared experience wrap like a woollen scarf around my shoulders, soft and warm. Part of me is surprised that, after her avoidance of me these last few months, she so readily believes me; yet her trust makes my heart soften in relief.

She pipes up again, her enthusiasm apparent.

'I've got another idea. Why don't I call the ward and pretend I'm a friend of one of the other mothers who gave birth today? Then I can find out the other babies' names and pass them on to you. We can do some sleuthing together.'

'It's ridiculous, Bec. It'll never work.'

She humphs. 'Alright. Well, if the medical staff are so cocky, they should be willing to prove they're right.'

'They're refusing to take me seriously.'

'You have to push harder.'

'Mark's talking to them now. I'm hoping he'll be able to sort all this out.' I hug the quilt to my chest, imagining my mother embracing me. Were she here, would she know how to help?

'I hope he can do something. But, Sash, you've got to act sane. Like I know you are. Remember – completely, utterly sane. Don't leave them any room for doubt.'

I'm sane. I know I'm sane. There is something, though, that is causing my heart to feel like a boulder in my chest.

'You don't think there's any way my baby could have died? They would have had to tell me, right?' I try to keep the tremor from my voice.

'Your baby's alive,' Bec assures me. 'And you'll find her. Or him. You've just got to search again.'

But her intonation sounds hollower than I've ever heard before. Does she really know that for certain? I have no choice but to believe her. I hear her swallow down the line.

'Sash, I'm so sorry I can't be there with you.'

I bite my lower lip. She *could* come, surely?

'I wish I could, really I do. But there's no way I can postpone a round of IVF for a month, not with the egg donor. The timelines are tight. I have an embryo transfer scheduled for next week.'

Last time we spoke, Bec disclosed that her eggs had been declared unfit for baby-making – scrambled, she had said with a heavy laugh. She and Adam had been spending hours sorting through scores of egg donor profiles, trying to select the description that most closely resembled her own physical characteristics.

'Sperm donor too?' I'd asked, remembering Adam's sperm weren't exactly top-notch.

'Adam has refused,' she said. 'He wouldn't want a child that wasn't biologically his.'

But it's okay for you to be a non-biological mother? I wanted to say. I kept quiet. I understood; she would do anything to have a baby. I'd been just the same.

It was only when Bec said they weren't planning on telling any future child they'd used an egg donor that I cleared my throat.

'You don't think the child will have a right to know their biological parent?'

'They'll be our child,' Bec said. 'No point in telling them.'

'What did the IVF clinic suggest you do?'

She'd laughed. 'The clinic wants the money. They let us do what we like.'

Maybe Mark had been right to refuse to go down the IVF route. So many ethical questions without a clear answer. So much room for hurt, and for mistakes.

'I understand why you can't come back to Australia right now,' I say, trying not to reveal the despair in my voice. 'You'll get pregnant soon, I'm positive.' I'm not, but I can't tell her that. We held the hope for each other for so long; I can't back out now.

Before I ring off the call, Bec begins to describe a torturous baby shower she was forced to attend recently: pin the sperm on the egg, guess the baby-food flavour, taste the chocolate bar microwaved into the nappy. Her story makes me want to scream. Clutching at the quilt draped over me, I try to listen, try to laugh at the right moments but it's impossible to feign interest. Doesn't she understand what I'm going through here?

Bec hears the crack in my voice and stops.

'You know everything always works out for you, Sash,' she says. 'So this will all end up fine, too. You'll find your baby really soon, I'm sure of it.' I hear her take a deep breath. 'Sash, I'm sorry I haven't been calling you. I've wanted to. It's just been too hard; you being pregnant and all. I hope you understand.'

And I do.

When she's off the line, I close my eyes and try to imagine the ebb and flow of breath in my chest. It used to help during the relentless infertility investigations. Now, in the thick heat of the room, my lungs are clamped tight like a stony seawall.

The quilt is cold in my lap. I clutch my phone to my chest, all too aware of the stretches of ocean, the thousands of kilometres, that lie between Bec and me.

TWO YEARS EARLIER

MARK

I'd seen Sash sad before. I mean, *really* sad. But there was something about the miscarriages that sucked the light from her face. We'd been trying for at least six years before then – six years of waiting; of frustration and tedium and heartbreak – and then everything happened at once.

It wasn't exactly a miscarriage, the doctors told her. It wasn't a baby, yet. They called it a *chemical pregnancy*. I got what they were trying to say, that there hadn't been a formed human inside her. Sash, of course, took it the wrong way.

'What am I, a nuclear weapons factory?' she said at the dinner table one evening soon after the first time. She was dicing into minuscule cubes, with a steak knife, the pork belly I'd spent hours perfecting.

'You were only five weeks,' I said. 'I guess this one wasn't meant to be.'

I was trying to help, make her feel okay about it all, but apparently that was the wrong thing to say too.

Her eyes dulled. Then her head dropped.

'I felt it inside me,' she said. 'It spoke to me before it left.'

I stopped chewing, mid-crackle. 'It did?'

It spoke to her, she said in a whisper. Unintelligible words, like the chattering of a child from the next room.

'Right,' I said. 'A child in the next room.'

'No,' she said, 'it wasn't defined speech. It wasn't full words or sentences. Maybe it was more of a sense of someone there. Barely audible, but present.'

My fork clattered as it dropped onto my plate. 'I don't get it.'

A presence. That was it. She couldn't explain any further. It wasn't something that could be firmly pinned down.

Sash isn't religious, not even spiritual. These sorts of things don't happen to her. Or, for that matter, to us. I've never heard Simon's voice in my head. I've had to conjure him up in my mind each time I make a decision; imagine what he would say, what he would do. I told Sash I didn't understand, that she needed to explain it again.

But she didn't have an explanation. All she knew was that she hadn't imagined it.

Knowing her, how could I not believe her?

I decided to plant a sapling. For Sash. For the baby. It was the least I could do.

Down at the bottom of our property, on the edge of the bush, I dug a hole in the dusty ground. It wasn't quite visible from the house, so she'd have to search it out if she wanted to grieve. From what I could see, she'd already spent a lot of time grieving over a pregnancy that was not meant to be. I would never have told her that, of course. Instead, I tried to get her to focus on the future, on things she could control.

Over the summer and into the autumn, she continued to blame herself. Hardly surprising – she likes to blame herself for everything. One day it was the sip of champagne at a work function that did it, the next the spoonful of gorgonzola pasta I'd made for our anniversary. I never knew what to say. I was pretty sure she was wrong, that it was sheer bad luck, but she's the doctor. Wouldn't she understand more than anyone why things had gone wrong?

That winter, she became obsessive. Getting pregnant was all she could think about. It took her mind off Damien so I was happy enough to listen as she ran through her new fertility-boosting methods.

No more food or drink she deemed unhealthy – dairy, wheat, alcohol, caffeine. Frankly, there wasn't much left she could consume. Then there was the yoga practice. The exercise. And, worst of all, the Chinese herbs she boiled up on the stove three times a day, filling our house with the stench of a rubbish tip.

I tried to point out that the extremes to which she was pushing herself weren't necessarily conducive to pregnancy. She refused to listen. What would I know? I hadn't felt a life take hold inside me, she said. No, I wanted to say, but I'm watching one slip past before my eyes.

After the second miscarriage, that winter, with flakes of snow melting to water as they hit the grass outside, I chose a candlebark. The shovel nearly broke as I dug into the frozen ground. Still, it was important. It was all I felt I could do.

When I'd stamped down the soil round the sapling, I heard a rustle behind me. Sash, clutching two steaming mugs of coffee in her hands. She handed one to me, then pointed to a trail coursing down my cheek through the caked-on mud.

'You've been crying,' she said.

'Sweat.'

'It's too cold for sweat.' Cushions of steam puffed from her mouth.

'It's rain, then.'

She held an upturned palm in the air, feeling for drops.

'You haven't cried at all?'

I sipped at my coffee, shrugged.

'Oh my God.' She bit her lip.

Mist rose around us as raindrops began to spatter our skin like pinpricks. We never spoke about the chemical pregnancies – the miscarriages – again.

One evening the following autumn, on my return from work, I found her in the kitchen. She was slicing fresh limes from our garden on a wooden chopping board. Her eyes were alight like candles. I slid my arm around her belly.

'Do you have good news?'

'The best.'

The skin of her neck was tinged with salt.

'Congratulations,' I said. 'Fingers crossed this one sticks.'

'It's already stuck,' she said. She held up an uncut lime in her palm, the peel glistening. 'Would you believe our baby is already this size? I'm twelve weeks today.'

I pulled away, eased myself down onto the kitchen stool.

She wanted to surprise me, she said. I was surprised. She hadn't wanted to get excited, given the last two times. Of course she would have told me if it hadn't worked out. I wondered if she was telling the truth about that.

'Now we can be happy,' she said. 'You're happy, right?'

I was. But there was no way I was going to let myself get too excited until Sash held our baby in her arms.

I had been watering the saplings three times a week to keep them going through the tinder-dry summer. The kangaroos were getting to them over the chicken wire, stripping the leaves from the twigs. I built the fence higher, reinforced it with a double layer of wire. I hoped like hell it would be enough to keep the saplings alive until the autumn rains came down.

DAY 1, SATURDAY AFTERNOON

The porcelain of the ensuite sink is cold beneath my palm. I'm grasping onto it to keep myself upright as I use my mobile to call the labour ward. I'm hoping Bec's idea might just work.

'How can I help you?' A gruff, tight voice. Ursula has picked up.

I try to imitate Bec's musical lilt and hint of a British accent.

'One of my relatives gave birth today. I was just speaking to her and I got disconnected. Could you please put me through again?'

'What's her name?'

'She's my . . . cousin's wife. Her baby was born today. I got put through to the wrong mother before – Toby's mother?' I give an awkward laugh.

'I'm sorry, I need a name.'

I only have one other name to draw on. I say it aloud. Saskia Martin – the name Ursula called me by mistake. I only hope she's the other mother. There can't be too many other women who gave birth here today.

'Oh, you want to speak with Saskia. I'll put you through to her now.'

'Look, actually, don't worry about putting me back through,' I say. 'I'd hate to disturb her again. Maybe I'll come and visit her and the baby later this afternoon instead.' I'll track her down on the ward myself.

'I suggest you speak to her now. She might not be here this afternoon. Her baby was flown to St Patrick's in the city this morning.'

An emergency code rings out across the hospital loudspeakers. I cover the microphone on my mobile, a little too late, and hang up. I scuttle back to bed as fast as I can, conceal the phone beneath my pillow and fling the covers over me. Soft footsteps pad across the corridor. I press my eyelids closed. The footsteps pause at my doorway.

A low buzz sounds from further up the corridor. The feet tread away towards it.

St Patrick's. A few hours from here by road. I ease my phone out from under the pillow, find the number for St Patrick's and dial it. My heart is in my throat. I ask reception to connect me through to the nurses in the Special Care Nursery.

The tips of my fingers are tingling by the time a woman picks up.

'My name is Ursula,' I say. 'I'm one of the midwives from The Mater. I was after an update on the baby we transferred earlier today. Baby of Saskia Martin. How is he?'

'Oh, you mean she? She's doing well.'

A girl?

'Isobel, they've named her.'

This must be her. My baby. It seems I was right about having a girl after all. My heart soars like a bird catching an updraught.

'We were meaning to call and ask someone from your hospital how Saskia's pregnancy was allowed to go three weeks overdue? Saskia can't explain it herself. It's not your standard protocol, is it?'

Oh, no. My heart deflates like a flaccid balloon. There's only one thing of which I'm certain: my baby was born prematurely. Isobel is not mine. My only lead, evaporated. And it appears this hospital hasn't treated her mother adequately. It accords with how badly they have treated me.

'I've got to go,' I whisper and, without waiting for the reply, press the end button on my phone. My body is a wooden plank beneath the sheets as I squeeze my eyelids together, willing the tears away.

The engaged signal bleeps when I call Mark's number. Next I try Dad's mobile. He picks up on the second ring. I'm hyperventilating, the breath leaping in my throat.

'Sasha, you've caught me just as I've got home.'

'Dad, they think I'm mentally unwell.' I count my breath in and out, trying to slow it down. 'I think they're going to lock me up in the psych ward.' I stop, almost unable to believe it myself.

Dad is quiet for a few seconds.

'Is this about you not believing your baby is yours?'

'Who told you that?'

'Mark's worried.'

My brain thumps inside my head. Mark should be looking for our baby, not disclosing things about me to Dr Niles, or calling my father behind my back.

Dad begins to ramble on about the golf game he has planned for tomorrow. I know he's trying to pretend this isn't happening. He can't stand emotions; doesn't believe in them, he once said. I toy with the best way to get him onside. He's a retired accountant. He likes crosswords. When I was seventeen and wanting to attend the after-party of the school formal, I drew up a spreadsheet, a budget and a proposal. It worked. Perhaps this time I can appeal to his sense of logic again.

'Dad, this isn't something I've imagined. Things like this happen. And I would never make something like this up. It's almost like sexual harassment. Or assault. The statistics show women hardly ever lie about it. It's just that people prefer not to believe them.'

'Are you trying to say you were assaulted, Sasha?'

I groan. 'No, Dad.'

I realise in that moment how little my own father knows me. Maybe he never really has. When I was a child, he'd collect me from Bec's house long after dark, drive me home and be off to work again before dawn. I'd wake to an empty house and the smell of burnt toast. Lucia would pick me up on the way to school. I can't remember Dad ever cooking for me or helping me with schoolwork. We never even watched TV together. He was more at work than at home.

He did try a few times, I suppose. He attended one of my cross-country runs when I was a teenager, standing on the sidelines with parents he'd never met. He saw my final-year musical, *Mary Poppins*, where I played Jane. I always forgave him for his other absences. After all, I knew more than anyone how hard it was without my mother around.

The afternoon he told me she wasn't coming back, I was six years old, lying on my patchwork quilt in a trickle of sunlight. Bunny was putting Dolly and Bear down for a nap on my pillow when his shadow fell across the bed.

'You know Mum's gone?' he said. 'For good. It's just the two of us now.'

My newly grazed knee from where I'd fallen on asphalt began to ache. Dad left the room without another word. I stuffed Bunny beneath my pillow. Bear tucked the patchwork quilt around Dolly and told her she wouldn't see Bunny again for a while.

'Where's she gone?' Dolly asked.

'To a better place,' Bear said.

'When's she coming back?'

'No time soon.'

'What did we do wrong?' Dolly said.

'I don't know,' Bear replied.

All at once, the phone is heavy in my hand. Dad pauses for breath at the end of his recount of golf.

'I'm sure they think admission is going to help, Sasha.'

Oh, fuck. They've got Dad believing I'm mentally unwell, too. How the hell am I going to find my baby now?

'Being admitted helped your mum the first few times.'

'Jesus, Dad. How many times was she in there?'

'I don't remember . . .'

His voice is creaky. There's so much about his relationship with my mother that I don't know, that he refuses to talk about. He's so awkward that I can almost understand why she wanted to leave us. Almost.

'I should have listened to the doctors the last time, before I took her home,' Dad continues in a broken voice. 'Everything is my fault. I should have done things differently.' His voice fades to a whisper. 'Do you think you'll be able to forgive me, Sasha?'

I shift on the mattress.

'Look, it's not really about that, Dad. This is about the hospital making a mistake with my baby. But I'm sure you did the best you could.' I fiddle with my quilt, tugging at a hole in the stitches to loosen the threads. 'And so did Mum.' It's not true, but it's the best I can come up with right now. 'Dad, I have to go – I have to find my baby. Do you understand? Right away.'

'Please try not to worry,' he says. 'Just stay calm. Everything is going to be alright. Look, I'll speak to Mark. We'll have a chat. Sit tight, okay? I promise I'll come and visit you in the psych ward very soon.'

I'm not even in there yet, I want to say, but he's gone, a dial tone in my ear.

I switch my phone to silent and stash it in the pocket of my gown.

Muffled voices sound from the hall. Dr Niles is returning to make her judgement on my mental state. I'm lucky her phone call took so long, buying me some much-needed time. Too late I remember her fountain pen on the floor. The back of my head sinks lower into the pillow, my heart thrumming.

Dr Niles enters the room looking flustered, followed by Ursula, who lingers at a distance from my bed, her back against the wall. Dr Niles bends down to retrieve her pen, smoothing her hair back into place behind one ear as she stands.

'So, as I was saying, when you come to us, we'll start some medication.'

'But there's nothing wrong with me.'

'The side effects are minimal.'

'I don't need medicating.'

All at once, I recall Bec's advice; the more I protest, the less sane I sound.

'We're all trying to help you, Sasha. You do know that, don't you?' There's the hint of a sinister tone under Dr Niles' smooth placidity. 'If you won't come in voluntarily, I'm afraid we may have to consider recommending you.'

Recommending me – as an involuntary patient. That's the last thing I want, or need. Dr Niles holds my gaze.

'Take your time to make a decision.'

'Where's Mark?' I ask.

'I believe he's attending to your baby.'

'What does he say about this?'

'He agrees with all of us.'

Mark. The one person I hoped would stick by me, no matter what.

My brain has turned to mist. I manage to get a few words out. 'I need to speak to him.'

'Of course,' Dr Niles says. 'Let us accompany you to his side.'

FIVE MONTHS EARLIER

MARK

We told Bill about the pregnancy on a warm, windy autumn night. He and I had just got home from the footy. Moths fluttered against the verandah lights outside as I handed him a beer and took a seat next to him on the leather lounge. Sash, stricken with the unfairness of all-day sickness, had just left the room to vomit.

'We're twelve weeks pregnant,' I explained to him. I'd expected congratulations, a warm handshake, even a nod of the head. Bill remained motionless on the couch, his jaw sagging.

'The timing's great, really,' I'd continued, as if Bill's response was normal for a man who had just learned he was going to be a grandfather for the first time. 'Sash has finished her pathology training. She'll qualify for maternity leave.'

Bill clamped his lips together.

'Sash is annoyed I won't get paid paternity leave, but at least the head chef should be okay about me taking a few weeks off after the baby's born,' I'd said.

Bill was staring out the window where stars, almost like fireflies, were collecting in the blackening sky.

'Is there a problem, Bill?' I asked.

His voice was so low I had to lean to hear.

'No, it's good news. Of course. But . . . after Sasha was born . . .' He cleared his throat. 'Sasha's mother became upset when they didn't let her see the baby. She thought something had happened. Rose was certain the doctors and nurses were keeping something from her.' He rubbed his palms together like he was trying to generate heat.

'Sash was fine, though, wasn't she? Nothing had happened.'

Bill shook his head.

'Sasha was fine. I knew the midwives were busy. I tried to stick up for Rose, really I did. But me demanding that the midwives bring Sasha to her room seemed to make her worse.'

'Sash isn't like her mum,' I'd said, perhaps a little too loudly.

He didn't seem to have heard me.

'Rose went a bit hysterical. From there she went downhill. That's where it all began.'

He stared at the sun-damaged backs of his hands, his fingers spread broad and long in his lap.

'Make sure you keep a close eye on her after the birth,' Bill had said finally, his voice hoarse.

I didn't put much stock in Bill's story at the time. If I'd have paid more attention, taken more care, maybe everything would have turned out differently. Just like with Simon, I suppose.

When Sash had walked back in, Bill jumped to his feet and clasped her hands between his.

'Congratulations, darling. Mark just told me the news. I'm so happy for you.'

Sash nestled herself into my arms on the leather couch. With her warm body pressed against mine, Bill's wide grin flicking between the two of us and the moon rising high among the stars, it was impossible to believe it would be anything but happily ever after.

DAY 1, SATURDAY LATE AFTERNOON

By the time Ursula has wheeled me to the lift, ridden with me to the fifth floor and pushed me into the nursery, Dr Niles is already standing beside a cluster of canvas partitions with sturdy frames, her hand wrapped around one of the poles. Ursula rolls the partitions into place one by one, forming a protective barrier around Toby's cot. Dr Niles pushes my wheelchair inside, then pulls the panels together behind me, ensuring there are no gaps so we are completely hidden from the nursery's view. Mark is folded over in a chair beside Toby's humidicrib, staring at the floor. He doesn't look up.

I clear my throat and Mark's head jerks back.

'Sasha.' There's darkness under his eyes. 'I'm so glad you're here.' He reaches for my hand and traces his finger over my palm as though he's reading it. He does it to calm himself when he's upset. 'You need to know it's best for everyone if you can try to believe Toby is our baby. Look.'

He reels off Toby's features, counting them on his fingers. Grandfather Bob's palms. Uncle Will's ankles. Cousin Emily's chin. I can't see the resemblances. Toby certainly doesn't look like a Moloney; at least, no Moloney I've ever met. Mark doesn't mention any features from my side of the family.

Dr Niles steps forward, a composed smile on her lips. Spikes of her red hair are sticking up like protruding horns.

'It's common to feel this way, Sasha. Many mothers talk like this. It helps if you can try to understand that we're all here for you. The rest will come later. You have your whole life to get to know him. To bond with him. To learn to love him.'

Ursula murmurs platitudes from behind me.

'What do you say, Sash? He's ours, isn't he?' Mark upturns his palms, outstretches his arms. 'All you need to do is tell them he's ours and this will be over. Dr Niles won't bother you anymore.'

I want to grab Mark by the shoulders and shake him. He's supposed to be defending, not betraying, me. He is right about only one thing: it would be so much easier to go along with them about Toby being our baby. Mark leans in front of me now, begging, pleading, almost on his knees in desperation, trying to make my life easier by convincing me to agree. It's what he wants for me, an easy way out.

He knows I've made hard decisions before. After Damien, I knew paediatrics wasn't the right career for me. At first, Mark tried to sway me. 'You're great with kids,' he'd say at every opportunity. He cornered me in the bathroom, in the laundry, in bed at night. At first, I just shook my head.

One night on the couch, in front of the TV, I exploded.

'You're not listening to me,' I shouted. 'I can't deal with the implications of getting it wrong in kids. Pathology was always top of my list. Paediatrics was a mistake. I've already decided.'

He sat dumbstruck for a while. Then he turned off the TV and took my hand.

'If you're finding paediatrics that hard, why not take an easier road? General practice. Medical research. A different field of medicine entirely. Pathology is a long, hard slog. You've said so yourself. Demanding. Stressful. Lots of exams. No guarantee you'll get to the other end.'

'Pathology is what I want to do.' I pulled away from him, took myself off to bed. And pathology is what I did. I love it, even more now that I've qualified and have started climbing the career ladder – my instincts, at least about pathology, were correct.

I check my mental state in an ordered list. No racing thoughts, no lowered or elevated mood, no strange ideas or beliefs, no suicidal ideation. I would know if I was mentally unwell, I'm sure of it. There are two things of which I'm certain in this chaos: first, that I'm sane. Second, that the baby in the crib in front of us is not mine.

I'm not going to back down. I won't give in to make this easier on everyone. I'll let myself be wheeled off to the mother–baby unit. It's hardly ideal; it will almost certainly prolong my search for my real baby and then, when I've found her, this admission being on my record may delay her return to my care. And it will put my career at risk. On discharge, I'll be referred to the Medical Board, placed on probation, forced to attend psychiatric check-ups, regular reviews. Mentally unwell doctors don't get very far in medicine. I might have to let go of my dreams of ascending the pathology career ladder. But, at this point, that feels like the least of my concerns.

In his humidicrib, Toby remains peaceful, asleep. He's the innocent one in all this mess. He looks nothing like my baby. I might have decided to mother him as best I can until he's reunited with his real mum, but at no point have I thought he's mine. And when I'm proven right, they'll realise there is nothing wrong with me at all.

Fuck them. Fuck them all.

'No, Mark,' I hiss, mustering all my strength. 'You know me. I don't make mistakes. I've fought so long and hard to have our baby and there's no way on earth I'm giving up now. I won't let anything stop me finding out the truth. This is not our child.'

Mark looks like he's going to cry. He nods at Dr Niles, who nods back.

'Then you'll have to come to us,' Dr Niles says, her smile flattening. 'Tonight.'

'If you insist,' I reply. 'I'll do whatever I must to find my baby.'

Dr Niles will be relieved she doesn't have to fill out the lengthy Recommendation paperwork to certify me now that I'm being admitted with my agreement. I wonder how long it will take me to convince her I'm sane.

'I'm afraid you can't breastfeed on the medication,' Dr Niles says. Amid the grief that hits me – failing to establish breastfeeding now means I'll likely never have a chance to breastfeed my real child – I'm partly relieved. At least there'll be no more agonising expressing for me.

'Finally, it's important that you obtain my permission before leaving the hospital grounds,' she says. 'Do you understand?'

I shrug.

'It's important you know that visiting the nursery is an essential part of your recovery. This will help you bond with Toby.'

Dr Niles gives a perfunctory smile. 'You'll be fine, Sasha. We'll make sure of it.' She undoes the buttons of her jacket, slips between the partitions and disappears. Ursula folds the partitions like a fan, then wheels them down the corridor to the other side of the nursery.

Mark is scrutinising me as if he doesn't know me anymore. He places a blanket on my lap and tucks it in at the edges like I'm a china ornament.

I'll find the truth. I'll eventually get out of there and find my baby, no matter what they say or do.

Mark leans in close and whispers in my ear as though it's the last time he'll get to speak to me.

'You don't need to fight so hard, Sasha. The doctors are on your side. You need to listen to all of them. Just follow their instructions. Please promise me you'll try.'

I still can't believe he doesn't trust me. Mark knows right away when I fib about liking his latest haircut or new clothes. Something about my eyes, he says, but he's never been able to quite put his finger on it. I thought he believed me, at first, about the baby. But the doctors have got in his ears, convinced him I'm wrong.

He's behind me now, his hands on the wheelchair handles, ready to push. He can't see my face.

'I promise,' I say through gritted teeth.

'We'd better get you back to your room, Sasha,' he says.

I wonder who *we* is. And he never, ever calls me Sasha.

DAY 1, SATURDAY DINNERTIME

Dr Niles comes for me. 'Psychiatrists don't usually escort patients to the psych ward,' she says, 'but seeing as you're a special case . . .'

I don't want to be a special case, but there's no point in fighting. I roll my eyes and sink lower into the wheelchair. I try to ignore the babies' wails as Dr Niles pushes me down the pink hallway of the maternity ward.

We take the lift down to the ground floor of the hospital. From there, I'm pushed along a walkway enclosed on all sides by rows of windows, seemingly to provide protection from the weather; or perhaps to prevent patients from absconding? Beyond the glass, a concrete loading dock lies in front of a multi-storey car park packed with cars. Before us, at the end of the passage, is a bland, squat building: the psychiatric department. The mother–baby unit is on the bottom floor.

Dr Niles shepherds me through wide double doors that slam shut behind me with a loud bang. This is it. Despite having been coerced in here under the guise of free will, I feel trapped.

A low murmuring from the nurses' station and the occasional baby's cry pepper the air. It's chilly in here. I tug my mother's quilt up to my waist. The ward still smells like a hospital, all chemically disinfected bathrooms and stodgy hospital food and the odour of something unnameable; what I think of as the waft of death. The same smell strikes me in the lab from time to time, perhaps from a freshly sliced specimen or a cluster of cells in a jar. It's the smell of rotting flesh, of ageing skin, of cells apoptosing into dust. The whiff in this corridor is faint but unmistakable. They must have had their fair share of deaths, even in here.

Dr Niles rolls my wheelchair along the hallway. The carpet is light grey; perfect for concealing dirt. They've painted the corridor pale green – supposedly a calming colour, I recall from my psychiatric rotation. The walls are lined with nondescript botanical prints, intended to be soothing and unobtrusive. Yet the lighting is so dim that shadows rear from alcoves and corners, each one seeming to hide a lurking threat.

'The nurseries,' Dr Niles says, indicating a cluster of small rooms with frosted glass doors as she wheels me past. 'This is where we sleep-train the babies. When Toby gets out of the nursery, we'll help him learn to sleep right here. He'll even have his own room.'

I don't want my baby to be sleep-trained in this dark, chilly place. I shudder, hoping Dr Niles won't notice. She pulls me to a stop at the end of the corridor, in front of the very last door.

'Your bedroom,' she says.

It smells like a motel: a tinge of mildew covered by the stench of ashtrays. Surely they don't allow smoking in here?

The air, in stark contrast to the corridor, is thick and moist, overheated like a sauna. I shrug the quilt off my lap and let it fall to my feet. There's a single bed in the middle of the room, bedside table next to it, chair under a round window set high in the wall, cupboard on the wall with a bar fridge alongside. Even a TV in the corner. Dr Niles indicates each shiny, plastic-coated feature with a weary hand.

'No minibar. And there's no way to adjust the temperature, I'm afraid,' she says, noticing my flushed face. 'You'll get used to the heat.'

'Can I please go to the bathroom?'

'The bathroom is free of charge.' She gives a twisted smile. I think she's trying to make a joke.

In the ensuite, the slick white tiles fixed to the walls still smell of bleach from the last clean. The grouting in the corners has darkened, collecting mould.

'I'll be back to take you to dinner,' Dr Niles says from the door. 'Oh, and you can keep your mobile phone.' She walks out.

Already I feel spied on. This isn't a place where secrets will be allowed. I walk to the toilet, sit down; my stitches, under the bandage on my belly, tug like they're holding me together. I press the heel of my hands into my eye sockets. In this moment, it all feels too hard.

A deep ache rolls through my abdomen as I ease myself to standing. In the polished stainless steel in place of a mirror, I can't make out any sense of an expression on my face. Instead, warped lines of silver split my features into pieces, like a Picasso woman. The water from the tap only reaches lukewarm.

In the cupboard beneath the sink, spare rolls of toilet paper are standing in an obedient row. I shove them aside to discover an array of yellow-lidded sterile urine jars. There's nothing of any use in here, either.

Then it catches my eye. One word, scratched into the wall between the stainless steel and the sink, as if by fingernails: *MINE*. I wonder who wrote it, how long it's been there, waiting for me? It's an omen, I decide. A message from one mother to another. It's easy to decode. I must claim my real child as my own as soon as I can.

I shuffle back into the bedroom and ease myself onto the mattress with a moan. Sweat drenches my armpits. Surrounding me, the walls are lined with clichéd Impressionist reproductions: Monet lilies, Degas ballerinas, Cézanne still lifes of fruit. Nothing by van Gogh in here, I note with a wry smile.

The ceiling looms above me. I wonder what it was like for my mother when she was admitted to a psychiatric ward more than thirty years ago. I doubt paintings like these hung on the walls of her room back then – more likely it was just an expanse of bland green. I can't believe my father kept the truth hidden from me for so long. I wonder how this knowledge will change my memories of her. Should I feel pity? Anger? Shame? Right now, there only seems to be a deep ache within my chest: how much I miss her presence, how much I wish she were here.

My mother must have felt so alone during her admissions, without me and Dad. Back then, mental illness was so taboo that she probably wouldn't have discussed her admissions with anyone, not even her friends. I can't imagine she would have talked about her feelings with Dad. I wish I could transport my adult self back in time and be there for her. Tell her how much I need her to get better. Tell her how much I need my mum around.

She'd left us by the time I was six. My strongest memory is of her reclining on her double bed with its brass bedhead touching the wall. She would lie on her side, smoking cigarette after cigarette, staring out the window into the front yard, a quilt tugged up over her thin frame. Sun would filter through her smoke, casting wave-like patterns on the cream-coloured walls as she would hold me tight against her, curled under her arm.

It was a lifetime ago. And now I'm a mother, and our lives are playing out in a strange parallel as I, too, lie here in a psychiatric ward, alone.

There's something familiar about this mother–baby unit room, I realise; something it has in common with all psychiatric units. The paintings are held fast against the wall. The phone cord is exceedingly short. The printed floral curtains are hung on a light plastic rail over the round window. There's no mirror to break into shards. And no way to escape.

Two women are sitting around a rectangular laminex table in the meals area. I avoid their eyes, lift my tray from a rack beside the kitchen door and limp towards them. I take a seat in one of the plastic chairs and, with hesitation, lift the lid on my meal. Sliced dry beef and gravy, limp carrots, wrinkled peas, all emitting the generic hospital-food smell.

The table overlooks a paved courtyard. There's a small garden bed studded with sprouting greenery, a blossoming apple tree in the far corner and a covered fernery along one side. Rain has begun splattering onto the slate pavers and dripping through the mesh awning onto the fern fronds below.

The woman seated to my right, her thin face framed by loose curls, is clinging to the edges of the tray. When she releases the tray from her grip, her knuckles turn from blanched white to salmon pink. She lifts the plastic lid, stares down at the semblance of a roast dinner dumped on her plate and grimaces. I don't blame her. The other woman, with golden hair draped across one shoulder, stands and returns her tray to the rack. She smiles at me as she leaves. I'm surprised; I had imagined the other inpatients scuttling away from me, fearful of associating with others who were mentally unwell. Perhaps I've underestimated women, the power of female friendship in times of need.

I've always struggled to make friends. I love the idea of having a group of close female companions, but I have no idea how to make it happen. By all accounts, my mother was the same; Lucia was her only friend. As for me, I have my work colleagues. Old friends of the family. And Bec, who has somehow managed to forgive my eccentricities over all these years.

The curly-haired woman remains at the table, pushing her soggy vegetables across her plate, tears collecting in her eyes. Postnatal depression, I conclude, not unkindly.

'Hi. I'm Sasha,' I say.

'I'm Ondine,' she says. 'Welcome, I suppose.'

'Nice to meet you.' I try to smile. 'How long have you been here?'

'Um . . .' She counts on her fingers. 'Six. No one seems to get out of here in under two.'

'Days?'

'Weeks,' Ondine says. 'They say they have to be sure we're safe to take our babies home.'

Weeks. My heartbeat slows to a sluggish pace. That can't be – won't be – me. Surely it won't take them that long to realise I have been telling the truth.

Ondine sticks her tongue into the gravy on the tip of her spoon then retracts it.

'You look pretty well, Sasha,' she says in a hesitant voice.

I remind myself to inhale, one breath at a time. 'I'm okay,' I reply.

Despite her shyness, she looks well, too. Her loose clothes are clean, her hair is washed and she has a tinge of tinted lip gloss on her lips. With her fine, curly hair and pale features, Ondine bears a resemblance to Bec.

'Are there many women admitted at the moment?' I ask.

Ondine shrugs. 'Maybe ten or so. It's hard to be sure. Most of them spend the day in their rooms. The woman who just left' – the blonde woman, I presume – 'she's heading home any day now. I can't say I've had much to do with any of the others.' Her cheeks redden.

Outside, the rain seems to be easing. My shoulders soften against the back of the chair. I've been holding them tight this whole, long day.

'Did I hear right that you're a . . . doctor?' Ondine's voice falters.

'A type of doctor. A pathologist,' I say, wondering how she could possibly know.

'And your baby? How is he?'

'I'm not really sure.' Damn this hospital, these doctors. I should have the right to know, to find my baby. I change the subject. 'You must have seen a few women come and go?'

'I have. There haven't been any other women who have arrived without their babies, though. I'm really sorry to hear about what you've been going through. It's not your fault.'

I gag as a lump of beef catches in my throat.

Ondine leans across the table and passes me a serviette. I spit the chewed-up gristle into it.

How many people know? And how have they found out? My cheeks burn like I've been slapped. 'What have you heard?'

'It's like the bush telegraph in here,' Ondine explains. 'I'm so sorry. I hate it. It's horrible. Everyone talks.' She dips her head. 'They said you think the baby in the nursery isn't yours. That's the extent of what I know. I wouldn't tell the staff too much if I were you. They might use it against you.'

'Thank you,' I say. 'I'll remember that.'

'Feel free to ask for advice on how to get out of here. I might be able to direct you to the right person.' She smiles thinly.

'The most important thing is that I find my baby.'

'So, no leads so far?' She brings her knife and fork together in the centre of her plate.

'No.' Rain now slams down on the paving outside.

Ondine is looking down at her cutlery, her irises dull.

'It's awful that your child is missing. You're going to keep searching, right?'

Someone else who seems to believe me. A thickness settles in my throat.

'Of course. Until I find her.'

Ondine's shoulders are drooped towards the tray.

'Isn't there part of you that doesn't want her to be found?'

Why would she say that? 'No. Not at all.' Concerned, I add, 'What about your child?'

Ondine's cheeks blush. She opens her mouth, but before she can reply Dr Niles enters the meals area, her face drawn into a frown.

'Time to rest, Sasha,' Dr Niles says, extending a finger at me.

Ondine bends further over her tray, her curls trailing against the plastic like the branches of a willow.

'Please let me know if I can help,' she whispers as I stand up and shuffle past her.

Outside the rain has thrust the flower stems to the ground. Cigarette butts are scattered across the paving. With a jolt, I notice the tinted windows, four of them, lining each of the courtyard walls. From the centre of the courtyard there is no way to see into the ward, yet from inside you could be observed from every angle. There's no way I'll be venturing out there any time soon.

Back in my room, sinking into the mattress and pulling the doona over my aching frame is a relief. Dr Niles taps a wiry finger against a plastic cup resting on my bedside table to indicate a clutch of rainbow-coloured pills: turquoise, vermilion, mandarin, butterscotch and one snow-white capsule. She tips the contents of the cup into my palm. They're the weight of a handful of popcorn. It takes me a few seconds to catch on that there's more than one psychotropic drug in this cluster.

'What are these?'

'Avanza, Risperidone, Temazepam. And Endone and Voltaren for pain.' She points at each one in turn.

An antidepressant, an antipsychotic *and* a sleeping tablet?

'It's not as rare as you'd think,' Dr Niles says, curling a thread of hair behind her ear. 'Postpartum psychosis. We see quite a bit of it in here. Even in doctors.'

Postpartum psychosis? If that were true, I'd be irrational, delusional, incoherent. Saying things that didn't make sense. Believing things that were clearly untrue. A shiver runs through me as I realise this is how I might appear. Even, perhaps, to Mark.

'We have to watch you take them,' Dr Niles says.

The tablets quiver in my palm.

'I don't need them.'

'If you take the tablets, you're more likely to be discharged quickly. Is that what you want?'

I pause. Getting discharged *is* important. Not nearly as important as finding my baby. Still, I do want to get out of here. I lift my hand to my mouth and raise my tongue so the tablets fall under it. I learned the trick on my psychiatric placement as a junior doctor, from a sweating, loquacious patient who whispered to me as the psychiatrist's back was turned. I swallow down a gulp of water.

'I need to check your mouth.'

I ease it open.

'Wider. Lift your tongue please.'

I tip my head to the ceiling.

'You need to swallow those.'

'And if I don't?' My voice is thick.

She frowns. I take another mouthful of water, loosen the tablets and swallow hard. The pills scratch at my throat on the way down, like razorblades. I clamp my lips shut to stop the urge to retch.

Dr Niles checks under my tongue once more.

'Good,' she says. 'Now, be sure to listen to the nurses. They know what they're doing. Everyone recovers eventually. The patients, that is,' she clarifies, as if I've accused her or her staff of being mentally unwell. She pauses at the door. 'And don't forget your induction meeting tomorrow. One o'clock. With me. Don't be late.' She sweeps out of the room, pulling the door shut behind her with a bang as if I'm a prisoner, interred for the night.

DAY 2, SUNDAY MID-MORNING

The shadows on the light grey carpet are long enough for me to realise I've overslept. My gown is clinging to my back and my sheets are soggy where I've sweated all through the night. There are two round wet patches over my chest where my breasts have leaked. The drugs have slowed my brain to crawling speed, blurred my vision, weakened my muscles. I begin to drift back to sleep. It's only when I hear a clearing throat that I realise there's someone seated beside my bed.

Mark.

'Darling.' He only uses this tone – meek, whining – when he's done something seriously wrong. 'Are you feeling any better today?'

'How the hell could I be feeling better?' The roof of my mouth is as dry as sandpaper, my tongue scraping over it.

'I'm sorry to hear that,' he says. I can see the concern in his eyes.

I run my fingers over my childhood quilt, which I've laid out across the bed. My neurons are starting to reconnect. There are things I need to know. I reach for his arm, lay my hand on his flesh.

'Did you know my mother had postnatal depression? That she was admitted to a psychiatric ward when I was a baby? Is that why you told Dr Niles about my miscarriages?'

He pulls his arm away, scratches at his neck.

'What? No. Why do you want to know about your mother?'

'My mother was in a psych ward, like me. Did you know that, Mark?'

He leans back into the chair.

'I don't know anything about your mother, okay, Sash?'

I shake my head to try and clear the fog.

'Maybe I can try and find out more about her. I could try and track her down, find out where she is now.'

Mark coughs. 'You've got a lot on your plate, Sash. Maybe when life has settled down.'

He's not going to tell me anything. I'll have to ask Dad about my mum. Mark resumes talking before I can speak again.

'I meant to tell you: my parents are coming to the nursery later today. I hoped you wouldn't mind.'

Mark's parents. They turned against me way back at the start of our relationship. We'd only been dating three months.

I had survived meeting Mark's entire extended family over a barbecue lunch at their house, and I was relaxing next to the fireplace as Mark and his parents said their goodbyes at the front door.

Patricia swept into the room, with Mark trailing behind her. Mark's father, Ray, was still helping the guests reverse their cars out of the driveway.

'What's this about Mark moving in with you?'

I glared at Mark. We had planned to tell his parents together, surprise them with what we thought they would take as good news.

Mark tucked his hands into his pockets. 'It's all for the best, Mum. Sash's friend just moved out of her apartment. She's been looking for a new housemate. It seems I fit the bill.'

Patricia's eyebrows rose like pointed arrows. 'You two hardly know each other. Don't you remember what happened with Emma? And you have no need to move out. You have free rent here with your father and me.'

Mark slowly shook his head. 'I love her, Mum.'

She leaned in close to Mark and hissed at him, just loud enough for me to hear. 'What about her mother?'

I hadn't realised Mark had told her about Mum leaving me as a child.

'Jesus, Mum.' He spoke much more softly, glanced over at me. 'She's not her mother.'

'Have you told your father about this plan to move out?'

'Dad will be fine. You two got engaged after dating for eight weeks.'

Patricia huffed and stormed out of the room.

I don't think she has ever forgiven me for taking her surviving son away. She's been cold and distant at birthdays, Christmases, even our wedding. Ray hardly speaks to me at all. I've accepted them, tried not to let her sullenness bother me.

'Have your parents seen Toby?'

'Not yet. They didn't want to disturb us, they said.'

My mother–baby unit room now feels cool; they must have turned the heating down.

'Mark, I don't want to be there when your parents come.' I lift the quilt to my shoulders.

'Let's talk about it later. I'm heading to see Toby soon. You can have a shower first. Then you'll come over with me, won't you?'

I sense I don't have a choice. Then my insides loosen a little as I remember my baby – my real baby – must still be in the nursery.

'I'd like that,' I say.

Mark launches into a description of Toby's condition – he's doing better than the doctors expected – then explains he's notified everyone on our list about the birth, but has informed them I'm not up for visitors yet.

'You said that?'

'I told them you were a bit tired, that you might be happy to see people in a few days. I thought you wouldn't want everyone to know.'

'You should have checked with me,' I say, but my heart unclenches. Another few days to regroup and work out my strategy for tracking down my baby.

I tug the quilt tighter around me. I need to convince Mark, as much as anyone, that there's nothing wrong with me. That our priority has to be to find our baby.

'I'm sorry for snapping. I am feeling better, Mark. Much better than yesterday. Do you think you could talk to Dr Niles? Ask her to stop the medication, for a start? I don't want to be so tired.'

'Of course, darling.' He gives a tight smile.

'And tell her again how unnecessary it is to have me in here.'

'Of course I will.' But his voice wavers on the final word.

Under the stream of lukewarm water, my breasts throb. They're lumpy and tender, more swollen than they've ever been. I give a gentle squeeze. Off-white milk dribbles from my nipple, coursing over my abdomen and slipping away, across the tiles and down the shower drain. My milk has come in.

What a terrible, terrible waste. Except, I suppose, it doesn't have to be.

With Mark waiting in my room, I rifle through the bathroom cupboard for the sterile urine jars. Holding one beneath my nipple, I begin to express, just like Ursula taught me. The colostrum flows more easily today, squirting out with each compression as if I'm milking a cow. After ten minutes, I have a quarter of a jar of cream-coloured liquid. As I hold the container to the light, I realise that this sample will be contaminated with the drugs in my bloodstream. This one I will need to discard. From tomorrow, I will avoid the tablets. Then I can secrete the jars in the back of the bar fridge, in the small freezer, perhaps wedged behind an ice tray to keep them hidden from view.

Expressing will mean my milk doesn't dry up. When I find my baby, I'll have frozen enough to keep her going until she learns to suck. I'm sure it's what any good mother would do.

I try to sense my baby as soon as Mark pushes me through the nursery door and into its sauna-like heat. I swear I can feel a presence, a warm, sweet pulsation, nearby. My baby was definitely premature, one of the only things I'm certain of, so she must be in here somewhere, being held by another mother perhaps? As much as I try to sense my baby, there's no way to home in on her location by intuition alone. I have more searching to do. There are only eighteen babies in here – ten in humidicribs, eight in open cots – so it can't be too hard to track her down. I scan the cots and humidicribs for faces, hands, feet, anything that may appear familiar, but Mark's wheeling me too fast and the babies are blurring into a kaleidoscope of whirling colours, heaving torsos, moving limbs. Before I can ask him to slow down, he pulls me to a stop in front of Toby's cot, Ursula waiting alongside.

'Here we are,' Mark says.

Ursula looms over my wheelchair.

'We've been waiting. I knew you'd want to be here while we take out his IV.'

Toby is lying still, staring at the roof of his crib, his eyes blank.

'He's had sucrose,' Ursula says. 'Like lollies for kids. Numbs the pain.' She turns to the bench to prepare her equipment: a dressing pack, antiseptic, a bandaid. I could have done this job myself.

Around the nursery, other parents stand beside their babies' cribs changing nappies, cuddling their newborns, chatting and laughing as though this is some sort of social gathering. At least they don't appear to be watching me today. They don't give any indication that they understand how serious their babies' conditions are; how precarious life can be. And they can't appreciate what Mark and I are going through, how our baby is suffering without us, what poor Toby is enduring without his real parents by his side.

Ursula moistens the dressing on the back of Toby's hand and pulls the IV from his skin. Toby freezes, his arm wobbling beside him, then gives a slight cry of confusion. Ursula presses on the bleeding hole with gauze.

'I guess you've seen this many times before.'

I nod. 'I was going to be a paediatrician.'

'And you switched to pathology?'

Out the window, a bus careers through a large puddle, spraying an arc of water onto the footpath.

'Change of heart.' I don't mention the incident. I've never even told Mark the whole story.

Toby has settled, gazing in my direction. The tape on his cheek, holding the nasogastric tube in place, is peeling off at the edges. It will need to be replaced before too long. Ursula points to his bellybutton.

'I'm sure you know premature babies are particularly susceptible to infection. I'll need to explain the signs of umbilical infection for you to watch out for.'

I know all about the signs of infection. Since Damien, I've been extra careful about sterility, almost to the point of obsession.

'You can tell Mark,' I say. When I turn, Mark is no longer there. I suppose he left at the sight of human blood; he says it's different to his animal rescues somehow. 'I'll go and get him.' I struggle to get out of the wheelchair.

'It's too early to be up and about,' Ursula says, her hand on my shoulder almost pushing me down. 'It's only the second day after your caesar.'

'It's fine,' I say. 'I'm not in much pain.' After all, this is the opportunity I need to scout around.

Ursula is about to argue when she's called away.

'Don't go anywhere,' she says.

As soon as she is out of sight, I press my arms to the armrests, groaning. There is no choice but to bite my tongue between my teeth and bear the pain. I may not have another chance.

The nurses' station is briefly empty. My eyes flick from humidicrib to humidicrib as I shuffle towards the other end of the nursery, attempting to look unobtrusive. So many babies, all shut in their hot, sterile cages, trapped along with their parents' despair. I'm searching for a familiar feature that would confirm a genetic connection: a curve of the chin, the rise of a cheek, an expression; anything that would allow me to be certain that this was my baby. But more than that, I'm looking for the connection that is more than a constellation of physical features – a presence. A knowing.

I'm nearly at the end of the corridor of humidicribs. Again, no luck. How can it be that she isn't here? Could Ursula have already moved her to an open cot? My baby wouldn't be big enough to have her temperature regulated yet, surely? Or has she been moved someplace else?

As I turn the corner to the cluster of open cribs in the smaller nursery wing, I hear Mark's voice from a small alcove. He's speaking with a woman with an accent; American, I think. I conceal myself behind the canvas partitions beside the visitor toilets, trying to still my breath.

'There have been discussions at a high level within the hospital,' the woman says in a careful drawl. 'The psychiatry team feels it's unwise to pursue the DNA tests. But the obstetric and paediatric teams have been speaking and we thought it would be appropriate to at least offer you the DNA tests anyhow, if you wished. You would need to be aware that the lab we use takes several days to get results back. It's not like in the States where it would take only a day or so.'

This is our chance. This is wonderful news. A surge of warmth flows through me. Mark is still on my side. Mark will ensure there is scientific proof that I'm sane. Mark has always convinced me he was a person who would love and accept me just as I am.

The first night we met, when I mentioned my mother having abandoned me as a child, I had been concerned Mark would think less of me. Instead he laid his hand on mine. 'She's the one missing out,' he said. 'If she knew you now, she would love you. I know she would.'

How could I not have believed he was the one for me?

The woman behind the partition continues. 'Of course, none of us feels DNA tests are necessary. A mix-up is impossible. We're mainly concerned that performing the tests could potentially worsen Sasha's mental health, feed into her delusions. Dr Solomon and Dr Niles have already discussed this with you, I believe?'

I wish Mark would hurry up and insist on the tests. I can hardly stay on my feet. I'm exhausted. Thank God it's almost over. When the results are back, they'll have to believe me. I bend forward to hear his response when a hand catches me on my elbow. Ursula.

'You need to come with me,' she says. 'Your baby needs a nappy change.' Her grip is unyielding, forcing me out of hiding, shepherding me back to Toby's side. 'Your son is waiting for you.'

I'm alone, wiping the last of the tarry-black faeces from Toby's red buttocks as he lies against the humidicrib mattress, the open wall of the cot pulled up over my head, when Mark rounds the corner of the nursery, an elegantly dressed woman with long blonde hair by his side. Her woollen skirt meets her black leather boots at the knees. A pink stethoscope with a small plastic unicorn clipped to it hangs against her cream blouse. *Dr Amanda Green*, her hospital badge says, with a yellow smiley face sticker. *Paediatrician*. She's what I would have been in another lifetime.

After introducing herself, Dr Green leans against the bench. A familiar yet unplaceable floral scent wafts off her skin. Her perfume is pleasant enough – perhaps an American brand? She begins to describe Toby's health in detail.

'He's doing very well. He should be ready to go home in a few weeks.'

I shiver and snap the side of the humidicrib back into place. 'Two weeks?'

'Perhaps. Let's wait and see. I believe you're a doctor?'

'Yes.'

Dr Green gives a benign smile. 'Then I'm sure you'll understand when I say DNA tests aren't necessary.'

I suck breath deep into my lungs.

'We have to do them,' I say, then with Bec's words echoing in my brain, 'I insist.'

Mark reaches for my hand and presses his fingers into my palm. *Let me do the talking*.

'We understand, Dr Green. We trust you.'

'Wait,' I say, but Mark squeezes harder.

'We need to follow the doctors' advice, darling,' he says. 'Dr Green had a premature baby herself. She understands what it's like, how hard it is. Remember, you've always said doctors know best.'

Mark has missed the fact that I'm a doctor, too. I've spent most of my waking adult life in hospitals. I know how cognitive bias can cloud judgement. Once a formulation has been made, a diagnosis reached, once hospital staff have closed ranks, there's little chance of convincing them to change their minds.

This is why I so desperately need Mark to be on my side about this.

'You said we should do DNA tests.' I squeeze back. 'You said it was the only way to know for sure.'

'It's best to be guided by the professionals. You've always said that yourself. They all think it's better this way. Dr Solomon, Dr Green . . .' His voice peters out. 'Besides, Toby has had so many tests already. Enough is enough, don't you agree?'

I shake Mark's hand from mine. This is unbelievable. How could he be so callous? Tears begin to well in my eyes. I've been so stupid to trust him; to think he trusted me.

Dr Green addresses Mark. 'Dr Niles will speak to you later today.' Then she turns to me with a wide smile. 'Sasha, I presume you've been informed of our privacy and confidentiality policy. Parents aren't permitted to inspect other babies in the nursery. I'm sure you understand. I need to warn you that there are consequences for not following hospital procedure.'

Before I can reply, she walks away, past the cribs that have been covered with padded quilts while I've been focused on changing Toby's nappy. His is the only humidicrib without one. They must have done it to obscure my view of the other babies. My heart stiffens.

As soon as she's out of earshot, Mark frowns.

'Sash, you know how much it's taken to get our baby here. Fuck, you've *got* to believe he's ours. You have to.'

My chin drops and I shake my head.

'After all this time, after everything. How could you, Mark? You need to speak to Bec. She believes me. She's seen stuff like this before.'

He glances down at the back of his hands.

'I'm sorry, Sash. Everyone I've spoken to agrees with me.'

Has he conferred with Bec? Who else has he spoken to?

For the first time, I wonder if Mark might have something to do with the babies being switched. But although he wanted a son, he's also wanted his own biological child for so long. Surely he'd favour a biological daughter over a non-biological son? No, he couldn't be implicated in this mix-up – it simply doesn't make sense. So why is he fighting me? Does he believe we're more likely to get our baby back if we go along with the doctors? Or has he just lost hope? He lost the fight to save his brother all those years ago. Maybe he doesn't believe we'll ever be reunited with our baby?

'We can find our child, Mark,' I reassure him, sitting forward in the wheelchair. 'It's not like Simon. We *can* find our baby.'

'Simon? What's he got to do with this?' Mark's cheeks flush scarlet. He snatches up his jacket. 'This has nothing to do with him. And Toby *is* our baby, Sasha. You need to stop this. Right now.'

As he storms from the nursery, a nurse at the desk glances back at me to assess my response. I lower my head until only the crown of my scalp is visible. No doubt she's writing it all down, making notes.

Toby's eyes have fallen closed, his lashes fluttering against his cheeks. He snuffles in his sleep. His bony chest rises and falls so fast, like a bird's. His fingernails are long, extending past the end of his fingertips. I suppose they grew inside his mother. She'll have to cut them soon before he scratches himself.

I sense someone beside me.

'Time for kangaroo care,' Ursula says. 'Skin to skin.'

Poor Toby. He may not be mine, but for now there's no one else to hold him and give him the love he deserves. His mother – where is she? Does she have the same questions in her mind as she holds my baby, trying to love her in return? I can only pray there's someone with my baby, holding her, giving her affection until we can be reunited. Until the two of us can be together again.

Ursula places Toby under my shirt, against my chest. Despite being such a small baby, today he feels like a reasonable weight. I can feel his bulk against my chest. His skin is as soft as raspberries. He's warm, so very warm. His heart beats through his ribs against me, almost like the heartbeat of the baby I had inside.

Clasping him to me, I prise his toes apart, checking to see if he has Mark's webbing. I'm not sure what I'm hoping for. I check left, then right, then left again.

Nothing.

I shift him to one side, then the other, examining his ears. The lobes are definitely attached to the skin of his scalp, like Mark's and his father's; nothing like my free-hanging ones that dangle with heavy earrings.

So, he doesn't have Mark's toes. Mark was right about his ears. The ultrasound could have been wrong about my baby's sex. Maybe Mark is right about me being mentally unwell. There are some facts that stand me apart, though. I've studied this stuff. I've seen enough patients to know poor mental health when I see it. I'd have enough insight to recognise if I was struggling, if I was psychotic. And I'd do something about it – take their medication, listen to Dr Niles, do what I was told. That's why I'm certain I'm right, no matter how many times they try to tell me otherwise.

Toby has slipped into sleep, his cheeks a dusty pink. I watch the rise and fall of his chest against my own. In this moment, with the warm weight of him resting on my skin, there's nothing else to do.

DAY 2, SUNDAY MIDDAY

Toby is deep in slumber when Brigitte, the mother of the baby under the blue lights, hobbles into the nursery. Her hair hangs down her back in two loose plaits like reins. She takes a seat beside her son's humidicrib, opposite Toby's, and removes his padded quilt from the perspex. Finally, someone who might understand.

'Sasha, wasn't it?'

The blue light gives her skin a wan, eerie glow. In his cot, her son, Jeremy, caws and arches his back. She slides her arms inside and rests her palms against his skin.

'There, there.'

He quietens and softens on the mattress.

'Damn jaundice,' she mutters. 'I wish his level would go down. I just want him to be okay so I can get him home. Hospitals are dangerous places, don't you think? So much could go wrong.'

It's hard to know how to reply.

'His colour doesn't look too bad from here.'

'It's the blue lights. They make everything look better. He's yellow all over when you get him out.'

Brigitte's eyebrows are creased, her forehead lined, as if with waves about to break. I feel like I should rest my fingertips on her temples to smooth out the skin. Her face looks haunted.

'He was too small, you know,' she continues in a monotone voice, her eyes transfixed on her baby. 'He stopped growing in my womb. First they stuck gel in me. Then the infusion. It turned my womb into a battering ram. You've seen it, I suppose?' She doesn't wait for my nod. 'Then he flew out of me before I was ready. He tore me all the way to my bottom. They had to stitch me back together afterwards. I didn't get to hold him for almost an hour. But when I finally had him in my arms it made it all worth it.' Her brow ripples as Jeremy's face contorts with a sneeze. 'I can get past all that. As long as he's okay.'

We're comparing birth stories. I suppose that's what new mothers do. My turn. I pause. How much to tell? What to say? I tell the barest threads, the ones I've already recounted to her. The blood clots. The emergency caesarean. I stop. She spurs me on, her hand firm on her baby's back.

I tell her everything I can recall from my hospital notes. The amount of blood I lost. The rapidity of my heartbeat. The volume of fluid they pumped in through my veins. Massive lumps of blood concealed behind the placenta. I don't remember any of it, but it must be true. I add in a detail that wasn't in the notes: Mark was with our son the whole time after the birth.

It must have been in that brief fragment of time when the switch was made. I don't mention the last part.

When I look up, Brigitte's whole body is trembling, her hand quivering against Jeremy's aquamarine skin.

'Sorry,' I say. 'Was it too much?'

'No,' she says. 'Not at all.'

She's the first person I've told. What I don't tell her is that I heard Lucia's voice, as calming as water lapping against a bank, as I lay drenched in blood on the hospital bed. *My darling, oh my darling. Just breathe.*

We sit in silence for a while, Brigitte stroking her son's back through the portholes, me running my fingers down Toby's bony spine. He is a little like a cuckoo, the wrong baby bird in my nest.

'Were you trying long for him?' Brigitte says.

My fingers pause on Toby's neck.

'Years,' I say. 'We were going to keep going until we had no choice but to stop.'

'Us too,' she says quickly, her hands coming to rest on the crown of her son's head. 'We even talked about adopting. Seeing him now, I'm so glad it didn't have to come to that. Which of you does your son look like?'

I stare at her.

'You or your husband?'

I scan the cribs lining the corridor as if they could provide the answer. Mark is right. I've never been good at lying.

'My husband says he has my nose and his eyes. You?'

She smiles, a lovely smile that illuminates her whole face, making her look so alive despite her haggard features.

'Everyone's been saying Jeremy is the spitting image of my husband, John.'

She draws her phone from her pocket and spins the screen to me. It's a black-and-white scanned photo, presumably of her husband, in a white christening gown and cap, with dimpled cheeks, bald head and chubby limbs.

'Jeremy's him all over.'

An alarm squeals from my phone. The meeting with Dr Niles, back at the mother–baby unit. I mustn't be late.

'Are you heading back to your room?' she asks, her hands cupping her baby like a present.

I nod as I replace Toby, still sleeping, in his cot. 'Visitors.' I roll my eyes.

'Don't let them exhaust you,' Brigitte says. 'I guess I'll catch you on the postnatal ward. I could pop in later to say hi if you want. Which room are you?'

I snap Toby's porthole covers into place, trying to hide the tremble in my hands.

'I can't remember the number. I'm sure I'll see you back here soon, though.'

Brigitte offers me a gentle smile as I trundle out of the nursery, my heart thundering. Perhaps I'm not as bad at lying as I've always believed.

I must be late. I rest my elbows on the nurses' station and try hard to project an aura of serenity in spite of my racing heart.

'You're on time.'

It's Dr Niles behind me, her lips pressed into a small smile. She directs me into a cramped interview room, only just big enough for a small table and four chairs. The door closes behind her with a harsh click. The room resembles a prison cell with its lack of ventilation and grey stucco walls. The downlights are luminescent like interrogation lamps. I have to squint to read the notice pinned to a noticeboard: *Our staff are here for you. Our aim is to help, support and understand you.*

'My idea,' Dr Niles says, following my gaze. 'I'm here for the patients. As we all should be.' She takes the seat nearest the door. It's a safety measure, like she'll have been trained. I used to do it, too.

I pick the seat opposite her. Less of a threat from me. She can play out her interrogation fantasies now.

Smoothing her ginger hair down flat against one side of her head, Dr Niles wordlessly passes two sheets of paper to me: a weekly schedule.

Monday – group therapy
Tuesday – video: caring for your baby
Wednesday – yoga
Thursday – morning: walk; evening: spirituality practice
Friday – free time

On and on it goes, and over on the next page.

'Two weeks of schedule?' I grip the base of the chair.

'We plan ahead here.'

'But what if I get discharged earlier?'

She raises her sculpted eyebrows.

'Let's wait and see how things play out. It's important that you know our sessions are compulsory. We record attendance.'

My fingertips are turning numb.

'I'm here for two weeks.'

'You could think of it as a bit of a holiday,' Dr Niles says. 'All mums need a holiday.'

I try to slow my breath by concentrating on the motes floating under the downlights. The hovering specks are like cells under my microscope, each one a tiny sliver bearing no resemblance to the whole.

Dr Niles clears her throat and I snap my attention back to her. I need to keep my head on the main game. Dr Niles won't help me find my baby. She will, however, be responsible for declaring me sane and discharging me, both important steps in bringing my baby home. I bring my head forward with a coated smile.

'You like dogs.'

'How did you know?'

I point at the *I heart Rottweilers* printed in small maroon lettering on the front of her shirt.

She glances down at her chest.

'I wear this on Sundays. My partner and I breed them. My top bitches are Henrietta and Goldilocks.'

'Lovely,' I say, although I'm more into cats than dogs.

Her eyes scrutinise what I know to be my straggly hair, my cracked lips, the black circles beneath my eyes.

'You shouldn't be in a rush to get out of here, Sasha. I suggest you attempt to learn more about others. And yourself.'

She rambles on without waiting for my reply. 'I know it can sometimes be hard as a doctor to let yourself be the patient. You need to trust me. With a combination of the medication, some downtime and group therapy, plus seeing Toby in the nursery, you'll be feeling better in no time. I'll visit you early every morning where possible and have a chat. See where I can be of assistance.'

I don't know how she can possibly help.

'We all need a little extra care at times. As psychiatrists, we have mandatory supervision. We discuss difficult cases in a group. Sometimes the other psychiatrists bring their personal issues up too. Their infertility. Their marriage problems . . .' Her voice trails away. 'No one is immune from distress, Sasha. We are all human.'

As she stands to usher me out of the room, I pipe up. 'Maybe you can show me some photos of your dogs one day.'

'Lovely.' She gives me a slight wave with her hand and steps away.

The dogs are a good start. If she sees me as a person, even as a colleague, rather than a patient, she's more likely to let me out sooner rather than later. But how little she comprehends me. How little anyone does – even Bec. I set my shoulders straight. In my state of forced complicity, I must remember not to allow the hospital staff to tear me down. What I can do is use my time here wisely. I need some semblance of a plan.

I have it, I realise with a start at the misleading sign on the noticeboard. I will go behind their backs. I will order the DNA tests myself.

CHILDHOOD

MARK

Our childhood wasn't so bad, but you couldn't call it idyllic. Dad ruled the house with his belt. Simon always seemed to be in trouble. I was usually the one getting him out of it.

When we were eight, Simon pinched ten dollars from our aunt's purse to buy a comic book. I denied it, but Mum and Dad knew it was one of us. Dad was ropeable. As he stormed out to the bedroom to get his belt to whip us both, I tugged ten dollars from my piggy bank.

'Hey,' I said, holding the note up as Dad approached. 'I'm really sorry. It was me.'

Dad twisted the belt round and round his fist.

'Lucky for both of you that you fessed up, Mark. I'll pass on the belting . . . this time.'

I spent the rest of our childhood protecting Simon from Dad. In high school, some of the kids tried to target him, labelled him *fatty*. I tried to teach him to act cool, let him hang out with my friends, invited him to all the best parties. I didn't mind that he tagged along behind. He was amusing to hang out with, fun to play video games or watch movies with. I liked him. Being his twin felt like a blessing, a gift. We were always a team of two.

One night, when we were seventeen, I dragged Simon to a party. In an uncharacteristic turn of events, he managed to pick up a girl. I left him there, pashing her, and took a cab home. But at 4 am, Dad woke me up: Simon still hadn't returned. Dad was about to call the cops.

When Dad had retreated to the kitchen, I snuck to the front door and slammed it shut, then thundered to Simon's room, crept under his doona and thrust it over my head.

'You're grounded, Simon,' Dad shouted from the bedroom door. 'You only just missed a whipping. Mark would never do something like this.'

From beneath the covers, I mumbled a reply.

Simon was grateful when he snuck back in at mid-morning.

'Thanks, Mark,' he said. 'I owe you big time.'

Even after we left school, Mum was always comparing Simon with me. Simon didn't make the state basketball team. He didn't date the *Home and Away* actress. He didn't get the Apprentice of the Year Award.

'You two are so different, aren't you?' she would say to us from time to time. 'I guess it makes sense. You are non-identical, after all.'

Simon would shrug, his cheeks falling flat. I'd wink at him, try to make him feel better despite Mum's snide remarks. He'd smile shyly back at me. I knew he always tried his best.

Simon had become an apprentice carpenter by that stage, working with Dad on his developments.

'He isn't up to standard,' Dad used to say to Mum when Simon was out of the room. 'He needs to shape up his work.' Then he'd scan his eye over my carefully arranged cooking creations. 'I think you'd be good with a hammer, Mark,' he'd say. 'Wish you'd come work for me.'

'Simon will get better,' I'd always reply. 'You just need to give him time.'

'Time is all he has on his side.'

Then everything changed.

Simon began to head to bed earlier than before. He declined my invitations to parties, saying he wasn't feeling well. He began to lose weight. In the bathroom, the bristles of his toothbrush were stained a pale shade of pink. There were smears of blood on his pillowcase in the mornings. I didn't say anything. I'm not sure he would have listened to me anyway.

The following week, I playfully punched him on the arm. A violet bruise sprang up almost straight away. It was still there a few weeks later, mottling, turning greyish-black.

'You should get that looked at.'

He humphed and picked up the Game Boy console.

I still blame myself a little, even after all these years. Maybe if I'd pushed him harder to see a doctor, getting treated earlier might have made a difference. It took another month to be diagnosed, another eighteen months of him enduring chemo, watching him shrivelling to sinew and bone. As Mum and Dad shrank into their clothes with each setback, I wished it was me in the hospital bed.

After the funeral, Dad spent his evenings staring at the blank TV screen, downing stubby after stubby. When he failed to heed

Mum's requests to stop drinking, she would leave the room in tears. Why couldn't they see I was the one who'd lost more than anyone? He was my twin; my other half. Back then, I couldn't see how hard it must have been for them, losing their son.

The night Simon passed away, I made a promise to him. I swore that I would live my life as if it were his own. Two lives, essentially, to make up for the one that Simon had lost. Whenever I have to make a decision, I think of what Simon would have done, and I follow his lead. It hasn't been easy, I'll admit. But I always stand by my word. And his companionship – of a kind – has stood me in good stead for all these years.

As for Simon's funeral: I was too upset to give a speech. Dad gave the eulogy. I did help to carry Simon out of the church, though. He had always been solid, yet bearing that coffin, my hand slippery on the silver rail, was like carting air. I imagined that the two of us were floating into the sky, helium balloons adrift on the wind, into the upper stratospheres of the earth.

I know what Simon would have done with Sash. He would have stood by her, supported her. So that is what I remain committed to doing. I will not give up on my wife.

DAY 2, SUNDAY MID-AFTERNOON

Mark catches me outside the nursery door.

'I'm so glad you've decided to come, Sash. Mum and Dad will be here any minute. I know it's been tough going for you, but it's a big day for them, finally meeting their grandson.'

He guides me through the sea of humidicribs to Toby's cot, which is now also covered with a padded quilt: lurid orange with bright purple spots. I assumed the quilts were to stop me from seeing the other babies. Was I wrong?

'I've just spoken with Dr Niles. I told her you were keen to get out of the unit.' His hand is like a parrot's claw on my shoulder, piercing my skin. 'She thinks it should be okay for us to go out of the hospital for a few hours at some stage. I can take you for a drive. Maybe we can get some dinner. Won't that be nice?'

A familiar 'Yoo-hoo' reverberates from the other side of the nursery. It's Mark's mother, Patricia, waving as she marches towards us, her hand held upright like a policewoman directing traffic. Her favourite cashmere shawl is slung over her shoulders. Ray, Mark's father, trails behind her, his hands tucked deep into the pockets of his jeans. He nods at me, then looks away.

'Sasha, my dear,' Patricia says. 'Sorry to hear you haven't been well.' She doesn't hug me, but instead leans down to place a kiss on my cheek as though I'm a china doll.

'I'm fine,' I say, my eyes fixed on Toby.

Early on in our relationship, Mark would defend me when his mother made underhanded remarks. I failed to notice that at some point in the last few years this had stopped.

This winter, his mother had addressed me as she carved into the neck of a roast chicken at the table's head.

'You'll be breastfeeding, dear? And having a natural birth, I presume?'

My empty plate was a pale moon. The eyes of Mark's relatives were all on me. *Of course*, I wanted to say, but my mouth was too dry to speak.

'The main thing is for our baby to be healthy,' Mark said. 'I don't care how it is born or what it's fed.'

I gave a silent cheer.

'Of course,' Patricia said, laying the slices of meat flat on a tray.

I only noticed later that he said nothing about me.

Standing erect beside Toby's cot, Patricia inspects the padded quilt.

'What is this? Is this one of your creations, Sasha?' Before I can reply, she tugs it away, then places her hands on top of the humidicrib, tapping her acrylic nails on the plastic. 'How's our baby boy?'

'The paediatrician said he'll be fine,' I say.

'Such a pity he was born so early,' Patricia says. 'Still, at least he's getting your breastmilk. That'll help him get stronger, won't it?'

Mark rubs his nose.

'Sasha can't breastfeed, Mum.' Finally, his attempt at a defence.

'I see.' His mother is the wolf from *Little Red Riding Hood*, dressed as Grandma, licking her lips.

'Ray and I were struck by Toby's likeness to Grandpa Bob in those pictures you sent through, Mark. You met Bob, didn't you, Sasha?'

I shake my head. But then I do recall meeting him years ago, early in our relationship. He was living in a nursing home with end-stage Alzheimer's. He had low-set, sticking-out ears, widely spaced eyes and a long nose. I don't remember his earlobes.

'Look, Ray.' Patricia points to Toby. 'They're Mark's pudgy toes. And the chin is yours.' Her lips draw upwards, exposing her capped teeth, as white as a shark's. 'He's the spitting image of Mark as a baby.' She leans to me. 'I thought Mark was a gorgeous baby. Everyone else thought he looked like a squashed cabbage. They didn't tell me that until later, of course.' She gives a clattering laugh. 'When will you be released from that other place, Sasha?'

'She's not in jail, Mum,' Mark mutters.

'Not long now,' I say. 'Mark has promised he'll get me out.'

Mark won't meet my eyes.

Patricia's gaze falls on Toby.

'Sasha, dear, don't worry if you're not let out before Toby comes home. We'll be able to help Mark out. We can even move in for a while, if needed.'

Mark picks up my hand and squeezes it.

'Thanks, Mum. Sasha and I will discuss it. We'll let you know. I guess we're going to need all the help we can get.'

Mark, his mother picking over me like a vulture, his father ineffectual there beside them. The babies, judging me with their unfocused eyes, knowing how badly I've failed my child. Tears well in the corners of my eyes. I don't want any of them to see me cry. I loosen myself from Mark's grasp and head for the nursery door. I'll retreat to the unit, have an early night. Patricia speaks from behind me.

'The poor thing. She's tired, I imagine. Goodbye, Sasha,' she calls. And then, seconds later to Mark, 'How are you coping with her?'

I don't wait to hear his reply.

DAY 3, MONDAY MORNING

With the sun already above the windowsill, I climb gingerly up on the chair underneath my window, heave open the curtains and rub a thick layer of dust from the glass. Spread out below me is a tiny garden backed by a wooden fence. A magnolia tree stands like a queen in the centre, mauve and white flowers bursting from buds. Jonquils break through the claggy ground in clusters. Sparrows pick at the bottle-green lawn, spotted with dandelions. I wish I could be out there, lying flat on my back in the sunshine. I sigh and unwind the window to the end of its cord. It doesn't open far, but it's enough to catch the scent of freshly mown grass.

With my palm against the glass, cold soaking into my skin, I call Bec again. I simply can't accept that she's told Mark she doesn't believe me. She's the only person I can think of who might be able to help me now.

'Sash!'

Last night, in my dreams, I saw deceased babies lying on a concrete floor. I'm not in the mood for pleasantries.

'Bec, is there any chance my baby might be dead? I still can't find her. Do you think they could be trying to hide what happened from me?' I clutch at the windowsill.

Bec's voice is slow and soothing. 'You're catastrophising. There's no way a hospital could arrange a cover-up of those proportions. Everyone will realise there's been a mistake soon and this will all be over.'

'But I've looked, Bec. I checked the humidicribs again since I spoke to you. My baby's not there, I swear.'

'So, check again. She'll be there. She's got to be somewhere, Sash.'

I shake my head. There's no way for her to understand what it's like here, where I'm supposed to be pretending to love a baby that isn't mine.

'The worst thing is they're still refusing the DNA tests. Mark is agreeing with them. And they've coerced me into being admitted to the mother–baby unit.'

Bec gasps.

'You haven't spoken with Mark?' I say.

She pauses. 'Let's just say we didn't see eye to eye. I thought he'd eventually come around and take your side. I'm going to ring whoever's in charge and tell them how fine you are.'

'It's okay, Bec. You don't have to do that. Besides, I doubt my psychiatrist would listen to you either.'

'Oh, Sash. This is awful. I just wish there was more I could do.'

'Just having you believe me is enough.'

I can feel her smile, her warmth and trust, down the line.

'Give me some time, Sash. I'll come up with a plan. And in the meantime, it's in your best interests to get out of the mother–baby unit as soon as possible. So, while you wait, you might as well cooperate with them, do what they want you to do. Spend time with the baby they're saying is yours. Make them think you're getting better. You're not going to be any use to anyone shut up in there. Just keep it simple and say that you now know that baby is your son.'

'You think that will be enough?'

'I hope so. As for your real baby – I know you'll find her. I promise.'

She sounds much more hopeful than I feel. Could her jealousy about my fertility affect her judgement? I decide not to tell her my DNA-testing plan. Best to keep the DNA tests to myself for now.

Out the window, the wind thrusts dandelion seed heads high in the air. Spring has always been my favourite season. The promise of new life. Of hope.

My mother loved spring too. She loved blossoming flowers, their perfumes and unfurling heads. It was springtime when she left us.

After she'd gone, my father refused to talk about her. He would never mention her name in those days, even when my boyfriends showed up at the front door with bunches of roses on dates. 'Nice . . . flowers,' he would say carefully. *Rose, Rose, Rose*, I've wanted to scream at him over the years, just to get a reaction. Anything to have him acknowledge she ever existed.

I wish my mother were here to support me now. It feels like she may be able to help me, know how to make this right. Maybe Bec can help me track her down. She knew my mother, too. And, unlike my father, Bec won't lie to me.

'Bec, I need to ask you some things about the past.'

One of my earliest memories is of lying on my belly on the back lawn, inspecting a line of ants trailing towards my mother. She was seated on a garden chair under the hills hoist, smoking cigarettes even as raindrops started to fall from the sky. I was soaked through by the time my father scooped me into his arms and carried me inside.

The knowledge I need the most is that just because my mother left me doesn't mean I'm going to be an inadequate mother myself.

'Of course. Anything,' Bec says, her voice delayed down the line from London.

'Did your mum ever say anything to you about why my mother left?'

I clamber down from the chair and press the heels of one hand against my forehead, unsure if I really want to know the truth. I sense a slight pause. Bec's reply sounds almost rehearsed. I wonder what she has to hide.

'No, Sash. I don't know anything.'

I hadn't expected any different, but it's a surprise how disappointed I feel.

'Nothing about where she went when she left? She never got in touch, did she? Or give any clues about where she might be now?' Surely there must be some clue in my mother's disappearance that could help me track her down.

'Sorry, Sash. Mum never said anything.' There's a catch in her voice, as if she's tearing up.

It's the seven-year anniversary of Bec's mother's death in a few weeks. At Lucia's wake, I attempted to comfort Bec as stiff-lipped relatives in matronly black dresses clustered at the edges of the hall, biting into curried-egg sandwiches and exchanging whispered commentary on Bec's lack of progeny. Mario, her father, didn't attend. He had left Lucia when Bec was a baby and hasn't been heard of since. Bec will never forgive him for that, she still says.

As for me: I don't know if I'll ever be able to forgive my mother for leaving me as a child, for not being here – particularly now, when I need her most. Heat flares in my chest.

'You're so lucky with your mum. She was perfect.'

'Mum wasn't perfect,' Bec says. 'Remember her squeezes?'

Lucia would hug us until it was hard to draw breath. She smelt of olive oil on her apron, garlic on her breath, a hint of rose soap on her fingers.

'My darlings,' she would say. *'Bellissime.'* It was just a word back then. It took many years before I found out she was calling us both beautiful.

Lucia taught me to cook fresh tagliatelle from floured pasta dough bundling together on her warm fingers. She would place her hand on mine to stir the bolognese. When she slurped her concoctions from the edge of the spoon, she would purse her lips and wink at me.

Bec's mother was perfect enough. If only the same could be said for mine.

'Can I ask you something, too?' Bec's hesitant tone pulls me back to the phone. She's always been so strong, independent. She hasn't needed me for anything and almost never asks for help.

'Go ahead.' I owe her the chance to ask me questions, even though it's hard to imagine what she could possibly need from me right now.

'Did you have a feeling when your baby was an embryo? Like a sense it was going to stick?'

No.

She continues without waiting for my reply. 'Because we've tried everything. I don't know what else I can possibly do.'

There's a pause as I try to craft an appropriate response.

'I think maybe I was trying *too* hard,' I say in the end. 'Perhaps it helped when I stopped being so rigid about my diet and exercise and everything.'

Bec sighs.

'I have a confession. I might have started on some hippy-dippy stuff. Did you ever try that sort of thing?'

I never told Bec, but I pursued every natural therapy around. After repeated failures to get pregnant, I had let go of my absolute faith in Western medicine. I would have tried anything, even standing on my head for a year if I'd thought it would have helped. I drank foul green spirulina that I vomited all over the kitchen floor; I allowed sticks to be burnt on my pressure points by a kind Chinese medicine doctor. I even visited a psychic in a caravan laced with crystals. Without prompting, the psychic deduced I'd suffered two miscarriages and that before the year was out I would give birth to a girl with golden curls and dimples. She gave me what no one else could: hope. Mark had frowned when I told him the story. 'You're becoming one of those people you make fun of. What's next? Witchcraft?' I didn't tell him about the business card a friend had given me only the week before for a witch with a four-month waiting list who lived in the mountains.

'What are you trying, Bec?'

'Just acupuncture. You know, the stuff with a modicum of evidence.'

As for pathology, it's the opposite of hocus-pocus, a science that can be digested, memorised and regurgitated in a stable, unchanging form. I suppose that's why I switched out of paediatrics after Damien. There's an evidence base for pathology: reams of books, articles, research, enough to fill a whole university. But working in pathology has taught me a thing or two over the years that can't be found in any textbooks. Such as we're all essentially the same underneath our thin coat of skin.

'Bec, just keep believing, okay? You never know when you might get there. You only need one embryo, after all.'

Deep down, I suppose I knew that some of the natural fertility methods I used were ridiculous, without any grounding in science, but I couldn't help myself. I had to pursue them because of the personal narratives I'd read online, or heard from my patients, the stories that tables and graphs couldn't encapsulate, the cases that didn't obey the laws of science. Those stories of hope were seared deep in my brain, reminding me of the limits of the scientific method I held so dear. I knew there were some things that couldn't be easily explained away.

'Thanks, Sash. You're proof that it can work out even when it seems hopeless – you've had your baby. And when you find her, you'll be so happy. Don't give up.'

Bec has always known the right thing to say. When my mother left, no adult would discuss it. My dad didn't want to talk about it. It was Bec who explained it to me. She drew a picture of the world showing my mother on the opposite side of the globe.

'Why did she want to go and live there?' I asked.

'She thought it was the best place to be.'

'But she'll be all alone.'

'That's the point,' Bec said. 'And then when she's done, she'll want to come back and see you.'

I didn't really understand it back then. I guess I still don't. Part of me is the same child I was all those years ago, trying to make sense of it, wishing my mother would swing through the door, overjoyed to see me, happy to finally be home.

Time to begin my plan.

My suture line smarting beneath the bandage, I drag the chair into the ensuite and jam it under the door handle. I take a seat on the closed toilet lid. At 9 am sharp, I dial a DNA-testing company, DNA Easy, one I've just sourced off the internet. The online reviews, mostly from fathers confirming the paternity of their children, say it's reputable. I'd thought about asking my old medical friend, Angus, for advice. He was a bumbling pathology registrar with thick glasses when I met him. Now he's a multi-millionaire, heading up a private DNA-testing company in every state. I'd clicked on his contact number, still in my phone after all these years, but I just couldn't press the call button. His questions would have been too hard to answer. Pathology is a small world, DNA testing smaller still. An anonymous DNA company will be far more discreet.

My hands shiver as the dial tone rings. I feel like I'm calling to ask for a date. A young-sounding man answers. Jim.

'I'm enquiring about DNA testing.' I try to keep my voice steady. *Proof is power*, I remind myself, even though, rightly, knowledge should be enough.

'So, paternity testing?'

'No, not paternity. Maternity testing, I suppose.'

'Let me see if we can do that.' I imagine most of their calls relate to paternity testing, made by disgruntled men. I hear his muffled voice in the background before he's back on the line.

'Is it after IVF? Or is it for you and your mother?'

I slide my palm over the shiny porcelain on the underside of the toilet, searching for something to grasp onto.

'IVF.' That must be one of the reasons people request maternity testing: to check the IVF clinic hasn't pulled the wrong embryo out of the freezer by mistake.

He details the process. They'll send a cheek swab for the baby, the baby's father and me. I'll have to mail it back to them. If the baby's father doesn't agree, I don't need his consent. A forensic sample will be fine.

'A forensic sample?' My voice rises. I wish our pathology training had taught us the realities of DNA testing, rather than just the molecular biology. I can't believe I don't know the practical details.

A sudden knocking at the ensuite door makes the chair under the handle rattle.

'Sasha, it's time for your pills. Can you open the door?' One of the nurses. Damn.

'Out soon,' I call. Then, 'Sorry,' I whisper into the phone.

My heart loosens as Jim lists the pros and cons of various forensic samples. I scribble notes on the back of Dr Niles' weekly schedule.

'A used handkerchief yields ninety-five per cent success. Nails are good. Hair is usually the last thing we try because it needs to have the roots attached. Blood is quite good – say if your partner's cut himself shaving. Or else toothbrushes are very successful, but they need to have been used daily for two to three weeks.'

There's no point ordering a cheek swab for Mark. He'll never submit to a sample voluntarily. His hanky? He often carries it around for his hayfever. I have no idea how I'll get it from him. All I know is I'll have to act quickly. Toby will be discharged and sent home from the nursery before too long. Then it'll be that much harder to convince everyone he's not ours.

In the polished stainless steel above the sink, I am once again a sea of silvery waves, but with some imagination I can just make out a semblance of my uncertain face.

'How long do the results take?'

'Max of two or three business days. So, if you get the samples back in the next few days, you should definitely have the results by next week. Maybe Monday.' Jim confirms he can mail two test kits and a sterile plastic bag for a forensic sample to Dr Moloney at the hospital's address.

'Can you send them Express Post? And could I have a spare kit – just in case?'

Jim is happy with that. He takes my details, repeating each one after me. Fortunately I've memorised my credit card number. Billing address: my house, far away from here. He doesn't sound fazed when he confirms he's sending the test to the mother–baby unit – giving my name as a doctor seems to have done the trick.

There's another rap on the door. The chair slides away and clatters against the tiles.

'I said, I'll be out in a tick.'

'No need to shout, Sasha.'

It's Dr Niles outside the door. I hang up on Jim without saying goodbye.

When I emerge from the ensuite, Dr Niles is seated on my bed, tapping her foot against the thin carpet like a schoolteacher. Pain sears through my belly as I take a seat beside her. I try not to wince, reminding myself that this level of pain is standard for such an operation. I certainly don't want any more painkillers dulling my mind. Dr Niles' stare bores into me for the longest time, as if she can see my thoughts.

'Are you feeling any better on the medication?' she asks finally. She's missed a spot with her foundation; a cluster of freckles is visible on the bridge of her nose.

'I'm feeling good,' I say. 'Great, in fact.'

'No side effects or other concerns?'

'Nope.' I don't mention the dry mouth, the headaches, the blurred vision I got after the first batch of tablets. I don't mention that last night I hid them in my cheek and spat them down the sink. The nurses weren't as vigilant as her. I decide to spare Dr Niles the effort of having to feign interest. Instead, I follow Bec's plan. I paste a smile on my face as I say, 'I know now Toby is mine.'

Dr Niles frowns and jots down some notes. Squirming inside, I smile harder and squeeze my fingers into my palms. Is it possible I've said the wrong thing? Dr Niles looks up to the window high in the wall, her eyes glinting like gemstones as she remembers something.

'The narcissi are blossoming,' she says.

I inhale the morning air.

'Jonquils, you mean.'

'They're narcissi.'

'Mark's the gardener,' I say, wondering if this is some sort of a test, 'but I'm pretty sure they're jonquils outside the window.'

Dr Niles glances around the room. I've hung my clothes neatly in the cupboard, stacked my toiletries in the ensuite. There's no evidence of my presence in the room besides myself. Her gaze lingers on the shiny bedside table.

'Are you reading anything at present?'

'I'm not a big reader.' It's not true, but I'm reluctant to discuss my literary tastes with her. I have no idea what the right answers – the ones that will render me sane in her eyes – should be.

'I believe there's much to be learned from reading. Empathy. An appreciation of differing perspectives. And engrossed in a book, we can feel less lonely, if only for a short while.'

I give what I hope is an appreciative smile. Her gold-flecked eyes pull into focus, drilling in on mine.

'Sasha, is there anything you should be telling me?'

I press my lips together.

'You requested DNA tests?'

Oh, no. Surely she didn't overhear me. I inhale deeply.

'What do you mean?'

'In the nursery. And on the maternity ward.'

Dr Green. And Dr Solomon. I sigh in relief.

'Do you still wish to pursue this testing?' Dr Niles asks.

'No, I don't.' I say it in my strongest voice and she seems to believe me, writing it all down with her steady hand, her fingernails buffed to perfection. I curl my own nails deeper into my palms so she can't see they're bitten to the quick.

When she finally looks up, her eyes are hard.

'And I sincerely hope you would never consider pursuing independent DNA testing yourself?'

'No, of course not.' She looks dubious, so I continue. 'After all, Dr Green and Dr Solomon refused. And it would be against hospital policy.' The floral curtains billow in the slight breeze. 'And, of course, there's no need. Toby is my son.'

Her head tilts to one side. It's the way women always seem to examine me, with their eyes trained on the smallest movement of my lips, my fingers, my feet. They can't seem to place me, figure me out; and that's when I'm being my honest self. I must be confounding her now. I keep my hands clasped in my lap, my gaze turned to the sky.

When the silence extends into minutes, I can't stop myself. 'Is there any chance I can go home before next Monday?' The sooner, the better. The DNA results will be back then. They'll be more likely to believe me, to take the DNA results I've performed seriously, if I'm back home rather than still an inpatient in a psychiatric ward. Surely there's no reason to keep me in here?

Dr Niles shuffles through her papers with her careful hands. 'Let's talk about your husband. What can you tell me about your relationship?'

Why on earth is she asking me about this? Is it because she has issues of her own? 'He's had a chat with you, he said.'

Her fingernails trace the lines on the page.

'Do you believe he's happy?'

'He seems happy enough. We're both excited to be parents.'

There's no sense in telling her how things have cracked apart over recent years, how this baby mix-up seems to have driven a wedge even deeper between us.

'I suppose we got together because we shared the same values,' I add as Dr Niles' pen slides across the page.

'Such as?'

'Honesty.' I scan my brain for our marriage vows. 'Kindness. Persistence in the face of adversity.' And the one I almost forgot. 'Love.'

'The basis of a solid marriage,' she says, her voice smooth behind her thin lips. 'Although I imagine enduring infertility would have put all that to the test.'

'Perhaps.' I'm reluctant to disclose anything else. There's only so much she could have learned from a textbook, only so much she could know about my grief. The question, still unanswered by Dr Niles, thuds through my brain.

'So, do you know when I'll be allowed to go home?'

She snaps the file shut.

'Soon. Perhaps when the narcissi finish blooming.' Her orange hair glints in the morning sun as she steps towards the door. 'I have more questions for you, Sasha. But as group therapy is in thirty minutes, we'll have to end the session here, I'm afraid. Be certain you're not running late.'

A waft of hot, moist air blasts my face as I push open the recreation-room door. Large panes of glass run along one side of the dark room, framing the mesh-covered fernery of the courtyard. Abstract paintings line the opposite wall. At the far end is a makeshift library: a few couches and beanbags, and a cluster of bookshelves lined with hardbacks.

'There's an issue with the thermostat,' Dr Niles says, fiddling with a fuse box in the corner of the room. 'If I can't get it working, I'm afraid we'll have to reschedule.'

Only one other woman is present, already seated in a small circle of chairs: Ondine, the slim, silent woman from my first night here. Her curls are lanky, her skin as pale as cloud. Behind a pair of dark-framed glasses her eyes are rimmed with red. I take a seat beside her.

'Small group today,' I say.

Ondine nods.

'We should start our own mother's group,' another woman says, taking the chair on my other side. I recognise her from the kitchen the night of my admission. 'We can call ourselves the Mentally Ill Mothers.'

Ondine shudders.

'I, for one, am not mentally unwell,' I say. Perhaps this group will be another chance to assert my sanity.

'Maybe not,' the other woman says. 'But if we are, it's our mothers who made us this way.'

I'm not sure that's the case with me. I can't blame my mother's departure for all my failings. When I was an adolescent, Lucia tried to instil in me that my mother gave me the gift of a blank canvas. She insisted that, as the artist of my life, I was responsible for the final painting. And for every mistake.

'How have you been, Ondine?' Dr Niles calls from the far wall. 'You've missed our other group sessions.'

Ondine slides her hands beneath her thighs, her palms flat against the plastic seat.

'I haven't been well.'

'And that's why you're in hospital. To start working through some of your issues.'

Ondine has started to cry.

In the coroner's court, during the prolonged interrogations about Damien, the coroner's assistant, then the family's lawyers, each had their own questions of me, their own ways of attempting to squeeze me like a sponge as I sat before them, trembling. I remember staring up at the courtroom ceiling, trying to hold back the flood. Lucia had taught me the trick years before as I'd sat on her lap at the end of her bed. 'If you feel tears coming on, look upwards, my darling. You look up, your tears dry up too.'

Back then, I couldn't imagine a time when Lucia might have cried. Me, I cried almost every night of my childhood. It was only ever under cover of darkness, when I knew my father in the next room had fallen into sleep, and I'd wonder what had become of my mother, and whether I would ever see her again. Asking myself what I must have done for her to leave me.

The other woman leans forward in her chair.

'I hope you'll get to see your son again soon, Ondine.'

Ondine's head tips back towards the beams lining the roof, her mouth falling open like a corpse. The tear trails across her cheek.

I bring my hand to rest on Ondine's shoulder, but she stiffens. I remove my hand and replace it in my lap.

From the corner of the room, Dr Niles drops the fuse box door shut.

'Seems broken. We'll have to formally reschedule, I'm afraid.' She approaches the circle and settles herself into a chair. 'We'll make sure to arrange a replacement session.'

Ondine stands from her chair and gives a grim smile, then glides out the door.

'Her husband is refusing to let her see her son, Henry,' the other woman whispers to me. The bush telegraph of the hospital in action.

I can't imagine what on earth Ondine could have done. How bad would a mother have to be for her husband to forbid her from seeing their son?

Along the wall, light shifts and curls on the faded abstract prints, splodges and blotches of colour on canvas captured behind glass frames. All at once the sun disappears behind a cloud. The paintings darken, falling into dull, lifeless greys and navies and blacks.

'We'll have to work harder to get a group together next week,' Dr Niles says, coming to my side. We're alone now in the recreation room. The other woman's chair is empty – she has disappeared.

From the ceiling vent, cold air shunts against the top of my head.

'Looks like the air-conditioning has fixed itself. Have you got time to continue our discussion now?' Dr Niles leans forward over her crossed legs.

I'm not in the right headspace for talking to her again, so soon. Disturbing images from my nightmare are still flashing before my eyes. The dead babies settled in my vision the day of my coroner's court appearance as I was verbally prodded and poked. The same dead babies have haunted my dreams ever since. I need to make a believable excuse.

'I want to visit the nursery and check how my son is doing. Can we maybe catch up another time?'

'Of course,' Dr Niles says with a smile. 'And if you're not finding group useful, we can set up more one-on-one sessions instead. Let me know what you prefer.'

I would never tell Dr Niles, but maybe I would have benefitted from group therapy after Damien, all those years ago. But, for now, the Mentally Ill Mothers' Group is the last place I need to be.

DAY 3, MONDAY AFTERNOON

Toby's face is the colour of embers, his eyes clenched, as he shuffles his back against the mattress, startling himself awake. It's important to be here, beside his cot. That's what a good mother would do. Maybe they'll trust me next time I say I believe he's mine.

'Your baby is gorgeous.'

Brigitte is leaning over me, a hint of sweet perspiration emanating from her. Her hair is tied back into such a tight plait that the tiny lines around her eyes are smoothed out. With her moist lips and shiny cheeks, it's hard to believe she's given birth so recently. My own face must appear dreary in comparison.

'I never expected it to be like this with a baby,' she says, crossing the walkway back to her son and tugging back the baby-blue quilt from his humidicrib.

Mark finally informed me in an offhand manner that each of the quilts was sewn by the Hospital Women's Auxiliary, one donated to each premature baby as a gift. I think the elderly knitters imagined them being used to keep the babies warm, not to hide the babies from prying mothers.

I give Brigitte a stilted smile. Toby stares at me through the plastic, his eyes seeking out my own. He is beautiful, really, with his wholesome gaze and untamed hair. It would be so much easier if I could believe he was mine. I tug his lurid orange quilt back over the humidicrib.

'As soon as I held him for the first time, I fell in love,' Brigitte says, plunging her hands into the portholes and stroking Jeremy's back. I clutch at the plastic armrests, wishing I could say the same.

'It's better than I could ever have anticipated,' she continues. 'You have no idea how it's going to go when you're pregnant, do you? You hope for a healthy child. Anything could happen. There are no guarantees.' She shimmies her hands out of the portholes and eases the doors closed. 'I always wanted to have children. It's everything I dreamed of. How about you?'

During our years of attempted conception, Mark and I made naive plans for me to try being a stay-at-home mother. I would breastfeed, take a year or two off work. He would work overtime, double shifts, if needed. I'd pictured soft hugs, first smiles, contented naps with my baby by my side, strains of the nappy commercial *must be love, love, love* playing in the background.

'It's a little different to how I imagined.' It's not quite the right answer – not the one new mothers are supposed to give, anyway – but it's honest, at least.

Brigitte pulls a bundle of red wool from her bag and unfurls a knitted sleeve, almost complete. 'You seem like an attachment parent.'

I can't fudge this answer. I clasp the rail of Toby's humidicrib and squeeze the metal tight.

'What's that?'

'Oh, you know . . . baby wearing, co-sleeping, baby-led weaning . . .'

I shake my head slowly.

'So, what's your parenting philosophy? Are you a helicopter parent? Free-range parent? Authoritative? Slow?'

Authoritative? *Slow?* Clearly I haven't done enough research into parenting theories. They didn't teach those things in medical school, or in pathology training. Stupidly, I'd thought getting pregnant was enough to join the generic mothers club.

'I've honestly never thought about it.' Maybe if I'd had my mother around, it would've been something we discussed.

Her hand covers her mouth as she giggles. 'You're so refreshing, Sasha.'

'I guess I'm passionate about breastfeeding,' I say. 'I've been expressing every day, so when he's well enough to suck, we'll start trying.'

I'm glad to be able to say something that doesn't make me look like such an incompetent mother. Of course I don't mention the jars of my expressed breastmilk already accumulating in my mother–baby unit freezer.

'I see,' Brigitte says, turning to her knitting.

'Are you going to breastfeed?'

'I can't,' she says. 'Medical reasons.' She winds the thread around the needle and pauses. 'I'd always planned to have a homebirth. There were complications, so we couldn't in the end. The next one will be a homebirth, though.' Her smile is tight-lipped. It seems her validity as an attachment parent has been bolstered by the prospect of a homebirth. 'So, are you planning more children?'

There's nowhere to hide.

'Not at this stage.'

'So, he'll be an only child?' Her eyes settle, like a falcon's, on my face.

'I'm an only child. It wasn't so bad.'

I can't imagine having more children. Maybe my mother felt the same after my birth. For her, it seems that even one child was too much.

The creases in Brigitte's forehead disappear.

'I'm an only child, too. So is my husband. We've survived – no, thrived. I'm sure Toby will too.'

We exchange genuine smiles. Perhaps her superior tone has been covering a level of insecurity even deeper than mine. Brigitte counts the stitches in her row, then picks up the next thread.

'We have to put Jeremy in full-time childcare at three months when I go back to work,' she says. 'There's no choice, I'm afraid.' Her grip on the knitting needles loosens when I don't proffer judgement. 'And you?'

'We're going to wait and see how it all goes.'

I remove my sweaty palms from the humidicrib rail as Dr Green approaches Brigitte's side and switches Jeremy's ultra-violet lights back on.

'His blood tests show his jaundice levels are still elevated, Brigitte. We'll pop these back on for now and do some more tests to try to ascertain the cause.' Dr Green glances at me, the plastic unicorn clipped to her stethoscope swaying like a metronome. 'You two have a lot in common. It's lucky you have each other to compare notes. Someone who can understand.'

The walls glow aqua. We could be sea creatures, Brigitte and I, lurking together in the depths of the sea. When Dr Green is far enough away, Brigitte skewers her skein of wool with a needle and sets the bundle on her lap.

'Don't get me wrong, the doctors and nurses here have been great. Dr Green's good. Ursula has been especially helpful. You know she used to be in charge until a few years ago? But I don't think even she can appreciate how hard this is.' She startles as an alarm sounds from the opposite corner of the nursery. 'So much has happened. I was hoping to have him home already. But with the jaundice, needing the lights . . .' Her voice drops to a whisper. 'You won't say anything about me finding it hard, will you?'

'Of course not.'

She sniffs. 'I wouldn't want the staff to think I've got postnatal depression. I mean, not that there's anything wrong with having that.' One of her knitting needles tumbles to the ground, rolling across the floor. I bend down to reach for it.

'Postnatal depression would definitely be bad . . .' I hear myself murmur.

But then the lights appear to dim, a brown haze rising at the corners of the room, as if I'm a mermaid flailing on dry land. I collapse back on the chair and drop my head between my knees, blood coursing through my thudding brain.

'Deep breaths, Sasha,' Brigitte says, her face insipid in the aquamarine light when I finally lift my head again. 'Are you okay?'

'I'm fine,' I reply as my vision returns to normal. It's the blood loss, the fatigue, the stress causing me to feel faint.

'So, do you mind if I ask you something? You're a doctor, right?' Her fingers yank at a kink in the red wool. She's pulling the knot tighter by mistake. 'Jeremy will be okay, won't he? I couldn't bear anything to happen to him.'

'Yes,' I say, clutching at my thighs to hide the tremor in my hands. 'I'm sure both of our babies will be just fine.'

DAY 3, MONDAY EVENING

Twilight settles into violet night as I fold the baby-blue cardigan from my father, nestling it on the top shelf of my cupboard. Mark slides his head around the doorframe of my room.

'I've got something for you.'

'Isn't it past visiting hours?'

He sidles over the threshold and hands me a green shopping bag, then places a large Tupperware container on the bedside table. His hand is like a spider, creeping around my waist.

'Conjugal visit,' he says.

'No, thanks.' I push him away.

'Sorry, Sash. I was joking. Obviously.' He tries to smile.

I tip the contents of the green shopping bag onto my bed. Tiny white cotton jumpsuits, still with the discount store price tags on: *three for the price of one*. He could have done worse, I suppose; the clothes could all be in shades of blue.

'Can you please bring in some clothes for me, too?'

He proudly pulls a small leather bag from behind his back, filled with skirts, beaded jumpers and heels from home, as though I'm at a medical conference, not in a psychiatric institution. At least he's brought in my favourite black leather handbag.

'Thanks,' I say. 'Maybe some more trackpants and T-shirts, too?'

'Of course. I'll bring them tomorrow.' He points to the Tupperware container. 'Apricot slice. I thought you'd like it.' Then he points to the TV. 'Would you mind? It's a very special occasion. It's the first time in nineteen years Collingwood's got this far. I only want to watch the last five minutes, then I'll switch it off, I promise.'

I ease open the lid of the container. The top of the slice is glistening, with chunks of apricot protruding. I bite into a piece, expecting the familiar moistness. Instead my teeth catch on thick dough.

'Did you leave out the bicarb soda?'

He's reclining on my bed, arms splayed under his head for a better view of the TV.

'I hope not.'

'You know you won't be able to make this sort of mistake in your café,' I say in what I hope is a mock-serious tone. *Organismic*, he's called the organic food café he's been dreaming of; he's even registered the business name. Yet each time he's got a little further with the business plan, or begun scouting out venues, he's found excuses to delay: a sick relative, a busy work project or one of my miscarriages. I've encouraged him, badgered him, even threatened to move forward with the plans myself. He has steadfastly resisted my calls to action.

Sometimes I've wondered if he's avoiding plunging into it because he's afraid to fail in front of me.

'I'll have to be the pastry chef,' I say.

He flicks between channels in the ad break. 'And I'll be the barista.'

It's the standard patter we run through every time a dish of his goes awry, or the coffee beans burn in our coffee machine under my watch.

'How's the hospital food been today?'

I nibble at the edge of the slice. It may not be his best batch, but he made it for me.

'Awful.'

'Then I'll bring you in one of your favourite dishes tomorrow, okay?'

'That would be nice,' I say.

His eyes are soft, his hair falling across his forehead in a cowlick, his cheeks glowing under the downlights. He looks just like he did the first night we met.

'Remember Puerto Vallarta?' he says. 'The incredible food?'

I nod.

It had been Mark's idea, the trip to Mexico. I'd been hesitant – as a wholly unfamiliar destination, it wasn't a place I would have chosen – but after several weeks of munching on enchiladas and fish tacos, lazing on the beach and exploring tiny markets, I had to admit it: Mexico had won me over. The change of environment helped me forget about Damien. As we neared the end of the holiday, I was relaxed and refreshed. Ready for anything.

A week into our trip, while we watched the sun set from the balcony of our hotel overlooking the Bay of Banderas, Mark asked me to marry him. Staring into his deep brown eyes, I said yes without hesitation.

'Puerto Vallarta was a long time ago, Mark.'

'Goal,' he says with a fist pump. Then, turning from the TV, 'I'm sorry. I should have been more understanding.' His forehead crumples.

It isn't clear which episode he's referring to. His parents' visit? His refusal to authorise the DNA tests? All the small burdens of our marriage?

'Mum is really keen to come and stay,' he says. 'She can help out.'

I press my finger into the slice, feeling its solid mass.

'Have you talked to her since the visit?'

'On the phone. They were supposed to come to the nursery again today.'

So, he must have made the slice for them. I press the lid back on the container, sealing it tight.

As the months following the wedding slid past, as the touch of his skin no longer made me tingle with anticipation and the weight of the wedding band on my finger began to fade, things around the house began to change too. Only little things. An apple core, forgotten in the base of his backpack. A smattering of mugs perched on his desk. A clump of dirty clothes on his side of the bed.

I tried not to let it bother me. Instead, I came to realise that Mark carried unspoken expectations; that, as his wife, these tasks now fell to me. When I raised this with him, he lifted his winter jacket from where it had been strewn over the couch.

'I do clean up after myself,' he said. 'I can't help it if you always get there first.'

As the years stacked up like dominos, he began leaving wet towels in piles on the bathroom floor, forgetting to let me know when he was going to be home late from work, having a little too much when we went out for drinks. Each time I'd make requests of him, he'd promise that things would change. He did try his best, I'll give him that. But what I failed to understand until now was that it was too late; that nothing even slightly damaged could be made brand new.

He can't blame me for what I'm about to do.

'Sash, I hope you know I'll always be here for you.' His eyes are solemn pools until a roar emits from the screen and he turns back to the scrum of players wrestling for the ball.

I stuff the baby clothes back into the shopping bag, which I shove to the back of the cupboard. These aren't the sort of things I'll dress my baby in. Perhaps Toby can use them instead. Toby is exactly what Mark wanted: a son to call his own.

The siren sounds, indicating the end of the match. Collingwood has lost.

He switches off the TV with a firm click of the remote.

'Thanks for that, Sash. Maybe we'll win next year.' He swallows hard. 'So, you seem better, Sash. More like yourself. Are you . . . I mean, do you believe Toby is ours now?'

This is it. The crucial moment I've been waiting for, trying to build towards. It's why, tonight, I've held back on my anger, restrained myself from any rebukes. All at once I'm struck by the heavy droop of his eyelids.

'Oh, Mark . . .' The next words stick in my throat. I've never had cause to lie to him before, yet I seem to have no other choice. Finally the words roll from my tongue into the thick, humid air between Mark and me.

'Toby is ours.'

'Ours?' His face is a mask of relief.

'Oh yes,' I say. 'I know it now. Toby is, and always will be, our son.'

ELEVEN YEARS EARLIER

MARK

The night I asked Sash to marry me was one of the happiest of my life. She was standing on the hotel balcony in the balmy evening air, her eyes cast out to sea, her hair tumbling down her back. I hadn't planned to propose, but I was overcome by her beauty, her passionate spirit. With the bay stretched before us like shimmering glass, I imagined life with Sash would always be this good.

Back in Australia, I could tell my parents weren't at all happy about our engagement. They were concerned, Mum said. Presumably fearful of my response, she wouldn't, or couldn't, elaborate. I would have refused to listen, anyway, to what they had to say. Sash and I began to make wedding plans for the following year. Late-summer wedding, church ceremony, reception at a local restaurant. It was sure to be a blast.

Then it happened. The letter in the mail: the request for Sash to give evidence at the inquest into Damien's death.

She went stony after that, wouldn't talk to me about anything. The sparkle she'd regained in Mexico faded from her eyes. Within weeks, she dropped out of paediatrics training and joined the pathology program. I was sad for her. She was great with kids and would have been a superb paediatrician. I gave gentle hints that she should stick with it, wait six months, and see if she still felt the same. She ignored me, insisting she had always wanted to be a pathologist. There was nothing I could do or say to change her mind.

We went ahead with the wedding. It was a nice day in the end. I think that's how she'd remember it, too.

The inquest came and went. I cooked her dinners, rubbed her feet. But afterwards she remained quiet. She stopped going out at night. She stopped going out at all. She wouldn't talk to me about anything. She was dealing with it her way, she said.

I can honestly say I never thought about leaving her. I did, however, begin to wonder if I was the right person for her; whether someone else would do a better job of being her husband. Nothing I did seemed to help. I guess I was hoping that once we had a baby things would start to improve. She'd enjoy motherhood. She'd discover how great a mum she really was. I was hoping a baby would be a fresh start.

DAY 4, TUESDAY DAWN

A woman beside me clears her throat. I rub my eyes. From my window, dawn is breaking in wafers of strawberry and apricot through the open curtains. *Shepherd's warning*, my mother used to say. Seated on the chair beside my bed is Dr Niles. She asks me how I am.

Befuddled by sleep, I nearly launch into my 'Toby is mine' performance but I stop myself.

'I'm fine, thanks.'

Dr Niles nods. 'I apologise for being here so early. I have a few . . . personal appointments scheduled for today. I thought I'd catch you before I headed off.' She tugs open the curtains. 'And, look, about your friend – she's been phoning me every day. Can you let her know I've received her messages – and could you please ask her to stop calling?'

Bec. How I wish she were here. It's sweet of her to have tracked down Dr Niles' number to proclaim my innocence.

I know she's only trying to help but perhaps her persistence is counterproductive. In my clinical days, phone calls from relatives and friends were often frustrating. I'll have to ask Bec, politely, to cease hassling my psychiatrist.

'I'm still wondering about your plans to find your child,' Dr Niles now says.

I fix my eyes on the clouds, banks of colour piled in the distant sky. Better to say nothing. If I stay silent, there's less I can give away. I learned this ten years ago, in the coroner's court. As I sat rigid in the witness stand, my thighs pressed together, my fingers clenching the wooden rail, the barristers tried to trick me into letting out the truth about Damien by asking the same questions in different ways.

You don't remember what you said to the boy's mother?
Did you tell his parents he would be fine?
You didn't believe there was anything wrong with him?

Snippets of half-remembered conversations had become confused with dreams and images of Damien. Where was truth? Where were lies? Unable to scan the courtroom for fear of meeting the eyes of his parents sitting upright in the front row, I referred to my notes, flipping through them repeatedly as if they contained a hidden clue to the correct answer. The barristers had stood aloft like birds of prey, ready to swoop.

Damien had a temperature?
Yes. Thirty-nine point six.
He had a rash?

I remember the rash all over his body: blanching, confluent, salmon-pink. The rash of a virus, not a life-threatening bacterium.

What led you to exclude meningococcal septicaemia as a cause for his presentation?

I settled on a neutral response. *There was no evidence of meningococcal disease, either on history or examination.*

Did you perform any investigations?

I didn't believe they were warranted. I clear my throat.

Dr Niles perches on the edge of the seat, her thin eyebrows raised into points, the same as the barrister all those years ago.

'So, how is your mood?'

If I say fine, Dr Niles will know I'm lying. If I say I'm feeling low, she'll keep me locked up for longer. I fiddle with the fraying quilt.

'Not so bad,' I say.

Her gaze is resigned as she scribbles down notes. A plain gold wedding band encircles her left ring finger; strange, I haven't noticed it before.

'Now, perhaps we can revisit the topic of your infertility?' she asks without glancing up.

I inhale. On this topic, at least, surely honesty is best; it's unlikely to bring my mental state into question any further.

'It was a challenging time.'

Dr Niles uncrosses her legs.

'Tell me more.' For the first time she seems interested in what I have to say.

I'm about to launch into a summary of the medical treatments Mark and I underwent – medication, injections, having Mark's sperm put directly through my cervix and into my womb – when Dr Niles interrupts me.

'My main question is: had you ever talked about when you might stop trying?'

I'm thinking about telling her the truth – that I was planning to break up with Mark until I fell pregnant for the third time. I even had the break-up speech all planned. Kate, our marriage counsellor, was going to be the facilitator, the conduit for Mark to understand how serious I was about the two of us having a trial separation. I wrote the speech out in longhand and rehearsed it in the mirror until I could recite it by heart.

It has all been too much, everything we've been through. I've been pretending for so long that things are fine, that I'm okay. Surely you can see we aren't happy the way things are. A separation is the only option. I hope one day you'll understand.

There's a knock at my door. One of the nurses enters before I can respond, clutching an Express Post parcel. She holds it up to one of her ears, jiggling hard.

'This arrived for you, Sasha. We had to sign for it — were you expecting something?'

I need to deflect any suspicions they might have. Perhaps it's time for some new-mother babble. 'How lovely. The baby toys I was expecting from my great-aunt Maude. She's so sweet.' I try to keep my hands steady as I grasp the package. The nurse smiles at Dr Niles as she leaves the room.

I breathe a private sigh of relief. My performance must be paying off.

'How special that you have a close relationship with your great-aunt,' Dr Niles says. 'We all need family support in times of crisis. It's a shame your own mother is not in your life.' Dr Niles squints as the rising sun falls on her cheeks. 'But perhaps we'll leave it there for now. I'll see you again tomorrow. In the meantime, Sasha, perhaps you could try being a little kinder to yourself.' She tries to smile as she stands to leave. 'None of us is perfect, you know.'

When she's gone, I retreat to the ensuite, pressing my back against the door to keep it closed. My chest tightens. What a relief it will be to finally prove I'm right.

I lay my woollen jumper across the floor and tip the contents of the package onto it. There are three swabs enclosed, as well as a sterile plastic bag and consent forms. I read the instructions. One cotton swab for myself. Its sterile dryness almost makes me gag as I roll it against the moist inner surface of my cheek. I fill out the details on all the swabs and paperwork, including my home address. Now that Dr Niles is onside, I'm confident enough that I will have managed to get myself discharged by Monday, when the results should arrive. I place the rest of the paraphernalia deep in my handbag, my heart a hummingbird inside my chest.

From the nurses' desk, Ursula watches me cross the nursery, her arms folded over her chest. I shift my handbag onto my opposite shoulder, hidden from her view.

Toby's face is whiter than it was yesterday, his toes tapping up and down like a metronome. His hands are curled against the mattress, standard newborn blue at the tips. I check his observations chart. No, he's okay. Everything is in order.

There's a commotion from outside the nursery. The door squeals open and a trolley is whisked in by several nurses. Dr Green hurries alongside, pressing a mask over a baby's face. Several staff, Ursula included, follow them into the resuscitation room opposite the nurses' station.

All at once the night of the birth comes to me. Was it really just over three days ago? It may as well have been a thousand. A memory. The ambulance ride as blood dripped out of my insides and into the sodden pad between my legs. The bleeding had stopped by the time the ambulance arrived at the hospital. I fell into a restless slumber on the narrow bed. Then, chaos. Wetness, again, between my thighs. Sheets drenched with a scarlet flood. The midwife falling silent as she examined me. Other midwives scurrying. The birth room filling with medical staff.

It's all I can recall for now. Perhaps there will be more memories to come.

I look around. The nursery is deserted. It's too early for visitors. This is it.

Toby is asleep as I plunge the swab into his mouth, wiggling it against the inside of his cheek. He grimaces and shuffles against the mattress. Then his eyes spring open. He begins to wail. I stuff the swab in my handbag and snap the porthole shut, dampening his cry.

No one emerges from the resuscitation room. I have more time.

I stride as fast as my stitches allow to the end of the long corridor of humidicribs, lifting quilts, peering through the perspex, inspecting faces and bodies and limbs for any semblance of my baby. She must be here. I sense her. I feel her nearby. I know I'll recognise her as soon as I find her.

As I flit from cot to cot back towards Toby, a heaviness gathers in my limbs. None of these babies is right. I feel my baby's presence nearby. Where on earth is she?

There's only one cot left. Jeremy's. But I've examined him before. Haven't I? I know I haven't paid as much attention to the baby boys' cots as the girls'.

Cards line the benches beside Jeremy's humidicrib, inscribed with messages of hope and well wishes, though for some reason they're all in the same large, clear handwriting. A flurry of soft toys is stacked in one corner. Photographs of family members are blu-tacked to the wall. So many mementos of love.

On the opposite side of the walkway, the bench beside Toby's cot is empty. I should be making an effort, however feeble, to celebrate the birth of a baby, even though he's not mine. I wonder what I could buy. A soft toy? Too cutesy. A photograph? Too personal. Heat surges through my body as it comes to me: a foil balloon, standard hospital fare, imprinted with *Welcome baby boy* or some other such banality. Perfect.

Jeremy is curled up on his side, facing away from me, a peaceful bundle of chubby limbs and a clutch of smooth, pale-brown hair. The fluorescent lights above him have been switched off for now. As I move to the opposite side of his humidicrib, his head shifts. A sheaf of fringe falls across his forehead. He has long, delicate eyelashes, watermelon cheeks and a dimple below his lower lip. His nose is upturned like a mountain peak. His eyes peel open to reveal irises of shimmering cornflower blue.

His gaze is fixed on me as if he knows me. The air sticks inside my chest. I can hardly breathe. I push open the door of his humidicrib and encircle his hands with mine, warmth emanating from his skin. He is a younger version of Mark, one I've seen in my husband's baby photographs, only with blue eyes instead of Mark's brown ones. My heart flutters in my chest. The hospital *was* right about something. I did have a son. A beautiful, beautiful baby boy.

'Oh, Gabriel,' I whisper. 'I've finally found you.'

Behind me, the squeak of a shoe on laminex. Ursula, palms pressed against her hips, peers over my shoulder.

'What do you think you're doing?'

I release my grip on Gabriel and withdraw my hands from the portholes, golden heat still lingering on my skin.

'I was just . . .'

'You're not permitted to touch the other babies, Sasha. You're not even supposed to be near them. What were you thinking? This must never happen again or there will be serious consequences.' Ursula clenches her teeth.

For a brief moment I nearly say something. *I think this is my real baby.* But I catch myself in time. I need to tread so carefully.

'You must keep the quilts over them at all times,' Ursula says. She lifts the baby-blue quilt back across Gabriel's humidicrib, hiding him from view. 'They keep visual stimulation and excess light to a minimum. We've got to keep these babies healthy, don't we?'

I had believed the padded quilts were to stop me from seeing the babies. But the quilts weren't to do with me at all; I'd misinterpreted their purpose. How wrong I've been, it seems, about so many things.

Keep the babies healthy, Ursula said. The other baby, the one being resuscitated – could Gabriel deteriorate like that baby has? I don't trust much about this hospital, certainly not their ability to keep my son safe from harm.

'Is that other baby okay?'

Ursula nods, surveying the sea of humidicribs stretching down the length of the nursery. 'Why do you ask?'

'Everyone seems so busy all the time. I worry that things might get forgotten. Or missed.'

'Everything is fine.' Ursula clears her throat. 'There's no need to think that baby's infection will spread.'

Infection?

Oh my God. I remember now. A nasty bacteria, *Serratia*, spread through this nursery like a wildfire a number of years ago. I suppose I've been repressing the memory, knowing what it could mean for my baby. The outbreak was leaked to the media, made the national papers. Several babies were transferred to the city, a couple died. I had to supervise their post-mortems. Was Ursula the nurse in charge at the time? It was suggested that it may have been due to poor hand-washing. As a result, this hospital instituted new infection control measures, the newspapers said. I can only hope nothing like that will ever happen again; certainly not while my son is in their care.

Ursula is inspecting the empty bench beside Toby's cot.

'You must bring in some personal items for him.'

Toby. He must be Brigitte's real son. A simple switch. An innocent mistake?

'I will. As soon as possible.'

As for Gabriel, I need a memento of him, a reminder that he is real, that I haven't imagined him, that he is mine. What can I keep to remember him through the long, solitary nights until we can be together? The photographs tacked to the wall are all of Brigitte and her husband's family. The cards come from people I don't know. And the soft toys mean nothing without my baby beside me.

Ursula continues sternly, 'If you can't afford baby items right now, I'm sure we can arrange a social worker to see you.'

'We're okay.'

'Because I know how stressful finances can be.'

There's a ladder in her stocking; a loose hem on her skirt; sticky tape on the arm of her glasses. She used to be the nurse in charge here, Brigitte said.

When Ursula's shoes have squeaked away, I lift Gabriel's quilt, my eyes transfixed on my glorious son. It doesn't matter whose mistake it was; not now. All that matters is that my son has come back to me.

Before I do anything else, I need to get the proof. I open the portholes and manoeuvre another swab gently into Gabriel's mouth. He sucks at it with his full, pouting lips as though it's a source of milk. My heart cracks for the thousands of moments I've already missed – and what I'm so close to regaining.

I push the swab to the bottom of my handbag. I have to keep myself together. Wait until the proof is back. It will require all my patience.

The drawer in the bench beside Gabriel's humidicrib is half-open. I sift through it. Beneath some spare nappies and face washers is a clear plastic zip-lock bag, labelled in black permanent marker with the name *J. Black*. Inside the bag is a fleshy, wrinkled cord with pinky edges and a cream-coloured clamp at one end. Gabriel's umbilical cord. I stash the zip-lock bag in my pocket and curl my hand around it. It's what connected the two of us when he was in my womb; I doubt Brigitte will notice it's missing. Surely I have the right to this memento. For now, it is all I have of my son.

I'm hovering over him, taking in every dimple and wrinkle and fold, when I smell her behind me: Brigitte, the sweet tang of sweat lingering on her skin.

'How's my baby today?' she says, peering over my shoulder.

Gorgeous. He's gorgeous beyond belief. She doesn't wait for my reply.

'Do you think he's even yellower than yesterday? I thought it was gone but now I think the jaundice is actually getting worse. See?' She points with nails tipped with coral pink.

His torso does have a yellow sheen, but I can't say if it's worsening or not. Fortunately Brigitte must think I was inspecting him as a doctor, not a mother.

'I don't know if his jaundice is worsening,' I say. I berate myself for not having examined him properly before, despite being only two metres away this whole time. But this is, in its own way, a relief. I've been close to him these last troubled days. I haven't really left him alone.

'Tell the nurses,' I add. 'You can't take any chance.'

Given how run off their feet all the nurses seem, I can't be certain they'll examine him properly unless Brigitte informs them about his jaundice returning. And there are so many possible reasons for his jaundice; I can only hope they investigate him thoroughly.

'I don't know,' Brigitte says. 'I'd hate for them to think I'm one of those paranoid first-time mothers.' She runs her tongue over her teeth. 'They're already watching me closely enough.'

'They're watching you?'

She tightens her jaw. 'It's nothing. I went through a bit of a rough time before I got pregnant is all. I've told the staff they don't need to worry about me.'

'They've been worried about you?' I'm using the interrogative techniques I learned in medical school – repeat the last few words of a patient's sentence and they're more likely to elaborate.

Brigitte, however, doesn't respond as expected. She freezes, a thin line of tears accumulating along the lower rim of her eyes. Perhaps she is depressed, after all.

'I'm really sorry,' I say in a rush. 'I get it. I'm not going through the best time myself.'

Maybe she also believes there's been a mix-up? Even if she doesn't, she more than anyone has the right to know. I make the snap decision to confide in her.

'I've just realised Toby –'

Out of the corner of my eye, I see Ursula's head rise above the nurses' station. She's still watching me. I'm certain she's too far away to hear me, but who knows what distance sound travels in this stifling place?

'– has been too cold,' I whisper. 'I don't suppose you're any good at sewing? Could you help me fix up my old patchwork quilt for him?'

'Of course,' Brigitte says, dabbing at her eyes with her fingertips. 'I can teach you before Jeremy is discharged, if you'd like.'

'Great.' I keep my voice as casual as I can. 'Any idea when you're going home?'

'The plan was for discharge later this week. Do you think his jaundice will delay his discharge?'

I make the calculation. The DNA results will be back Monday, at the earliest, making later this week too soon for Gabriel to go home. I can only hope his jaundice will keep him admitted until the DNA results are back.

'I don't know. But don't forget to let the nurses know you're concerned about his colour. I saw a baby die from jaundice a while back. It was horrific.' It's not true, but Brigitte can't know that.

'I won't forget.' She wrings her hands in her lap. 'And Toby? When's he being discharged?'

'I don't know. Maybe a few more weeks.'

Brigitte bites the inside of her cheek.

'At first I was begging them to send Jeremy home, but now I'm starting to think they might be discharging him too soon, before he's truly fit to go. I just want him well – that's all that matters, in the end.'

There's no way she'll cope with the news of the baby swap at present. And she doesn't seem to have caught on to what I've deduced about Gabriel. Fortunately I seem to have alarmed her into telling the nurses. Once they examine him properly, I'm hopeful his jaundice will keep him hospitalised until Monday, when the results will confirm the truth. I'll tell her then. And as soon as I get the DNA results sent off, I'll speak to Bec. I need her help to work out what to do.

For now, I'm melting under Gabriel's gaze, so full of forgiveness, so full of love. It doesn't matter that they all think I'm wrong. Not now that I've finally found my son.

'What are you doing?'

Brigitte has only just left when Mark catches me beside Gabriel's cot again, admiring his flawless skin, his cherubic lips.

'I'm keeping an eye on Brigitte's son for her. He might be a bit sick.' Brigitte didn't hang around after our conversation. I'm not sure where she's gone; hopefully she's already speaking to the nurses about Gabriel being unwell.

I trail Mark back to Toby's cot.

'How's he doing?' Mark asks.

'I hope he'll be okay.'

He follows my gaze to Gabriel's cot.

'I meant *Toby*.'

'Oh, he's doing fine,' I say. 'Just fine.'

Out the window, in the playground across the road, a young boy climbs to the top of the steep slide and careers headfirst to the ground. His father, having missed his descent, scoops him up and pats his back like a drummer.

'You seem brighter,' Mark says. 'I'm glad.'

'I'm sleeping better.'

'Thank God for the tablets, hey?'

I give a thin smile, clutching my handbag against my chest. Mark thrusts his arms into the humidicrib where Toby lies on his side, and tucks a cloth nappy along the length of the baby's spine then between his legs to ensure he remains in place. During my pregnancy, he used to arrange my pillows around me in a similar way.

'Look,' Mark says, his eyes still on Toby, 'if you don't want my mum to stay with us, I'll tell her no. I understand.'

'I'd prefer it was just the two of us at home.'

He slides his arms out of the portholes.

'No worries at all. I'll let Mum know.' He places his arm around my shoulder, a yoke around my neck. I pull from his grasp and remove a tissue from my pocket. This is a chance to get his DNA.

'Blow your nose, sweetheart. You're sniffing.'

'*Sweetheart?* Since when have you called me that? And I'm not sniffing.' He ignores the tissue.

I stuff it back in my pocket. Out the window, the playground is now deserted. The boy and his father have gone. Empty chip packets flit across the tanbark in a small whirlwind. The child-restraint chain on one of the swings glints in the sun in short bursts like Morse code.

Mark goes to the bathroom. His leather jacket is draped over a chair. I thrust my hands into the pockets: keys in one, sunglasses in the other. I unzip the small pocket on the inside. My hands come to rest on a used handkerchief, lying snug against the seam. Thank God. This part of my plan should work at least. I drop it into the sterile plastic bag and secrete it in my handbag beside my other loot.

Across the walkway, Gabriel implores me to stay with his luminescent eyes. I can't bear to leave. My heart aches as though it's been cut open. *I'm sorry, my darling. This is the only way. I'll be back as soon as I can.* I imagine kissing him on his forehead, sliding my lips down the bridge of his nose and onto his glistening cheeks, one by one, a butterfly kiss. *One day, my baby, one day soon it'll be your dad and me at the bottom of that slide, our arms outstretched, catching you.*

DAY 4, TUESDAY MORNING

I've placed all my hope in my father. I want him to be my courier, an essential part of my plan. It will make it that much more difficult to get the DNA tests back to the lab if he isn't willing to help out. He's already cited his tax return, golf tournaments, basically anything he could think of to get out of seeing me in the psychiatric ward. It's taken all my tactical negotiation to get him to visit me again.

'The women in here aren't really unwell,' I said on the phone. 'Think of it as a ward for mothers and babies.'

'That's the problem,' he replied.

It's late morning when he edges into my room without knocking. He's dressed in a suit and tie as if he's attending a job interview. Approaching my bed, he swivels his head from side to side like he's about to be ambushed.

'I'm the only one here, Dad.'

He perches himself on the end of my bed, as far as possible

from where I'm propped up against my pillows. He pulls out the crossword from his pocket.

'You wanted to see me?'

He must have been just as awkward with my mother as he is now with me, making things worse without even trying. He's incapable of having insight into my needs, I can see that clearly now. My poor mother, in a psych hospital without the support she needed.

Words spill from my lips before I can properly think them through.

'That night Mum left. I don't remember much. Did she even say goodbye to you?' The question has emerged from a void in my core. The words hang between us in the air.

Dad underlines a clue on the crossword, the ink from his pen seeping deep into the newspaper.

'I was . . . She'd spent the day with you,' he says.

I see her on her double bed, enfolded in my patchwork quilt. Her eyelids flicker open, then close again. Her arms reach for me, standing beside the bed. Her hands are warm, so warm in mine.

'And when did you realise she'd gone?'

He runs his hand through the thin hair combed over his bald patch.

'Sasha, why did you want me here?'

I haven't considered telling him about Gabriel, but he's the only blood relation I have these days, and surely sharing genetic material involves some degree of trust. Though perhaps he knows more than he's letting on about my mother; maybe he'll help me track her down if I tell him the good news. Surely she'd want to meet her grandson? Before I can recognise the folly in it, the words have formed on my lips:

'I've found my baby.'

Dad smooths the newsprint flat against his thigh.

'Thank God.'

He gives a crooked smile, his body trembling with relief. I unfurl my legs. I'm not sure how he'll take it. But I know it's always better to tell the truth.

'Jeremy, they call him.'

His crossword flutters to the floor.

'No, Sasha. Toby is your son.'

'The hospital's wrong, Dad. Another baby is mine.'

His face is the colour of the hospital sheet as he reaches to the carpet. He folds the newspaper up and tucks it into the inner pocket of his jacket.

'Sasha, I'm sorry. I don't believe you. You need help. Professional help.' He drops his head into his hands. 'Look, I won't mention this to anyone. I'll leave it to the people looking after you. They're the ones who know best. They're the ones who know what to do.'

Is this what he was like with my mother, too?

'I shouldn't have visited.' He rises from the chair. 'I wish there was more I could do to help. Let me know if there's anything that comes to you.'

The return Express Post package, filled with the evidence I need, is hidden beneath the quilt. The idea that my father would help me prove that Toby isn't my child now seems ridiculous. Clearly I'd overestimated Dad's abilities. He isn't capable of doing this for me even if I were to work up the courage to ask. I will have to figure out another way to post this parcel back.

Dad pauses at the doorway, his body rigid, his shoulders set in a line.

'Your mother would want you to get help, you know.'

White heat burns in my chest. Mark, my husband, is meant to be supporting me. My mother, the one who abandoned me, should be here too. As for my father, with his awkwardness and cold distance: he exemplifies everything that is wrong with my family.

'But Mum *left* us. How much would she really care? We don't even know where she is, right?'

The words hit their mark. Dad turns away so I can't see his face. His neck stiffens.

'Dad? What is it? What aren't you telling me?'

His shoulders rise and fall.

'I was at work, you know. She called me to tell me she didn't feel well.'

There's a long pause. When I speak again, my voice is a child's, quavery and uncertain.

'What are you talking about? You mean the day she left? Was she sick?'

He emits a noise like a strangled sob.

'I didn't think to call an ambulance. I rushed home. I didn't think at all.'

My body turns icy, my fingertips numb, like during the experiments we did in medical school, immersing our feet in freezing water to test our tolerance to pain.

'An ambulance?'

His eyes scan the ceiling.

'By the time I got home, she was lying still on the mattress. She was cold. So cold.'

I don't understand. I don't want to understand. He clears his throat.

'I tried to warm her up. God knows, I tried . . .'

Dad has always said Mum left us. She wasn't around; never would be. She'd gone away. That's what I'd always understood. How could I have constructed a memory of her slipping out the door into the night?

'What are you saying, Dad? Did something . . . happen to Mum . . .?'

Dad drops his head. 'I know I should have told you. I know that.'

'She's *dead*?'

'I'm so sorry. I'm afraid she left us both. For good.' He brings up his hands to cover his eyes.

A cluster of questions resounds through my brain to a dull beat. But before I can hold them back, they all tumble out.

'How did she die? Why did this happen? Who else knows?'

Dad shakes his head. He opens his mouth to speak, then clamps it shut again.

'We'll have this conversation next time, I promise. I'll come back when things are a little more settled.' He drops his hands from his eyes to his mouth. 'She loved you so much, you know.'

Blackness gathers inside me as though I'm descending towards the ocean's depths. I stare down at the back of my hands. How similar are they to my mother's? I will never have the chance to know. Something is breaking inside me.

From the corner of my vision, a sliver of movement. Dad, slipping from my room without saying goodbye. I call out, but he doesn't turn back.

In the wan morning light filtering through the curtains, I track dust motes drifting through the air. The hardest question of all, too hard to ask but impossible to ignore: *where was I, Dad, while you rushed home from work? Where the hell was I?*

DAY 4, TUESDAY LUNCH

I'm still feeling dazed a couple of hours later. My mother's death, the flashbacks of Damien and my birth, have spun out my centre of gravity. As I lift the plastic lid on my meal, it slips from my grasp and clatters to the tabletop. The dried-out lasagna shudders under my knife. I crush the peas beneath my fork, forming a green pile of mush, before I replace the lid with a clang. I'm not hungry; not at all. How the hell could Dad have been keeping this from me the whole time? How could he have thought it was the right thing to do? And why is he telling me now?

Ondine gives me a wary glance as she enters the meals area. With her hair pulled back in a neat ponytail, her glasses perched on her nose, and a white cotton blouse, she looks schoolteacher-like, almost authoritative.

'I won't stay long,' I say. 'Feel free to eat here, if you'd like.'

Ondine hesitates, then slides her tray onto the table beside me. She removes the lid, then begins to push her lasagna from one side of the plate to the other. Outside, in the courtyard, a flutter of wind catches a cluster of white blossom petals from the slate, thrusting them up against the window beside us.

'Any luck finding your baby?' Ondine asks in a stilted voice.

I shake my head. Amid my father's disclosure, I'd briefly forgotten my mission. I straighten my back. My mother is long gone. Part of me had always known I would never meet her again; in fact, until recently, I had never had a desire to. All my father's revelation has done is confirm that belief. My own baby is my priority now.

'How's your son?'

Ondine shrugs and drops her head. I rest my fork onto the plate.

'I'm sorry.' Stupidly, I've forgotten she doesn't have him in her care. An image of Gabriel, his bright-blue eyes and pale skin, floats into my vision: my purpose, my love. 'You know, it doesn't matter how long it takes if you get him back in the end.'

She sniffs. 'I don't know if I even want to see him.' She hangs her head. 'I'm so worried what I might do.'

'What do you mean?'

'Zach, my husband, won't speak to me anymore. He says I'm a monster.'

'Whatever you did, it can't be that bad.'

At the table, Ondine is silent.

'We've all done things that could be considered monstrous,' I say. What I did with Damien, for example; what I'm always trying to forget. 'Ondine, you're not a monster.'

She stares at the apple tree in the courtyard, its branches floundering in the wind.

'Everyone else thinks I am,' she mutters.

I take a chocolate freckle from the bag she proffers.

'I was a childcare worker,' she continues. 'I looked after so many children. I don't ever want to do that work again. Here, I'm safe. If I stay in the unit for good, I'm not a risk to anyone.'

The chocolate crunches between my teeth. I shift my chair closer to her.

'Do you think you might feel better when you get your son back?'

She looks down at the unpalatable meal before her.

'He was screaming so much. I thought he was unhappy. I thought I was doing the right thing.' She stops, her mouth agape.

I don't need to know what she's done. I've heard every possible variant of her story during my medical training. 'You're human,' I say. 'Babies are stressful. Whatever happened, I'm sure your husband will forgive you one day.'

Ondine clamps her mouth shut.

I could tell her, or I could stay silent. There's an impulse to share my news with someone who might understand. Bec is supportive, but she's not here beside me. Telling my father was pointless. There's no way Ondine could have anything to do with the baby swap; she feels like a safe confidante. And she is one of the only people, apart from Bec, who hasn't judged me for anything. Plucking another freckle from the bag, I suck at it, allowing the hundreds and thousands to fall away as the chocolate dissolves on the roof my mouth. Ondine, more than anyone, might understand.

'I've found my son,' I say softly, swallowing hard at the molten chocolate coating my mouth.

She stares, eyes wide. 'Wow.'

'Do you believe me?' Whether she does or not, it's a relief to confide in her.

She places her palms flat on her thighs.

'I don't know what to believe these days. But that's great news. What's he like?'

'He's so beautiful. And I'm going to get him back, one way or another.'

'Of course you are,' she says with a sad smile. 'I wish there was some way I could help. Is there anything I can do?'

'I'll be okay,' I say, placing my hand on her bony arm. 'I think you've got enough going on right now. I know our babies will come back to us. One day, one way or another, we'll both have our babies in our arms.'

FOUR YEARS EARLIER

MARK

We'd been trying to get pregnant for five years when Sash suggested we attend marriage counselling. I resisted. There was nothing wrong with our marriage, I was certain of it; at least nothing that a beach holiday and some romps in a hotel – or a baby – wouldn't fix. Sash wouldn't budge. She had already made the appointment and she insisted I come with her.

We only saw the first counsellor once. Serenity. She had floaty sleeves in a material Sash later identified as chiffon. There were a few crystals on her desk. Sash sat slumped in the wooden chair in the lavender-infused air. When Sash said we timed intercourse around ovulation, Serenity flicked back her sleeves.

'So . . . have the two of you tried having sex just for the fun of it?'

I sat up straighter and winked at Sash. She glared back.

'Clearly she doesn't understand infertility,' Sash later said in the car on the way home. 'Who has sex just for the fun of it when it needs to be timed? We have to try someone else.'

By this stage, Sash had moved onto tablets to help her ovulate. I could tell she was stressed about the failing fertility treatment. I understood how hard it was for her. It was hard for me too, though. I have to admit, when she would glance up from her piss test and declare today was 'one of the days', it did tend to make sex feel mechanical. But I always tried my hardest to play along.

Sash suggested a second marriage counsellor, a dour-faced, balding man in a pastel-coloured room. Wilfred dissected our childhoods in minutiae, drawing tenuous connections between childhood trauma and infertility.

'Load of bullshit,' Sash said as we emerged onto the street. 'Was he seriously blaming our parents for us not getting pregnant?'

'It wasn't about blame, Sash. It was about understanding.'

'Then why wasn't he making any sense?'

Wilfred was no good either, according to Sash. Too old. Too Freudian. Too analytical. Frankly, I thought that might be exactly what Sash needed.

Finally the fertility specialists suggested we start intrauterine insemination: injecting my sperm through Sash's cervix into her womb. I gave my consent in the end. It was as invasive as I could tolerate. I wasn't prepared to put her life at risk from IVF. I'd read about the possible complications in the booklet from the clinic. General anaesthetic. A needle piercing the wall of her vagina over and over again, potentially causing haemorrhage and infection. Risk of her ovaries being hyperstimulated. Clots in her legs and lungs.

I never told Sash why I refused to go ahead with IVF. She was so desperate for a baby by the end that she would have pretended the risks were minimal and dismissed my concerns. I agreed with her about one thing – a baby would have been nice. But having Sash as my wife trumped a baby by far. I'd already lost Simon. I wasn't prepared to risk losing Sash, too. Eventually, after failed cycle upon cycle saw Sash collapsing into tears, I insisted we stop trying. It was natural or nothing, I said. I didn't tell her I was afraid she might die, that going any further might kill her. Sash hadn't lost a sibling. She would never have understood.

That's when we started seeing the third counsellor, Kate. She welcomed us into her office with a compassionate smile. The room was wood-panelled and laced with the scent of freshly brewed coffee – we could have been in a café.

Sash laid the bones of our relationship before Kate, and described how much we both wanted a baby. And how, according to Sash, we'd stopped talking about the important stuff long ago.

After listening to my side of the story, Kate reinforced my idea that our marriage, rather than a baby, was the priority. That, with time and effort, we could make our marriage whole. Sash slunk down further in her chair. It appeared she didn't like hearing that. It was odd, I suppose – Sash was the one who had dragged me there.

I had the script for our next counselling session with Kate written out in my head. Sash and I could start to map out our futures together, child-free. My café dream had been discouraged by my parents years ago. 'You need to provide a stable income for your wife and future children,' Dad had insisted, and Mum had agreed. Not that Sash needed me to provide for her, of course. But I'd seen Mum and Dad's point, and let go of my café dream for the time being. I knew the food industry was tough, with no guarantees of success. I didn't want Sash to think she had to rush back to work after a baby in order to support all of us. I didn't love the restaurant where I was working – the menu was conservative, staid and bland – but at least I brought in a steady, reasonable income, enough to feel like I was contributing.

I never discussed my decision to let go of the dream with Sash. She seemed so excited about me running a café, I let her believe it was about to happen any day. Frankly, it was a relief to see her smile about anything. But now, with a child-free future on the cards, I finally felt free to pursue my longstanding café goal. I also hoped our future plans would involve overseas travel, expansion of the veggie garden, four-wheel-drive trips around Australia. Things we'd been putting off for a long time while we'd been waiting for a baby to join our family.

Beyond that, though, I wanted to use our counselling sessions to discuss Sash's dark side. Her obsession with getting pregnant. Her black moods around the time of the inquest, which she still refused to discuss, even years later. The stuff her father had told me about what had happened to her mum, which he hadn't even told Sash. I thought she had a right to know the whole truth.

The day before our second appointment with Kate, Sash confronted me after work. She told me she had cancelled the counselling. I stared at her glowing face, her rosy cheeks, so like the Sash I had fallen in love with all those years ago.

She was pregnant for the third time. My breath evaporated like steam. We never saw Kate again.

My mum had hinted for years that Sash wasn't the best choice for a wife. When Mum heard about Rose leaving, she became concerned that maybe Rose's instabilities were heritable. Wouldn't Sash be at risk of abandoning her family, too? I refused to listen. Sash had always seemed stable enough to me. And I believed I could support Sash through anything. *In sickness and in health* – that's what I'd promised.

When Sash declared our baby wasn't ours, I'll admit I found it hard to believe, but for a time I gave her the benefit of the doubt. It was only as Dr Niles confronted me outside Sash's hospital room, to explain that she was certain Sash was suffering from postnatal psychosis, that my chest compressed like a wrung-out sponge. Finally, it hit me; Sasha wasn't anywhere near okay. Of course I cared about her. Deeply. We'd been a team for so long. I wanted her to get better. But, with Dr Niles' steely glare set on me, I realised in that moment that what I cared about more was Toby. And myself.

DAY 4, TUESDAY LATE AFTERNOON

'Stop here, Mark.'

A mass of headstones stands before us, backlit by the setting sun. Mark pulls the car to a stop at the back of the cemetery. I've been granted a few hours leave from the mother–baby unit and, with the DNA tests in need of posting, I've suggested a drive. Mark initially acquiesced, but now he's staring at me, incredulous.

'Why here, Sash?'

'I need to stretch my legs. Get some fresh air.'

'Behind a cemetery?' He squints at me.

The closest Express Post box to the hospital is just outside the cemetery gates, on the main road out of town. It isn't visible from the car park on the opposite side. In this relatively small town, I can't think of any other place where I can post a package without Mark seeing me. I know a shortcut through the graveyard. Mark won't follow me; he can't stand cemeteries.

And he won't have a clue what I'm up to. He might be suspicious, but I'm now down to last resorts.

'Just give me five minutes. Please.'

'Should I be worried about you, Sash?'

'I need some time. Dad told me some stuff about Mum.'

His neck jerks back. 'What did he tell you?'

'I think he was telling me she's dead.'

'Oh, Sash . . .' His head droops to the steering wheel.

'I'm okay. I just . . . need a few moments in a place where I can get a sense of her.'

I ease myself out of the car and close the door before he can say anything more.

Stones crunch under my shoes as I curve along the cemetery path in a wide arc. Has Mark known about Mum this whole time? What else is he hiding from me?

A shimmering word catches my eye, inscribed on a headstone: *Rose*. It's my mother's name carved into the white marble in a silvery, gothic font. I check – it's not her grave. Until this morning I hadn't even realised she had one. My fingers, clutching my handbag, start to tremble. My mother, dead? I suppose a small part of me has always wanted to see her. Confront her. Demand to know why she left. Now it sounds like I will never have that chance. I try to stuff the visions of her pale face to the back of my mind. I have more pressing issues at hand.

I'm about to keep walking when I notice the word *Tobias* carved into the same marble headstone. I trace the names and dates. It's a family from long ago.

Rose Jane. Deceased aged 6 weeks. 3/1/1866.

Theodore Thomas. Deceased aged 2 months. 8/12/1866.

Beloved children of Mary Agatha and Tobias Matthew. Forever at peace.

But how could they have known their babies were truly at peace? And what about these parents, long dead – how did they bear such a loss?

The first dead baby I saw had translucent skin shedding from its muscles, fingers and toes still fused together, eyes not yet open. I knew, then, what I was fighting for, and what I was fighting against. How hard nature could be, how unforgiving. The baby's parents were farmers, familiar with death. They were stoic enough to bear the loss. I couldn't have been that strong.

I check the dates on the gravestone again. Two babies deceased, less than a year apart. How did their parents possibly manage to go on?

I clutch the iron railings edging the grave, my palms numbing from the sudden cold. But then, that was Mark and me. We lost two babies not even a year apart.

The first child's voice had been with me for the duration of my short pregnancy. It was muffled, low-pitched, reciting imperceptible words. It was like a one-sided conversation heard through a semi-closed door, almost like a child playing in their bedroom, beyond the line of sight. Harry, I would have called him.

The second voice was quieter. I had a hunch this one wasn't destined to stay, but I played along anyway, booking upcoming ultrasounds, obstetrician appointments, blood tests. Matilda. On the day the pregnancy ended, I was lying on the couch after lunch when I sensed a white light rising from my pelvis towards the ceiling. I knew she was gone.

Mark didn't want to discuss the miscarriages or the voices or the light. He didn't want to hear anything about it. I didn't press him. What would have been the point? He did a reasonable job of holding me as I wept at night. And he planted the trees. After that, we never discussed the babies again.

A thin sheet of darkness settles on the gravestones, shadows stretching long across the path. The thrum of traffic in the distance mingles with the swish of plastic flowers in vases perched beside headstones, colourful windmills spinning in the breeze, rustling weeds on unkempt graves. The wind catches my belly through my thin jacket, prickling my skin. I zip it closed all the way up to my chin.

My eyes flick from grave to grave. *Edith. Frederica. Arthur. Muriel.* Born in a time when medicine was too primitive to save them, these babies didn't stand a chance. Their parents were blameless. Unlike my mother. Unlike me. I've let Mark down in so many ways. Not only did I lose Harry and Matilda, I've also come so close to losing our son.

I remove the Express Post package from my handbag and stuff it under my jacket, close to my heart. It's a bundle of hope swathed in bubble wrap; hope that one day in the future I'll be cradling Gabriel in my arms, all of this a distant nightmare.

A flash of orange from the roadside: our car's locking device. Is Mark coming to find me?

I press on, scurrying past more headstones, my shadow a thin pillar spreading out on the ground in front of me. The main gates of the cemetery, wrought iron with gothic swirls, rise before me like sentries. A thick chain and padlock encircle them. I glimpse the yellow Express Post box outside, on the nature strip beside the road. I shake the bars of the gates. The chain holds fast. My heart palpitates.

Before I turn, a flicker of silver glints in the darkness. A small, unlocked gate, propped open with a brick, next to the main gates. My escape.

I slip through it and out onto the footpath. The tangle of country-town peak hour has eased, cars thinning out like the end of a factory line, headlights sliding past in the dusk. My pocket vibrates. Mark.

I pull out the package. It weighs heavy despite its contents: three mouth swabs plus Mark's handkerchief encased in the sterile plastic bag. I slide the parcel through the mouth of the letterbox, the flap flinging closed with a thud.

A car horn blast erupts from the other side of the cemetery. Mark, again. I head back through the small gate and along the main path, old stone vaults and gaudy crypts and solemn headstones lining the way.

At the front gate, a fluorescent yellow poster has been tacked to the brick wall. I've seen the signs before, plastered on posts all over town, advertising an annual memorial service for people who've lost babies: stillbirths, miscarriages, SIDS, the whole conglomeration of grief. *A time for remembering*, the poster reads, *where parents recite poetry, tell their stories and release yellow balloons of hope*. I don't think I ever fully processed my failed pregnancies. Perhaps Mark never had the chance, either. One day, not too far in the future, I could be a parent huddling in a cluster at that service, holding Gabriel against my chest, releasing the yellow balloons from my hand, free to float high into the dusky sky.

DAY 4, TUESDAY NIGHT

The nursery is quietest at night. Minimum staff – two nurses, at most, and only one at the desk when the other takes their tea breaks. With the lights dimmed, the babies seem to sense they should be sleeping. Their cries are timid, an accompaniment to the soft hum of machines in the background. No visitors; the other mothers are sensible, at home in their beds, resting up for when their babies are finally discharged and come home for good. Me – I have no desire for rest. Evenings are the best times to watch my beautiful son. And I'm doing what they told me – spending time with him, in order to bond.

I'm seated by Toby's cot, observing Gabriel across the way. He is peaceful, nestled on his stomach in a bundle. *Wait for me, Gabriel*, I whisper. *I promise I'm doing everything I can to get you back.*

I'm about to sneak across the walkway to have a closer look at him when my phone vibrates. Bec. I've been waiting for her to return my call.

'How are you, Sash? How was your leave from the mother–baby unit?'

She knew about that? Has Mark spoken to her again?

She speaks before I can answer. 'Mark told me you were granted leave. I've been calling him, trying to tell him there's nothing wrong with you.'

'I bet that's going well.' It sounds like she's only trying to help.

She lets out a short, hesitant laugh. 'So was it good to get out of the unit for a while?'

'We made it brief.'

After the cemetery, I was shivering by the time I returned to the car. Mark was happy enough to take me back to the unit. I told him I felt much better, communing with my mother. He didn't seem in the mood to talk about Mum, so I didn't push it. Maybe the drive hadn't been such a good idea, was all he said as we made our way back to the hospital.

'There's good news, Bec,' I say, sitting up straighter in the vinyl chair. No one is nearby, but I still lower my voice. 'I found our son.'

'Oh my God! Sash! That's incredible. What's he like?'

'Blissful. Divine. A miracle.'

'Oh, Sash. That's amazing. Well done. I'm so glad for you.'

She does sound glad. I'm relieved. Perhaps she is more able than I would have been to let any residual infertility jealousy go.

'Is there something bothering you?' Bec adds. 'You don't sound that happy.'

'It's just that the hospital has been talking about sending him home later this week. If he goes home, it'll be that much harder to get him back.'

'Crap.' Bec pauses. 'So, we need to think like detectives.'

I pinch the bridge of my nose. This isn't a game.

'We're doctors, not detectives,' I say.

'I know, I know. You're right.' She inhales. 'Okay. Let's use our medical training, then. You've done an examination – and you've found your baby. What's the most important part of making a diagnosis? What have we neglected to do?'

'Um . . . history-taking?' I'm not sure where she's going with all of this.

'Exactly. You need to speak to the suspects. Question them about their motives. Their alibis. Speculate about who did this. Then we can work out further investigations and management.'

'It sounds a little . . . tricky.' It's the kindest way I can say that I think her plan is ridiculous.

'I can try and help over the phone. You give me a list of suspects. We can work through it together, see if we can rule them out, one by one.'

'But couldn't it just have been a simple mix-up? A genuine mistake?'

'I suppose,' Bec says slowly, 'but there's no harm in trying to figure out if anyone has a motive. And maybe one of them has a clue about how it could have happened?'

Dr Niles springs to mind. I remember the phone call she had to take about a embryo transfer. I had assumed it was about a patient, but now it sounds like it might have been a personal call.

'I think my psychiatrist could be trying to get pregnant.' I glance across the walkway to where Gabriel lies still. 'She said you've been calling her.'

Bec is silent for a moment. 'Sorry, Sash. I'm not going to stop calling her. Someone needs to protest your sanity. It's so unfair, how everyone's treating you. I can't even imagine if it were me going through this. I would have lost it by now.'

For a moment, I had questioned Bec's loyalty. But I trust Bec more than anyone; more, even, than Mark.

'Thanks, Bec. But I think you might be annoying her.'

'Bad luck for her. She's annoying me. I'm not sure she's involved in your baby mix-up, though. Wouldn't she just take a baby if she were that desperate? Switching babies doesn't make sense. And surely a psychiatrist in a special-care nursery would raise some eyebrows. But you should check her out anyway, just to be sure.'

Her plan is starting to make sense.

'There are some other potential suspects. One of the midwives seems to have taken a dislike to me. The other two doctors refuse to believe me. And there's the woman who believes my baby is hers. Toby must be her real son. I haven't dared tell her about the mix-up yet.'

Bec's tone is decisive.

'You should check them all out, then get back to me. But I can't imagine that baby's mother could be responsible for this.'

'Mothers can be responsible for lots of things.'

I wonder suddenly if Bec knew about my mother. Has she been lying to me, too?

'Bec? Something else has come up. Dad told me about my mother . . . Did you know she was . . . dead?'

Bec is silent. When she finally speaks, her voice cracks.

'I'm so sorry, Sash. Mum told me years ago, right before she passed away. She begged me not to tell you. Before then I had no idea. I promised Mum I wouldn't say anything.'

I know it's not Bec's fault; I don't blame her.

'Did Mark know too?'

'No, I don't think so.'

I'm not so sure. It's something about the way he stares at me from time to time, his eyes filled with pity rather than love.

'Do you know the details? How she died?'

'I know nothing, Sash. Only that she passed away when you were young. I truly wish I knew more.' She sounds sincere.

'But you'd tell me if you knew anything else, wouldn't you, Bec?'

'Of course,' she says at once.

How could I doubt Bec? She knows everything about me, from my embarrassing schoolgirl crushes to me wetting my pants on the first day of high school when I couldn't find the bathroom. She's remembered the stories for all these years. She would never lie to me. And I know she would never betray me.

'Look, I should get back to work in a minute,' Bec says with a sniff. 'But did I tell you Adam and I are coming home for Christmas this year? It'll be great to see you.' There's an undertone to her voice, the grief of infertility with which I'm all too familiar. 'It's horrific what you're going through, Sash. Thank God you'll have him back any day now.' She clears her throat. 'But Sash? You're okay, right? Your mental health?'

'Absolutely.'

'And things with Mark are okay?'

I've spent so long hoping Mark would change. Hoping he'd open up to me, wishing he'd show he cared about the pregnancies we lost. But he wasn't there for me, and now, when I need him more than ever, he's still not here.

'It's not going so well,' I say.

'Mark does love you, you know,' Bec says.

'Not enough.'

One morning years ago, when I was a teenager, Lucia ushered me to her bedroom. She indicated an enormous artwork strung above her bed, the canvas slathered in black, gold and vermilion welts. She pulled me onto the doona beside her and squeezed me against her bosom. She told me she had never been able to decipher how her ex-husband, Mario, had manipulated the colours so that in one light it appeared to represent an autumnal sunset and in another an image of blood seeping from an open wound.

'When you choose a husband, be careful,' she said. 'Make sure there is nothing he loves more than you.'

Bec's voice pipes up above a shrilling nursery alarm: 'Listen to me, Sash. Mark's a really good man. Better than most. Marriage is what gets you through the hard stuff. The easy parts take care of themselves. Remember, no marriage is perfect.'

Lucia would pull out her wedding album once a year on the anniversary. As she pored over the photographs of her wedding day, she would tell stories of the women Mario had seduced over the years. Miriam. Bernadette. Carolina. Scores of them. She knew what he was like before she married him. What she had learned after ten years of marriage she intoned to Bec and me on a regular basis: 'People don't change, my darlings. They just reveal who they really are.'

Bec is waiting for me to speak. I manage to croak, 'It's easy for you to say. Adam's a way better husband than Mark.'

'No, you're wrong, Sash. Adam works ninety-hour weeks. He sleeps at the office most nights. We've hardly seen each other in months. I'd do anything for a husband like Mark.'

I've always viewed Bec and Adam as the perfect couple, Adam the perfect husband. When he posted thoughtful anniversary messages on Facebook, I nudged Mark in the ribs. When he bought her a car for her birthday, my insides hardened. When Bec disclosed that Adam was doing all the housework after her miscarriage, I lost it at Mark: 'You haven't even cried.'

Mark glared at me until my blood ran cold. 'How would you know?' His eyes were so dark I never mentioned it again.

Bec sniffs. 'Okay. I gotta get back to work. Tomorrow, make sure you start work on our plan. Until we speak again, Sash – please take care.'

DAY 5, WEDNESDAY EARLY MORNING

I wrap my arms around my baby, cocooning him against my chest. Mark gazes at me with adoration, his arm slung over my shoulder. It's a warm summer's day. A mild breeze nuzzles my neck as we sit side-by-side on the park bench by the lake close to home. Things couldn't be more perfect.

Then the rain begins. Fat, heavy drops of liquid land on my scalp, my arms, my face. My skin chills. I reach to cover my baby's head, to protect him from the rainfall, but as I glance down I see his hair is coated in clots of scarlet. On my right, streams of red liquid drip down Mark's face, his lips frozen in a silent scream. My body begins to give way, my skin and bones and muscles liquefying to maroon, and my son slips from my grasp. I tumble beside him into the puddle beneath the bench, both of us pooling into blood.

The nightmare jolts me awake. I lie rigid, sucking air into my lungs. I'm in my bed in the mother–baby unit. Not home. Not yet.

A shuffle from the cupboard, then the plop of something falling to the floor. Slivers of early-morning light cut through the open curtains, piercing the dusty window, falling onto Mark, who is kneeling above a pile of my belongings, his face a guilty mask.

'What are you doing?'

'I could ask you the same thing.' He flings the last of my clothes from the bottom shelf of the cupboard onto the floor. 'Tell me where they are, Sash, and I can go.'

He brought those clothes in for me from home, just like I asked. Jeans, tracksuit pants, T-shirts, windcheaters, my comfortable clothes. Now it all lies in crumpled piles on the floor.

'What the hell are you doing with my stuff?'

He reaches into the pocket of his jacket, yanks out two pieces of crinkled paper and drops them on my bedside table. Dr Niles' schedule, with my notes about the DNA tests scribbled on the back.

'Where did you get that?'

He drops his arms to his sides. 'The other night. I found it right here.'

'And how did you get in just now?'

'I told the nurses I needed to see you urgently. I'm here to help. To find the DNA tests. To protect you from yourself.'

'I don't need protecting.' I sit up. 'Mark, you know I've let go of the need to do the testing now.' Thank God I already sent the DNA samples back. What he mustn't find: the zip-lock bag, Gabriel's umbilical cord secreted within it, concealed in the pocket of my jeans. Mark has already thrown that pair on the floor.

We're interrupted by a click at the door. Dr Niles marches in, her shoulders hitched back, her head erect. She surveys my belongings scattered like body bags across the room.

'Mark's helping me with the washing,' I explain.

Dr Niles glances between us, her head tipped to the side. Mark grabs handfuls of my clothes and begins to shove them back into the cupboard.

'May I speak to Sasha alone?' Dr Niles says. 'It's time for our morning chat.'

I want to pretend all this isn't happening: my baby being mixed up, me being locked in a mother–baby unit, my husband not supporting me, my mother apparently dead. I want to be anywhere but here.

Mark's eyes stray to Dr Niles' schedule on the bedside table. He sighs and casts me a backwards glance. Mark isn't my knight on horseback; he never will be.

'I'm here for you, Sash,' he says to me. 'Whatever it takes.'

As he stalks from the room, it's hard to imagine his words hold much weight.

Seated in the chair under the window, Dr Niles rubs the back of her neck.

'It appears you're getting better, Sasha. Your room is quite a mess, but' – she checks the notes in her lap – 'you are making connections here. Friends, I believe.'

Friends? Ondine is an acquaintance, a companion on this journey of horror. Friends are people I would trust with intimate details of my life, my marriage, my hopes and fears. It will be a while before I place Ondine in that category. Still, if that is what Dr Niles wishes to believe, I suppose it can only help me get discharged sooner.

Bec's face flashes before me, a reminder of my mission. I need to check Dr Niles' alibi.

'Do you remember the day you admitted me?'

She nods, her face quizzical.

'Can I ask why you were running late to see me?'

Her face clouds. 'I had a personal appointment that ran into the afternoon. I apologise again. I came as soon as I could.'

That call Dr Niles made, about an embryo transfer, is still weighing on my mind. It's worth asking a final question.

'Is a baby something you want, Dr Niles?'

She frowns. 'Why is knowing that important to you, Sasha?'

'I understand why someone would want to have their own baby,' I say.

'So do I, Sasha. Sometimes we just have to accept we can't have the things we most want.' She clears her throat. 'But we're here to discuss you and your needs. Perhaps you can tell me more about your own desire for a child.'

I can't believe she has anything to do with the baby swap. 'I think Mark always wanted a baby more than me.'

'I see.' She fiddles with her tarnished gold wedding band as she speaks. 'I sense things with Mark are . . . tense?'

'We have our days. Same as any married couple.'

'Perhaps,' Dr Niles said. 'And what is holding you in this marriage, do you think? What is it about Mark that makes you want to stay?'

I slump back against the pillows. I used to have a list in my head for the times I felt like ending the relationship. He makes me laugh (*occasionally*). He'll be an amazing father (*if we ever get pregnant*). All the good men are taken by now (*though surely there's one or two left*).

The truth? My fertile years had fallen behind me like Gretel's breadcrumbs and had been eaten by the birds. In my desperation to get pregnant, I'd forgotten to lay a trail for myself to lead me home. There was no way I was going to raise a baby alone. By staying with Mark, with access to his sperm, I still had a chance at getting out of the wilderness.

'How do you think Mark will cope if you're discharged?'

Cope? Is she joking?

'He'll be fine.'

She lifts her eyebrows. Perhaps I was right when I suspected Mark was responsible for me being in here. Does he see me, a mentally unwell wife, as an impediment to his work? To his relationship with the baby he believes is his son? Would he prefer I remained an inpatient for now?

Mark had come along to our marriage counselling appointments without grumbling. I shouldn't complain, I suppose. Many husbands would have refused outright. At least Mark was prepared to show up.

After two unsuccessful attempts at finding a good enough counsellor, I chose Kate at random from the internet. She had a sensible name. Plus she looked sincere in her photograph on the website. I hoped she'd be the one.

After listening to both of us, Kate laid out our relationship in a clear timeline: jazz club, marriage, infertility, miscarriages. At the end of Kate's summary, Mark began to speak of his desperation to have a child. My heart began to thump so loudly, I was certain both of them could hear it. Mark neglected to tell the counsellor we were taking a break from trying. I neglected to tell either of them I wasn't going to recommence it. My dreams for a baby? I was already starting to let them go.

'I wouldn't blame Mark for leaving,' I said when Mark paused for breath. 'If I were him, I think I'd leave in these circumstances.

Things would be easier for him with someone else. A more fertile woman. A more fertile wife.'

'It's important you stay focused on each other, on your strengths as a couple,' Kate said, before Mark could reply. 'No relationship is easy, especially with children. And even with just the two of you, you're still a family. You can nurture each other in the same way you would a child.'

It was sound advice. Yet with Mark's long, irregular chef hours and strident pursuit of pregnancy, it was becoming increasingly obvious that he saw me more as the womb for his child than as his wife. He threw himself into his work with more energy than he ever brought to our marriage, as if he wanted to hide from our difficulties. No matter what was to come, I knew he would stay with me out of duty. A husband wasn't what I wanted, though – not if I wasn't truly loved.

Three weeks later, right before our next counselling appointment, I wiped a clear spot in the fogged-up mirror of our ensuite. Staring at my reflection, a wave of nausea ran through me. Then a pang arose from within as my guts were wrung like a sponge. I turned to the toilet and heaved. Kneeling before the bowl, I ran through my period dates. I'd become so accustomed to the clinic monitoring my cycles I'd failed to realise I was overdue.

In a reflex action, I reached for the pregnancy tests in the bottom drawer of the bathroom cabinet. My hand shook as I held the stick in the stream of my pallid urine. The second line showed up pink.

Just for a moment, I was despondent. I wouldn't be separating from Mark anymore. Then I was triumphant. Surely things could only improve between Mark and me now that we had the baby we both had planned.

I postponed the counselling with a feeble excuse, something about needing more time to reflect on the strengths of our relationship. Mark took me at face value. I hid my morning sickness from him and waited until I was twelve weeks gone to let him know. No sense getting his hopes up again.

'The ultrasound is tomorrow,' I said, as I stood at the kitchen bench slicing limes. 'That's why we don't have to keep going to counselling anymore.'

'I guess not,' he said, his eyebrows slightly creased. 'Congratulations, Sash.'

The insides of the cut limes glistened like emeralds as he pulled me towards him and lifted me off the ground, hugging me tight. I was happy, wasn't I? After all, this was everything we'd been waiting, hoping, striving for, wanting more than anything, for so very long.

DAY 5, WEDNESDAY MORNING

I rush down the corridor, hoping there won't be a black mark against my name for tardiness. Everything I do wrong might hold me back from being discharged. And getting out of here – and getting home – is essential to having Gabriel back. I'll need to be seen as mentally well before they let me have custody of him. Today's scheduled activity is yoga. I won't be able to participate so soon after the caesar, but I suppose it's the attendance that Dr Niles is interested in.

For the longest time, yoga was my method of relaxation. I used to love the heat in my muscles as I held the poses, the tingle of breath moving through my body, the flush of my skin at the end of class. That is, until I became pregnant, when every movement sent a searing rod of pain through my pelvis, even as the teacher urged me to bring my legs higher up the wall, ease into the discomfort and feel the burn.

The women glance across from their warrior poses as I enter the recreation room. A carpet has been laid out with blue yoga mats and the chairs are stacked against the far wall beside the bookshelves. I pick up a mat and give a small, involuntary yelp at the sting in my stitches. As usual, I seem to have overestimated my capacity.

The teacher encourages me to lie flat on my back, close my eyes and meditate on my post-baby body. Meditate on my post-baby body – is that supposed to be a joke?

I ease myself down onto the thin rubber mat near the windows and place my hands on my chest, watching them rise and fall with each breath. Women around me exhale, sweeping into various arrangements – angry cat, tree, crab.

At the window, fern fronds scrape on glass. A shadow flickers from behind my closed lids. Opening my eyes, I see Ondine, her face red and blotchy, tiptoeing out the door. The teacher, her backside held aloft in a downward dog pose, hasn't noticed.

I shift onto my side and ease myself to standing. The other women hold their inversions steady, together resembling the panorama of a mountain range. I was never as agile as these women. I'll leave them to their cats and trees.

The rec-room door clicks shut behind me. A stifled sob drifts from the bathroom in the corridor. I press the door open, squinting in the dazzling light reflected against the tiles. Ondine's handbag sits on the bench beside the sink, a beige-coloured envelope protruding from the top.

'Are you okay?'

'Sure.' Her voice is thick, mucusy, from behind the cubicle door.

'You don't like yoga?'

'Not much.' She gives a quiet guffaw. When she emerges from the cubicle, her face is stained with tears.

'I just got a long letter,' she says, pushing the envelope deep into her handbag. 'From Zach. He wants to see me. And he wants to bring Henry.'

'That's great news. When are you going to see him?'

'I don't know,' she says, washing her hands. 'It's hard, after what happened. I want to see them both. I want to be back with Henry. But I'm scared.'

'What are you scared of?'

She blanches. 'That I'll have thoughts about killing him again.'

'Show me a mother who's never imagined killing her child,' I say, 'if only for the briefest fraction of a second. In anger. Or fear. But there's a chasm between thought and action, Ondine.'

'I did act,' she says, her voice so soft I have to bend to catch it. 'I started to.' She clutches her handbag to her chest and gives a deep sob.

'I'd hardly slept for a month. Henry was screaming. His bottom was filthy for the tenth time that day. I ran a bath. He was in my arms when I imagined him under the water. His face, submerged. How much quieter he'd be. He wouldn't struggle at all.' She gives a sharp inhalation. 'Zach walked in as I dipped him below the surface. He'd had a sense something wasn't right when he left for work that morning. He pulled Henry from my arms and breathed air in his mouth.' She gives an involuntary shiver. 'At least Zach is communicating with me again, even if it's only by letter. And it looks like Henry is going to be fine.'

A tingle passes between us as I place my hand on hers.

'I hope you can forgive yourself one day,' I say, not entirely sure who I'm addressing.

She gives a wry smile. 'I guess I'll never win the world's-best-mother award.'

'You're good enough.' As Ondine stands up straight before the mirror, I'm finally starting to believe it about myself.

'At least I was honest,' she says. 'At first, I told the staff I was so tired that he slipped under the water.'

'What made you tell the truth?'

'I didn't want to lie anymore.' She dips her head.

'Being honest always helps. And Henry needs you. When you feel ready, you should see him. He'll be so glad to see you.'

Her cheeks crease into a small smile. 'I'm sure it won't be long until I feel better. Dr Niles says the tablets will start helping soon. Are you taking tablets?'

I pause, examining the parched, split skin of my fingers, drained of moisture by the nursery antiseptic handwash.

'I'm supposed to, but I haven't been taking them.'

'You haven't?'

'I can't stand medication. You won't say anything though, will you?'

'Of course not.'

Ondine is trustworthy. She's an ally. She believes me.

'Let's skip the rest of yoga,' I say. 'I have a better idea. Would you like to meet my baby?' I want to show him off.

'I'd love to,' Ondine says, running the sleeve of her sweater across her cheeks. 'Let's go see your son.'

The nursery door slides open. Babies wail from every corner, their high-pitched cries drowning out the low beeps and whirrs of machinery. Fluorescent lights flash on screens in every colour of the rainbow. I press a hand to my nose to block the smell of soiled nappies and curdled formula.

'This way.'

I lead Ondine to Toby, the small bundle of him that lies immobile, his chest spluttering up and down in his plastic cage.

'This is the baby they're saying is mine.'

She stands over him, peering into the crib. 'Not yours, I agree.'

'You won't say anything, will you?' I suddenly blurt. 'I don't want to panic anyone yet.'

'Of course not.' She looks almost hurt that I've suggested it. 'So where is your baby, then?'

There are no visitors at the humidicribs nearby; no nurses, either. I press my finger to my lips and point to where my Gabriel lies.

Ondine tiptoes across the corridor, then crouches down in front of the cot, flicking her eyes back and forth between Gabriel and me.

'He looks exactly like you.'

I smile. 'I know.'

'Congratulations,' she says. 'You should be very proud. He's beautiful.' She gently leads me back to Toby's cot.

'I've been trying to think how it could have happened,' I tell her. 'There was a case in France where the nurse mixed up the babies by mistake. I mean, the name bands could slip off, couldn't they? And be wrongly replaced?'

'I guess. Though it seems like protocols are strict enough here. All the nurses I've met in the mother–baby unit are so thorough. It'd be almost impossible for an accidental mix-up to occur.'

'But people are human, aren't they? I mean, we all make mistakes.'

As I glance at Toby's shiny hair, his flat nose, his grey-blue eyes, it strikes me how similar he looks to Damien. The barrister's voice ringing through the coroner's court chamber still echoes in my skull in the dark hours of the night. *Do you recall Damien's parents alerting you to an unusual purple lesion behind his right ear on the evening in question?*

In the witness box, I held my breath in my throat and clung to the wooden railing to stop my hands from trembling.

To this day, I remain unsure of the correct answer. And I'm still not certain if I made the right decision in my reply.

I tipped back my head and, with my hands as solid as rocks on the railing, spoke decisively.

Did I see the purple lesion? I don't recall.

Ondine clicks open one of Toby's portholes and reaches in with a delicate hand. She places the nail of her index finger around the name band encircling his wrist and tugs.

'It's tight, Sasha. Hard to break. And it can't be slipped off.'

'It could be cut, couldn't it?'

'That would take intention.' She places her hand on Toby's forehead. 'Who on earth would want to do something like that?'

Hot breath on the back of my neck. It's Mark. I didn't notice him entering the nursery. He doesn't seem to have overheard us. He addresses Ondine.

'Hello, I'm Sasha's husband, Mark.'

Ondine smiles. 'Hi, I'm a friend of Sasha's.' She rests her hand on mine. 'I'll leave you to it. I'm sure you two have got a lot to discuss.'

Mark stares after her, then at Toby, running a hand through his hair. I sink into a chair beside Toby.

'I've got some good news for you, Sash,' he says, drawing his mouth into a smile, a lock of hair falling back over his forehead. 'I didn't have time to tell you the night of the birth. Work offered me to buy in. It's a great opportunity to take a lead in the running of the restaurant. Take it in a new direction. A little more upmarket, perhaps.'

His irises are the muddy brown of the hot spring we swam in years ago in the central Australian desert. The pond appeared shallow from the bank, yet when we tried to find our footing, we were continually pushed back to the surface, aloft on enormous bubbles of gas emerging from deep underground, until we could do nothing but lie suspended on our backs in the sandy emulsion. It was fun back then, floating free, nothing solid beneath our feet. Nowhere safe to land.

'But you don't even like what they serve there. Don't you prefer organic food? And what about starting your own café? Your dream?'

Mark's forehead creases. 'I let go of that idea long ago, Sash.'

'You never told me that.'

He frowns. 'You didn't want to know.'

I clutch the armrests. When did he become a stranger?

'But I thought it was still your dream.'

Mark's mouth droops as he shrugs.

'I suppose it's congratulations, then,' I say.

'I told them I'd discuss it with you before I accepted.'

'It doesn't sound like there's anything to discuss.'

'Great, then. It's settled. We'll be making a lot more money down the track.'

He's thinking about money at a time like this?

'It's enough for you to stay home with Toby longer than we planned. Only if you want, of course. I don't want to force you to do anything.'

I want to spend all the time in the world with Gabriel.

And once I get him home, I will never dare leave him alone again.

DAY 5, WEDNESDAY LUNCHTIME

I glance up to see Brigitte's face before me, as pale as sea foam. I hadn't noticed her come in. I've been standing beside Gabriel's cot for what must have been an hour but feels like mere seconds since Mark left to call his work.

'Your baby is beautiful,' I say, glad to be at least partly honest. But there's something else. His skin is the colour of ripe mandarins, too dark for his fifth day of life. Yet he's not under the fluorescent blue lights. 'Do the nurses know Gabriel's jaundice is getting worse?'

She glances up, squinting. 'Gabriel?'

My hand recoils from the plastic.

'Sorry, I meant Jeremy. Sorry. My sister has just had a baby, Gabriel.'

'Sister? I thought you said you were an only child.'

Shit, she's quick.

'Bec is my best friend. We grew up together. She's like my sister.'

She nods, seemingly satisfied.

'Gabriel is a lovely name.'

Brigitte folds Gabriel's quilt and places it on the bench. I wish I were the one aligning the edges to make it just so. The colours accentuate the blue of his eyes. He'll look gorgeous wrapped in it when I take him home.

'The nurses are doing a blood test,' she says. 'If the results come back okay, I'm hoping for Friday.'

It sounds like they're investigating him adequately, at least. But they're still talking about Friday? That's only two days away. I was hoping his discharge would be delayed beyond the end of the week. There's no way the DNA results will be back by Friday. And is it really safe to be sending him home when he looks like this?

'The worst thing is that I haven't been able to get in contact with John. He has no idea about any of this.'

Her husband, she informs me, is currently stationed in remote Papua New Guinea, out of mobile range. He won't be back for at least a week.

'He's going to get a surprise when he finds out he missed the birth,' I say.

'He sure is. He chose the name. He's going to adore our baby.'

So will Mark when he comes to accept the truth.

Brigitte rests her hand on Gabriel's folded mat.

'For a long time, it looked like we wouldn't be able to have a child. It was the mines, I always thought. The heat, the dust, the chemicals wrecking John's sperm. That's when I started looking into lifestyle and diet. We experimented with a few things. I started studying naturopathy.' She fixes her eyes on Gabriel. 'Now here we are.'

'Isn't it hard with your husband away so much?'

'No. Not really. He gets leave every few months. And the company pays for me to meet him in exotic locations several times a year. We spent our babymoon in East Timor.' She gives a contented smile. 'Anyway, I think having a partner at home is overrated. My girlfriends are always whingeing about their husbands. I get to cherish every moment I have with John when he's home.' She pauses. 'But what about you? Does your husband ever annoy you?'

I survey the old photo from our central Australian trip that Mark has blu-tacked to the wall beside Toby's cot. It's of the two of us crouching beside a flooded Lake Eyre. The water extends for miles in every direction as if impassable, yet it was only ankle deep.

'Mark and I are having some issues.'

Brigitte tugs at her long plait.

'I wouldn't have guessed. Has that been going on long?'

I rarely talk about my marriage to anyone but Bec, but waiting here in this nursery hour after hour creates an unnatural intimacy. It's getting harder and harder to keep things to myself.

'I guess it started when I couldn't get pregnant. All those years we thought we'd never have a baby –'

'– but you can work it out, right?'

I turn away and pull my brittle ponytail loose. 'I suppose so.'

'I mean, you wouldn't want to be a single mother, right? Not if you could help it?'

Single mother. Words I've never imagined could apply to me. For years I'd believed I was incapable of being a mother at all. After all, I hadn't been shown how. Would I be able to stay around for my child even when it all seemed too much? When

I finally came around to the idea of motherhood, I was relying on Mark to be the good enough parent, the one who would make up for all my failings. The idea of being a single mother – the only parent in the house – has always made my shoulders lock fast. I saw how hard it was for my father. I don't know if I'd be any better than he was at meeting my child's emotional needs.

'I was raised by a single mother,' Brigitte says without waiting for my reply. 'Don't get me wrong, it was fine. It isn't what I want for my child, though. You know, it's funny, it never occurred to me before that some people might see my life as like a single mother's. I mean, when John is away, I'm home alone for weeks at a time.'

'You don't get lonely?'

She shakes her head.

'And you don't get scared of being alone at night?'

Brigitte's cheeks become even paler as she picks up her needles and rectangle of knitted wool.

'Some nights.'

'Because you've got a baby.'

'Yes, and after . . .' She brings her tongue into the large gap between her front teeth as if she wants to stem the flow of words, then continues quietly. 'I had a bad experience. Something really terrible happened before I got pregnant. Thank God that's all over now. I'm looking forward to a fresh start.' Her body gives a slight jolt. 'Damn!' She unpicks a dropped stitch then begins to knit again. 'I just want Jeremy to be okay,' she says.

She's really not going to take it well when I tell her about the baby swap. It's the kind of news nobody wants to hear. But she'll need to know soon, and when the time comes there'll be nothing I can do to soften the truth.

Brigitte threads the wool around the ball of yarn in a haphazard pattern.

'And how is Toby going?' Her voice is bright, but there's an edge of despair beneath it.

I cross the walkway and press my palm on the orange quilt on top of Toby's humidicrib in a semblance of ownership, inspecting once more the photograph of Mark and me.

'Really great, thanks.'

If it comes down to it, I can do single motherhood. *Don't worry, Gabriel, I'll be a good enough mother. You'll be safe with me.* As soon as I can prove he's mine. But how am I going to secure the proof I need before Friday? I don't have time to muck around with this covert sleuthing. I need a more concrete plan.

'I'm glad Toby's doing so well,' Brigitte says. 'Our babies. That's the only reason we're here, after all.'

I'm sitting in the most secluded corner of the hospital cafeteria, where the windows are coated with white mesh. There's a gentle hum of staff members conversing. At other tables, visitors sip at cappuccinos and nibble at sweet cakes. Only just visible behind some pillars, on the opposite side of the cafeteria, are two women playing peek-a-boo as they bounce their babies on their knees. I'm not supposed to be in here – Dr Niles' rules – but I need a break from the confines of the nursery and the mother–baby unit. And I need some privacy for what I'm about to do.

I call DNA Easy. Jim answers after one ring.

'I'm desperate, Jim,' I say. 'I need the DNA results.'

'Of course,' he says. He checks his database. 'I can see the results were posted today.'

Already, quicker than anticipated? This is brilliant news. 'When will they arrive?'

'We guarantee two business days. So, Monday at the latest.'

'Monday is too late,' I say. 'Can you just read them to me over the phone?'

'I'm sorry,' Jim says. 'For legal reasons, we can only provide a written copy of the results.'

My heart plummets. 'No. I must have those results today. Can you email them to me, please?'

Jim's voice tightens. 'An email address hasn't been supplied with the form. I'm afraid our policy is extremely strict on this matter.'

I forgot to fill in a box, and because of my oversight and a senseless bureaucracy I will potentially delay my reunion with my son.

'I apologise,' Jim says.

I see my father's number light up on my phone. 'Forget it,' I say to Jim and take Dad's call.

'Dad.' I whip the white froth of my hot chocolate into the brown liquid.

'Sasha. There's something I need to tell you. I wanted to say it yesterday, but . . .'

He trails off. What else is he going to thrust upon me? All I hear is his breathing for several seconds before he continues.

'Your mother loved you. I know she wouldn't want you to think badly of her. She did what she thought was best. For both of us.'

'I don't understand,' I stammer down the phone. 'What are you trying to say?' Yet part of me is one step ahead and doesn't want to hear.

'She . . . she took pills, Sasha. She took the whole box.'

The dull hum of the cafeteria fades to silence. *Pills.* I remember them, a splash of pretty colours, spread out across the quilt like a rainbow.

It takes a few moments for the pain to hit. My mother killed herself. She couldn't bear to stay, not even for me. I wasn't enough for her.

'I'm only telling you now because I don't want anything to happen to you.'

I place the spoon on the saucer with a clang.

'I'm not like her,' I hear myself say. 'I've never been like her.'

I don't smoke. I don't have postnatal depression. I won't neglect my child. I am never going to kill myself. There was a time, though, that dark, lonely time when I thought I could have.

After Damien's inquest, I was dragging myself to work each day, seeing children who weren't ill and trying to smile at their parents in a reassuring way. In the evenings, I'd come home and collapse on the couch in front of the TV. There was one particular day that had been more trying than most. A baby with light-brown curls, sick with pneumonia, who reminded me of Damien. As I listened to the baby's chest, I was back beside Damien again, watching as the ambulance brought him back to the emergency department. It was the morning after I had first seen him. He was still conscious, but covered in the purpuric rash of meningococcal septicaemia, plaques on his torso, his face, even on his drooping eyelids. His eyes were haunted, like those of an animal that knows it's about to die.

After I'd finished treating the baby with pneumonia, I feigned a migraine and left work early. Before Mark was due home, I went to the garage. I pulled our tallest ladder into place beneath the beams. The rope was behind the hot-water heater. I was reaching for it when Mark grabbed me from behind.

'Sash, what are you doing?' He yanked the rope from my hands. 'You need to come with me.'

He dragged me into bed, tugged the doona over us and lay beside me cradling me in his arms. The following morning the ladder and the rope were both gone.

Looking back, I don't know if I would have gone through with it. I don't think I could have. But I just wanted the pain in my head to cease, the wrench in my gut to evaporate, the tightness in my chest to vanish. I wanted to disappear.

Mark hadn't let me. It strikes me now: he must have known about my mother. He knew about it all along and he kept it hidden, too.

'Sasha? Are you okay?' Dad is waiting on the phone.

No.

'I'm okay. I'm fine.'

'There's something I need to show you. I'll bring it in next time.'

'What is it?'

'You'll see. I'll be there soon.'

Another quilt? A photo album? Another reminder of the mother who didn't love me enough to stick around.

After Damien, I wanted to give up because I didn't have anything to fight for. That mistake nearly cost me everything. But this time, it's different. I will fight to the death for my son.

DAY 6, THURSDAY EARLY MORNING

The nursery thermostat has been turned down. My skin tingles in the cool air. As I trundle through the nursery towards Toby's cot, I try to forget what I've learned about my mother. Overnight I was plagued by images of her, of my childhood. I've hardly slept. My eyes are red and puffy, with thick black semicircles beneath them. Fortunately I was able to shift my morning session with Dr Niles to the evening to give my eyes a chance to return to normal. I don't feel up to making excuses about my appearance quite yet.

I feel the eyes of the staff on me as I pass their desk. No doubt they all knew. Not just Mark. The doctors. Everyone. It's why they've been so worried about me. Why they've been so quick to admit me.

Brigitte is already seated by Gabriel's cot, a forced smile on her face. She nods to the seat beside her. It looks like she's been waiting. Waiting for me?

'You could have said something,' she says.

My throat tightens. I don't want to sit down. 'What do you mean?'

Colour drains from my vision, the blue lights of Gabriel's cot shifting to black, Brigitte's face fading to the stark white of the nursery walls. At last I take a seat beside her.

'You could have told me you have postnatal depression. There's no shame in it. Lots of women have had it. I would have understood. I mean, I understand now. But I wish you'd felt comfortable enough to tell me.'

So she doesn't know about the swap yet – that's good news. But how has she concluded that I have depression, when it's postnatal psychosis they admitted me for? Did she get the idea from Mark? Thank God she's got it wrong. Colours begin returning, and when I look up Gabriel's cot is turquoise, Brigitte's face a familiar pale cream.

'I'm sorry. It's hard to talk about,' I say. That is the truth.

'Are you getting better?'

'I'm fine,' I say. 'I've been through worse.'

'That's no good,' she says. 'I understand. I've been through tough times myself. It's good to hear you're getting the help you need.' She blinks. 'Do you have a family history of depression?'

Has Mark told her? My nose starts to run. 'My mum.'

'I'm sorry,' she says. 'Is she okay now?'

I wipe at my nostrils, hesitating. Saying it makes it more real, somehow. 'She's dead.'

'That's horrible. Was it . . .?'

Mark must have told her. I slowly nod.

'Did you ever feel like that too?'

'Only once,' I say. I may as well confess everything. There's no harm discussing my past with her. Who knows – it may actually help to be honest. 'Years ago.'

'Even so, that's awful. I'm sorry. You must have been going through a rough time.'

'Yeah . . . Some things at work . . . it was all a bit much.'

'Pathology must be stressful.'

Mark didn't tell her everything, then.

'Mmm. One of my patients died while I was doing paediatrics. I took it hard.'

'That's tough. I'm really sorry. How are you going now? Do they have you on medication?'

'Um . . .' I decide there's no harm in telling her about the medication. I won't mention the expressed milk I've been freezing. 'I actually haven't been taking it.'

'You haven't?'

'I'm sure you know what it's like. The horrors of Western medicine.' I try for a small smile.

'Yes,' she says, pushing her hands into Gabriel's humidicrib and smoothing down his stray wisps of hair. She sounds a bit calmer. 'I know what it's like. I mean, I've been doing everything I can to make sure I don't get depressed. Kinesiology, homeopathy, chiropracty, everything.'

'Chiropracty?'

'My spine is out of alignment since the birth. Jeremy's, too.'

As she runs her fingers along the length of his back, I can almost feel my hand caressing his soft skin. I flick open the porthole of Toby's humidicrib and cup my hand around his cool scalp, a porcelain bowl beneath my palm.

'So, will you take Jeremy to the chiropractor?'

'Yeah, when I get him home. Maybe you should think about taking Toby? Babies born by caesarean are particularly at risk.' She opens the side of Gabriel's humidicrib and lifts him to her chest. I can see that he's still jaundiced, but at least he's receiving treatment. And at least this might mean he'll be in the hospital a little longer.

Gabriel shuffles in Brigitte's arms. She runs her palm over his torso, down to his belly.

'I can't wait until he's out of here. He needs homeopathies more than anything. We'll be starting the vaccinations soon.'

'What vaccinations?'

'Homeopathic ones, of course. He'll be healthier than any kid injected with Western vaccines. I can't believe the toxic rubbish some people are prepared to give their children.'

I bite at my bottom lip, forcing myself to stay quiet. I understand why someone like Brigitte would choose natural medicine, but I can't agree with her approach to vaccinations. Fortunately, I'll have Gabriel back soon enough. Then I'll protect him with everything he needs to keep him safe and well. For now, I stretch out my hand in what I hope is a casual gesture.

'I don't suppose you'd mind me having a hold of him?'

She stares, not seeming to understand.

'Jeremy. Could I have a hold?'

She stands and lifts Gabriel onto her shoulder. Her face has become a mask, unreadable.

'Um . . . I don't think so. Sorry.'

'They're saying I can only hold Toby for brief periods. It might help me feel better to hold another baby.' It would definitely help me feel better. And I'll only need a second or two to check his toes for webbing. Another piece of proof. 'Please?'

'He's unwell,' she says coldly. 'They're saying his jaundice level has risen. He's under triple lights now. I'm only allowed brief cuddles before he has to go back in.'

Damn. I'm having no luck with my attempts to check the toe webbing.

Brigitte turns to look out the window. Perched on her shoulder, Gabriel has a tiny smile on his lips, a smile just for me.

'He's going to be okay, isn't he?' I try to sound casual.

'The doctors say he should be fine.'

She frowns and clamps her lips shut. Does she suspect something? I remove my hand from Toby's head and tug it out of the crib.

'Who told you about me having postnatal depression?'

'No one told me. When Mark said you hadn't been discharged yet, his eyes said it all.' Brigitte turns to me, so I can no longer see Gabriel's face. 'What's it like in there?'

I shrug.

'What did you have to do to get locked up?' Brigitte sways from one foot to another like a tree buffeted by wind in an attempt to lull Gabriel to sleep.

'I'm not locked up. I went in there voluntarily.'

'Jesus, you're brave. When they tried to talk me into going in, I refused.'

That catches my attention.

'They tried to talk you into it? Why did they want to admit you?'

Brigitte stares down at Gabriel nestled in her arms, her eyes dull. He would be warm, so warm against my skin.

'Did they think you were depressed?' I press her. That would explain her tears, her coldness. I have to restrain myself from reaching for Gabriel's arm as it dangles from Brigitte's.

'No,' she says, her eyes all at once alight. 'There's nothing wrong with me. I'm fine. But you haven't answered my question. What about you?'

Is it possible she told them the same thing as me and they didn't believe her either? Before I can think, I've blurted the truth.

'They didn't believe me when I said I didn't think Toby was mine.'

She freezes mid-sway. Her eyes widen in alarm.

'That's why you're in the mother–baby unit?'

I nod slowly, goosebumps prickling my skin. Perhaps I've said too much, too fast. It seems she hadn't worked out there's been a mix-up at all. And I haven't questioned her about what she knows. Mark is planning to come to the nursery a little later today. I still have time. I've been patient with Brigitte, but it's my chance to ask some questions of my own.

'Did you see anything the morning of Jeremy's birth? Anyone acting suspiciously?'

She steps away from me, shielding herself with the humidicrib.

'Not a thing. Ursula was here with me and Jeremy the whole time.' She beckons Ursula at the nurses' station. Has she realised I think Jeremy is my son? As Ursula approaches, Brigitte speaks slowly, staring at me all the while.

'It's good you're getting help. But I don't think I've ever seen you hold Toby.'

'He hasn't been well enough.'

Ursula reaches our side. She gives both of us darting glances.

'You two look like you're getting on. Maybe it'll turn out to be a good thing Jeremy won't be going home as soon as we'd thought.' She is standing oddly still as she addresses Brigitte. 'I'm sure Sasha appreciates the company, Brigitte.'

Brigitte bites at her bottom lip.

'I'd like to get Jeremy home as soon as possible. Tomorrow, please, like Dr Green first planned.' She points to me. 'Sasha is saying Toby is unwell, too. She seems to think he's too sick to hold.'

'We'll get Jeremy home as soon as we can,' Ursula says, turning to me with a frown. 'But Toby is well enough to hold. You do know that, don't you, Sasha? You only need to ask.'

A trickle of morning sun seeps through the nursery's window onto the back of my neck.

'Yes, I know.'

Ursula's face is set in a grim smile.

I need to get out of this stifling, oppressive place. As if on cue, an alarm beeps on my phone.

I try to smile. 'I'll be back as soon as I can to give Toby a cuddle. But it's time for group therapy. I must go. I'd hate to be running late.'

DAY 6, THURSDAY MORNING

Ondine and I wander out through the main hospital entrance, past a row of shops: laundromat, newsagent, café. A group of teenagers loiter on the footpath beside the bus stop. Miners' cottages stretch in neat rows far into the distance.

I had arrived at the rec room to find a sign sticky-taped to the door. *Walk cancelled due to staffing issues. Free time this morning.*

'I don't suppose you want to go for a stroll anyway?' Ondine said from beside me.

'Do you think it's okay? Dr Niles insisted I wasn't allowed to go anywhere except the nursery while I was admitted.'

'You're right. They don't want us leaving the unit. But they were going to take us for a walk.' Ondine shrugged. 'It should be okay. The security here is pretty lax. They're never even going to notice we're gone.'

I gave a broad smile. 'Okay.'

Now, falling into step beside her, my cheeks prickling in the morning sun, it feels like this walk is exactly what I need.

'The cemetery is to the right,' Ondine says. 'Let's head for the lake?'

We head left. A mother pushing a pram appears further along the footpath.

'Do you mind if we cross here?' Ondine says.

We make our way to the other side of the road. Neither of us glances in the direction of the woman and her pram.

'Any luck getting your son back?' Ondine asks.

'Not yet,' I say. 'But my plans are in the pipeline. It won't be too long now.' I don't want to jinx myself by saying too much. 'How about you? Are you surviving the unit?'

She considers this for a moment. 'Only just.'

'What's the worst part?'

'Everything. The other women. The staff. Even the crying babies. It's easier to stay in my room with my head-phones on.'

'What do you listen to?'

'Nothing,' she says, giving me an unexpected grin. 'Just my own thoughts, I suppose.' She speeds up, pressing on towards the lake.

As I catch up to her, the brown water sweeps into view. Since the return of rain these last few years the reeds lining the lake's banks have been swallowed up by the rising water. Their tangled, dusky-green stalks now lie submerged, occasionally rising to skim the surface like sea snakes.

'And what do your thoughts say?' I ask Ondine.

'That I'm the most unwell person in there. That I don't deserve my baby back. That I should be locked up for life.

Which is what I want, anyway.' She stares towards the lake, where joggers travel the perimeter of the water.

'Your son needs you to be well, Ondine. You need to get better and get out of here for him. One day, when he's old enough to understand, he will forgive you for everything. I promise.'

'That's hard to believe.'

'Of course. But you don't always need to believe your thoughts, you know.'

She gives a slight shake of her head. 'How about you? How are you going?'

From nowhere, memories surface from the night of the birth. My baby's heart thumping on the monitor. The trolley, me lying flat upon it, careering through cold, white corridors on the way to theatre. The fumes of alcohol-based antiseptic. The barb in my back. Then the repeated attempts to find my baby's heartbeat. Dr Solomon, his panicked voice: 'She needs a general anaesthetic. Right now.' The dry rush of oxygen pushing through my lips. The propofol stinging my arm as it slid up the vein in an icy stream. The shimmering reflection of my semi-naked body in the operation spotlight. Mark, standing beside me as the room faded to blackness. They didn't used to allow partners into the operating theatres. I suppose the rules must have changed. I'm certain it was his presence I felt at the last moment. There wasn't time to say goodbye.

All at once, an image of a baby's dead body floats into my vision. I startle and trip, only just catching myself before I fall. The vision dissipates as dust rises from under my feet.

'Are you okay?'

'Yeah.'

Ondine stops at the edge of the lake in the shade of a eucalypt. She reaches down to pick up a stone from the path. 'I suppose you think I'm really crazy.'

'No,' I say. 'Not crazy at all.'

'Not even in your professional opinion?'

'I stopped seeing live patients a long time ago.'

On the lake, ducks bob their heads in the water. I bend to pick up a flat rock lying on the path, the size of my palm, groaning with discomfort as I straighten.

'Many of us are crazy in some ways,' I add.

'You're not.'

The rock is a good weight, a good shape, for skimming. I shift the rock between my fingers, feeling the curves and edges, trying to find the right hold.

'Sure I am. Or, at least, I was.'

'What do you mean?'

'I guess I thought about ending it.'

'Your life?'

'I *thought* about it. That's all.' I don't tell her how close I came. How much I wanted to die. 'I'm really glad I didn't, though.' The last bit is true.

Ondine's eyes are dark as she studies the shimmering surface of the lake.

'I'm not at the point of being glad I'm alive,' she says.

I squeeze the rock tight in my palm. 'You will be,' I say.

I skim the rock. It catches the surface of the water, skipping two, three, four times before sinking to the lake's depths, sending out concentric circles that spread wider and wider until they fade into stillness once more.

When I worked up the courage to leave the courtroom all those years ago, it was a spring day. Bees were buzzing in the gardens. Pollen was thick in the air. Damien's parents had been standing at the front entrance of the coroner's court. His mother was round-shouldered, her face puckered in fury, while his father stood erect, a piercing glare on his face, his arm pressed into the small of his wife's back, holding her upright. Their eyes trailed me as I passed.

I thought about stopping and apologising. But what could I say, really? There was nothing I could do that would take their pain away. I would only make it worse. Better not to try at all.

When I reached my car, I glanced over my shoulder to find them still staring. Damien's mother pulled away from her husband and started screaming.

'After what you did to my son, you don't deserve to be a mother . . .'

For the longest time, I believed her. The miscarriages were my punishment. It was all my fault.

Ondine drops the stone in her hand to the ground with a dull thud.

'So, Dr Niles is talking about giving me ECT.'

ECT – electrodes on her temples, plastic mouthguard between her teeth, subtle jerking of her limbs, high-voltage electricity flowing through her brain. *Don't do it*, I want to say.

'Could you wait, give it more time?'

'I don't know,' she says. 'But you're right about my son needing me to be well. I suppose I need to try everything, if only for his sake.'

If she can do it, so can I. Dr Solomon is supposed to be visiting me before lunchtime. I grab Ondine's elbow. 'Let's get back. I'm going to try and figure out how this happened to my son.'

DAY 6, THURSDAY LATE MORNING

I'm checking on my breastmilk in the freezer, ensuring it hasn't thawed, when Dr Solomon knocks on the door. I let the freezer flap fall shut, swing the fridge door closed and manage to compose my face.

'Found you,' he says. 'This building is like a labyrinth. I tried to track you down yesterday without success. And the heat in here. Unbelievable.'

Needing to rule him off my list of suspects, I requested a visit yesterday but he rescheduled for today. I haven't seen him for five days, since I was transferred from the postnatal ward. Dr Solomon's brusque manner hasn't changed in that time. I've been looked after by so many doctors and nurses, yet no one has really cared about me at all. How terrible to be a patient in this system. How terrible to be a doctor too; to lose one's humanity amid the burdens of overwork and stress.

When Dr Solomon points at my belly, I lift my shirt to show him my dressing. He peels it off to reveal my scar; all that remains is a clean red line just above my pubic bone.

'Good,' he says, easing my maternity cotton underwear back into place. 'You're fine to go home from my perspective. I'll put in a good word for you with Dr Niles. She mentioned she's thinking of sending you home tomorrow.'

Home tomorrow. A shock to me, but a brilliant one. I thought I would be forced to remain in here for days to come. Maybe my performances with Dr Niles have been more successful than I've given myself credit for.

'Excuse me, Dr Solomon?'

He pauses at the door.

'Can you please tell me a little more about the birth?'

His mouth stiffens.

'I'm sure you are aware it was a standard emergency caesarean. Under a general anaesthetic, yes. Emergency, yes, but there were no complications. Your baby came out perfectly. A little oxygen once he got up to the nursery, I believe, but that's not unusual.' He goes to turn the door handle.

'So, the midwife would have been with my baby the whole time?'

He sniffs, his fingers still gripping the handle.

'Of course. One of our midwives was at the birth. Ursula. She escorted him upstairs.'

'He couldn't have been left alone at any time?'

'I find that very unlikely,' Dr Solomon says. 'Frankly, I'm concerned you're still fixated on this. I'm afraid I'll have to mention it to Dr Niles.'

My knuckles whiten in my lap.

'Please, you don't need to say anything to Dr Niles. I was only curious. I know Toby is my baby. I know Mark was with him from his first breath. I'd just like to ask –'

'Your husband couldn't have been there for your baby's first breath.'

Dr Solomon releases the door handle and tips his head back against the wall, almost touching Monet's lilies.

My heart squeezes tight. 'What do you mean?'

'Relatives and partners aren't allowed in the operating theatre if a caesarean requires a general anaesthetic. Surely you know that? Your husband was asked to wait upstairs in the nursery. I went up there myself after the surgery to tell him everything had turned out successfully.'

My fragmented memory of Mark holding my hand as they injected the milky white liquid into my veins, as they held an oxygen mask against my face, as the ceiling petered from white to grey to black – had that all been constructed by my mind? My heart judders in my chest.

'He might have observed the resuscitation in the nursery, but not the birth. Standard hospital protocol,' Dr Solomon adds.

I press my knees together hard until they hurt. Perhaps I placed too much faith in Mark and in my own mind. But the hospital's culpability – their understaffing, numerous unantici-pated emergencies and dismissal of my concerns – are not in my imagination. I've heard rumours of hospitals concealing things before. I might be just one more woman they want to stay silent.

Dr Solomon digs his hands deep into his pockets. Could he have been involved in conspiring to keep the baby swap under wraps? I don't want to ask him directly where he was all Friday night and Saturday morning. He's smart enough to see through me right away.

'Did you see anyone acting suspiciously in the operating theatre?'

He rocks back on his heels. 'No, Sasha, I didn't. And if I had I would have alerted a staff member.'

Personally, I'm not so sure. But I can see his patience is wearing thin.

'Was there anyone else responsible for my baby between the operating theatre and the nursery?'

'Probably. Nurses.' He sighs. 'But your baby had identification tags put on him when he was first born. Ankle *and* wrist. They're still on him, I presume?' His mouth twists into an incredulous line as he leans towards the door.

I throw my hands in the air.

'What happens if the tags fall off? Surely whoever replaced them could have got it wrong. I can't believe this hasn't been investigated further. Have there been any other baby mix-ups at your hospital?'

Dr Solomon's eyes are like lily pads floating on a shimmering pond.

'You know we're not permitted to cover up adverse incidents these days, Sasha. There has never been a baby mix-up at this hospital, or any other hospital I've worked at. It's an extremely rare occurrence. Which is why we've been so greatly concerned about you.'

After Dr Solomon has left, I contemplate whether I've blown my cover – whether tomorrow is no longer likely for my discharge.

But there's always the possibility he'll forget; or that he won't be bothered with the paperwork – I'm one more 'difficult' mother among many. Hopefully wires will be crossed in the hospital's bush telegraph, the message fading along the line.

No time to dwell on these possibilities for now. I need to see my son.

In the annexe outside the nursery, I scrub the rim of my cuticles and the webs between my fingers with nursery disinfectant, wincing at the sting, then wash it off with streaming water. Better to get everything out of the cracks; who knows what bacteria could be lurking in their depths?

In the nursery, I find Mark with his hands pressed against Toby's humidicrib. His hair is slicked back and he's wearing his baggy chef pants. Surely he hasn't been in to work?

'He's doing well,' Mark says, a solemn smile on his face. He nods at a plastic bag resting on the bench. 'I cooked you something.'

I peer inside the bag. A container of homemade gnocchi. I'm grateful, but he should know better. 'Food is forbidden in the nursery, Mark. The risk of infection is too high. You need to take more care.' I tie a knot in the plastic bag. 'Dr Solomon came to check on me earlier. He told me everything. Why did you lie to me after the birth?'

'I don't know what you're saying, Sasha.'

'You lied to me about staying with Toby the whole time.'

'I've never lied to you.' His voice thickens. But he won't meet my eye. Yet another betrayal by Mark. He's not going to tell me the truth. I'll have to let it go for now.

Through the perspex, Toby's cheeks are rosy, becoming plumper. He could almost pass for a full-term baby. I feel Mark's hand on my shoulder, pressing the flesh between my collarbone as though he's reaching through my skin. I can't read whatever message he's trying to impart.

'I went into work briefly this morning. And they're going to need me back there next week.'

'Weren't you going to take two weeks off after the birth?'

'They're short-staffed, Sash. There's nothing I can do.' He shifts his hand to massage the sinewy tightness of my neck. 'Nothing's turned out quite like we planned.'

Come Monday, I know he'll be back in the restaurant kitchen, dicing beetroot, searing cutlets, slicing herbs. Straightforward, honest work. He'll be more at home there than in here where beeping machines and numbers and the colour of skin each reveal only a fragment of the truth. I shrug his hand away.

'How was work, then?'

'Fine.' His voice is bland.

'What exactly have you told them?'

'That our baby came early.'

I stare at Toby, his fists opening and closing, clasping at air.

'Nothing about me.'

He doesn't reply.

'They might give you more leave if you told them.'

'Maybe.' He loosens his shirt at the neck. 'Hopefully you can come home soon. They're talking about tomorrow as a possibility.'

I wish everyone would stop talking about me behind my back.

'Maybe,' I mutter. I should be delighted to be heading home. But going home to Mark, my old house, my old life, doesn't feel like such a great thing after all. 'And becoming a partner in the restaurant – have you given them a final answer?'

He turns his face away, shaking his head.

I check Toby's chart. His temperature is stable. His heart rate is normal. He's soared through the first six days of prematurity with ease, despite not having had the comfort of his mother's touch.

Mark is watching me.

'You don't have to be his doctor too, you know. All you have to do is be there for him. You're his mum, remember. I know you can do that.' He tries to smile.

At last I can see the truth. It's never been only me that doubted my capacity to be a mother – my ability to be there for my child. All these years we've been together, Mark has been worried about how I'll cope, concerned I'll end up like my mother.

'You knew about my mother, didn't you? You thought I'd top myself and leave you alone with the baby.'

He has such a sad stare on his face that I'm stunned into silence.

'You know I adore our son,' he says quietly. 'I can't believe I get to be his father. I'm sure you'll grow to love him, too. And I know you would never leave us alone.' His phone alarm sounds, a reminder of Toby's feeding schedule. 'The nurse just checked his nasogastric tube is in position. Maybe it'd be good for you to do this feed.'

He hands me a bottle of formula he has already warmed and heads to the formula room to heat the next batch. I don't know why I'm finding it so hard to trust him. Of course he hasn't switched Toby and Gabriel. He has no motive, no intent. I pour the formula into the syringe. According to the nurses, it's a perk of me being a doctor, that they trust me with this task so early in our nursery stay. They think it will help with bonding, too. Lifting Toby's nasogastric tube high above the humidicrib, I watch the liquid drain along its length, down through his nostril like a white-skinned snake. Without thinking, my eyes travel to Gabriel.

Brigitte is knitting by his side, her needles piercing the red rectangle perched on her lap. A thread of wool, like a trickle of blood, trails down the side of her leg into a bag on the floor. Ursula is fiddling with Gabriel's lights. Her tunic is the grey of a prison warden. She has her back to me.

Gabriel kicks his legs up against the walls of the cot and raises his arms high in the air. Every part of me wishes I could breastfeed him. My nipples tingle. I feel the wetness before I see it, dribbling from my breasts, leaking through my bra to form two patches of dampness, instantly visible on my white cotton shirt. It's a reflex, a natural bodily response to seeing my beautiful baby. It's not under my control.

Brigitte looks up from her knitting. Her eyes flick from me, to Gabriel, to the wet circles on the front of my chest. Her needles freeze mid-stitch. Oh, no. Now she'll presume I've had a let-down reflex because I'm still obsessed by her baby. I'm going to get into trouble again.

She taps Ursula's sleeve and hisses something indecipherable. Ursula turns to inspect my shirt, snaps the doors of Gabriel's humidicrib shut – *not so hard*, I want to call – and heads for the cluster of nurses at the nursery desk.

I pour more formula into Toby's syringe, but it's too much too fast, and it overflows, spilling out across the floor in a milky puddle. I crouch to try and wipe it up, but no matter how many tissues I pull from the box I can't seem to get it all.

Ursula is suddenly in front of me, her grey torso blocking my view of Gabriel. She waits until I stand, clutching the sopping handful of tissues.

'I believe I made it quite clear you are not to inspect other babies.'

'I wasn't doing anything.' My tongue sticks to the roof of my mouth.

'Nevertheless, your reaction' – her eyes take in the front of my shirt – 'requires us to put precautions in place.'

Metallic sounds screech from nearby. The other nurses are tugging partitions around Gabriel's cot, around Brigitte too, concealing both of them from me.

'If I see any further concerning behaviour, I'll have no choice but to remove you from the nursery,' Ursula finishes.

'Is he alright?'

Ursula's eyes narrow. It strikes me that I haven't yet ruled her out as a suspect in the baby swap.

'Were you here with Toby the whole time the morning of his birth?'

'Of course.' She wipes at a thin line of perspiration on her brow.

'And did you see anything suspicious?'

'No, Sasha. In fact, the only person behaving strangely this whole time has been you.' She wrinkles her nose before backing away towards the desk, her eyes never leaving me.

'What's going on?' Mark emerges from the formula room clutching the freshly warmed bottle of milk in his hand. 'Why are they putting up the screens?'

His eyes bulge as they fall on the wet patches on my chest, and I explain the conclusion Ursula and Brigitte have jumped to.

'I know it looks bad,' I say, yanking my cardigan tighter. 'But I don't get things like this wrong.'

Mark falls into a chair beside Toby and drops his forehead into his hands. His voice is almost inaudible.

'Maybe the time has come to accept that sometimes, Sasha, even you do.'

I press my knuckles into my eyes until pinpoints of light dance before me. I will not give anyone the pleasure of seeing me cry.

The lime-coloured paint is peeling from the plasterboard in chunks. The sinks are green porcelain, the toilet seats black plastic. The nursery bathroom doesn't look like it's been redecorated since the 1970s, and it smells like it hasn't been given a thorough clean since then, either.

The other parents never use this bathroom; they seem to prefer the modern one beside the lifts. I've been coming to these cubicles and locking myself in for quiet time, space away from prying eyes.

I scan the ceiling. They don't have cameras in here – or listening devices. Nothing obvious, anyhow. Fluorescent bulbs flicker like train tracks. But I'm soon startled when the bathroom door creaks open. Heels clack against the tiles. Crap.

When there's a click of the lock in the cubicle beside mine, I make a dash for the basins. As I shake the water from my hands, the other cubicle door opens. It's Brigitte. Her skirt is hitched up on one side. Her hair hangs loose around her face.

'I can explain about the let-down,' I say. 'It's a bodily reflex. I didn't mean anything by it. It's not even under my control.'

'I get that it's been hard for you,' she says, not looking at me. 'But I'd prefer you stay away from me. Okay?'

'I'm just trying to figure everything out. I'm not trying to steal your baby.'

'I'll make sure you don't get the chance.' Her eyebrows are knotted together.

I have to ask how long I've got to make things right.

'When will Jeremy be leaving hospital?'

'Please just stay away from him. And me.'

How the hell am I going to stop him from leaving? It's not until the door slams shut behind Brigitte that it hits me: in her rush, she's forgotten to wash her hands. It's important. I wonder if she realises how important it is, especially after the *Serratia* outbreak several years ago. The bug may still be contaminating the taps, the door handles, the shiny surfaces. But if I go after her, she'll only make some other accusation against me; stalking, perhaps.

I crumple against the basins, being careful not to touch the porcelain with my sterile hands. This whole time I've done all the right things. Yet Brigitte has the one thing I want, the one thing I can't yet claim: my child. My son.

My only option: to stick with my original plan. Pretend I believe Toby is mine. Rule out the final suspect. Wait for the DNA results to come back. Then show everyone how right I was all along, and how cruel they've been to me.

DAY 6, THURSDAY LUNCHTIME

Back in the nursery, I find Toby asleep, his lips fallen apart to reveal the darkness of his mouth cavity. I take a cotton ball and moisten it with clear, salty water, then run it over each of his eyelids. He winces and tips his head back, away from me. Then, behind me, I hear a rustle.

It's my father, laden with plastic bags in either hand. I wasn't expecting to see him today. He stoops to kiss me, meeting my cheek with his whiskery one, then stretches out the bags to me.

'Bought you some baby clothes,' he says. 'From the friend of a friend of mine. She thought you might need them.'

'Thanks, Dad.'

He peers at my face.

'You know, you have your mother's eyes.'

'I don't think I'm like her at all.'

Dad's nose crinkles. He reaches into his pocket and tugs out a piece of paper, folded into quarters, heavily creased.

'I should have told you everything years ago. I meant to. I'm so sorry. This – this is the last thing I've kept from you. I've been saving it for when I thought you were ready. This is for you.'

I unfold it. My mother's handwriting.

'What is this?'

'Read it.'

I thought I'd love being a mother. I was wrong . . .

It's her suicide note. I can't believe he's giving it to me here and now. I know my father is out of touch with his emotional side, to say the least, but surely he knows this is beyond callous. I don't want to read any more – I can't. I fold the note back up and pass it back to Dad. 'I . . . I don't want this.'

'Sorry, I didn't mean for you to read it right now,' he says. 'Just thought you should know the whole story, especially as you're a mother now. I can see I should have told you everything a long time ago.' He tries to hand the note back to me.

'I know you're only trying to help. But I don't ever want to read it.' I push the note back into his palms.

Beside me, Toby startles in his sleep, his limbs shuddering behind the plastic.

'I figured it out,' I say. 'Everything.'

Dad draws breath. 'What do you mean?'

'I remember now.' Lying beside her, the drowsiness descending on me. Listening to her stop breathing. Her arms around me, turning cold. 'I was there when she died, wasn't I?'

Dad slumps into the chair beside Toby's cot.

'You really should have told me everything long ago, Dad.'

He is trembling. 'They said the drugs she gave you wouldn't have any lasting effect. Once you got through the worst of it, they told me you'd be fine.'

Drugs. What drugs?

There was a cup. A shining silver cup that caught the sunlight. Full to the brim with brown liquid.

Chocolate, darling. Chocolate milk. Nice and warm. Drink up, darling. Drink up.

Her slurred words. Her dank breath.

The liquid filled my mouth with warmth and coated my tongue as it drew down into my core, as though I was submerged in a bath of chocolate. I had lain down beside her, curled my body into her cool one. She pulled me tight against her, breathing against my neck. I had already become accustomed to the smell of her vomit on the quilt.

Now everything will be better. Everything will be okay.

I was with her. Of course everything was going to be okay.

Let me fix what I have done. And forgive me for what I'm about to do.

I always forgave her. She was my mother. I loved her more than anyone. I thought I always would.

My vision blurs. I think part of me has always known. The part of me that has tried so hard to forget.

'How could she do that?' I gasp.

Dad's head droops onto his chest.

'I can't explain it, Sasha. She was . . . sick.'

My body feels empty, like a void, like the far reaches of outer space.

'How close did I come to dying?'

'The doctors said it was touch-and-go.'

It feels as if that dark liquid is now bubbling up inside me and foaming out my mouth.

'You didn't protect me. You left me with her. Why didn't you know what she was going to do?'

'I'm so sorry. I had no sense that something wasn't right that particular day. It wasn't like nowadays. People didn't know how to talk about it.' He buries his head in his hands.

An alarm sounds from further down the queue of humidi-cribs. A moment later a flurry of hospital staff enters the nursery. Dr Green attends to the baby with her stethoscope as Ursula takes charge, directing people with a pointed finger.

'There must have been some signs she wasn't right,' I mutter.

Dad sits with his back slumped to the unfolding scene, oblivious.

'She seemed fine to me.' When he lifts his head from his hands, his cheeks are coated with tears. 'I know I should have told you, but how do you tell someone their mother . . . I just hope you can forgive me one day.'

The nurses rush the sick baby into the resuscitation room. Right at this moment, I would do anything to evaporate into the air and be carried out the window, away into the sky. I can only hope that at some point in the future I will be able to recall the details of what it was like being held fast in my mother's arms, with her only wanting, and loving, me.

FOURTEEN YEARS EARLIER

MARK

When it became obvious that Simon's chemotherapy wasn't working, the doctors began looking for a bone marrow donor. The money was on his twin: me. But when the tests came back, they said I wasn't a match. My heart seemed to stop. I'd failed him. I didn't even get a chance to help him out.

And then, to my family's horror, the doctors couldn't find another donor.

The last time I visited Simon, he was in his single room in the hospital with a view over verdant parklands. At the time I didn't know they gave the best room to the terminal patients.

'It's over, Marky Mark,' he said. 'Better say your goodbyes.'

'Don't be ridiculous,' I said, wringing my hands. 'You can't give up. Anyway, what about the finals?'

'Damn Collingwood. They're never going to make premiers.

At least, not in my lifetime.' He chuckled at what he thought was a great joke.

He still looked okay to me, perched against the pillow, his face not quite the colour of the sheet concealing his bony body. If he wasn't around anymore, I would no longer be a twin. I'd be an only child. I'd have no one to protect. No one to look out for. Nothing would be the same.

'Don't say that,' I pleaded.

'I can say what I want. You try and stop me.' He laughed again, like it was another joke.

'You can't give up. It's not your time.'

'There's a point when you have to say enough is enough. When it's okay to let go.'

I clenched my hands into fists.

'This isn't that time,' I said.

Simon's eyelids fell shut. I thought he was trying to get me to stop hassling him. Later, I wondered if it might have been the drugs; he was in a lot of pain. Whatever it was, I stormed out of the room. I wasn't ready to let him go.

When Mum called me later that night to tell me he had passed, my face prickled with intense heat. The doctors said he had been ready to die. He was at peace.

Maybe he was ready. I never would have been. The thing I wish most; the thing I'd give anything to change? I wish I'd had a chance to hear his final words. I wish I'd had a chance to say goodbye.

DAY 6, THURSDAY EARLY EVENING

A thick, harmonic noise fills my room. It's the women chanting in unison from the recreation room, their voices resonating all the way down the corridor. I should be there, but I've started packing on the presumption that they'll still permit me to go home tomorrow. Despite my let-down reflex in the nursery, and my questioning of Dr Solomon, I haven't heard that my discharge is off the cards. Maybe, as I hoped, staff haven't communicated their concerns with each other – the hospital bureaucracy working in my favour, for once. Hopefully that will remain the case until I'm well out of here.

The hard, shiny surfaces of my room – the bedside table, television cabinet, table and chair – remain devoid of my possessions. The cupboard is a different matter, and my belongings, shoved in on top of each other after Mark's frenzied search, tumble onto the carpet like guts spilling from a wound as I open the door.

My phone lets out a shrill from my pocket. Bec. I hover my finger over the accept button until the last moment.

'How are you coping, Sash?'

'Not great. Has my dad been in touch with you?'

'No. No one has.'

Now I can see why Lucia had been so kind to me. All the adults pitied me – everyone must have.

'Dad finally told me the whole truth about my mum.' I pause. I never thought I'd have to say these words about my mother. 'Did you know she killed herself? And she tried to kill me, too?'

Bec inhales sharply. 'What?'

'She drugged me, Bec. She wanted to take me with her.'

'Jesus Christ. What the hell? Why?'

I have no idea. I doubt I'll ever know.

Then it comes to me, something else I've suppressed for all these years. Lucia, licking a glob of dough from a wooden spoon, her eyes sparkling as she picked up the jar of sugar from the bench. I had mistaken the white crystals for salt.

'Mistakes, my darling. Don't feel bad. We all make them. Me, as well. I should have ended the pregnancy like Mario suggested.'

But ending the pregnancy would have meant aborting Bec. Surely that's not what she meant?

'Your mother too,' she said as she spooned the sweet dough into the bin. 'She felt having a baby had been wrong for her.' She pulled me tight against her. 'But believe me, Sasha, you are no mistake.'

All the nights I would sob into my pillow after my mother left, Lucia would find me. She would send my father next door to babysit Bec and she would climb into my bed and wrap her arms around me, pressing me into her thick, warm body, murmuring words I didn't understand. She smelled of garlic and rose soap and love.

'I think Lucia knew what my mother tried to do.'

'She never told me.' Bec's voice is almost a whisper.

I do believe Bec. I know I probably shouldn't, but I do.

'Mum was always asking why I wasn't more like you,' Bec says. 'She loved you more than me.'

'Nonsense,' I say. Lucia never introduced me as her daughter. Lucia never took my mother's place. I never called her Mum, even though I would have liked to.

'You were her only daughter,' I say. 'She wanted the best for you.'

Bec gives a sniffle. 'I miss her, Sash. All the time.'

'Of course you do.'

And in some strange way, despite everything, I miss my mother too.

As if reading my mind, Bec murmurs, 'Your mother loved you, you know.'

'Right. That's why she tried to . . . you know.'

'Sash – we're all capable of doing the wrong thing.'

At least I can relate to that.

'Damien,' I sigh. 'I can't believe I did that. He's my biggest mistake.'

'Sash. That wasn't anyone's fault.'

Technically, Bec's right. She was in the courtroom when the findings were handed down several weeks after the inquest.

'I hope you're not still thinking about that,' she continues. 'Don't you remember? The coroner said his death couldn't have been prevented. Nothing you or anyone else did would have changed the outcome. It was an unfortunate death caused by a deadly disease. You weren't at fault.'

There's only one problem; Bec doesn't know that my mistake wasn't just missing his life-threatening diagnosis. It was what I failed to do when the coroner interrogated me.

'Sash, more importantly – your baby. Any progress?'

I push Damien to the back of my mind, where he will always remain.

'It's going terribly, Bec. They've put up partitions around Gabriel's cot so I can't even see him. They seem to think I'm going to *hurt* him. It's still looking like he's going home tomorrow and I can't bear the thought of not seeing him every day. I don't know what I'm going to do.'

'Breathe, Sash, just breathe. It's going to be okay. I know it's been stressful, finding out about your mother. How are you going with eliminating suspects?'

I take a deep breath and run through the list in my head.

'Brigitte, who thinks she's Gabriel's mother, and the nurse Ursula corroborate each other's stories. They were both in the nursery all morning and saw nothing suspicious. Dr Solomon and Dr Niles are off the list, too. And it's not Mark, of course.'

Bec snorts. 'I told you.'

'So, the only person left is Dr Green. The paediatrician.'

'It's always the person you least suspect,' Bec says. 'Or an accidental mix-up like you thought at first.'

'Or I'm just mentally unwell.'

'Don't even think that, Sash. You've got to have faith in yourself. It sounds like no one else does. Except for me.

Stick to the plan. Everything will be fine, okay? Together, no matter what happens, we'll work it out.'

When we've hung up, I run through the list of tasks left to do before I am discharged. Number one: question Dr Green about her alibi the night of Gabriel's birth. Number two: pack the zip-lock bag with the umbilical cord. For now, it's tucked inside my bra, as close to my heart as anything has ever been. Number three: get rid of the breastmilk in the freezer. There's no way I can get it home without Mark knowing. Besides, Gabriel will be more than capable of breastfeeding when he's back with me. I've achieved my aim of not letting my breastmilk supply run dry, so there's no need for the frozen jars anymore. Number four: say goodbye to Ondine. She's more than an acquaintance now. I would call her a friend.

As I wait for Dr Niles, the curtains in my room flutter in the evening breeze. The flowers printed on the white cotton fabric aren't quite right. Carnations and violets never bloom in the same season.

At last Dr Niles appears in the doorway, her phone clasped in one hand, her fountain pen in the other. She seats herself on the chair under the window.

'How are you, Sasha?'

'I'm fine.' I start to chew my nails but stop myself. 'No worries at all.'

'You must be pleased Toby is doing so well.'

'I am.' I make myself smile.

She begins to drone on about a medical student from years ago, a previous patient. The flowers on the curtain shift and sway in the wind until my ears prick at the word *suicide*.

'. . . I realised it had been right in front of me.' Dr Niles stares hard at me, her amber eyes darkening. 'Have you had any suicidal thoughts since you've been with us, Sasha?'

'No.'

'It's just that, given your history . . . And I was led to believe you had an episode about ten years ago?'

'Who told you that?'

Mark. Betraying me again. I'd trusted him not to say anything to the medics. He should have known how greatly his disclosure of my suicide attempt to a medical professional could have sway with the Medical Board – more so, even, than a diagnosis of postpartum psychosis – and how it would affect my career.

'Whoever told you was mistaken,' I snap.

'You were never on antidepressants then, either?'

'Well, yes. I suppose I was.' She's again missed a spot of foundation, over a pale patch of skin on her temple. 'After a tragedy.'

Dr Niles rests her hand in her chin. 'A child who died.'

A sob wells within me, but I fight it back. 'A baby.' Dr Niles joins me on the bed and places a hand on mine.

'I'm fine,' I say, sitting up and forcing a smile. 'It was such a long time ago.'

She fixes me with a pointed stare and removes her hand.

'You're not the only one who's ever made a mistake. We all do. Even the best of us.'

'I was wrong.' It's hard to say aloud. 'And I don't think I can ever forgive myself.'

After the coroner had handed down his findings, after the exoneration, I remained fixed to the seat. If I stayed like this, still and unmoving, I could pretend I was a relative of the deceased, or simply an interested stranger. Not the doctor responsible for Damien's death. In all the mess, I had forgotten who I was pretending for. Was it for his family, or for me?

Dr Niles turns to me. There are deep creases around her eyes, the legacy of all she's seen. Has helping other patients allowed her to get over that one patient's suicide? Am I part of her healing?

'For the record, self-compassion requires practice. It's one of the hardest skills to learn. For a doctor. For anyone.'

'I'm fine, really I am,' I lie, crossing my arms. 'I hardly think about it anymore.'

'Uh-huh.' Dr Niles smooths down her hair. 'And I presume you are taking the medication every day, as prescribed?'

'Of course.' I try to look incredulous.

'And it is helping?'

'I guess so.'

'You think Toby is your baby.'

It's a statement, not a question, and I know the correct response.

'Absolutely.'

'And you don't feel like harming yourself?'

'Of course not.'

'You'll let me know if that changes? I don't want a repeat of my previous mistake.'

'Neither do I.' I give her a brief, conspiratorial smile. It's amazing what doctors will see if they want to: a success story, a shot at redemption. And of course, as a doctor, Dr Niles sees herself in me.

'I should also warn you, Sasha . . . Don't be alarmed if you begin to develop the desire to be beside your baby every moment.'

She goes on to describe primary maternal preoccupation, a well-recognised psychological state where the mother and baby merge into the equivalent of one being for a short period of time immediately after the birth, a stage in which the mother is attuned to her child's every need. The onset might be delayed for me, she explains, but I should still expect it to occur.

My mother was in a place like this, separated from me when I was only six months old. Did she miss me while we were apart? Or was she relieved to be free of the endless demands of a small baby? Perhaps it was her times in the psychiatric ward that convinced her it would be better to take me with her when she died.

Dr Niles' eyes fall on me kindly as though she understands. Perhaps she does, after all. She stands, smoothing down her skirt.

'I'll reassure your husband you're fine. He's been worried about you.'

At the window, the curtains billow about, and we're both momentarily distracted.

Dr Niles goes to leave, but pauses at the door.

'You're doing very well, Sasha. You have had excellent reports from the staff I've talked to. You've made such good progress, and in less than a week. I'm happy to authorise your discharge for tomorrow. I'll let the nurses know.'

I attempt to smile. How much I have had to keep inside to deceive those around me, in order to be perceived as mentally well.

Dr Niles rests her hand on the doorframe. 'You'll be glad to know that as your symptoms have resolved so quickly and have had no effect on your medical work, I'm not mandated to mention your admission to the Medical Board. And we were both right, by the way. I looked it up. Jonquils are a species of narcissi.'

'They're nearly out of season,' I say.

'Yes, but I can still smell them as I pass the open windows. I suppose I'm imagining it. Though some fragrances linger more than others.' She gives a brief wave goodbye, switching off the light on her way out of the room.

I keep the smile on my face until her footsteps disappear, then let my mouth drop. I tug the curtains open so I can see a sliver of night sky, stars, a new moon sparkling through the darkness for me.

DAY 7, FRIDAY MORNING

I've come to the nursery this morning with a plan. Before I go home, I need to hold my son. I have to take this chance as I don't know when the next one will come.

Gabriel's cot is still surrounded by partitions, only this time they're not completely closed. Catching a flicker of him under the aqua lights in the gap between the screens, my nipples prickle, followed by a hot flare of breastmilk pooling in my bra. The fluid leaks onto my T-shirt, but after yesterday I've realised the importance of wearing black.

Ursula, hunched over a baby in an open cot on the far side of the nursery, is the only person visible when I look around the corner; the other nurses must be at handover. I creep back to Gabriel's cot and peer through the crack in the partitions. Empty, except for Gabriel. I slip inside. Through a thin crack between the panels, I can see all the way to the nurses' station. I'll have more than enough time if anyone approaches.

Gabriel lies still, his mouth curled into a slight smile, his eyelids closed, his long lashes brushing his cherubic cheeks. It's hard to assess the extent of his jaundice under the blue lights. I reach over to lever his toes apart. Webbing would be a scrap of proof that would force even Mark to take note.

Yet again, before I have a chance to check, there's a creak and the partitions are thrust open. Mark's clean-shaven face peers between the screens.

'I've been looking everywhere for you.' He takes in Gabriel, then me with my hands thrust through the portholes resting on Gabriel's feet. His mouth gapes open and closed like a goldfish.

'What the fuck are you doing?'

I yank my hands from the humidicrib and snap the portholes shut. 'Nothing.' I push past Mark and into the open part of the nursery.

Mark slams the screens closed and begins to pace back and forth in front of me. He looks like a caged animal; a lion, perhaps.

'I thought you understood you have to stay away from Jeremy.'

'It's not what you think,' I say.

He continues pacing back and forth, muttering to himself.

'You don't need to tell anyone,' I say. 'I haven't done anything wrong.'

He stops still. 'How many times have you been near his cot? How many times have you touched him?'

'This is the first.'

He resumes the pacing, his hand pressed to his forehead.

'Please don't tell anyone,' I say.

He stops and stares at me as if I'm some sort of a threat. A chill runs down my torso to my feet, which are frozen to the floor.

'Please don't tell. *Please.*'

His body is rigid.

'It was a mistake.'

'A mistake.' The lines around his nose and mouth deepen into crevices.

He won't believe me until I have irrefutable proof. The only thing left is to try and lie.

'Jeremy was crying and crying and the nurses were busy and no one was helping the poor baby, and I thought it was the least I could do to help Brigitte out and –'

'You weren't trying to hurt him, were you?'

'Of course not.' How could he even suggest it?

'You can't do anything like this again. You understand?' His mouth clamps shut as Ursula makes her way towards us.

'Is there a problem here?' Ursula tugs at the neck of her pinafore as she addresses Mark. He gives her a small smile.

'Sasha has been telling me how well Toby's doing.' He doesn't look at me. 'Isn't he, sweetheart?'

'Yes,' I say. 'He really is.'

Ursula recedes into the background. Mark, his knuckles paper-white over the humidicrib's metallic rail, is peering down at Toby like he's a priceless jewel.

'You need to believe me, Sash. Toby is our son. That thing he does before he sneezes.' He looks up, crinkling his nose. 'And the crease in his brow.' He points to the space between my eyebrows. 'You have the same.' He stares at me, his pupils dark tunnels travelling to nowhere. 'Please promise me you'd never hurt a baby.'

'You wouldn't ask that if you really loved me.'

'You don't get it, do you?' His voice is soft, frightening in its quietness. 'I *do* love you. That's why I lied, why I told you I was with him the whole time after the birth.'

Ursula stares in our direction, but she's not looking at Mark and me. Her gaze is fixed on the window beside Toby's cot where hailstones as large as golf balls have begun volleying down.

'I wasn't allowed in the operating theatre,' Mark continues, staring at the thundering hail. 'They made me wait outside, so I went straight to the nursery. As soon as he got up here, I stayed with him, during the resuscitation, during everything. I didn't leave him alone.'

I don't know who to believe anymore.

'Was me getting locked up your doing? Did you want me in here so you could quietly become a partner in the restaurant without having to worry about your mentally ill wife disturbing you? Like those husbands who used to have their wives committed to asylums when they'd had enough of them?'

'You're acting crazy,' he says, his hands tightening on the rail. 'I've been doing everything in my power to get you out of there.'

Outside, on the street, cars are reducing their speed in the hail. Time itself has slowed. We've entered a parallel universe where things aren't as they're meant to be. Then the hail stops. Fluttering, twirling, rising into the air on a wind current, then swirling to the asphalt, are snowflakes; an extremely unusual occurrence for such a warm spring.

'I suppose the reason you told Dr Niles everything about me is because you love me too, right?'

Mark shakes his head. 'What are you on about?'

'You told her about Damien. About me being suicidal. About the foetuses talking. Why did you have to tell her everything?'

Snowflakes now stream from the sky in clusters and gather on the roof of the bus shelter, the concrete footpath and the road before they're crushed to sleet by passing cars.

'I didn't tell her anything. Except about the foetuses. She dragged that out of me.' Mark's expression blurs into all the other versions of his face; the occasions he's given me his wooden smile, the times he's avoided my gaze.

'You knew about my mother this whole time, didn't you?'

'Sash, *please*. I really don't know what you're talking about.'

'I can't believe a word you say anymore.'

Mark snaps the humidicrib doors back into place. His face is knotted into a shape I've never seen before, beyond worried or frustrated, bordering on disgust.

'I'm supposed to be taking you home this morning.' He glances at Gabriel's partitions. 'I think I'd better give you some space to clear your head.'

He doesn't know the half of what is in my head.

When Mark has departed, I examine Toby. He is quiet. His limbs are creamy white, his breathing shallow and rapid. His eyes flicker in the weak light. Is he too still? Is there something wrong?

I inspect his chart. I'm not happy with his observations. There is a variability in his temperature and his heart rate. It's a subtle increase – I can see why the nurses have missed it – but it's there.

Dr Green, the paediatrician, is making notes at the nurses' station. I haven't spoken to her properly since Sunday, when she refused the DNA tests. I call her to my side. Her heels clip on the floor until she halts at Toby's crib, her hair falling into clean, straight lines. Her pleasant floral perfume wafts over me.

'Is there a problem?'

I point to his chart and indicate the fluctuations, the abnormal patterns.

'I thought you ought to know.'

She traces the lines on the graph. Then she opens Toby's crib, palpates his abdomen, rests her stethoscope against his chest. When she's finished, she glances up at me.

'You've only just noticed these . . . irregularities?'

I nod.

Dr Green grabs the chart and heads back to the nurses' station where she picks up the phone. I was supposed to be questioning her about her alibi and motives, but I can hardly do that now. Toby needs someone by his side. Lucia wasn't my birth mother, but she was there for me. I can be there for Toby this morning. He is innocent in all this and he needs someone to love him today.

I look down at the crib. Toby's chest and abdomen look like they're working at odds with one another, one blowing out as the other sucks in. Paradoxical breathing. A bad sign.

After Damien, I stopped trusting my instincts when it came to illness. I decided intuition wasn't one of my strengths. Possessing so little confidence in my abilities, each time I was confronted with another sick child I ordered more and more lab tests, X-rays, scans. Why I left paediatrics: I realised the tests couldn't protect me from myself.

Toby, though; he looks different to yesterday. He looks unwell. Dr Green approaches again, this time her cheeks pale.

'Let's take him into the resuscitation room,' she says. 'I need to pop a drip in, take some bloods, then start some antibiotics. We'll have more room in there.'

Putting in an IV, taking blood tests, starting antibiotics; it's what I should have done for Damien. Instead I sent him home – and to his death. Back in those early days, I had been certain I could never make the wrong call.

Dr Green lifts Toby and passes him to me.

'You carry him,' she says. It feels like far too long since I last held him. His skin is clammy and cool. I could easily rest him in one hand, but I cradle him in two to support his spine. His arms and legs loll about like he's a rag doll. I press his small frame against me to keep him warm.

Dr Green walks alongside me. 'I remember how hard it was, seeing other babies struggling when my daughter was improving. Mark mentioned I had a premature baby?'

I nod, remembering the day I was admitted.

'Cassie. Would you believe I felt guilty when she was doing well?' She pauses a beat. 'I felt guilty about everything back then. I'd even convinced myself her premature birth was my fault. It's taken me longer than I thought to let go of my self-blame, to realise it was chance. Just one of those things. Not my fault at all.'

The resuscitation room is hidden behind an opaque sliding door. I had hoped I'd never find myself in one of these again. The walls are stacked high with shelves of equipment: syringes, needles, masks, boxes of medication. Everything a sick baby could need. The resuscitation cot, covered in various dials and switches, stands in the middle of the room, pushed up against one wall. Two gas tanks are strapped to the back, ready to pipe oxygen or air to the sick baby. A heat lamp hovers above the cot like an emergency helicopter. It's been years since I worked in paediatrics; I could no longer resuscitate Toby according to best practice standards. He is in the hands of the medical staff now.

Dr Green shuffles between shelves, tearing open plastic packets, setting up a cannula tray. I lay Toby out on the mattress of the resuscitation cot. The heat lamp is turned up to maximum, prickling my forearms as I stroke his head. On the wall, flowcharts detail the steps of resuscitation. A whiteboard still shows the times and doses of the last baby they brought back from the dead.

Dr Green's eyebrows are creased in worry, her hands shaking ever so slightly as she primes the IV line. 'I wish someone could have given me a healthy baby, rather than a premature one.' Her rich floral perfume mingles with her sweat in the confines of the tiny room. 'It's not fair for anyone – parents, babies – to have to suffer in this way. That's why I do this work, you know; to ease other people's pain.'

She hands me a small tube of clear liquid. 'You give him this sucrose while I insert the drip,' she says. She leans over Toby on the resuscitation cot mattress and takes his tiny arm; it's no thicker than her thumb. Her fingers leave white imprints on his skin as she bends his wrist back. His veins become threads of violet, poking out. I use one palm to hold his chest, the other to drip the sucrose into his mouth. Despite the heat lamp, he's cold all over. I clamp his wrist with my hand. His mouth opens and closes as he gasps and swallows the sugary liquid. Dr Green taps a bulging vein with the back of her fingers, then pricks his skin with a needle. Toby screeches.

'It's okay,' I say, a layer of sweat springing up on my forehead. My pulse is racing.

Toby's squeals reverberate through the room. My fingers spasm and cramp, but I don't loosen my grasp of his chest or the sucrose tube.

Finally, the needle is gone, replaced by a screw-on cap and the line of plastic IV tubing. Dr Green fills a few tiny vials with Toby's rose-coloured blood, her eyes watering. 'I always wanted a big family, you know. As soon as Cassie was born, I became obsessed with the idea of having another baby straight away. I think part of it was to prove to myself and everyone that I could do it right the next time. But when I saw what Cassie went through in the nursery, one child felt like enough.'

Toby is whimpering now, his wails rising and falling like a church organ. A deep, almost familiar furrow forms between his eyebrows as Dr Green tapes his arm to a splint. Feeling his skittish heartbeat against my palm, my head spinning and my feet all at once unsteady under me, I let go of his chest and flee from the room, no longer knowing which direction to run.

The nursery is empty; no staff or visitors are around. Outside, snowflakes are still tumbling to the ground. I slip back through the crack between the screens to find Gabriel asleep in his crib. His skin is shining blue under the lights. I press my forehead to the perspex. He is starting to settle into chubbiness, his face rounding out, rolls developing at his wrists. I click open one of the portholes and reach in to touch his skin.

'I knew it.'

Ursula. Her shoulders are drawn up to her ears like a serpent ready to strike.

'You are well aware you are not permitted near this baby.' She steps forward, a black stethoscope swaying over her chest like a hypnotist's watch. 'I was all for you bonding with Toby,' she says. 'I thought you had every chance of getting better, Sasha. I even stood up for you when the other nurses wanted you banned from the nursery.' She fixes her eyes on Gabriel. 'But this time, you've really gone too far.'

With her hand pressed against my shoulder, Ursula propels me out of the partitioned room towards the nursery exit. She directs me through the door and plonks me in a chair in the hallway beside a plastic fern.

'Wait here,' she instructs.

Opposite me, photos of babies born in this hospital cover a pinboard, a mass of chubby faces, double chins and wide eyes. The babies I know aren't on that board. Not yet, at least.

Toby, in the nursery, his feeds travelling through a tube in his nostril all the way to his stomach, handled by strangers day and night.

Gabriel, with the woman sitting by his cot day after day believing he's her son, calling him by a name that doesn't fit.

Finally, me cradling Gabriel against my neck, inhaling the sugar-sweet scent of his skin.

Three babies, four names: Damien, Gabriel, Jeremy, Toby. Only one of them mine.

The tight furrow between Toby's eyebrows, the one Mark is convinced is mine; it couldn't be genetic, could it? Surely there's no chance Toby could be my son?

All along Dr Niles has said she's seen women with similar reactions to mine, especially after a traumatic birth. They dissociate, struggle to bond with their babies. Toby doesn't feel like mine. And I've tried, haven't I? Tried to love him, tried to feel something for him. Nothing came.

I count the number of times I've properly held Toby. Once. Once in seven days.

Perhaps it's like they've said: it could be my fault. Perhaps I haven't tried hard enough.

If Toby were my son, I could live with Mark's silent reproaches.

And I could learn to live with my massive mistake.

What the hell am I supposed to do?

The nursery door squeals like a whining dog as it opens and closes on its hinge. There's no reply to the question in my head, or in my heart. As for Damien, I've been carrying him with me for years now, waking from nightmares and clawing at the doona. Mark stopped asking why.

In the coroner's court, I said I had no recollection of the lesion behind Damien's ear. But I do. I checked the spot the night before he died, trying to make it blanch with my index finger. But it wouldn't. It was still there when I lifted my hand from his skin. I had put it down to a birthmark his parents had never noticed. He didn't have any others – I did check – and one lesion wasn't enough to order more investigations, or so I believed at the time. I'd learned at medical school the meningococcal rash was always the last thing to come up before death, but Damien didn't look like he was about to die – not that night, at least.

Yet the biggest problem wasn't missing the significance of the lesion. It was what happened next.

The coroner interrogated me about the mark. I froze. My incompetence was on vivid display in the courtroom, illuminated for his parents, the media, assembled strangers, even myself. It had felt like I'd only had one option. My response has echoed through my head every night since then, in my weak, tinny voice.

I don't recall.

'I'm so sorry, Damien,' I whisper into the hot, humid air of the corridor. The words hang in the ether, around my head, but when Toby's solemn face hangs before me, so similar to Damien's own, I wonder whether Damien might be ready to let me go. And I pray I will come to accept Toby – the son I might have spurned for reminding me of Damien, of my mistakes – in his place.

As the nursery door slides open and Dr Green stands before me with a stern expression on her face, it all comes to me; what I should have known this whole time, what I no longer need a test to confirm. What I hadn't wanted to believe.

One more thing to add to the long list of my mistakes.

My heart contracts and loosens beneath my ribs. I slump off the plastic seat, onto my knees, unable to bear my own weight, but Dr Green has rushed towards me, catching me before I fall.

The carpet beneath my knees is grubby, tainted with old, dark stains. I shudder. It's not too late. Some women don't bond with their babies for months, or even years. Or ever. It might take me an awfully long time to learn to love Toby. At least this way he and I will both have a chance.

I haul myself to my feet.

'I need to see Toby,' I cry. 'I need to hold him. Please. You have to let me see him.'

Dr Green shakes her head. 'There have been some questions raised about Toby's illness,' she says. 'I'm afraid we'll have to ask you not to visit for now.'

'Please. I didn't do anything to Toby. I can see I've been wrong. If I can just hold him –'

'I'm sorry,' Dr Green interrupts. 'Really, I am. But for now, we have no choice.' She ushers me past the long sink towards the lifts. 'We'll let you know when you can visit again.'

My knees are so weak I feel like I'm going to collapse. This can't be happening; not when I've finally discovered the truth.

I've done so many things wrong. But I'm not my mother. I haven't purposely caused Toby any harm. I can love my son and be a better mother than I expected of myself, a better mother than my own. I hope to God it's not too late for Toby, or for me. My legs begin to slide out from under me.

I feel a hand beneath my armpit, keeping me upright.

'Time for you to come home, Sash,' Mark says.

For the first time in a long while, he's here when I need him most.

DAY 7, FRIDAY LATE MORNING

My chest feels hollow as Mark helps me into the car outside the main hospital entrance. I shouldn't be going, not when part of me is being left behind.

The trip home is quiet. Mark is playing a new CD of experimental jazz that makes me want to scream. Once we hit the outskirts of town, I scan the shoulders of the road where pockets of snow lie, melting in the spring sun that has emerged from behind the storm clouds. Occasional animal carcasses line the asphalt, rotted beyond recognition, feasted on by insects until they're nothing more than lumps of bone and fur. I wonder what Mark would do if we were to see an injured animal now; whether he'd ask me for help to save its life. The thought of a joey sucking at a teat, unable to draw in enough liquid to sustain its life as its mother grows cold, is almost too much to bear.

In the overhead mirror, the baby capsule we'd set up weeks ago rests in the back seat like an empty egg carton.

'Mark?' I feel I owe him an explanation.

He nods.

'This has made things really hard for you, hasn't it?'

We leave the asphalt and hit the dirt road, stones striking the under-surface of the car as the suspension shudders beneath us.

'I thought this would be different.'

'Me too,' he says.

Wind turbines on the distant hills whip around like kitchen beaters. We pass a farmhouse washing line, a fitted sheet billowing in the wind. Then the house with the front yard chock-full of rusting cars, tractor bodies and scrap metal. I turn up the heater and stretch my legs out under the dashboard. We're getting close to home. I need to say it now before it's too late.

'Something happened after you left . . .' But the whole story is somehow too difficult to put into words. I try again. 'I'm sorry for making your life hell. I think I've been wrong. I've made a mistake. I do think Toby is our baby. We'll be able to get to see him soon, won't we? We'll be let back into the nursery? I need to hold him. He's going to be alright, isn't he?'

Mark sighs, and his hands loosen on the wheel. 'I'll go back and see Toby this afternoon,' he says. 'Dr Green seems to think he'll be fine. Hopefully they'll let you see him again very soon. Everything is going to be okay.' I think he's talking more to himself than to me.

Cherry blossom petals crumple under the tyres as we turn into our white stone driveway. The snowstorm hasn't hit this far out of town. Our house looks almost unfamiliar after the week away, its lace awnings and carved verandah posts, its deft Edwardian style all at once too elegant for these forest surrounds, as though it's been transported here from the inner city on the back of a truck, then dumped in the middle of the bush. We're encased by trees on all sides, our house invisible from the road. *Situated in a magical clearing*, the real estate agent had proclaimed. *A bushfire death trap*, Mark had corrected. I had insisted that we snap it up anyway, swept up in the fantasy of a bush retreat, as though serenity was something that could be bought, or owned.

Mark spent the first five years in the house whingeing about the wiring, the floorboards, the sloping ceilings. 'Old houses,' he'd mutter as he clambered into the manhole. He preferred modern houses: clean lines, straight roofs, everything ordered and under control.

Me, I loved houses that had history. Atmosphere. I could almost sense the people who had lived in this house before us. There was nowhere I would rather be. After eight years, it felt like home.

Once we're inside, I see that clusters of dust and hair have been swept into piles up and down the hallway. It must have been Mark. He's never appreciated the importance of vacuuming or sweeping before mopping. I glance at the statue of a pregnant woman on the hall table. I bought it as a present to myself, early in the pregnancy. To commemorate the nine months, I said at the time.

Above the table hangs a Monet reproduction, *Water Lilies and Japanese Bridge*. It will have to go. Empty walls will be enough. We had them freshly painted in preparation for the baby. Clotted cream. Mark let me have my choice of paint.

I kick off my shoes and inspect the ceiling. Stringy cobwebs dangle between the cornices and our stained-glass light fittings.

In the lounge, bunches of wilting flowers line the mantelpiece – gerberas, lilies and carnations – their petals already brown at the edges. They smell of mould, of death.

'I thought I'd leave them for you to see when you got home,' Mark says. He hands me a stack of greeting cards. They're from friends, work colleagues, extended family, each containing cheery messages of congratulations and well wishes, all filled with hope. Nothing dark. Nothing real. I toss the worst of the cards into the fireplace.

The presents have been left in a ceremonial pile on the lounge suite. Rattling toys, organic-cotton clothes, a set of *Baby Einstein* DVDs. Mark picks up a pale-blue onesie and holds it against his chest for size.

'I've put your tablets next to your bed,' he says. 'So you won't forget.'

'I haven't even been taking them,' I say.

Mark drops the onesie to the floor.

'Why not? Oh my God. Can you please tell Dr Niles when you see her? I don't want to have to tell her myself.'

'She discharged me. She said I'd recovered.'

But Mark only shakes his head as he ducks beneath the doorway and leaves the room.

When I'm sure he's gone, I spread my mother's patchwork quilt over the back of the couch. The red of the fire engines matches the burgundy leather. The quilt is the perfect length and width, even if the childlike fabrics don't quite suit the décor of the house.

Later, we stand side-by-side in the kitchen preparing lunch, almost like old times. After a week away, our kitchen feels sterile, with stainless steel appliances, glossy grey cabinets and clear benchtops. It's as though I'm back in the lab.

There's still some leftover gnocchi from the batch Mark made. The boiling water spits onto the stove as he bundles handfuls of white dough into the saucepan.

'I saw a tawny frogmouth last night,' he says.

'Uh-huh.'

'It was sitting on the tree stump by the garage. I got all the way up to it. I almost touched its feathers. It wasn't until the last moment that it flew away.'

I cut through a tomato, the blade a scalpel in my hand as it cracks on the glass chopping board. The juice spatters up at me.

'Careful,' he says.

The kitchen cupboards fade from grey to black as blood drains from my head. I ease myself onto a stool.

'You know what they say,' Mark says with a smile. 'If you can't take the heat, get out of the kitchen.'

I place my hand over the scar above my pelvic bone.

'I was joking,' he adds. Then, gentle: 'Are you okay?'

I don't reply. He stirs the boiling pot.

'Dr Niles rang,' he says. 'She wants to see you back at the mother–baby unit this afternoon.'

'So soon?'

'She insisted. Look, if you don't go to the appointment, there's the risk she'll readmit you. Involuntarily this time.'

A sparrow flutters away from the birdbath in the yard.

'And Toby? Any word on how he is?'

'I haven't heard from Dr Green.'

'Couldn't you just give her a call?'

'I don't want to hassle her, Sash. She's busy. I'm sure she'll be in touch as soon as she can.'

'Maybe we can go and see Toby after I see Dr Niles.'

'I don't think so, Sash. We need to wait for the paediatrician's okay.'

There's something he's not telling me.

'Why does Dr Niles want to see me? What did you say to her?'

'Nothing,' Mark says. 'She sounded worried about you.'

Shit. She's heard about my interest in Jeremy. I'm going to have to convince her all over again that I believe Toby is my son.

'You must have said something.'

'I'm trying to help you, Sash, I promise. The last thing I want is for you to be readmitted.'

Sitting around the table with the quiet women munching on their soggy hospital meals like a prisoner. Sobbing in the bathroom, with the lukewarm water dribbling down my back. Pinching my eyes shut in meditation, the women around me shuffling and sniffing.

Mark drains the gnocchi into the colander in the sink. Steam rises, fogging the kitchen window. I picture Toby, all alone in his humidicrib, and bury my face in my hands.

'I'm not up for lunch,' I mumble.

'Let me know when you're hungry. I'll heat some up for you.'

In our bedroom, Toby's dirty clothes lie in a plastic bag on the bed beside my suitcase, ready for me to wash and fold. I press one of his jumpsuits to my face. It smells faintly of soil, like the downy tan and white bird feathers I used to collect on my bushwalks back when we couldn't get pregnant. I would press them into my pocket and hold them tight as though I was clasping magic in the palm of my hand.

I try to picture how our room will look when we get Toby home. I'll keep the new breastfeeding chair by our bed. The change table should fit under the window. And we can move his cot in here. He'll be able to sleep beside us, on my side of the bed.

Clothes spring out at me as I unzip my suitcase. As for my cupboard, it's a mess: tops and pants tangled in clumps and spilling from the open drawers. Wire clothes hangers are scattered on the ground.

'Couldn't you have tried to keep my stuff in order?' I call out to Mark. Hidden at the back of the top shelf, I find my mother's quilt. Mark has already removed it from the couch.

I retrieve the zip-lock from the front pocket of my suitcase. The umbilical cord is even more blackened and shrunken than when I last examined it. I prise open the plastic bag. The shrivelled black lump of cells no longer has a smell. I carry it into the ensuite and toss it in the bin. There's a creak behind me.

Mark is in the doorway, brandishing his jacket and a letter, *DNA Easy* on the header, in his shaking hands. A vein throbs on his forehead.

Shit. The results have arrived earlier than I expected. And I'd forgotten that, hoping I'd be discharged early, I'd asked for them to be sent to my home address.

'That's addressed to me.'

I reach for the paper, but he snatches it away.

'You did the tests. You went behind my back. You weren't even going to tell me. How could you?'

My knees tremble.

'It's complicated.'

'It doesn't seem complicated to me. No wonder you're so sure Toby is our son. I don't even need to read these to know the answer.'

He crumples the letter in his palm.

So he hasn't read it. I feel no need to read it either. I already know what it will say, the results in bold black type accusing me of yet another mistake. Now I can only hope that Toby will recover.

Mark stuffs the letter in the pocket of his jacket. 'And me? Did you take a sample from me?'

The floor tiles are a monotonous pattern, white-and-black squares like a chequerboard, endlessly repeating. The pattern was Mark's choice. I never told him I couldn't stand the design.

He curses under his breath.

'If Dr Niles hadn't insisted I keep things calm for you at home . . .' He draws in a breath, tightens his hands into fists. I can smell his breath, sweet and sickly, from beside me.

'You hid my quilt earlier.'

Mark eyes me. 'It's a child's quilt, Sasha.'

My heart sinks in my chest, my stomach rising to meet it. *'Mark.'* My whole body shakes until I'm almost rocking. 'We need to talk.'

Mark stuffs his hands into his pockets. I could hold back, say nothing and live the life we've made for ourselves in our house secreted in the bush like a fire bunker. It would be safe. Comfortable. Adequate.

I see people gathering in front of us, like in the genial photographs adorning the walls of the living room: my father, friends, work colleagues, extended family, all of them clustered, their eyes drawn into thin lines. How can I disappoint them all like this?

I never allowed myself to imagine life without Mark, not even in the weeks before the wedding when the pressure of a husband living life for his dead twin began to weigh heavy on me.

'Don't back out now,' Bec said as I wallowed in martinis at my hens' night. 'You'll regret it.'

No relationship is perfect. Bec had been right about that. Marriage keeps you together through the bad times. Like now, I suppose. It's just that we haven't been happy together for so long.

'I . . .'

Mark holds up his palm to me, shaking his head.

'I wanted to . . .'

There's so much I want to say about the ways in which we have failed each other, but it almost feels like too much to discuss. He doesn't open his mouth so I continue.

'We haven't been honest with each other.'

Mark's cheeks are sunken into his skull, his eyeballs into their sockets.

'This isn't you, Sash. It's your hormones speaking. Or your illness.'

My hands quake on the bathroom sink.

'I've been thinking about this for the longest time, Mark. It seemed easier to keep going, see if things got better between us once you were happier, once we had a baby. I've been pretending for so long that everything is fine, that I'm okay. You have, too. Surely you can see both of us aren't happy the way things are. I can't do this anymore. I hope one day you'll understand.'

I stop, nothing left to say.

'I've been trying so hard to be the husband you wanted.'

'I can't be the wife you need.'

He turns to me. He looks devastated.

'You can't save us,' I say, 'any more than you could save Simon.'

His face tightens.

'Simon shouldn't have given up. He shouldn't have let go. I told him that on the night he died.'

In that moment, with his eyes on fire, his mouth set in fear, I no longer recognise my husband. I wonder who he has loved and whether he has ever loved me at all.

'Fuck this,' he says. 'I'll wait for you in the car.' His feet thump down the hallway runner to the front door.

He's right. This is fucked. All of it. I want to be with my baby. I want to hold Toby. Above all, I should have the right to see my son.

Toby. He's a good baby; better than I deserve. We will have a bond, finally, that feels real and true. He'll get better every day. He simply has to; he's already suffered so much, and I can't bear to even contemplate losing him now.

A rush of bile slides up my throat. I need to hold him. Then I'll be absolutely certain he's mine. I only wish there was another way to find out.

DAY 7, FRIDAY AFTERNOON

'How are you, Sasha?'

Brigitte is behind me in the hospital foyer, clutching her handbag in one hand, her plastic bag full of knitting paraphernalia – red wool, needles, knitted squares – in the other. 'The sooner we all get home, the better, huh?'

Why is she happy to speak to me now? She must not have been told I was found again beside Jeremy's cot. And after what's happened with Mark, I'm not too sure home is where I want to be right now. Mark and I barely exchanged a word on the drive here. When I left him waiting in the car, he looked ashen. I wonder if he even trusts me to attend my appointment with Dr Niles.

I push Mark out of my mind and try to be generous to Brigitte.

'I'm sure Jeremy will be going home soon.'

'Maybe.' She bites her top lip. 'How's Toby today?'

'He's having some antibiotics. I hope he's going to be okay.' I'm due at the mother–baby unit, where I'll attempt to placate Dr Niles before heading to the nursery. I'm desperate to check on Toby's condition. If they still deny me access, I'll have to work out another plan to see him. So the last thing I want is to keep talking to Brigitte. She was right to be fearful and suspicious of me; there's no point in trying to rekindle any connection we might have made early on.

Before I can slip away, Brigitte gives a wide smile. 'Ursula just told me everything. I'm so sorry. I had no idea what you were going through. If I'd known you thought my baby was yours . . .' She keeps smiling. 'It must have been horrific for you. I'm so glad you've come around.' She appears genuine in her concern. 'By the way, I noticed your quilt is a little threadbare. I'd still love to help fix it up, if you'd like.'

I hesitate, and Brigitte sidles closer.

'Look, I've been thinking about everything that's been going on for you. I've been doing some research. Did you know the very first humidicribs were made from metal?'

I pull Mark's jacket tighter around me, the one he insisted I put on when I began shivering in the car on the way to the hospital.

Brigitte babbles on. 'Apparently back when they first started putting babies in humidicribs, mothers kept abandoning them. They'd leave their babies in the nursery and never come back. So they started making humidicribs out of glass. The mothers visited every day. The doctors put it down to mothers being able to bond with their babies because they could see them better.' She drops her voice. 'Maybe they were wrong? Maybe it was the glass itself that helped? It's a natural material, not like perspex, or metal. Maybe you should ask for a glass humidicrib?'

There's not even the hint of a smile on her lips.

'I mean, you can see your baby much more clearly through glass than through perspex, right? Who they are. Who you want them to be.'

I wonder how her mental health is, and whether naturopathy and chiropracty are really keeping postnatal depression at bay.

'Thanks, Brigitte, but I'm okay now. Everything is okay. But I've got to go.'

She takes a step back.

'I'm glad to hear you're feeling better. I've been meaning to tell you, by the way. I love the name Toby. Names are funny, aren't they? I've always thought people grow into them until there's no way they could have ever been called anything else.' She stares at me with curious eyes.

I feel a flush of heat and loosen my shirt at the neck. If the situation were reversed – if she'd touched my baby without my knowledge – I'd want her to tell me. I take a deep breath.

'I'm sorry, I –'

'It's fine,' she interrupts. 'You don't need to say another word. I know what you're going to say. And I know what it's like. It's so easy to do the wrong thing sometimes. When you wish things were different. When you want to start over. When you feel like you have no other choice.' She scrabbles in her pocket. 'I've been meaning to give you my number. It would be great to catch up when we get our babies home. Jeremy's being discharged any day now. I was concerned I might not get to see you before I left, so I got your number from your notes. I was sure you wouldn't mind.' She passes me a scrap of paper. 'I'd love to stay in touch. Maybe our sons can be friends.'

'My medical notes? How did you get them?' Alarm bells are sounding in my head.

She purses her lips. 'I only got your phone number. They keep the medical records of women like us, the mothers whose babies are in the nursery, on the postnatal ward. Nurses' station, top drawer on the right. Easily accessible when the nurses are busy. You know what it's like.' She winks.

Her handwriting on the scrap of paper is familiar somehow. Then I remember: it's the same large, clear lettering that was filling each of the cards beside Jeremy's cot. Why would she have written letters of congratulations to herself?

'I've really got to go,' I mumble.

Brigitte is still rummaging through her handbag.

'The books said they used to call premature babies weaklings in the olden days, back before humidicribs. I guess it let everyone justify the way they would leave them to die. Can you believe it? Thank God it's not like that now. Our babies couldn't be luckier. And neither could we.' She pulls a tiny red knitted jumper from the depths of her handbag and places it in my hands. 'I made it for Jeremy,' she says, 'but I think Toby should have it.'

I run the pads of my fingers over the braided neck, the woven wrists. It's merino, softer than it looked from a distance. It's too big for Toby's minute torso, but I'm sure he'll grow into it soon enough.

'That's very kind,' I say. 'Are you sure you don't mind?'

'Absolutely,' Brigitte says, flashing her friendly smile again. 'And be sure to stay in touch.'

*

I pause in front of the wall of monitors in the mother–baby unit where a dozen speakers screwed to plasterboard emit the sounds of babies in a separate room. The speakers are used for sleep-training. The mothers stand outside the door, listening to their child's cries, attempting to recognise signs of distress. I never paid much heed to the speakers when I was admitted. Now I press my ear to the closest one. Snuffles. A wail. Silence. Then a piercing cry that echoes through my chest. I would never want my child in a place like this.

'Sasha, hello.' Dr Niles' coffee breath wafts towards me when I turn to find her standing at my side. 'Thank you for coming in at my request.'

She herds me into the interview room beside the nurses' station, where the air is once again hot and thick. I shrug off Mark's jacket and perch on the plastic seat with my spine erect. The downlights are interrogation spotlights on my face.

Dr Niles sits in the chair opposite me. She lifts her pen above my file, the nib as sharp as a barb. I wonder how much she knows about my now-resolved obsession with Jeremy. *We are here for you*, the sign above her head reminds me in bold, black type.

'You haven't been taking your medication.' A statement, not a question.

'Mostly I have,' I lie. 'When I remember.'

She glares at me.

'You must take your tablets regularly. Otherwise we may have to consider readmitting you.'

'No problem,' I say, rising to my feet. Her fingernails are sharp against my skin as she takes hold of my arm and gestures to the chair. All I want is to hold Toby in my arms to know that he's okay; yet it appears I have no choice but to sit back down.

'There's something else we need to discuss,' Dr Niles says. 'You showed particular interest in another baby in the nursery. You asked to hold him.' This isn't a question, either.

I frown.

'You deny it?'

'I just wanted to see what it was like to hold a baby that was a bit bigger than Toby,' I say carefully, not entirely sure if this is an adequate answer, but it's the best I can do right now.

'You wanted to hold a bigger baby.' The sharp nib of her pen is poised above unmarked paper on the desk.

'Yes,' I say, spotting my chance. 'I didn't expect Toby to be so small. He's very delicate. And frail. I feel like I could crush him with my touch.'

'Crush him with your touch.' Dr Niles squeezes her fingers into the shaft of the pen so the skin under her nails turns white.

Oh, shit.

'No,' I say, 'that's not what I meant. I mean that I don't want to hurt Toby. You see, I only want the very best of everything for him.' I cast my eyes to a poster tacked to the wall, a serene mother breastfeeding her baby, a placid smile on her face. 'Like my milk, for example.'

'You were planning on breastfeeding Jeremy?'

The walls of the tiny room feel as if they're closing in. My top is soaked with sweat, clinging to my back. I feel like a caged animal in an experiment, observed through one-way glass, a single spotlight trained on me. Perhaps I'm like those rhesus monkeys that clung to constructed mothers in the experiments. The monkeys favoured cloth mothers over wire ones, I recall.

'I would never breastfeed Jeremy. He's not my baby. I don't know what else I can say to make you believe me.' A line of sweat trickles from my temple. 'I've known ever since you admitted me that Toby is my baby. You can ask anyone. They'll tell you. I've visited his humidicrib every day. I've expressed milk for him even when you said I couldn't. I've bought him presents . . .' I realise there isn't much more to say. My voice fades until it's almost choking. 'I do love him.'

Dr Niles observes me as a scientist would have observed those monkeys. She envisages me as a wire mother, I'm sure of it.

'Is Toby okay?'

'I'm not aware of all the details. You'll have to speak to the paediatricians.'

That's what I'll do as soon as I possibly can. None of this should have happened, this hospital horror show. My chest constricts.

'Mark is responsible for all of this, isn't he? Me being admitted in the first place, and telling you all about my past.'

Dr Niles blinks. 'Mark has been your most ardent supporter.'

'But he's been lying to me the whole time.'

'I doubt it.'

Mark's face forms in front of me. His guilt-ridden frown as he crouched on the floor of my room, searching through my belongings. His desperate stare as he tried to keep me from being admitted by encouraging me to pretend nothing was wrong. His wide-eyed horror as he discovered the depths of my obsession with Jeremy. The roses, the home-cooked gnocchi, the apricot slice. Finally, his face as it was on our wedding day: shining eyes, flushed cheeks, lips crinkled into a smile. Is it possible he's been fighting for me this whole time?

'Then who? Who told you everything?'

Dr Niles raises her pointed eyebrows.

'Bec?'

Dr Niles gives a slight shake of her head, her hair falling back into place. 'Is Bec that friend of yours? The one who finally stopped calling me?'

'My father, then.'

'I haven't spoken to your father.'

'Surely not Ondine.'

Her eyebrows crowd together. Not Ondine, then. There's only one other person who knows me and my mistakes. But she has nothing to do with the mother–baby unit.

'Brigitte?'

Dr Niles' face is blank.

'But why the hell would she do that?'

She shrugs.

My brain sorts through what I've told Brigitte, what I haven't, as if I'm trying to sift through a pile of flood-damaged papers that are falling apart in my hands. I can't understand why she's been speaking with Dr Niles. Nothing makes any sense.

'I have to go,' I say.

There's something going on here. I need to figure out Brigitte's motives for betraying me to Dr Niles. Perhaps if I read her medical notes, I'll gain insight into her motives. Then I can finally try to see my son.

Dr Niles snaps the top of her fountain pen back in place.

'I'm sure you're aware we have significant concerns about your safety around the babies, Sasha,' she says. 'Believe me, from now on we'll be watching you very closely indeed.'

FOUR MONTHS EARLIER

MARK

The night I popped in to tell them Sash was pregnant, Mum was at the sink, wringing water from a sponge. Dad was at the dining table, a handful of empty stubbies before him.

'What on earth are you thinking?' Dad said, his words slurring into each other. 'Simon would never have done this.'

When Simon died, their criticisms of him evaporated. He became revered, remembered as the perfect child; the perfect son. It didn't bother me. It was how I'd always seen him anyhow: the greatest brother; my best friend. The only problem was that, for my parents, I was left behind to make all the mistakes. It was a bad move to open my own café, they said. To marry a woman whose mother had abandoned her family, who might do the same. Now it seemed having a baby with Sash was the worst decision of all.

But I had one trump card left.

'It's a boy.'

I wasn't sure it was a boy, of course, but I had a strong feeling the twenty-week ultrasound would prove me right. Intuition didn't strike me often, but when it did, it was always correct. Like how I knew Sash was the woman for me from the very start.

As for the baby, I was certain Mum and Dad would be thrilled about a grandson. The baby would be like another Simon all over again. Not a replacement, but a form of solace.

I was right. Mum dropped the sponge into the soapy sink and clapped her hands on her cheeks.

'A boy? How delightful. Hear that, Ray? It's like a gift from Simon. A baby boy.'

Dad plonked his stubby on the table and stood to shake my hand.

'Congratulations, son. A grandson to carry on the family name.'

Driving home that evening, I was speeding through the countryside when I was overcome with a surge of heat in my body. I had the oddest sensation someone was in the passenger seat.

'Simon,' I said aloud, knowing it was ridiculous to address my long-dead brother but needing to speak to him anyway. 'Thank you for the baby. We're going to be a family now, Sash and me.' I listened to the engine hum in the silent night. 'I have my own life to live now, bro. I can't live your life as well anymore. But I still want you to be beside me. Like a mentor. A guide.'

On the roadside, I spotted an enormous shadow on the approaching rise. As I drew closer to the knoll, I could make out a kangaroo in the headlights, erect. A male, standing alone.

I'd seen him in the area before, but never this close. He was big enough to smash the windscreen, take me with him to our graves.

I applied the brakes, skidded to a stop beside the roo. He swivelled his head, taking me in. His fur glistened red in the headlights. His eyes were pinpoints of light rimmed with black. There was something of a challenge in his gaze; an expectation. A total absence of fear.

Before I could unclick my seatbelt, he turned and leaped over the fence into the thick blackness of the bush. I emerged from the car, blinking in the darkness as I peered after him. There was no sign of him amid the host of thick trunks. I was tempted to follow him in, but something held me back.

Sash. She needed me. She always would.

The asphalt crunched beneath my feet. The leather car seat was still warm. Sash. And the baby in her womb. I had to head back home. Both of them were waiting for me.

DAY 7, FRIDAY LATE AFTERNOON

I stride to the lift, take it to the first floor: the postnatal ward. I haven't been here for nearly a week, not since the morning after the birth. The corridor and nurses' station are deserted. I only need a moment.

Top drawer on the right, Brigitte said. I sidle behind the desk and pull open the drawer.

The two blood-red folders I'm looking for are at the top of the pile. S. Moloney. And B. Black.

I hesitate at the folder marked with my name. No doubt there are a multitude of offensive, inaccurate observations to sift through. I sigh. I'm in a hurry. Mark is still waiting for me in the car, I presume. I don't want him to suspect that I'm trying to see Toby. And I'm certain to be interrupted by another patient or a nurse at any moment. I don't have time to care what the hospital staff say, what they think, about me now.

I take out Brigitte's folder and flip it open to the first page.

Brigitte, naturopath, single. Two miscarriages, one stillbirth at 24 weeks.

So much she hasn't told me. So many times she didn't tell me the truth.

I turn the page. Handwritten in capitals, underlined in red: *ALLEGED SEXUAL ASSAULT BY UNKNOWN ASSAILANT IN HER HOME PRIOR TO PREGNANCY. NOT FOR VAGINAL EXAMINATIONS UNLESS ABSOLUTELY NECESSARY.*

I close the file. I don't need to read any more.

'I'm sorry,' I say aloud. It's directed at Toby but it could be for Brigitte, for all of us, all women with our secrets and necessary lies.

My mind churns.

Brigitte questioned me about my parenting, my plans for more children, my marriage.

She prevented me from seeing Jeremy after I raised the possibility of a baby mix-up.

She gave me a hand-knitted jumper for Toby.

Hardly firm evidence of what she might have done.

I try to reassure myself that I could never switch my baby with someone else's. But I know I can barely imagine what Brigitte has been through.

An announcement sounds on the hospital loudspeakers: *Code Blue, Special Care Nursery.*

Toby. No. This can't be happening.

I shove the folder in the drawer and slam it shut, then scurry down the corridor to the lifts and press the number five button again and again. Finally the lift doors open and I tumble in. On level five I scrub my hands over the sink, then I move towards the nursery door. It slides open with a whirring sound. Brigitte stands before me. I almost knock her down in my haste to enter. She averts her gaze and steps into the foyer, towards the lifts. I have no time to talk to her now.

Through the open nursery door, I hear chaotic sounds reverberating from the resuscitation room: urgent voices, beeping monitors, squealing alarms. Through the glass panel on the door, I can see medical staff clustered around a trolley in the resuscitation room, their huddle obscuring the baby being resuscitated from my view.

Ursula approaches me at the door, her face pale. 'You'll have to wait in the hall,' she says, yanking at my elbow.

'Is it Toby?'

'You'll have to wait,' she repeats. She presses me back, out through the nursery door and annexe, into the cool corridor. 'Take a seat.' Her face has a weary, haunted look. 'We're not letting any parents in right now. I'll come and speak to you when I can.'

How could I possibly sit? I pace the threadbare carpet. My fingers are frozen from shock. I thrust my hands into the pockets of Mark's jacket. Inside the leather, my fingers catch on a crumpled ball of paper. I pull it out. A snow-white letter, the one Mark stashed in his pocket back home. The DNA results. I lean against the photo board on the wall and unfurl the pages. This is what I thought I had to wait for. What I thought I'd needed all along. What I risked everything to obtain. Mark said he didn't even bother to read the results.

My heart hammers like a drum. When Mark pulled out the letter at home, I had thought I didn't need to read it either, that I could trust my intuition. It's only now that I realise I need definitive evidence, to prove to others as much as to myself who my child really is. I need more than my heart, more than my brain or my gut can know. I need the certainty that scientific proof can provide – that Toby is, after all, my son.

With trembling fingers, I smooth the sheets of paper flat and hold them out in front of me. I hesitate. A small part of me doesn't want to know. But I realise that now there is no turning back.

I look down at the results. My eyes blur and the paper shakes in my hand. The DNA results are not at all what I expect.

Brigitte. She must have switched our babies.

Jeremy – Gabriel – is my son.

From the resuscitation room, the clamour of voices settles to a whisper, then dense silence. Staff emerge from the nursery in small groups, their heads cast low as they pad along the corridor. Dr Green follows them out, her gaze on the lifts. None of them has noticed me standing by the photo board.

I cling to the wall to steady myself. When the nursery has cleared, I stuff the results back in the jacket pocket. My heart is racing.

I make my way towards the nursery. As the door slides open, Ursula's torso is a solid trunk before me.

I try to weave my way around her. 'I need to see my son.'

'It's not the right time.' Her hand on my shoulder is a crab claw, gripping tight, as she proceeds with me to the furthest corner of the annexe, behind the sink, away from the nursery door.

Ursula. She's treated me poorly since I was admitted. Does she know about the mix-up?

'Was it you?' I say. 'Did you know Toby wasn't mine this whole time?'

'We've been through this.' She looks down and flattens her pinafore across her thighs.

'You knew. You knew and you did nothing?' I wrench the letter from my pocket, wave it in her face. 'I have proof, Ursula.' I unfold the paper and slam it against the wall, point at the results in black and white. 'Look. Jeremy is my son. Like I said all along.'

As Ursula inspects the letter, her chin sags. She pauses, as if to consider her options, then starts slowly. 'I . . . She has no one, you know. She's all alone.'

'She said she has a husband. Friends.'

Ursula shakes her head. 'There is no husband. Brigitte is single. And she has no friends.'

The cards that surrounded Jeremy's cot, all with the same handwriting – Brigitte did indeed write every one.

There's only one way I can see this will be resolved. 'Let me take Jeremy home. None of this has to be exposed. Otherwise I will bring it all into the open: the hospital's culpability, your knowledge of the situation. You will lose your job.'

Ursula presses her back to the wall, her eyes falling to her feet.

'How could you let her get away with it?' I say.

Water drips from the taps into the metal sink, a steady beat.

'I . . . It wasn't Brigitte.' She swallows, her voice thick. 'I made the swap.'

Ursula? My heart threatens to stop. It feels as if blood is coagulating in my chest.

Huddled against the annexe wall, she appears almost pitiful. Her explanation starts haltingly. 'The hospital stripped my supervisor role from me after the *Serratia* outbreak. They shoved me into an antenatal clinic rotation as if I was in disgrace. That's where I met Brigitte, on her first antenatal visit. She was twenty weeks by the time her pregnancy was discovered. She'd been in denial about what happened, I suppose – the rape.' She spits out the word as anger flares in her voice.

'Despite her repulsion at how she became pregnant, she couldn't face a termination. She struggled the whole pregnancy. Of course she did. Who wouldn't? She was so afraid she wouldn't be able to love her son after he was born. We bonded. We understood each other. I told her about something similar that had happened to me, years ago; something I'd never told anyone. We became close. Friends, almost.'

I listen to Ursula in silent disbelief.

'I arranged her induction with the hope that I would be on duty at the time of the birth. It turned out perfectly. The labour ward was short-staffed, so I was called into work early and Brigitte was allocated to me. As soon as her baby was birthed, and I laid him in her arms, I knew her fears were founded. He looked nothing like her. She didn't say a word; just turned her face to the wall.

'She was so torn down below that she had to have stitches. While that was going on, I took her baby to the nursery. She looked relieved as I wheeled him out of the room in his crib.

'Later, when I took her to see him, she didn't want to approach his humidicrib. Instead she started to look at the other babies. I warned her against it, told her it wasn't a good idea, that it wasn't even allowed. She should have been focusing on her own baby. But as soon as her eyes fell on Jeremy, she was in love in a way I knew she could never be with her son.' She pauses as a staff member exits the nursery. The nurse glances in our direction then continues to the lifts.

The words hurtle out of me. 'But I loved my son. Even before he was born. How could you – how could she – do that to me? To my family?'

A darkness spreads over Ursula's face as she straightens her spine against the wall. 'I knew *you* could love any baby. I read your notes while you were in the caesar. I had them faxed over from the Royal. You were desperate for a baby. I've seen it with many women. After infertility, after trying so hard and for so long, you would have been happy with any child.

'When Brigitte made a suggestion for me to swap your babies, I thought it was an offhand comment. It was only when she offered me a reasonable sum that I realised she wasn't joking. And I was desperate.' She bends over, her hands coming to rest on her thighs. 'It's not so easy to get by these days. You're a pathologist – you wouldn't understand what it's like as a nurse in a public hospital. Our pay and our conditions get worse every year – and then I was demoted. *You* try to pay the bills, the mortgage, after that. *You* try to survive. And Brigitte had been a nurse – she understood perfectly what I was going through.

'But now Brigitte had financial compensation, because of what happened to her. She could afford to pay me. It was so easy, you know. Easier than you would think. The name tags almost slipped off them both. I'd attached them to their wrists myself. It was simple to write new ones and discard the old.

'After, it all unfolded as I'd hoped. Brigitte was insistent that she get to know you, ensure Toby was going to a good home. She was happy that you would do a good enough job raising him. She only started to become wary of you when you asked to hold Jeremy. I fobbed off her concerns and didn't tell her of your suspicions until she witnessed you having the let-down reflex.

I'd been hoping you would eventually come to believe that you had been mistaken. You were the only person who noticed there was a problem. Really, the biggest problem was you.'

Ursula's piercing gaze, like a bird ready to swoop, startles me from my frozen state.

'Someone else should have noticed. The babies were different gestations. Hitting different developmental milestones.'

'We all see what we want to see. Isn't that right?' she says.

Dr Solomon. Dr Niles. Dr Green. Even Mark. It was easier for them to believe I was mentally unwell than to see the truth.

'Was it you who told Dr Niles on me? Who told her I thought Jeremy was mine?'

'You were doing the wrong thing. Breaking the rules of the nursery. Of course Dr Niles needed to know.'

I shudder. 'What exactly did you tell her?'

'I simply told her what happened, and what you told Brigitte. Nothing but the truth.' She counts the facts off on her fingers as she speaks. 'That both you and your mother had been suicidal. That you weren't taking your medication. That you felt bad about a child's death. That you tried to hold Jeremy. That you told Brigitte you wanted to hold him. That you had a let-down reflex when you looked at him. That you still considered Jeremy your son.'

'What about my marriage? What did you say to Dr Niles?'

'What Brigitte passed on. Dr Niles is having problems of her own, I believe. Marital problems. Infertility. Perhaps she believed she could learn something from you.'

There is nothing I could teach Dr Niles, except perhaps what I have learned from pathology: that everyone has something wrong with them under their thin coat of skin.

'And Toby. Is he okay?'

Out in the corridor, from near the stairwell, a desperate wail. It's a woman's cry. Ursula's head jerks towards the sound. 'I have to go. Wait here.' She steps back, straightens her pinafore then hurries in the direction of the stairwell.

She hasn't answered my question. But I can take this chance to see my Gabriel. I slip through the nursery door, hurry along the corridor to his cot and thrust open the partitions.

His humidicrib is empty. Where is he? Surely he hasn't been discharged. He was jaundiced, a little unwell. He needed to stay in hospital, receive medical care.

On the mattress, a syringe half-full of clear liquid. A discarded IV cap.

I clap my hand to my mouth, suck in air between my fingers.

Toby was sicker than Gabriel. Wasn't it Toby being resuscitated? So why isn't Gabriel in his cot?

Oxygen tubing, attached to the wall, is strung out like a snakeskin across the ground.

Please God, no. It can't be him. It can't be Gabriel. My son.

A minute bloodstain on the sheet. From putting in an IV? I touch it with my fingerpad.

I slump against the bench, my hand sliding off the humidicrib as my legs buckle from underneath me and I slither to the ground on all fours.

The cold vinyl cuts into my knees. My forehead meets the ground in a futile prayer. This is floor that he gazed upon. His skin cells will be on this vinyl. A cell memory. I run my palm over the surface, collecting flecks of black and grey dust, and the precious ones, the white flakes of skin. I kiss at my hand.

There is dust and dirt on my lips. But his skin, too. It feels dry and warm.

I use the humidicrib rails to haul myself to standing and run my fingers across its metal rim, the buttons that have kept him alive, kept him warm.

The perspex is smooth. Too smooth. I want to shatter it to fragments so sharp they could pierce my heart.

I lift the side of the humidicrib and press my face into the small cotton sheet. He is still here with me, his scent of honey and cinnamon and hot buttered toast. I breathe him in deep, right to the base of my lungs.

The sheet sticks as I try to pull my head free. I tug and it lifts away with me. I fold it into a tiny square and stuff it down my bra, next to my breast, where it will be safe.

I lean over and cradle the mattress in my arms, between my elbows. I press my lips to its plastic cover, which could almost be a baby's skin.

I stroke the plastic, slippery beneath my palm, and imagine my baby is here with me. I think he's too hot. He needs cooling down.

The face washers are kept on a shelf at the base of the humidicrib. I wet one under the cold tap in the sink beside the cot and go through the motions of wiping his forehead. He's cooler now. He's more comfortable. Maybe he's going to be okay.

An alarm sounds from a cot across the way.

The plastic is sticking to my elbows. I wrench it off, haul the mattress back into place. This isn't my baby. This isn't him at all.

I snap the side of the humidicrib closed. I must see Gabriel. I need to cradle him, hug him. Hold his cold, dead body in my arms.

*

The resuscitation room is empty. The emergency is long over.

The heat lamp perched over the resuscitation cot is still on but there's no baby beneath it. I bring my face to the mattress. I can smell him here, too, can feel his presence through every pore of my skin. I must have missed him by the slimmest fraction of time.

The cot creaks as I drop my face against the sheet. The heat from the lamp above sears my skin.

This is where he lay. Where he took his last breaths.

With my head at an angle, on the whiteboard on the wall I can make out times of procedures. IV insertion. Intubation attempts. CPR. Doses of drugs: suxamethonium, propofol, adrenaline, amiodarone, bicarbonate. Medication vials half-empty on the benchtops. Opened plastic packets like lolly wrappers on the floor. They gave him everything they could to try and keep him alive.

I cry out. It was all I wanted, all I asked for. A baby. A family. Someone to love and to love me in return.

I don't know how to bear this. Please, Mum, please help me. I don't know how to make this right.

I peer through the fog filling the room, imagine Lucia's face before me, imagine her stroking my back, telling me everything will be alright.

Gabriel trusted that I would find him. He cried for me. He expected me to be there to comfort him. I failed him.

Through my tears, I listen for him, for his cry, for his voice.

Nothing but silence.

A scuffle from the door. Ursula, her face a blank mask. 'You really shouldn't be in here.' She assists me to stand.

'Please,' I say, grasping for the side of the cot, trying to hold fast. 'No.'

'You must come this way,' she says. She prises my fingers, one by one, off the cot rail. With her hand steady in the small of my back, she directs me into the nursery.

My mother. What might she say? That I tried too hard. That I pushed too hard to have a baby. That somehow this was all my fault. Had this been her, she would have let go, let her ending come. I'm not like her. I don't want ends. I want beginnings. They have to understand what they've done, each of them. Not Brigitte, though. I understand what she did. And she didn't mean to make my son sick. It's all too much, too quick to process. What I do know is it's the hospital who should pay. I should bring *them* down. Bring them down for all the other women the system has failed to believe across the years, the women who've been mocked and dismissed and ignored. Bring them down for what's been done.

Ursula presses me on to where Mark now stands by the nursery door, his jaw rimmed with stubble, crumpled clothes hanging off his broad frame. He was supposed to be waiting for me in the car. What is he doing here? And, I find myself asking again, how much does he know about our son?

He grabs my arm, pulls me close. 'Sash, look.'

A squalling baby, its face red raw, its hands clenched.

I pull away from him. 'Leave me,' I say. 'It's too much.'

His hand is firm on my clothes. 'Look.'

The name tag.

It's Toby.

'He's doing okay, Sash. He's just been moved to an open cot,' Mark says.

In my resident days, the doctors used to say that closer to the door was closer to home.

Toby's forehead is sweaty under my palm. My finger slides down the bridge of his nose, to its peak. His cry eases a little.

Toby is not my son. But he needs a mother, a mother who wants, loves, adores him. Who loves him unconditionally. Like Lucia loved me. I wonder if I can be enough for him, and him for me.

'Shh,' I say, 'Shh, Toby. Hush.'

I pull the wraps around him, not too tight, and lift him to my chest. He's heavier than I imagined as he settles in against me, his face paling to a shade of peach. His arm grasps at me, takes my pinky in his hand, the creases of his palm folding over me so I can't let go.

His eyes are the colour of shimmering twilight. Around the outer rim of his iris, a deep ocean of blue, impenetrable. *Can I ever truly know you? And can you ever know me?*

Toby looks back at me.

I think I could hold him like this for the longest time.

Then, a commotion at the door.

Brigitte charges into the nursery. Her blue floral dress hangs loose on her thin frame, her shoulders hunched like an old woman. Her long dishevelled hair is shaken from its tie and dangles down her back.

Ursula steps forward from the nurses' desk as if to comfort her but Brigitte turns her back on her and swivels in my direction. 'How dare you?' she screeches.

I clutch Toby to my chest. He doesn't deserve any of this.

'It was you, wasn't it?' Her jaw is tight, the whites of her eyes a deep red. 'They're saying he died from an infection. You infected him.' Spittle flicks through the gap between her front teeth.

'No,' I say, 'I haven't done anything wrong.' All at once it comes to me, how this has come about. I saw Brigitte forget to wash her hands in the nursery bathroom. Inadvertently, it appears, she is responsible for the death of a baby. My son, who I carried with me for thirty-five weeks. I should be beyond furious, I suppose; yet what I feel is a blanket of horror cloaking me, like in those times I have made catastrophic mistakes.

Brigitte's face is contorted with grief. She hisses, too soft for anyone but me to hear. 'You know what I did, don't you?' She searches my expression. 'Given the opportunity, any good mother would take a chance to rewrite the past.' Louder now: 'How come this baby gets to live? You don't even love him. I've seen the way you look at him.'

Mark steps forward but he's too far away to reach us. I hadn't noticed how close Brigitte has managed to come. She's right in front of me now, her stale breath catching my nostrils as she reaches towards me, her arms outstretched.

'Give him to me,' she says. 'I can love him more than you will.' She leans in.

I step back, hugging Toby to me. She encircles him with her hands and tries to wrestle him from my grasp, and with the vigour of grief she's so strong that I don't know if I can keep holding him, if I have the strength to never let him go. Her fingers dig deeper into his wraps as my hold on him loosens, and as she pulls he begins to give way.

For a moment, with the slipperiness of my palms, the lightness of Toby in my grasp, I contemplate letting him slide into her arms. It would be almost like letting go of a breath, or a sneeze, something released involuntarily, to give him over to her soft hands, softer than mine, her nails more baby-friendly than my bitten-down quicks and my dry, cracked skin. With her hands, her grip, she would be able to hold him more tightly, more easily, more like I think a mother should.

My mother. She held me tight as she slipped into darkness. I remember her arms pressing me into her cooling chest. She had wanted to take me with her. For some reason, I didn't follow her. I stayed alive. And despite everything, I have continued to choose life. Even as I remained unsure whether I could be different to my mother, I chose to have a baby. My doubt in my mothering ability lingers. But I know I will do anything, everything I can, to make sure I never hurt my son.

Brigitte scrabbles for him, yanking at his wraps. I press Toby firmly to me. Even though I couldn't love him for so long, didn't even consider him mine, I know I gave him what I could. I can only pray that he will forgive me for my failures one day.

A vision of Toby pulls into focus: the depth of his gaze, his subtle frown, the way he closed his fingers around my pinky.

I am his mother. She gave him away.

She gave him away to me.

'He's mine!' My voice is strong and clear, echoing through the nursery. I give a jolt and step back from Brigitte.

Her grasp slips from Toby, her empty hands clutching the air in front of her.

My baby, finally in my arms.

I press him to me, so warm against my chest. His heart is beating at the same rate as mine; we're in synchrony.

Mark holds Brigitte by her wrists. She swivels her head to Ursula, standing by the nurses' desk. 'Help, Ursula,' she calls. 'I need your help again.' Ursula gives a slight shake of her head and reaches for the phone. An emergency code comes over the loudspeaker and, almost immediately, security staff dash through the door. They surround Brigitte as she collapses to the ground. They drag her, kicking and screaming, away.

In my arms, my baby begins to cry, his screams pulsing through my chest. I cradle him. 'Shh, shh,' I whisper into his ear, stroking his back up and down, down and up. 'Everything will be alright.'

At the nurses' station, Dr Green speaks frantically on the phone. Mark shouts at Ursula, flinging his arms about as she huddles against the wall. I can't hear what either of them is saying.

I feel compassion for Brigitte, for what she's been through, for the desperation that drove her to forsake her child. I know she will seek redemption eventually. As for me, I have redemption of my own to seek.

Toby's screams begin to subside. He pauses longer and longer between his cries until he's whimpering, then snuffling. I study his face as I rub gentle circles on his chest, finding features I'd noticed in quiet, hidden moments and forgotten until today. The curve between his nose and eyes. The shape of his eyebrows, thicker in the middle, thinning at the edges. The gentle crease under his lower lip.

I press him to my cheek and kiss him, on the crown of his head, the curl of his ear, the rise of his cheek, all of his parts coalescing to form a whole. 'I'm so, *so* sorry,' I say. He settles into silence and softens in my arms, staring up at me, his eyes shiny and clear, willing me to be his mother and to love him, and, after so many days, hours, minutes, I finally believe that I can.

SIX MONTHS AFTER BIRTH

MARK

The windscreen wipers shift left to right in a jerky beat, lulling Toby to sleep. He's been an easy baby, even easier for Sash than for me. He tends to fall asleep in our arms, or in the carrier when we take him for walks around the lake.

In the rear-vision mirror, I can see him strapped into his capsule in the back seat. His eyelids droop until they're closed. Against the windscreen, the rain comes down in sheets, pooling over the road.

I glance back at Toby. His nose, long and proud. His hair, swept to one side, highlighting his wide forehead. His neck tilted at an angle, exposing his earlobe joined to his head.

Impossible.

He looks exactly like Simon.

I turn my eyes to the road, where a sulphur-crested cockatoo is pecking at the ground beside a rotting kangaroo carcass.

Fixated by the image, I miss the curve of the road and speed across the shoulder. With no time to brake I swerve, the wheels skimming across the dirt at the roadside, the steering wheel slipping from my hands. The car spins out of control and I wonder if we will stop, and when, and what it might feel like for it to end here, now, but then the car squeals to a juddering halt.

Rain hammers on the roof. Toby begins to whimper, a soft cry that fills the cabin in the quietness of the bush. I shift my limbs in the seat and check on him. It looks like we're both okay. The cockatoo flaps across the road, squawking. Everything is going to be fine.

Except it isn't. Not really.

There are so many things I can't tell Sash. I'll never be able to let on about this accident, for starters. Nor that Bill told me years ago what her mother did, what she tried to do to Sash. Or my deathly regret that I never got to know Gabriel.

How wrong I've been. About Sash. About everything.

I'd read the DNA results when they arrived at the house but, thinking Sash had deliberately engineered the results to confirm her suspicions, refused to believe them. I only deduced what had happened in the nursery as I took Brigitte's wrists in my palms, her fingers clawing for what I had thought was my biological child. Sash was cradling him, loving him in this new way before I could. I knew instantly that all of us would be best served by my silence. I can't say I understand Sash's decision, but who am I to judge her choice, after all she's been through? That first evening, after she'd claimed Toby, I briefly told her what I'd concluded in a private moment. I didn't ask her anything more. I didn't need to know the details. I'd already said and done enough.

Besides, everything that has happened is at least partly my fault.

The morning Toby was born, I lied to Sash. I had gone home. I told myself that after the night we'd had, I needed rest. I was exhausted. Wrecked. Back in the cocoon of our house, I tried to cook something for Sash. The smoke alarm woke me from my slumber. I took the ruined ragout from the stove, had a shower to wash away the stench of the joey and, on the way back to the hospital, bought roses and some food at the cafeteria for Sash.

Sash was still asleep when I left the roses by her bed. I headed back to the nursery, planning to see our son. But my limbs were like iron bars. I couldn't force myself to go inside. The thought of seeing our baby pale and naked under artificial lights, tubes fed into him to keep him alive; it was too much like what I'd seen with Simon. I wasn't prepared to watch our son go.

Maybe if I'd stayed with him like I'd promised Sash I would; if I hadn't failed him on his first day of life; if I'd told Sash the truth from the start, before it all began; maybe then, everything would have been alright.

Simon, and Gabriel, I couldn't save. Now I have Toby. Him, I can protect.

I reach behind me to the back seat, unclip Toby and pull him into my arms. He shuffles against me, his eyes still shut. I hug him to me as the rain beats down on the roof, carrying dirt from the duco onto the road, carrying our mistakes into the bush where I hope, in time, they will turn to fertile ground.

NINE MONTHS AFTER BIRTH

A flock of yellow balloons hovers above the crowd gathering on the oval. Mark has Toby strapped to his chest as he strides towards me. He's been taking care of Toby during my job interview. He is committed to being a stay-at-home dad. The restaurant, and the café, are out of the picture. Our family comes first, he says.

'How did you go?' He hands me his own small bundle of balloons to hold them by their shiny strings, then pecks my cheek. I give an encouraging smile.

'Fine. I think I've got it.' The pathology company in the city doesn't know my history. It's anonymous, safer than working in a smaller town, given everything we've been through.

People cluster in a loose circle on the damp grass. As always, I scan the crowd for long, plaited hair, piercing eyes, a gap between front teeth. I look for her everywhere now. She will come back for him one day. I wouldn't blame her. That is what I would do.

336

Ursula cornered me after Brigitte had been taken away.

'You never tell anyone anything,' she said with an almost apologetic smile, 'and I'll make sure Brigitte never does the same.'

I knew, even then, that there were no guarantees.

Mark struggles with the clip to unhook the baby carrier from his chest. I fiddle with the clasp. As Mark loosens the straps, Toby wakens momentarily, stretching an arm towards me. Mark lifts him and delivers him into my embrace.

Toby is heavier now. Warm, too, despite the coolness of the late-afternoon air. He is alive, so alive. He gives a faint sigh, his breath tinged with the sweetness of breastmilk. I wipe away a streak of white above his upper lip then stroke the fuzz of hair on his scalp. Does a child ever really belong to a mother? For now, at least, he is mine.

'I got five balloons.' Mark removes the carrier from around his waist, stretches it across my belly and clicks it in place.

'Five?'

His face softens. 'The two we lost early on. And then one for Simon. One for Damien' – I hadn't realised he'd remembered his name – 'and one for . . .' His voice trails off. He doesn't say the name. He doesn't have to. We both know what happened; what I did; what I should have done.

I wrap my hand around Mark's bony one, clasping the balloons. 'Thank you.' What I want to say is: thank you for finally taking my side, after everything at the hospital. Thank you for not questioning my decision to raise Toby as our own. Thank you for giving us another go. So many things remain unsaid between us. But *thank you* is enough for now.

He stares towards the goalposts at the far end of the oval, their long shadows falling like gravestones over the dewy grass as the light begins to fade on the edge of town.

It's like Bec said. Mark is a good guy. I'm lucky, I suppose. At least he didn't leave when it all got too hard. Adam, on the other hand, left Bec six months ago, right after she finally became pregnant, saying he wanted nothing to do with the child. After falling apart for a while, she decided to move back to Australia. Bec is committed to being a single mother, and to telling the baby about the donor egg.

'When she's old enough to understand. I'm fine about using a donor now. A child's a child; what difference does it make who their biological mother is, right? Better any baby than no baby, from my point of view.'

I almost told her, then. At the last moment, I held my silence. But I'll be there for her as she makes her own motherhood journey, like Lucia would have wanted for both of us.

A hush falls over the crowd. It's time.

We form a large, loose circle. Others begin to release yellow balloons into the air: first one, then another, freed by their owners, curling on airstreams, floating higher and higher into the falling dusk.

Mark plucks one string from his cluster, closes his eyes and mouths inaudible words. The balloon soars from his hand, diminishing into a small egg, then a pinpoint, before our eyes.

'I used to think it was a dishonour to release him. Like he would be forgotten, I suppose,' Mark says. 'Now I know I can say goodbye.' He presses a yellow ribbon into my palm. 'Your turn.'

Damien. I think of him less and less these days. He no longer occupies my nightmares. He's a dream-baby; an afterthought; a wish that things could have been different all those years ago.

I thrust open my palm and liberate him. He soars into the air, towards the clouds, until he's just a speck in the darkening sky.

The next two balloons are easier. I recall the voices I heard in my head: Harry and Matilda. Their squeals of delight, the faint chattering. Their spirits are already free. I say a silent prayer as they drift high above us: *May you find a family who loves you as I did. May you find a happy home.*

Ondine's face surfaces in my mind. Now that she's again living with her husband and son, she has reclaimed her own happy family. After her medication finally kicked in, she was able to avoid having to endure ECT. We catch up for coffee and chats regularly, in our own incarnation of the Mentally Ill Mothers' Group; we call ourselves the Mad Mums.

Mark passes me the final balloon. It hovers overhead in the space between us. His eyes, creased and struggling to meet mine, say everything.

I reach for his hand and coax him to hold the string with me. He acquiesces, drops his head. 'For Jeremy,' he says.

'Gabriel.' My smile flattens. A sob spills out of me. 'Her baby.' I press my arms tight around Toby, hugging him.

'He was *ours*, Sash.'

Mark is right. He was, for such a short time.

'Sash, look.'

The balloon has pulled itself from my grasp and is floating above us, luminescent in a shaft of setting sunlight, as though lit from within.

Mark wraps his arm around my shoulders and leans into me. We watch the balloon as it soars into the sky, towards the stars, until it is no longer visible.

He takes my hand, squeezing neither too soft nor too hard. 'Come, Sash. It's time to go.'

'You go. Give me a minute.'

He wanders back to the car, his feet laying trails in the grass. The crowd begins to disperse, until it is only Toby and me standing alone under the deepening blue sky.

Toby shuffles against me. I look at his beautiful face and remember the times I wasn't sure if I would ever love him; the time I hadn't known whether he would live or die; the way in which we claimed each other's hearts at the last possible moment.

A chill pulses through the air. I pull down his red woollen jumper, the one that's finally the right size, and tuck his blanket securely over him.

He snuffles and nuzzles into me. I kiss the top of his forehead, his fuzzy hair tickling my nose, and whisper to him, 'I'm so glad we found each other.' Then, pressing him close to me, I mutter words of adoration in his ear. He shifts his head, almost smiles, squeezes my finger tight. I smile back and, almost imperceptibly, whisper his name.

Toby.

My baby, Toby Gabriel.

ACKNOWLEDGEMENTS

My deepest thanks to all those who have provided support and encouragement over the years. I could not have done it without you.

To my learned teachers – Mrs Mason, George Papaellinas, Antoni Jach, The Story Suite's Mark Dickenson, and the RMIT Professional Writing and Editing staff, especially Ania Walwicz, Michelle Aung Thin, Olga Lorenzo and Penny Johnson – thank you for teaching me what I needed to know.

To my sage mentors and supporters – Inga Simpson, Toni Jordan, Kate Torney, Alison Arnold and Elizabeth Whitby – thank you for pushing me further than I believed I was capable of travelling.

To my dear friends, fellow writers and readers – Rosalind McDougall, Yolanda Sztarr, Jennifer Coller, Kali Napier, Mark Brandi, Imbi Neeme, Bella Anderson – my heartfelt thanks for all your pertinent feedback and advice. To my loyal writing group – Jennifer Porter, Margaret Kett, Caitlin Ziegler, Jasmine Mahon – thank you for your vital encouragement and incredibly insightful comments. To my fact-checkers – Kate Irving, Amanda Furber, Evan Symons – thank you for picking up the important things. To the Tifaneers, thank you for your support. And to Kym Riley, I am so thankful for your faith in me, for your invaluable suggestions and for listening to my brainstorming over many years.

To Varuna, The Writers' House, and Queensland Writers Centre, enormous thanks for your faith in me.

To Grace Heifetz, I am indebted to you. Thank you so much for giving me much-needed time and space to develop this work, and for your tireless patience and support. To Kimberley Atkins, thank you for your belief in and enthusiasm for my writing. And to Tom Langshaw and Rebecca Starford, thank you for getting me over the line.

To Mum and Dad, thank you. To Annie, thank you. Finally, to Milly and Sebastian – thank you. I am so grateful for you all.